THE GOLD OF PANCHO VILLA

I knew that in the thirty-five or forty years it had been buried, the cowhide would be decayed and rotten, so I forced myself to work slowly. I carefully removed the dirt down to where I could see the hide. I had to widen the hole before the entire top of the bundle was exposed; then with my hands I carefully cleaned all the dirt off.

I can't describe the feeling that swept over me as I reached down to fold back the old cowhide. I've never experienced anything like it. I looked up at José. He was shaking from head to foot, and I wasn't the calmest man in the world at the moment, either.

"See, my brother, it is as I have told you," said José, trembling but triumphant.

"Yes, it is, José. Now hand me the lantern." I carefully unfolded the hide, and the first thing I saw was the leather bag. Holding the lantern in one hand, I opened the mouth of the bag with the other. Inside it were more gold coins than I had seen in my whole life. I raised the folded hide higher, and there were the gold bars, uniformly stacked. The bars were cold, but the touch of them sent a tingling sensation all through my body.

"Look, José, isn't that the loveliest sight you have ever seen?" I whispered.

THE
GOLD SEEKERS

J. Mark Bond

LEISURE BOOKS ☯ NEW YORK CITY

Dedicated to my old friend, the late, great John Wayne, whose appreciation of HALF A TREASURE inspired me to expand the book to its present form. Here's to ya, Duke! In his memory, and that of others who have lost their lives to cancer, a percentage of my profits from the sale of this novel are being donated to cancer research.

A LEISURE BOOK

Published by

Dorchester Publishing Co., Inc.
6 East 39th Street
New York, NY 10016

Printed in the United States of America

Part I

"HALF A TREASURE"

Dear Mark:

This story is too good to not be true.
Where did you stash the gold?

I certainly enjoyed it. I'm sure
others will.

Sincerely,

John Wayne

Chapter 1

"SENOR MARK, I would not lie to you; if it is not as I have told you, I will let you cut off both my arms," the Mexican finished breathlessly.

"Easy, José, tell me either in English or Spanish. I can't understand that jargon. Now, start all over."

"*Bueno.* Many years ago, when my Papa was a soldier with Pancho Villa, one day they made the big raid and robbery. Almost they get caught. To make the get-away, they bury all the gold and silver. What Pancho no savvys is, it is only a short distance from where they bury all the gold to the village where my Papa lives. Very soon my Papa takes the leave to visit his family. While on this visit, Papa, my brother, and me, we go dig up the treasure, and bury it in our patio— five big mule loads of the *oro* and *plata*.

"Never have we sold even one peso. Always they suspect my Papa of stealing the treasure. Always we have been afraid to sell the gold, for when you are poor, and there is no work, how can you explain having so much money? We would be killed, for then they know for sure we steal gold. After my Papa dies, then I come to the States to try and find someone I can trust. For two years, since 1967, I work for you in the mines. Now, *compadre,* if you will go with me to Mexico, I will make you a very rich man. Half of the gold and silver I will give to you. Then you sell this and come back and buy the other half, and my brother and me will slip away from our village and go to Mexico City and live like rich people. *Si, Señor?*"

"Look, José, this calls for a little study. Suppose I give you

7

my answer in the morning?''

"And if your answer is 'Yes,' *mañana*, we vamoose. *Bueno, Señor?* Already the gold and silver is buried for too many years. I should have told you before, but I have to be sure, *compadre*."

"We'll talk about that in the morning, José. I've got a lot of thinking to do tonight."

José grinned an ingratiating grin and took his leave. As soon as he left, I called my foreman, Tex Murray, and asked him to come by the office. When Tex arrived, I posed a question on which an awful lot depended. "José's been working for us for two years now, Tex, and you've been exposed to him day after day. I want your honest opinion. Just how reliable and trustworthy do you think he is?''

"I know this much about him," Tex said, "he's loco about you, absolutely devoted to you, and I believe you can depend on anything he tells you."

Then I told Tex the story José had told me. "Quite a story, isn't it?"

"That it is," Tex nodded, "but damned if I don't believe the ugly little devil. I've worked Mexicans for many years, and I know they can be slippery as eels, but I've found that once one of them becomes attached to you, he's truthful and loyal. If I were you, I'd give careful thought to his proposal. He thinks you are the only man in the world to work for, and believe me, as far as José is concerned, you two are *amigos*."

"Then you think I ought to buy this proposition?"

"I think you're a damn fool if you don't," said Tex. "It's always possible he simply wants free transportation home, but knowing José as I do, I'll sure buy his story."

"Okay, Tex, you've sold me; but under one condition: You're going with us. If José's story is true, I'm going to need all the help I can get. You remember Jim Dunlap, who owns the big ranch at Casas Grande?"

"You introduced me to him a couple of years ago," said Tex.

"Jim is always ready for an adventure. I'm going to call him and see if he can get away for a few days. Jim has ranched in Mexico for twenty-five years and he knows the country as

few white men ever will. In addition to that, he's one of the best bush pilots I ever ran across, and if José really has the treasure, we might want to fly it out.''

"Sounds like a good idea," Tex agreed, "and as far as I'm concerned, the sooner we get going, the better."

We agreed to be packed and ready to leave by 9:00 the next morning. Then I placed a call to Jim. It took three hours to get through to him. "Jim, you old son of a gun, I'm entering into a deal that staggers the imagination and if it proves as fruitful as I expect it to, I'm sure as hell going to need your help."

"Don't underestimate my imagination," said Jim, "Shoot! I'm listening."

"It's a long story, Jim, and I can't go into it over the phone; but Tex and I and another fellow are heading South early in the morning on a mission that will take us through Chihuahua and fairly deep into Mexico. We ought to make Chihuahua around dark, and I'm wondering if you can meet us there and hear the whole story?"

"Sure thing," agreed Jim, who was never one to waste words. "Let's check in at the Hilton and meet there."

"It's a deal," I said. "Come prepared to be gone several days."

That done, I set out to find José and tell him I'd decided to go along with him. I wish all my missions were as easy to accomplish as that one was. By the time I got within a block of the Chavez Bar and Grill, it became evident to me that José had anticipated my answer. The noise that reverberated around the neighborhood told me that this was no ordinary celebration. José's farewell party was well under way and it was unquestionably going to be a booming success. When I reached the bar and stepped inside and looked around, I could have sworn that every Mexican in town was present, and not a sober one in the lot.

I threaded my way across the room until I found José's table. All that was visible of the little devil were his grubby hands, with which he was trying to encircle the waist of a fat barmaid who was sitting on his lap. He was such a runt that the girl's excess poundage spilled out on all sides of him, and

9

his short arms could hardly reach halfway around her. I stepped to one side of the chair on which he was sitting. The minute I caught sight of his face, I knew that he was drunk from stem to stern; but he wasn't too drunk to recognize me as a new and important link in the long chain of circumstances that was giving him cause for celebration. As soon as he focused his bloodshot eyes on me, he pushed the girl off his lap and staggered to his feet. "*Señor* Mark, my *amigo!*" he greeted me, trying to execute a sweeping bow. I reached out and steadied him to keep him from falling flat on his chin.

"*Amigos! Amigos!*" he cried out, clapping his hands to gain the attention of the roistering crowd. "This is *Señor* Mark, my good *amigo*. Two years ago I came to the States a poor Mexican with no job and no *dinero*. Then *Señor* Mark give me a job in his mines. He pay me good and treat me like the brother. *Mañana* I take him to Mexico with me to visit me and my family. My home is his home for as long as my brother will stay. We will show him what hospitality we have in Mexico—*mucho* tequila and mescal. She is going to be one big fiesta, I think. Now I buy the drinks for all, to drink to the health of my *amigo, Señor* Mark, *un bueno hombre—Salud!*"

Cheers rose from the motley crowd as Francisco, the bartender, helped himself to a double swig and then began pouring drinks for the others. That was the first of several toasts drunk to me; and preceding each round, José managed to get to his feet and tell the assemblage what a great guy, a good *amigo*, and a fine *Americano* I was. After half a dozen rounds, I finally succeeded in getting the old boy by the arm. I paid the bill, and steered José out to my car and poured him into the front seat. Then I drove around for a while to expose my passenger to some fresh air and give him a chance to sober up a little. During the drive, I got him to retell his story. He repeated it word for word, just as he had related it earlier in the day. There was not the slightest deviation in the retelling. The little seed of doubt that had been lurking in my mind dissolved. Anyone who would repeat a story as accurately as José did, as drunk as he was, was bound to be telling the truth.

I told José that I had decided to go with him, tht I'd talked to Tex and he was going along with us, and that we'd leave at 9:00 the next morning. Then I drove him to my house so that I could put him to bed, keep an eye on him, and try to get him into shape to get rolling in the morning.

Things had happened so fast that it was not until I stopped the car in the driveway that I gave any thought as to what I would tell my wife about the venture on which I was embarking. I fully expected her to hit the ceiling, boot José out, and take me into custody until she could personally escort me to a head-shrinker. As usual, Nita was to do the unexpected. It was well after midnight when I got José off to bed. After hiding his clothes in order to make sure he didn't slip out during the night for more fire-water, I went in and told Nita the entire story.

"I think you and Tex are loco," she commented, "to listen to such an improbable tale, much less believe it; but Mark, I've got to admit that José's story is as fascinating as it is fantastic." It was as simple as that. You can never tell about women.

When Tex showed up in the morning, all set to hit the road, José was one sick Mexican. For a wholly different reason, I didn't feel like the top of the morning myself, what with such a daring decision to be made on such short notice, my session with José, and the various preparations to be made for the trip. However, we managed to get underway on schedule. Several cups of coffee and a good breakfast at a cafe in Las Cruces left us all feeling considerably improved, and the goose was hanging high by the time we reached Juarez. Obtaining our tourist papers there presented no problem.

The drive from Juarez to Chihuahua is one I've made many times—so many times, in fact, that I'm on a first name basis with a thousand and one cows and burros along the way, who for some reason or other prefer to stand on the highway rather than under the mesquites which nature has so abundantly provided for their comfort and convenience if the confounded beasts only had the sense to take advantage of them.

We got to Chihuahua at dusk, registered at the hotel, and

found that Jim was already on hand. I called him and asked him to join us in the dining room for a drink and dinner.

Tex and Jim's meeting a few years earlier had been a brief and casual one, with little more than an exchange of greetings, and now that we were all to engage in a joint venture, I was curious to see how they would react to each other. Jim, a crusty old bachelor and rancher, sizes a fellow up and forms an opinion right off the bat, and once he's made up his mind, nothing short of a stampede will change it. My concern was groundless. The two of them hit it off as if they'd enjoyed blood brotherhood all of their lives.

After dinner, we went up to Jim's room, and I told him the story José had told me. He wasn't too impressed. He had spent twenty-five years ranching in Mexico, and had heard many such tales of buried treasure. In spite of his skepticism, however, he agreed to go on with us and check it out. He had brought along his four-wheel drive pick-up, two automatic shotguns and a .38 revolver. "Now, is there anything else?" he asked. "If not, get the hell out and let a man get his rest. It's about 700 miles to where we are going, and we'll leave at 5:00 in the morning."

"Let's take a walk before we turn in," I proposed to Tex, as we left Jim's room. "We need to stretch our legs and limber up in preparation for the hard drive ahead tomorrow."

"I second the motion," said Tex, "and besides, it'll give us a chance to enjoy some of the local scenery." I'd been around Tex long enough to know that when he referred to "local scenery," he didn't mean landscapes—he meant females.

Just across a narrow one-way street from the hotel was the town plaza, an ideal place for an evening constitutional. Several small bands of serenaders were softly playing Spanish love songs, and dozens of pretty *señoritas* were strolling about in groups of twos and threes. As we walked past them, the two *Americanos* received many an admiring, provocative glance. Knowing Tex's weakness for a pretty girl, I piloted him back to the hotel before the provocation reached the saturation point.

12

It seemed to me I had barely closed my eyes when there was a series of knocks on my door. I managed to get to my feet and stagger to the door in my sleep. When I opened it, there stood Jim, fully dressed and looking as fresh as a sunrise. "Wake Tex and José," he said in a voice loud enough to wake everybody in the hotel, "and while you three are dressing, I'll go down and order breakfast for all of us."

I had less trouble rousing Tex and José and getting them down to the coffee shop and ready to roll than Jim had with the coffee shop personnel. After what seemed like an hour's delay, and a half dozen mistakes in the orders, we were finally served. The orders were still mixed up, but rather than go through the whole deal again, we ate what was put before us.

Despite Jim's intention to leave at daybreak, it was around 8:00 before we pulled out of Chihuahua and headed South for Jimenez. José and I rode in my car, and Jim and Tex followed in the pick-up truck.

It was dark when we got to Durango, and we congratulated ourselves on making as good time as we had, considering a detour we hadn't counted on. José told us it was only about 125 miles to the village where he lived, and he was all for pushing on; but we were all dog tired, and agreed it would be better to spend the night at a motel in Durango, which almost proved our undoing.

When I knocked on José's door the next morning, I got no answer. I was pushing open the unlocked door when Jim came along. Together we looked into the room. José was nowhere to be seen, and it was obvious that his bed had not been slept in. "What do you suppose has happened to him?" I said to Jim.

Jim's reply was characteristically brief: "The little son of a bitch just wanted free transportation home." There was little doubt about it; it looked like I had been played for a sucker.

Regardless of highs and lows, life has a way of going on. Jim, Tex and I went into the café to have breakfast. Jim ordered coffee, but he was too mad to eat. Tex was just as mad, but he didn't allow his fury to stand between him and his appetite. In between bites of a hearty breakfast, he swore that if he ever caught José, he'd cut his throat, in addition to inflicting numerous other forms of torture, drawing and quartering being the most humane among them.

Black as the picture looked, I still found it hard to believe that José had lied to me. Except for the clothes he had on, his possessions, including the souvenirs he had bought in the States and which he prized so highly, were still in his room.

We had just finished our breakfast and walked out of the cafe when a policeman on a motorcycle drove up. "Is one of you *Señor* Mark?" he asked.

"My name is Mark," I said, half glad and half sorry to be able to qualify for the doubtful honor, for I was both hopeful and fearful of what was coming next.

"Let me see your passports," he said. When he had examined them he asked, "What are you doing in Mexico?"

"We're on vacation," I told him.

"Do you know José Torres?" he asked me.

When I answered in the affirmative, the policeman unraveled the mystery for us. It seemed that after the rest of us had gone to sleep, my *amigo*, José, had decided to sneak out and renew old acquaintances at the local cathouse. After a few drinks too many, a chronic occurrence with him, he started bragging about the money he had made in the States. Also was he not the best dressed man present? Furthermore, he felt that royalty was honoring the presence of peons; and since no one present was worthy of sharing his bed with him, why should he pay for the drinks? "Then, *señor,*" the policeman explained matter-of-factly, "was when the big fight she starts. If you want to pay 300 pesos, I will turn José out of the jailhouse."

I didn't haggle over the $24.00 fine; I looked upon it as one of the best bargains I had ever had offered me. I paid the 300 pesos at once, but it was about three hours before José was turned loose. When he finally came dragging back to the motel, he looked as if he'd got his money's worth. He had a beautiful shiner and two badly scratched cheeks which the madam had given him to remember her by. As outraged as Jim and Tex and I were, José looked so ludicrous that we couldn't resist a few good belly laughs when we saw him. He looked like he had gone through a Texas tornado with a wild-cat under each arm.

"Señor Mark, my *compadre,* I am very sick and sorry," he apologized, all the wind gone out of his sails. "It will not happen again. On the grave of my mama, I promise. If I can have a cup of coffee, I will be ready to go. If only my head she did not sound like a drum!"

It was about noon when we got started on the last 125 miles of our journey. The road was good for about eighty miles; then we turned off the highway onto a country road that was jaggedly rough. After driving for an hour, we came to a good sized village. I was sure we had reached our destination, but my confidence received a rude jolt when José announced, "Eet is only twenty-five more miles from here to my house, but the road she is not so good from here to Loreto." That was an understatement if I ever heard one. No equipment had ever been used on the so-called road, it had never had any maintenance, and very seldom did a car travel over it.

The crude road ran through cactus and around arroyos. When we came to a high center, we would have to take out across the desert and carve our own road. It was the roughest stretch I'd ever encountered. We were three hours covering the twenty-five miles.

Just before sunset, we came around the side of a mountain, and there, across a large arroyo, on a small rolling plateau, was Loreto. It was a pretty village that looked down over a peaceful valley, and it had a picturesque plaza and an ancient mission. A narrow, crystal clear river flowed through the valley. The place looked like an oasis, wholly unspoiled by tourists or commercialistm. The village had been built by the Spaniards over 300 years ago, and Indian slaves had been used to work the rich gold and silver mines that abounded in the area. José estimated the population to be about 1,500. As our red and white car drove along the narrow alley-like streets, curious eyes peered out of every door and window.

We drove directly to José's house. His wife and children gave him a warm welcome, but were plainly embarrassed by the presence of strangers. Of José's seven children, only a little five-year old girl would talk to us. José told everyone that I was the rich *Americano* he had worked for in the States, and that we had come down because I was interested in mining properties around Loreto. We had previously agreed to this story, to explain our presence.

It didn't take long for word of our arrival to spread around the village, and within an hour, *el presidente*—the equivalent of an American mayor—of the village had sent an invitation for us to have dinner at his home that night.

José then directed us to the only hotel in Loreto. It was of ancient vintage and poorly furnished, but its patio was a thing of beauty. The hotel had no electricity or plumbing, nor did any building in the village boast such modern conveniences. Of all the primitive places I've been in, Loreto took top honors.

José insisted on staying at the hotel with us. After all, he had not left his village a peon, and was he not now back with a little money? Also had he not become the *compadre* to the *Americano* who owned the big mines and also the big new red and white car, such as never before had been seen in Loreto? This was José's finest hour and he proposed to make the most of it. José's brother, Juan, was in the mountains, herding the goats. It would be two or three days before he came home. Until his return, there was nothing we could do about the treasure; but José intended to use those few days to live it up and impress his fellow villagers.

When I say we all had tub baths, I use the word "tub" in its old-fashioned sense. The water had to be carried from the river and poured into wash tubs. Then we shaved, put on our best clothes and called at the house of *Señor* Vargas, *el presidente*.

Our host met us at the door. He was a big, burly fellow, with an unctuous manner that made you feel like reaching for your wallet and keeping both hands on it. His home was as spacious as it was old. It consisted of eighteen or twenty rooms, all of which opened onto the oblong patio, which was about a hundred feet wide and two hundred feet long. The patio was one of rare and exotic beauty. Here and there were palm, orange, and lime trees; vines and fragrant colorful blossoms grew everywhere.

"*Señor* Vargas," I said in all sincerity, "I compliment you on your fine home and your gracious patio and its beautiful flowers."

"Thank you, *Señor*," said Vargas. "The credit goes to my three daughters, who are all more beautiful than the flowers."

El presidente led us into a huge room filled with all manner of tanned animal skins and large pottery vases, and as he pulled a bell cord, he invited us to be seated. A maid promptly appeared, bearing a jug of mescal and a dish of limes. We sat around the table, enjoying our drinks as *Señor* Vargas told us the history of Loreto. The maid's announcement that dinner was served interrupted a very interesting conversation.

The meal was delicious. No matter how rich or how poor they may be, the Mexican people are gracious hosts, and try to make you feel that their home is your home.

After dinner, *Señor* Vargas called his family in and introduced them. First came *Señora* Vargas. Like most Mexican women, she was short and on the heavy side, but her face showed lingering traces of youthful beauty. Close behind her was their son, Pablo, an engaging looking boy about seventeen. The two younger girls, both of them quite comely, followed—Marta, perhaps thirteen, and Sophia, who was fifteen or sixteen. Finally came the third daughter, taller than the others, and with an easy grace about her. She was the embodiment of every real and legendary beautiful and captivating woman through the ages, from Helen of Troy and Cleopatra right on down to Liz Taylor. "This," said *Señor* Vargas, with justifiable pride, "is my eldest, Maria." He shook his head regretfully. "What a shame there are no men in our village worthy to court her." Maria blushed becomingly.

Pablo was a friendly, straightforward lad, and we talked for a few minutes like old friends. Then Vargas ordered the jug of mescal brought in. Marta, burning with youthful curiosity over the fine car parked in front of their home, asked timidly if she and her sisters might go out and look at it. Her question inspired me to ask *Señor* Vargas' permission to take Pablo and the girls for a ride in the car while the others had a few drinks. I told him that one drink in an evening was just about my capacity, and that this would give me a chance to see the town. I knew Pablo and his sisters would enjoy the ride.

To my surprise, the old man was all for it. A second look at his expression, and I knew why. "Poor Maria." I read his mind—"almost twenty-one, and no man. Here is a rich *Americano* of thirty." I could see the dollar signs light up in his eyes all the way across the room. "Don't go too far," he said, "and be back in an hour; I have some mining properties I want to tell you of."

The average American kid's eyes wouldn't light up half as brightly if he saw a flying saucer from Mars complete with a contingent of Martians land in his own back yard, as those kids' eyes did when they saw the car. It was the most wondrous thing they had ever beheld. They were eager to get into it and learn all about it. The air conditioner was completely beyond their understanding. Their eyes had not seen and their ears had not heard anything to compare with such magical inventions.

Pablo's thinking must have been akin to that of his father. He took charge of the seating arrangements and ordered the two younger girls into the back seat, which was quite spacious enough for three or four. Then he told Maria to get into the front seat, after which he climbed in beside her and pulled the door shut. That, of course, placed Maria between Pablo and me, an artful bit of arranging on the part of a seventeen year old brother.

Pablo directed me up and down every street in the village, and each street seemed to be more filled than the previous one with wandering burros and goats. When I felt that time was running out on us, I persuaded a reluctant Pablo to point out the way home. It was too bad for the kids' sake that it was not daylight, so that their friends might have seen them. The ride would have been a triumphal tour and they would have left a trail of glory long to be remembered.

As we were getting out of the car, I asked Maria to show me around the patio. She was very shy about it, but Pablo and the younger sisters were as cooperative as she was shy. Out of the corner of my eye, I saw Pablo raise his elbow and give the two girls a gentle but meaningful jab in the ribs. The three of them said a brief thank-you and good night, and hurried into the house, leaving the moon-drenched night, the patio and the flowers in Maria's and my keeping. Maria took my hand.

"This night, with the soft moonlight, is so beautiful," she said, as we strolled over to a spot where orchids were blooming in wild profusion. She picked a blossom and turned to me, working its stem into the buttonhole of my lapel. "Everywhere there are orchids here," she said, "but always the beauty and mystery is about them that no other blossom knows. Of the many flowers that grow in this garden, my favorite is the orchid. That is why I give you this one."

The moonlight cast a mellow glow over Maria's face, and her black hair was shimmering as she lifted her dark, velvety eyes to mine, her lustrous lips slightly parted in a half-smile. The blossom-spangled background served only to accentuate her beauty. The garden was rife with beautiful flowers, but Maria was the loveliest and most exotic of them all.

"*Señor* Mark," she said, rolling my name over her tongue and breaking it into two syllables, "what has happened? Why do you look at me like this?"

"Maria," I said hoarsely, "your father spoke the truth. You are the most beautiful woman I have ever seen. I was only wishing I had known you long enough to take you in my arms and kiss you."

"But *señor,* the kisses are for the lovers, are they not? And besides, an important man such as yourself could never love a poor Mexican girl like me."

"Listen, Maria, I speak your language, but some of your customs are strange to me. In my country, we love a person for what he is. Maybe a girl is rich and the boy very poor, or maybe one is Mexican and the other American, or some other nationality. It makes no difference, Maria. Love is the same between everyone, the world over."

"*Bueno,* Marek; if you promise what you say is true, then I will kiss you—not as a lover, but as a sister."

If the kiss Maria gave me was a sisterly kiss, I wish I had ten thousand sisters just like her. Her arms were smooth and warm around my neck, and her lips as soft as rose petals and as sweet as wine. I tried to return her kiss, but very gently she pushed my face away from hers and darted toward the house. At the door, she turned and came back. "That is not the way I would kiss my brother," she said teasingly. "Now you may give me *your* kiss, Marek.'' I took her into my arms and kissed her. All too soon, she slipped from my embrace and ran toward her room. As she reached the door she swung around and said, with a mixture of naiveté and coquetry, ''Thank you for the ride. *Buenos noches,* Marek. I am so proud you are not my brother.''

I stood there bewitched for a minute or two. Then I managed to stagger into the room where I had left *Señor* Vargas, Jim, Tex, and José. Damned if I wasn't drunker than the four of them put together! I must have looked like a fool, with my mouth wide open and an orchid in my lapel, but I couldn't have cared less; the others were either too drunk or too gentlemanly to take notice of my bemused condition or of the flower that graced my lapel.

I was still in a mesmerized state when *Señor* Vargas broached the subject of the mines he wanted to show me the next day, and exacted my promise to go along with him. Tex had stayed sober enough to suggest that we retire for the night. We thanked *Señor* Vargas for his hospitality, and staggered out to the car. My intoxication was purely emotional, but it was every bit as real as that of my three companions.

Chapter 2

THE NEXT morning, I drove José to his house so he could change into old clothes before we left for the mines. I also wanted to look around and get a clear picture of the premises, since it would be dark when we came for the treasure. The adobe house was a hundred years old if it was a day, and consisted of four rooms, two on each side, with a hallway running through the center. The patio, which did double duty as a corral for the goats and burros and a vault for José's untapped resources, was about sixty feet wide and one hundred feet long. An adobe wall some ten feet high had been built around it and joined to each side of the house. There was no gateway or door leading into it; the only entrance was through the hallway in the house. Large flat stones covered the floor of the patio.

When José had changed clothes, he joined me in the patio and pointed out the spot where the treasure was buried. "The *oro*, she is right here," he said, pointing to one of the stones, "and buried very safe. Soon as my *hermano* comes with the goats, we will dig it up." I was anxious for the hour to arrive when we could get the job done, and hoped it would not be delayed too long.

When we got back to the hotel, *Señor* Vargas and Pablo were waiting to go with us and show us the mines. We used the four-wheel-drive truck, and it took us less than an hour to reach the first mine. What I saw was a revelation to me. I had never seen a mine that had been worked by the Spaniards. This particular propertly had been worked more than three hundred years ago, and they'd driven a drift about three hundred feet back in the mountain; then the vein dipped down and they had sunk a shaft almost two hundred feet straight down, following the ore. After that, the vein leveled off again, and there was another six hundred feet of tunnel before we reached the end of the mine.

I have seen a lot of dangerous mines in my lifetime, but nothing to compare with that one. At times, the drift was so small we had to crawl on our hands and knees; then when the vein swelled, there would be plenty of room to stand up. The silver and lead ore was running in dolomite, with a lot of loose shale overhead. When I reached the back of the tunnel, I found a nice vein of ore, cut my samples as fast as I could, and got the hell out.

Señor Vargas insisted on showing me another property on the north side of the mountain. I heaved a sigh of relief when I found that the second mine had solid rock overhead. The tunnel was only about three hundred feet. The potential for a producing mine appeared very promising, but I explained to Vargas that a lot of exploration was needed and that the assay reports would be the deciding factor.

When we emerged from the mine and sat down on a boulder near the top of the mountain to rest and smoke a cigarette, I looked across the valley and saw a truck moving along the mesa about ten miles in the distance. Knowing how remote Loreto was, and how few cars ever came there, I asked José to explain the presence of a truck that close. He told me that it was on the Durango-Mexico City Highway, and that as the crow flies, it was only ten miles from Loreto straight across to this highway and to the village of Aquelia. I learned from him that because of the mountains and the deep canyon through which the river flowed, there was no way to build a road without the aid of engineers and expensive machinery. Pack horses and burros could go straight across, but cars had to go around the circuitous route we had come. The road we had taken to Loreto was the one and only road into the village. It was no wonder that little village had a primitive, virginal beauty about it; it was as isolated and inaccessible as a Tibetan lamasery.

We got back to the hotel about 5:00, dropping the

Vargases at their home. I was dead tired, but enthusiastic over the potential of the mining properties Vargas had shown us. I'd never seen better prospects, or a more highly mineralized area, and I was sure a profitable mining operation could be started with a very small investment.

Pablo came tearing over less than five minutes after we reached the hotel, and told us that his father had forgotten to tell us that he expected us for dinner. We washed up, changed clothes, and drove back to Vargas' home. This time we went directly to the dining room. None of us had eaten anything since breakfast, and we were five hungry *hombres*. We applied ourselves to the food with such intensity that there was little time for conversation during the meal.

After dinner, Vargas took us into the den and had a jug of mescal brought in. He asked me what I thought of the mines, and I told him that his properties looked very good and I was definitely interested in beginning operation if the samples assayed as good as I expected them to. "I'll take the samples back to the States in a day or two and have them assayed, and come back within thirty days, ready to set up operations." That, of course, would give me the excuse I needed to come back after the other half of the treasure.

"That is fine," said Vargas, "but you must not leave until after Saturday night, for we are making the dance for you that night. It will be the big affair and all the village would be much disappointed if you do not stay so we can honor you."

That caught us by surprise, for it was now Wednesday night, and we had all hoped to be gone from Loreto before Saturday night rolled around. I looked at Jim for a cue. He nodded his head, so I accepted the invitation. Then I asked where the nearest telephone was. Since we were going to be delayed longer than we had anticipated, I wanted to call our families so they would not worry.

"It's at Durango," Pablo spoke up. A hundred and twenty five miles was a hell of a long way to go to use a telephone, but I knew Nita would be climbing the walls with worry if she didn't have some word from us, so I determined I must call her at any cost, and have her pass the word on to Tex's wife.

Vargas' ears perked up at the mention of Durango. "Are

you going there tomorrow, *señor?*" he asked.

"Looks like I'll have to if I want to place a telephone call," I said.

"Can *Señora* Vargas, Maria and Pablo and I go with you?" he asked. "For a year now we have wanted to go, but the *camione,* she comes to Loreto only once a week, and most of the time she is broke and cannot come at all. When she does come, she breaks down and cannot come back."

I'd had a little experience with those dilapidated, third-class Mexican buses and I knew what Vargas meant. I told him I'd be glad to have them go along.

"Mama, Mama," he shouted to his wife, eager to share the good news with her, "tomorrow we go to Durango with *Señor* Mark!" *Señora* Vargas was as happy over prospective junket as he was, and they promised to be ready to go when I came for them at 7:00 in the morning. A trip to Durango was something to wave flags about. Loreto boasted only three cars—a '36 Model Ford that belonged to the village doctor, *Señor* Vargas' '38 Buick, and a '52 half-ton truck that the police used (when it would run). Not one of them would have been able to make it even half way to Durango, and the *camione* was just as sorry and undependable as Vargas had credited it with being.

When we got back to the hotel, Jim congratulated me on having sold myself to *el presidente.* "It'll make our job a hell of a lot easier," he said, "and eliminate any suspicion." The four of us held a session, and in spite of José's being so enraptured with the hotel life, I talked him into moving into his home, taking the truck with him and keeping it there. My theory was that if he kept the truck at his house every night, we had a much better chance of getting the treasure loaded without arousing suspicion; and that Saturday night, after the dance was over, we could slip over to José's, dig up the gold, load it, and be well on our way before anyone knew what the score was. We agreed upon that as a workable plan, and I told the others that it was my purpose to buy enough beer and mescal to have every Mexican in the village so drunk that they would pass out before the dance was over, and leave our way wide open.

When I reached the Vargas place next morning, they were ready and waiting. While Pablo and *Señora* Vargas were getting into the back seat, I asked Maria if she would honor me by riding beside me. This was the first time I had seen her since she gave me the "sisterly" kiss. She was beautiful in a white and blue fiesta dress, and her father was plainly pleased that I was paying attention to her. Once more the cash register started ringing up dollar signs in his eyes.

Being *el presidente*, he rode in front with Maria and me. Whenever he caught sight of a peon or sheepherder along the road, he would lean over and blow the horn until we had passed them and were well out of sight. He made sure that everyone saw him riding in the big new car. He insisted that I stop at every village we came to, sought out the local *presidente*, and introduced me and boasted about what a big mining man I was, and that soon we would have the big mines operating at Loreto. We finally made it to Durango. We had been on the road seven hours. All of us were pretty hungry by that time, so I pulled up at a cafe and invited the Vargases to be my guests for lunch.

I gave my order, excused myself and went to the nearby telephone to call Nita. For once I got the call through without having to wait. I told Nita we'd run into a delay, but that all was well, and not to worry; to please call Jackie and pass the word on to her and to hold the fort until I got back.

After lunch we drove downtown, where *Señora* Vargas and Maria could do the shopping they'd been saving up for a year. Having nothing else to do, *Señor* Vargas, Pablo and I went along with them, and did a little looking around while the women shopped. In a dress shop, we were standing nearby when I noticed Maria admiring a lovely white evening gown and calling her mother over to show it to her. I heard the saleswoman name the price, and I knew it was far more than *Señora* Vargas could afford to pay. When the *señora* shook her head, Maria's face fell. She looked as if she was about to cry, she was so disappointed. Knowing that Vargas too had seen and overheard the incident, I turned to him and said, "*Señor* Vargas, will you give me permission to buy the gown for Maria?"

Vargas appeared to be humiliated and embarrassed. "*Señor* Mark," he bristled, "never has anyone had to buy the clothes for Pancho Vargas' family. Maybe we are not so very rich, but always we have better than anyone in Loreto."

"*Señor,*" I said, "I did not mean to question that. It was only a token of gratitude for being invited into your home that I spoke. The gown is so lovely and Maria so beautiful that they were truly made for each other. It would make me very happy if you would allow me to buy it."

"No, *señor,* my humble house is also your *casa* and never would I think of accepting any pay or gift for what little hospitality we can afford," he said. "And in Mexico, *señor,*" he added, "only when a man has the very serious thoughts does he ask to buy such a nice gift, and if he is worthy, then the *señorita's* papa gives the permission. Do you like Maria?"

"*Señor* Vargas, the dress is Maria's if you will permit me to buy it. I like her very much."

"*Bueno, bueno,*" he said. "Mama, Mama," he shouted, "come quickly, and bring Maria!" The two women came over to where we were standing. "*Mamacita,*" he said excitedly, "the *señor* has asked the permission to buy the beautiful and expensive dress for Maria. He understands our custom that only when a man intends the marriage does he ask to buy such a fine gift."

I don't know who was the more embarrassed, Maria or me. All the clerks gathered around to hear the conversation, and began showering us with congratulations in the emotional manner of the Mexican people. I was glad we weren't in a grocery store, for we would have undoubtedly been showered with rice. I hadn't bargained for this, and for once I was at a loss for words.

I turned to Maria and asked, "Maria, do you want the dress?"

"It is a very lovely dress," she said simply, "and always I have dreamed of having such a beautiful gown, but Marek, if you are not sure in your heart that you want to buy it for me, please do not buy it."

"I want very much to buy it for you, Maria," I said. I called the salesgirl and told her to fit the gown for Maria, and asked her to help her select shoes and a purse to match.

Vargas suggested a drink, and the Lord knows I needed one. The bastard had my back to the wall. I didn't know what to do. I loved my wife and boys and I respected Maria. I was really in a bind. I wanted to stay in Vargas' good graces until I could move all the treasure, and I couldn't figure out how to do this without hurting and humiliating Maria. Knowing the ways and customs of the Mexican people, I was aware of the shame Maria would suffer if this went any further.

We walked around the corner to a *cantina,* and Vargas immediately took over, shouting and blustering in his usual bad taste. In short order it seemed to me that half the people in Durango had learned that a celebration was under way, and came running. Free drinks didn't come along every day. Three drinks later my problem remained unsolved. I had a hard time getting Vargas away. He was riding high, wide and handsome, and he didn't want to let go of the reins; but when he found that I wouldn't stay any longer, he reluctantly came along with me. I paid the bill, and we went back to the dress shop, where Maria was to pick up her dress before closing time, and where we had all agreed to meet. It was a major undertaking, but I finally managed to get everyone in the car and took off for Loreto.

On the homeward drive, Maria sat very close to me, and as soon as darkness came, she placed her hand on my arm. I pretended to ignore the gesture, but she did not seem to notice. She was so happy over her new outfit that she talked gaily every time she could get a word in edgewise, which wasn't often, for Vargas' big mouth kept going like a triphammer during the entire drive.

We got to Loreto about 10:00 and I drove the Vargases home and helped them unload their packages. I had no intention of dallying, but Maria asked me to let her show me her flowers while the full moon was shining directly down on the patio. The memory of my experience two evenings earlier was all too vivid, and I was determined to avoid a repetition of it. I didn't want to be alone with Maria, but I could think of no excuse that would sound plausible, so I walked into the patio with them. *Señor* and *Señora* Vargas and Pablo grabbed all the packages and took off like a trio of scalded cats.

Leading me by the hand to a stone bench under a palm tree on the far side of the patio, Maria sat down and drew me down beside her. Despite my resolution to avoid any further emotional involvement, I felt the warmth and wonder of her lithe young body coursing through my veins like warm wine and quickening my pulse. Then she edged away a few inches, turned to me and raised her arms, cupping my face within her hands. "Tonight, Marek," she said, "is the happiest and saddest night I will ever have in my whole life, no matter how many years I may live."

I tried to think of something to say, but Maria did not give me a chance to speak. "You see, I know you have the wife in the States. This day when you made the telephone call, I cannot understand the English, but being a woman, I can see the love in your eyes, and by the smile and the kindness of your voice, this I know." I had given it no thought at the time, but now I recalled that the telephone was close enough to the table at which the Vargases were sitting so that my voice could easily have been heard.

"Please tell me, Marek, is she so much more beautiful than I? And do you love her so very much?"

"Perhaps not in the way you are beautiful, Maria, but to me she is very beautiful, and I love her more than any woman I have ever known. I have every reason to love her, Maria. She has given me two fine sons that make my life complete and happy. I have all that any man could ask for."

"Marek, I know you would not lie to me; this I can also tell by your face. And you are very strong and very sure. You are not really beautiful—handsome perhaps, to any woman who knows you—but kind and gentle you are. This has made me love you; and many more women will love you when in their hearts they know you as I do."

Again I tried to frame some kind of reply, but Maria placed her hand over my mouth. "Please let me finish. A Mexican girl, or any woman who really loves a man, can only love once. You will always be my only love; and each night I will pray to the Virgin Mary to keep you safe from danger, and should you ever become unhappy, to guide you back to me, for always I will be waiting. Each month when the moon is overhead as tonight, I will wear my pretty dress, and sit here where we are sitting now, and with the moonlight shining on me, you will always be here beside me, no matter how far away you may be; and nothing can take you from my heart. Now I shall say goodbye, for the night of the dance, I will leave my heart here in my house.''

She gave me a long kiss. I felt her tears against my face. She made no sound, and when she raised her eyes and looked into mine, they were shining like luminous pools.

''Maria, I don't know what to say,'' I stumbled lamely. Any words of mine would seem puny and inadequate after her tender and eloquent avowal of a love which I could not reciprocate and had done nothing to earn. ''I am sorry I have caused you so much pain. I did not realize that you would come to love me. I did not mean this to happen.''

''Please do not blame yourself,'' she said, ''You could no more help me loving you than you can stop the sun from rising.'' She rose to her feet and started to leave. ''Do not feel hurt. I would not have had it any other way. You have given me very much to be thankful for, very much that I would never have known. I now have your love, although it could not be all mine, to remember you by, and it will last me all the days of my life. *Vaya con Dios, mi novio, no me olvides, yo oro.*'' It is a benediction as beautiful in English as it is in Spanish: ''Go with God, my sweetheart, forget me not, I pray.''

Suddenly she was gone, and I was alone in the silver-flooded, flower-scented patio. I went back to the hotel, but there was no sleep for me. Never had I met a woman like Maria. I cursed myself for the hurt I had left in her heart. I vowed never to be alone with her again, although I knew we would be forced together at the dance. That was something neither of us would be able to prevent. It was hours before I finally drifted off to a restless sleep.

Chapter 3

EARLY THE the next morning, Tex came in and woke me. José had sent his eldest boy to tell me that Juan had come back from the mountains and was now at José's house. I dressed quickly, had a cup of coffee, and hurried over to José's. Jim and Tex stayed at the hotel, since we all agreed it would be easier to deal with Juan if only he, José and I were present.

José was waiting for me at the door and asked me into the room where Juan was having a drink of tequila. Juan was a typical peon, ragged and dirty, his hair and beard unkempt. He wore sandals made from old car tires cut to fit his feet. It was the same type of sandal worn by most of the natives in Loreto. There must have been an awful lot of old tires imported into Loreteo, what with the village having only three motor vehicles to its credit.

Juan seemed genuinely glad to see me, and we talked for an hour before José finally got around to telling his brother what my mission in Loreto was. Juan immediately became wildly excited, and almost incoherent in his talk. Finally, we got the old boy calmed down to where he would listen to José. Over and over, he kept asking José if he was sure he could trust me.

"Juan, for two years I work for *Señor* Mark in the States," José said, "and all the time he know I did not have the passport, but still he would not report me to the authorities; and all this time he paid me as much as any of the miners were paid. And Juan, when you write me for the *dinero* so Rosa, your wife, can have the operation which saved her life, I do not have this much money. It was none other than my *amigo*,

30

Señor Mark, who gave me the money to send to you. The *señor* I love like I love you, and you are my brother, and if you will let *Señor* Mark, he will be your brother, too. He will make us very rich. He has the big car and also the money to move and sell the treasure, and already he has made friends with *el presidente*, and tomorrow night they are making the big dance in my brother's honor before he returns to the States to have the ore samples assayed; and he will be back in thirty days, so you see, everything she is perfect, nothing can go wrong. After the dance, we dig up the treasure. Our brother takes half of it and sells it and will be back in thirty days and pay us our money.''

Juan didn't like the idea of my taking half the treasure and not paying them until I came back for the other half. He didn't like it at all. I told him that this was the deal that José and I had made. ''Besides, Juan, if I gave you even a partial advance, how could you and José explain where you had suddenly gotten so much money without having sold the treasure that so many people suspect you of having? Not only would that make trouble for you and José, but I could never come back for the other half.

José went on to explain to Juan the plan we had worked out. ''In ten days, me and my family will go to visit our mama in San Luis Potosi, and when *Señor* Mark sell the gold, he will call me by the telephone. Then our brother-in-law, Roberto, and me will come back here to Loreto in his car, and tell everyone that our mama she is very sick, and you and Rosa and your family will go with us to San Luis. *Señor* Mark will come there and pay us the money and we will go to Mexico City and live like rich people and never come back to Loreto. When the chance come, *Señor* Mark will come back here and dig up the rest of the treasure and vamoose.''

Juan still had his doubts, and José tried to dispel them. ''We will be so careful digging up the treasure, throw all the dirt on a tarp, and then fill up the hole, leaving the rest of the treasure there so *Señor* Mark can be sure to find it when he comes back. We will be so careful that even if they become suspicious, they could never tell that the patio had been disturbed.''

"*Si*, she sounds very good," said Juan, "but if *Señor* Mark and the others get caught with the gold, what happens then?"

"If we get caught, we will never tell where we got the gold, and if you and José are ever questioned, you must say that you know nothing whatever about it, and stick to that story no matter what happens."

"And you, *Señor* Mark, what of you and your *compadres?*" asked Juan.

"Don't worry about us," I told him. "If we do get picked up, we've got enough money to buy our way out."

Juan finally agreed, and we sealed the pact by shaking hands all around. The transaction was completed as far as José and Juan were concerned. José would help me dig up half the treasure, and from then on I was on my own.

It was almost noon when José and I took Juan back to the hotel with us, and introduced him to Tex and Jim. *Señora* Padilla, who owned the hotel, had seen us as we arrived, and came in to tell us she had bought some good steaks and would start cooking lunch at once. As soon as she had gone, I told Tex and Jim in English that the deal had been made and everything was all set.

Señora Padilla soon called us, and we went down to the dining room. The treasure wasn't mentioned during the meal. The conversation centered around the big dance the next night. When lunch was over, José and Juan went home to water the goats. Then we went back to my room and I gave Tex and Jim a rundown on the deal with Juan and José. Not until after he had heard me through did Jim show any real interest or confidence in José's story. "In the twenty-five years I've ranched in Mexico," he opined, "I've heard of so many buried treasures that I don't even believe in Santa Claus any more. I only came along as a favor to you, Mark; I have to admit that. And I was kind of looking forward to seeing the silly look on your face when you found out what a sucker you'd been. I wouldn't have missed that for all the chili in Mexico!"

"You're a man of little faith," I told him.

"Right now, I'm on the buying end," Jim said, "and I'm

willing at this point to bet every cow on my ranch that José really does have the treasure. But if he's lying, I'll personally cut the little son of a bitch as slick as a muskrat.''

Señor Vargas' knock on the door called a halt to our discussion. He had come over personally, he explained, to invite us to his house for dinner again that evening. ''Already I have ordered the case of cold beer,'' he said, ''so come at once and enjoy it before it gets hot.''

We drove with *Señor* Vargas back to his place, and had just parked in front of his house when the beer arrived. It was delivered by *Señor* Gonzales, who Vargas told us was the man who owned the dance hall and *cantina* where the big dance would be held tomorrow night. Vargas introduced us to Gonzales, and I asked him how much tequila, mescal and beer he usually sold during a fiesta. ''For sure I do not know,'' he said, ''but I would guess around a thousand pesos tequila and mescal, and maybe five hundred pesos of beer, and two hundred pesos of wine and Coca-Cola for the *señoras* and *señoritas.*'' I knew damn well that he didn't sell half as much as he claimed he did. But for my purpose, it sounded fine and I doubled the ante.

''Since the dance is being in our honor,'' I told him, ''we want to buy all the drinks for the evening. I want you to serve two thousand pesos of mescal and tequila, a thousand pesos of beer, and one thousand pesos of good wine and Cokes for the *señoras* and *señoritas.*''

''I will do so, *señor*,''beamed Gonzales.

''And I don't want any mixed drinks,'' I added. ''Don't serve Cokes with the mescal or tequila.''

''*Señor*, never are drinks mixed in Loreto,'' Gonzales assured me. ''I swear to this.'' That was good news, for I wanted to make sure every Mexican in the village was so drunk by the time the dance was over that we could walk off with half the village and the surrounding countryside, and no one would realize what was going on until we were past Durango.

That was the largest order Gonzales had gotten in many a moon and he was obviously pleased over it. ''Only one thing bothers me,'' he said, scratching his head, ''I do not have this much in stock, and I will have to buy from other *cantinas*, and once they know I have such a large order, they will raise their price. I wonder if you could advance me some of the money now, so I can be sure to have everything you have ordered, and be ready when the party starts, to be sure she is a big success?"

I shelled out $320.00, the equivalent of 4,000 pesos. Gonzales was as surprised as he was delighted to be paid in full in advance. And no one could have been happier than I to contribute all I could toward the success of the party.

"Gonzales," Vargas said, not being able to resist an opportunity to get into the picture and throw his weight around, "I warn you, I will personally check to see that you serve the full amount that *Señor* Mark has paid for."

"*Señor* Vargas, how come you think that I, Pedro Gonzales, would hold out on you?" Gonzales asked indignantly. "Pedro Gonzales, *señor,* is a man of honor, and every drop will be as the *señor* has ordered."

When Gonzales left, Vargas voiced his pleasure as well as his fears. "*Señor,* it is very big of you to buy so many refreshments for the dance in your honor, but maybe you should not have ordered so much, since our jail is very small, and I do not know where we can put all the drunks. With so much free drinks, it is bound to be more people drunk than sober."

On that last score I was in complete agreement with Vargas. Both mescal and tequila have a kick like a three-year burro, and as cheap as they are, two thousand pesos worth, plus the beer and wine, ought to have all the natives so plastered within a few hours' time that they wouldn't know the ceiling from the floor.

After we had had a couple of bottles of beer apiece, dinner was served. I've never enjoyed a meal more than I did that one. Everything was coming up roses. We excused ourselves early in order to get a good night's sleep, so that we would be ready for the big dance the next night. We also made it a point to tell Vargas that we were leaving Loreto soon after the dance was over, so that we would be able to have the samples in El Paso Monday morning when the assay office opened.

When we got back to the hotel, José was waiting, with an old miner he introduced as Pancho Ramero. Pancho was supposed to have a good placer mine he wanted me to see the next day. My time was free until the dance, so I agreed to go. It was better than sitting around the hotel all day.

The next morning José and Pancho made it to the hotel in time to have breakfast with us. We drove about fourteen miles up arroyos and over hills that only a four-wheel-drive vehicle could have traveled. When we arrived at the placer, I found an old stream bed covering the area at least three hundred feet wide and half a mile in length that Pancho had been panning and sampling. There was no water within five or six miles. Pancho told us that he worked and sampled at least eleven months a year, getting ready for the rainy season. He only had water enough to pan three to four weeks, but in that short period of time, he made more than enough to see him through until the next rainy season.

We shoveled about a yard of sand into the truck and carried it back to where we had crossed the river. We took turns panning until we panned the entire load. It produced between five and six grams of coarse gold. I don't know whether the yard of sand we took was a representative sample. If it was, Pancho had a real live gold mine right on this earth, not the pie-in-the-sky kind we're always hearing about. Any time a placer will run a dollar a yard, you're in business, and the sample we took ran at least seven dollars a yard.

It was 5:00 when we got back to the hotel. I cornered José and told him about all the free drinks, and to be damn sure he sat at the table with me, to make his drinks weak, and I didn't mean maybe. I also instructed him to park the truck as close to the front door as possible when he drove it home and to leave it there and walk to the dance.

Pablo soon came over to extend *Señor* Vargas' invitation to us to have dinner with him again that evening. We thanked him, but explained that we had to shave and bathe, and it was going to rush us to be ready by the time the dance started, so we'd have to decline the invitation. Pablo said he was sure his father would understand. "You and *Señor* Tex and *Señor* Jim are to be sure to come to the table my father

35

has reserved for our family," he said in parting, "and, oh, yes, we have invited two pretty *señoritas* as partners for *Señor* Jim and *Señor* Tex."

"And, Pablo," I said, "as a special favor to me, will you please ask *Señor* Vargas to make room for José and his wife, Melinda, at our table?"

Pable was sure his father could arrange everything.

When Pablo left, we went over the plan once more, to see if we had overlooked any detail. Everything dovetailed perfectly. Unless something unexpected turned up, we had nothing to worry about.

Jim voiced a fear that the dance would last all night, but I felt certain that with all the free drinks coming up, it couldn't last beyond 3:00 at the latest. We cut cards to see who got the first bath. Tex won, so Jim and I had dinner while we were waiting our turn.

After dinner, I asked *Señora* Padilla for our bill. "Since we are leaving after the dance, I will pay you now, and we will not have to disturb you when we are ready to leave." She shook her head in a gesture that plainly questioned the sanity of her departing guests. "I no can savvy anyone starting on a long journey after dancing all the night."

"*Señora*," I assured her, "we are leaving so early only because we have to be in El Paso early Monday morning to keep an appointment."

Each of us gave her a hundred peso tip. That was a lot of money for her to have in hand at one time. She looked at it with tender, loving care, thanked us profusely, and assured us our rooms would be ready for us when we came back. "Also, I will have my son, Pepe, to sleep by the door tonight," she said, "so you can get in after the dance, to get your baggage." Each night when all the guests returned to the hotel, the door leading from the patio to the street was locked and barred from the inside.

I thanked our thoughtful innkeeper, and stepped outside for a moment to have a cigarette and admire the patio and flowers. Jim interrupted my meditation by yelling out to me, "Do you intend to go to the dance? If you do, you'd better hurry and get your bath; none of the *señoritas* will dance with

36

you if you smell like a sheepherder.''

Before I had finished dressing, Jim came into my room to hurry me along. "We're already late. Get your damn coat and let's go!" I slipped my coat on and turned around.

"Damn! Kid," Jim exclaimed, "you sure look sharp! If I were as young and full of fire and vigor as you are, I'd have so many blondheaded kids running around here, they'd change the name of the village to Gringoville."

"I hope I never live to be as old and worn out as you are," I told him.

"Listen, you cocky bastard," he shot back, "I may be sixty years old, but by God, I'll live to decorate *your* grave." He growled like a sore-tailed bear all the way out to the car.

With only three cars in Loreto, we had no parking problem. I parked about a hundred feet from the entrance to the dance hall. At least fifteen Mexicans surrounded the car to offer us advance thanks for the free drinks and to tell us how welcome we were. After about five minutes of backslapping and handshaking, we made our way inside. The mob was even bigger than I had anticipated, and the dance hall much larger than I had pictured it. Tables, chairs and benches covered at least two-thirds of the floor space, leaving a big space for dancing. Colorful paintings depicting Spanish and Mexican scenes and customs decorated the walls and created a gay, fiesta-like atmosphere.

Señor Vargas met us at the door, embraced me as if I were his long lost brother, and led us across the room and to the front of the bandstand. He held up both arms, to get the attention of the crowd, and introduced me to the people of his village. "As you know, this dance is being given in honor of my good friend, *Señor* Mark. Early tomorrow morning at 5:00 *Señor* Mark is leaving for El Paso with his two foremen," (the only recognition he gave Tex and Jim, who were standing beside me, feeling about as useful as a couple of Hula dancers at a camp meeting), "and with him he is taking ore samples of two mines I have shown him, and if they are as good as the *señor* thinks they are, soon the big mining job will start, with work for everyone." The crowd cheered. "Now, if anyone with a mine will bring the samples to my house, *Señor* Mark will inspect them when he comes back to Loreto soon."

A buzz of voices eddied around the hall as Vargas paused for a moment before resuming. "And now, for the big surprise: all the drinks for the whole evening have already been paid for by my good friend, the *señor*. Everyone can drink all they want tonight, and everything is for free. Do not all of you think that my friend, *Señor* Mark, in whose honor the dance was made and who bought all the drinks, should be made to feel welcome?"

The crowd cheered loud and long. Finally Vargas raised his hands and quieted them. Then he turned to me, "*Señor* Mark, you are truly one of us, and the first dance you shall have the honor of dancing with the beautiful *señorita* of your choice. Which of the pretty *señoritas* will you choose?"

"*Señor* Vargas, you have asked me to do the impossible," I said, striving to rise to the occasion. "There are so many beautiful *señoritas* here . . . With your permission, I shall ask Maria. I am such an awkward dancer, and since I *know* Maria, perhaps if I step on her toes, she will not slap me."

Vargas looked so pleased I thought he was going to pop the buttons off his jacket. Not that I didn't know damn well at the time that the old bastard would have had a heart attack if I had chosen any of the other *señoritas*.

I turned and walked over to the table where Maria sat with her family. I had not looked in her direction during *el presidente's* introduction and speech. I had spent enough time in Maria's company to have grown accustomed to her loveliness, but when she and I exchanged glances that night, my heart stood still. The new white gown brought out the creamy color of her pearly, fine-textured skin, a heritage from her Spanish ancestors. A mass of dark hair framed an oval face that had a serene, yet exciting quality about it. Her blue-black eyes were alight with happiness, and her petal-soft ruby lips were parted in a radiant smile. I would probably have stood there gazing at her in open-mouthed wonder for the rest of the night if Vargas hadn't signaled the band to start playing.

Maria was a superb dancer. In a semi-trance, I circled the hall with her in my arms. My lack of skill on the dance floor was compensated for by her proficiency. It took some artful maneuvering on her part, but I didn't step on her toes even once. All too soon the music stopped. When we walked back to our table, Gonzales was waiting to see if we were ready for him to start serving the drinks. He told me he had hired many men, so everyone would get fast service. Pretty *señoritas* were sitting by Tex and Jim, and José and Melinda were also at our table. After I had been introduced to the *señoritas* and exchanged greetings with the others, we all ordered Bacardi and Cokes. Once we had been served, Vargas again signaled the band and the dance was on. I turned to Maria and asked, "Shall we dance?"

"Maybe later," she smiled. "Please not now, for I have just danced every dance for the rest of my life."

I danced with Sophia and then with Marta. The chief of police, *Señor* Flores, came over and asked Maria to dance, and requested my permission.

"Go ahead, *señor*," I said, and with that, Flores led Maria onto the dance floor. That gave me a good opening to talk to José, so I asked him to show me the men's room outside, and questioned him as to how things were going.

"Everything, she is fine," he assured me. "Juan has carried the goats back to the mountains, all but five of them, which I will walk back and forth over the place after we have removed the treasure;. then no one can tell there has been any digging in the patio."

We want back inside and tried to forget the business at hand and enter into the spirit of the fiesta. The hands on our watches had never moved so slowly. By 1:00, José was well on the way to getting drunk. Once again, I excused myself and motioned to José to come along with me. Tex and Jim followed us out. I gave José a talking-to that he'd never forget. He promised to stick to Cokes during the rest of the dance.

"How much longer is this shindig going to last?" Jim asked impatiently.

"Damned if I know," I said. "I'm surprised it's lasted this long. I've never seen so many drunk Mexicans in one place at one time." The three cops were running their legs off trying to break up the fights. The jail was already so full they were just throwing the drunks out and letting it go at that. I told the others that if it didn't break up by 3:30, we had better revise our plan. José could pretend to be very drunk, and Tex and I could walk him home, dig up the treasure, load it under the truck seat, drive the truck back and park by my car. Tex and I would then go inside, mix with the guests, and Jim could drive the car back to the hotel, load our baggage and drive back to the dance. In this way, any suspicion ought to be averted.

By 2:00 most of the celebrants were so plastered they could hardly stand on their feet. It was then that the band took its second break of the evening. The leader, accompanied by Flores, came over to our table and had a drink. "How much longer will the dance last?" he asked.

"As far as we're concerned, another thirty minutes will be long enough," I told him, hesitant to appear not too anxious. "We have to leave Loreto early in order to keep an appointment we have in El Paso Monday morning, and we'd like to get a couple of hours of sleep if possible."

Vargas finally succeeded more or less in getting the crowd's attention, and asked how much longer they wanted to dance. His question produced no constructive suggestion. However, Gonzales came to our rescue when he announced that there was only one more round of drinks left, so it was generally agreed that the party would end at 3:00. I slipped the band leader 200 pesos on his promise that he would not play after 3:00. With that agreed on, Tex, Jim and I relaxed and enjoyed ourselves more the last thirty minutes of our going-away party than we had during the entire evening. Our hour was almost at hand.

At 3:00, the band played the last number. After shaking hands with the few who were still able to stand, I asked José to walk with Jim and Tex to the hotel while I drove the Vargases home. *Señor* Vargas was quite drunk and quite happy. So far as he was concerned, the evening had been an unqualified success. When we reached the Vargas home, I helped the ladies out of the car, and unlocked the patio door, since the head of the house was in no shape to find the keyhole. Each member of the family wished me separate goodbyes, and invited me back again. Vargas almost blew his cork when Maria only held my hand and said goodbye.

"Maria," he shouted, "Is this the only way you know to tell your lover goodbye?"

"Papa," Maria said quietly, "*Señor* Mark and I said goodbye when we were alone."

Vargas was not only placated, he was pleased. "Mama," he said, winking at *Señora* Vargas, "our daughter, she is the shy one, no?"

Maria had held my hand while Vargas was having his say. I gave it a gentle squeeze and looked into her lovely eyes. They were glistening with tears. She started to say something, then bit her lip and, without a word, turned and ran into the house.

I walked back to the car and slowly drove to the hotel. Not until I saw Jim, Tex, and José, did I remember the job we had to do and that there was very little time left before daylight.

Chapter 4

BACK AT the hotel we finally succeeded in rousing Pepe and
getting him to let us in. Once inside, fear took hold of José.
He didn't think we had time to complete the job before daylight and wanted to wait until the next night. I asked him
how deep the treasure was buried. With shaking hands, he
measured about eighteen inches.

"Look, boys," I said, "let's handle it this way. It's only
eight blocks to José's house, and Tex and I will walk him
home. José will pretend to be so drunk that we have to carry
him. When we reach the house, Tex can get into the truck.
As sandy as this soil is, even being cautious and throwing the
dirt on a trap, I can dig the treasure out in a short time, and
while I refill the hole, José can carry the gold and stack it by
the door. José, you did park the truck close to your house, at
the exact spot we had picked out?"

"*Si, compadre.* I parked where you showed me. I can step
from the truck into the door of my house."

"That's fine," I said. "Once you have the gold stacked by
the door, I'll come out of the house and walk to the back of
the truck and embrace you as we say goodbye. This will block
the view of anyone who might be looking up the street. Tex
can have the seat raised and when we come out and walk to
the back of the truck, he'll open the door and leave it open.
The door will extend almost to the front wall of the house and
block the view of anyone who might be looking down the
street."

Jim and Tex were sure it would work. José was so scared he
couldn't be sure of anything. Jim handed Tex the .38. "And

42

if I hear you fire, I'll be there *pronto* with the two shotguns," he said. "I'll have all our luggage sitting by the door, and when I hear the truck start, I'll load the car and be ready to go. When we get underway, we'll let Mark go ahead in the car. Tex can drive the truck, and I'll ride shotgun."

Jim and José shook hands and said goodbye. At long last we were ready to go; the waiting was over. Once outside in the street, José began shaking with fear. We had to carry him bodily. On the way we saw only four people, all stragglers from the dance. When we reached the house, we took a fast look up and down the street. No one was in sight. Tex got into the truck, and I held José up and led him into the house. Once the door was closed, I was gripped by excitement. "José, make a light and bring me the tarp and shovel!"

José had such a bad case of jitters that he couldn't do anything. I lighted the lantern, picked up the tarp and shovel, and asked José to lead the way to the patio. "Where is it, José, where do I dig?" For an agonizing minute, I thought he had decided to back out. Then he walked to the southwest corner of the patio and started counting the large flat stones that covered the floor. He stopped and set both feet on an oblong rock. "It is here, my brother."

"Are you sure this is the right place?" I asked. I sure as hell didn't want to dig a dry hole.

"*Si*, the *oro* we bury here, and the *plata* there." He indicated a stone to the right of the one he was standing on.

"*Bueno*. Help me move this stone, and then spread the tarp." The soil was harder than I had anticipated. José ran into the house and brought me a pick. A few strokes with the pick and I started shoveling dirt onto the tarp. I had dug down about eighteen inches when the point of the shovel struck something solid. "What did your bury it in, José?" I asked.

"We laid a cowhide down and stacked the bars on it. The gold coins we put in a leather bag sitting beside the bars. Then we folded the cowhide over so that all the gold was covered. Then we filled the hole."

I knew that in the thirty-five or forty years it had been buried, the cowhide would be decayed and rotten, so I forced

43

myself to work slowly, so as to approach it with care. I carefully removed the dirt down to where I could see the hide. I had to widen the hole before the entire top of the bundle was exposed; then with my hands I carefully cleaned all the dirt off.

I can't describe the feeling that swept over me as I reached down to fold back the old cowhide. I've never experienced anything like it. I looked up at José. He was shaking from head to foot, and I wasn't the calmest man in the world at that moment either.

"See, my brother, it is as I have told you," said José, trembling but triumphant.

"Yes, it is, José. Now, hand me the lantern." I carefully unfolded the hide, and the first thing I saw was the leather bag. Holding the lantern in my one hand, I opened the mouth of the bag with the other. Inside it were more gold coins than I had seen in my whole life. I raised the folded hide higher, and there were the gold bars, uniformly stacked. The bars were cold, but the touch of them sent a tingling sensation all through my body. I had to stifle an impulse to cry out in sheer joy and excitement.

"Look, José, isn't that the loveliest sight you have ever seen?" I whispered.

"*Si*, my brother; but please hurry. Already is coming daylight." That warning brought me back down to earth.

I reached down and picked up a bar of gold. The bars were about five inches long, three inches wide, and two inches thick. I had never lifted anything so heavy for its size. There were nineteen bars, weighing between twenty and twenty-five pounds each. Once the bars were out of the hole, I could see that the leather bag containing the gold coins was so decayed that if I tried to pick it up, it would dissolve into dust. I didn't want to scatter the coins. I reached into the bag and took three of the large centenarios and put them into my pocket. The entire cache of coins probably weighed fifty pounds.

"I'll take ten of the gold bars, and leave nine bars and the coins. All right?"

"*Si, señor*, only please hurry!"

44

"All right. José, you carry these bars and stack them as close to the door as you can. I will put these nine bars back in the hole, with the coins . . . No, damnit, carry one in each hand." He had tried to carry five or six of the bars across his arm, and they were so heavy he fell over backwards when he tried to get up.

For once, I didn't have to tell him to hurry. By the time I replaced the bars and covered them over with the old cowhide, José was on his fifth and final trip. I threw a little dirt into the hole, and told him to jump in and pack it down while I shoveled. After I had replaced all the dirt, we took the tarp, folded it down the middle and shook it free of dirt. Then we painstakingly replaced the stone. After a careful look around, we were satisfied that we had left no trace that would indicate there had been any digging or disturbance.

I looked at my watch. It was five minutes after 5:00. We had been inside just twenty minutes. "Let's go, José," I said. I opened the door and stepped outside. I asked Tex if he had noticed anything unusual.

"Nope," he said. "A guy has been standing up there," he pointed up the street, "all the time you were inside, but he's probably a drunk."

"To hell with him," I said. "We have the gold, Tex. It's just inside the door. Load it while I tell José goodbye." José and I walked to the back of the truck. "Listen close to what I have to say," I said to him, "and this also goes for Juan. You be sure and tell him when he comes back. If we get caught, we will never tell where we got the gold, and don't let anyone scare you or Juan into admitting that you had it. Even if we should lose all of this, there's still enough left to give all of us nice bank accounts. And when you go to San Luis Potosi, be sure to leave the lantern full of oil, and the tarp and shovel where I can find them."

By that time Tex had got the gold loaded. "Let's go, Mark," he said.

As I embraced José, I realized that I had actually grown to love him as if he were my brother. "Take care of yourself, José, and I'll call you in San Luis in a few days."

"*Adios, mi hermano*," José replied, "*tien cuidado; te*

45

protejas Dios.'' Of all the blessings I have ever received, none was ever more sincere than that one. I knew it came straight from the heart. "Goodbye, my brother, be careful; may God protect you."

I climbed into the truck beside Tex and we drove slowly to the motel. "How much do you think the gold is worth?" Tex asked.

"I would guess over a million; and we left more than we're taking."

Jim had heard us approaching. He had the car packed and was ready to go. He motioned for Tex to turn the truck around and stop beside the car. When we pulled alongside the car, he asked, "Everything go all right?"

"Like clockwork," I told him. "There was even more gold than José had remembered."

"That's good, Mark. Now get your carcass out of that truck and hold the door, so I can get these shotguns in without the whole village seeing me." While Jim was accomplishing that feat, I got into the car. "Mark, you go ahead," Jim said, "and we'll follow."

I drove slowly down the street. About three blocks from the village was the arena where the bull and rooster fights were held. The road circled around the arena and across a large arroyo. Once behind that, we would have it made. As I started down the arroyo, I looked back; the truck was less than fifty feet behind me. I was ready to congratulate myself on a perfect job when I saw something that made me look a second time before I could believe my eyes. On the far side of the arroyo, parked across the road, was the old Dodge truck the police used. I couldn't think of any place we had slipped; but I knew something was wrong. Bad wrong.

I drove up to within thirty feet of the truck and stopped. All three of the village policemen were standing beside the truck, their hands on their pistols. As I got out of the car, Tex pulled alongside and stopped. I noticed that Jim had his head lying in the door, as if asleep or passed out. I decided to try to bluff our way through. Hoping to seize the initiative, I walked up to them and spoke. "That was one big dance, no? I am happy you all came out to tell us goodbye. I missed

seeing you after the dance, but I know you were quite busy.''
It was a noble experiment, but it didn't work.

Flores, the chief, snarled, ''Why you leave this early?''

''Look, *amigo,*'' I replied in Spanish, ''you yourself heard my good friend, *el presidente* tell everyone we were leaving at 5:00, and already it is after 5:00.''

''This I hear,'' Flores said, ''but why did you not sleep a little while as you say? And why you take José home and walk when you have the car? And why you stay so long in José's house?''

''José was sick, and I didn't want him to mess up the car, and when we got to his house he wouldn't let me leave without having a last drink; and when someone is as drunk as José was, these last drinks take a long time.''

''Maybe it is as you say; then again, maybe you have something to hide, for you stay too long in José's house.'' Now, I knew who had been watching the house while we were inside.

''Now, look, Flores, what could we possibly have to hide? You yourself watched all the time I was inside the house. Did I bring anything out with me? José has only one thing I want; his friendship.''

Flores wasn't convinced. He admitted that he hadn't seen anything suspicious, but added that it was dark and the truck was parked so close to the house he could not see very clearly.

Reasoning that Flores was leading up to a pay-off, I reached into my pocket and pulled out a hundred dollar bill. ''Flores, I had intended to bring you a new pistol when I came back. Here's a hundred, buy yourself one, or do whatever you like with the money. Okay, *amigo?*''

''I am not your *amigo*. I do not want your damn money, and Maria she is the fool to want either you or your money.'' It hadn't occurred to me, until I looked into his face, that the bastard was drunk and crazy jealous. If I have ever seen hate written in anyone's face, it was in Flores'!

''Now, wait a minute,'' I set out to calm him, ''you are all wrong. This very night Maria told me she would never marry anyone except one of her own people; and the way she looked at you when you were dancing, I believe you are the lucky one.'' Crossing my fingers when I told that whopper didn't ease my conscience in the least. Not because I had any qualms about lying, but because the lie involved a woman I admired and respected and would remember as long as I lived.

"I do not believe you," Flores snapped, "all you say is the lies."

For the first time, Alfonso the fat cop spoke, "Maybe he does speak the truth. I follow them to Senor Vargas' house like you tell me to, and Maria only shakes his hand like the rest of the family. I am too far, I cannot hear what they say, but it looked like she say goodbye to a friend, not a lover."

That cooled Flores down a little. "Maybe it is as you say, but still we will take them back to the village and when *el presidente* wakes up we will search them, for still I do not believe them."

"Are you ready to take them?" I asked Tex in English.

Flores jerked his pistol out and pointed it at my stomach. "Do not speak the *gringo*. I cannot understand."

"Flores," I said placatingly, "I only told my friend to go to the car and bring the bottle of good whiskey that we brought from the States, so we could all have a drink."

"We do not want your whiskey," he shouted. "I will fire if he starts to the car." I was standing between Jim and Flores. I knew that if I had been out of the line of fire, Jim would have blown the strutting idiot in two when he pulled his gun.

"Put the gun away, Flores, we're not going to cause you any trouble. We have nothing to hide, and we will go back to the village with you."

"No!" he shouted. "Felipe will drive the truck with the drunk one; Alfonso will drive the car with this one," pointing to Tex; "and you, *Señor Gringo,* will ride in the truck with me, so you will not escape." I wasn't buying any of that. I knew that once Tex and Jim were out of sight, the crazy bastard would shoot me in the back.

In his reference to Maria, Flores had unwillingly given me a cue that could mean the difference between life and death for me. I mentally asked Maria's forgiveness for the unworthy thing I was about to do. I hated to drag her name into this fray again, and in another lie, but I had to find a way to get hold of Flores' hand, and quick. "I will have to admit you are a better man than I am. I am embarrassed and hurt because Maria has chosen you instead of me; but as humiliating as this is to me, the *Americano* is still a man, and I want to congratulate you and wish you the best of luck. Are you man enough to shake my hand and accept my congratulations?'' I stepped forward and extended my right hand.

Flores changed the pistol to his left hand, and a smile, half triumphant, half scarcastic, broke over his face as he extended his right hand. As our hands touched, he opened his mouth to speak, and I wish now that I might have heard what he was going to say, but the words never came out. Since I had been out of the service, I hadn't had a chance to use the Judo I had learned in the Navy, and I was afraid my timing might be off. But never had I thrown anyone as hard as I did Flores. He hit the ground like a wet sack, and the impact jarred his pistol out of his hand. I'll have to give the son of a bitch credit for being tough. He was on his hands and knees when I got to him. With my left hand, I grabbed him by his hair, and started from my shoe tops with a right upper cut. When the punch landed, pain ran all the way up my arm into my shoulder. The sweetest sound I ever heard was the cracking of his jaw bone.

I turned around quickly. There was no need to hurry. Tex had his pistol rammed into Alfonso's fat belly, all the way to the cylinder. Jim had the shotgun out of the window, aimed at Felipe.

"By God, kid," he said, "you ought to have been a preacher or a politician. I thought you were going to talk all day. Something else—I want you to teach me that hold you just used on Flores."

"Right now?" I asked. For once, Jim was speechless.

I picked up Flores' pistol and told Tex to get Alfonso's and Felipe's guns, which were still under their belts. At that, the two of them became wildly excited. Felipe dropped down on his knees, begging and pleading for their lives.

I walked over to the car and got the fifth of whiskey that we had brought from the States and never opened. *"Amigos,"* I said to Alfonso and Felipe, "come have a drink with me; and don't be afraid. I will not let anyone harm you." If anybody ever needed a drink, those two Mexicans did. They were so scared they could hardly hold the bottle. I told Tex to drive the police truck off of the road, then pull all the wires off of the distributor, and leave their guns in the truck.

Confident by now that we weren't going to harm them, both men took another drink. Then they began to curse Flores for all they were worth. I let them swear for a while; then I interrupted and asked if they would do me a favor.

"*Si, si, señor;* anything you want, we will do."

"I want you to go together this very evening to the house of my good friend, *el presidente,* and explain all of this to him. Also tell him the only reason I knocked Flores out was that he was so drunk, and I was afraid he would shoot me. Now, both of you are policemen; please search the truck and car so that you can truthfully tell *el presidente* that we have nothing to hide, and that Flores was wrong and he only caused this trouble because he was so jealous."

"No, so, *Señor* Mark. Never would we doubt your word. We know there is no need to search. You have nothing to hide. That we know. And now you are free to go. Please accept our apologies. We and all of the village will be shamed by that son of a bitch of a burro. He was crazier than the jackass who eats the loco weed."

I reached into my pocket and got the one hundred dollar bill I had tried to give Flores. Neither of them knew how much it was worth. When I told them it was the same as six hundred, twenty-five pesos each, they were dumbfounded. They only made eight pesos a day, and this was more money than they had ever had at one time in their lives. "We cannot accept so much," they said, "when we have nothing to give you in return."

"I do not want anything in return," I told them. "You are doing me a big favor by going to *el presidente* for me; please accept this as a gift." Since I had put it that way, they couldn't refuse. I was not to worry, they assured me; they would take care of everything.

I gave them the fifth of whiskey and asked them, as another favor to me, to stand by until Flores came to. I still wanted to be his friend, I told them, and didn't want him to be left alone. They both gave me pumping handshakes and said they would be anxiously awaiting our return. Taking the bottle over to where Flores was lying, Alfonso gave him a hard kick in the ribs, and Felipe stamped on his hand. He didn't move. I knew he would be out for a long time, and by the time he did regain consciousness, I was pretty sure they would be so plastered they wouldn't know midnight in Paris from high noon in the Sierras.

I asked Jim and Tex if they were ready to go. "Hell yes," Jim said. "I've been ready ever since we stopped."

As I got into the car, Jim said to Tex, "Of all the snow jobs I've ever heard of, that one took the cake. Damned if Mark didn't make those two Mexicans think he did them a favor. He's a patient man. I would have bent a gun barrel over their heads."

After we had crossed the arroyo, I looked back. Alfonso had the bottle turned up, and Felipe was searching for it. We were in the clear for the present, even if they ran for help the minute we were out of sight. First, they would have to wake *el presidente* and tell him what had happened. Then Vargas would have to decide if he wanted to have us stopped. I didn't believe he would, but if he did, someone would have to ride a horse ten miles over to the village on the Durango Highway, and have the alarm sent out from there. There were no communications into or out of Loreto.

We were sure of at least a two hour start, but the twenty-five miles of rough road before we came to the other village had always taken three hours to drive. If Mr. Ford could have been along on that twenty-five mile ride, he would have been pleased with his product. We were only an hour and forty minutes driving it.

Few people were on the streets as we passed through the village. The dirt road beyond it seemed like a four-lane highway compared to the miles we had just covered. Then my worry set in, wondering if it were possible that Alfonso and Felipe had had time to give the alarm. I reached the highway quicker than I had expected, and heaved a sigh of relief when I saw there wasn't a car of a human being in sight. I'd been traveling at a pretty good clip and had to slow down and let

Tex catch up. He signaled that he was running at top speed.

It seemed only a matter of minutes before I noticed a large lake on my right. We were only seven miles from Durango. Tex began blinking his lights on and off and I slowed down. They went around me and motioned me to follow. As we approached a bridge that crossed a river about three miles from Durango, Tex slowed down. I followed him across the bridge, six miles east on a dirt road, north toward the highway, and across it to the same dirt road we had been traveling.

I finally got Tex stopped and asked him why we didn't take the highway to Torreon. Jim answered, "Look, Mark," he said, "This old road will intersect the highway going to Parral. This way we dodge Durango."

"That's *magnifico,* Jim," I said, sarcastically, "but I'm just about out of gas."

"What the hell you think I have in that fifty gallon drum in the back of the truck? It sure ain't buttermilk."

Before I could answer, they were off. In a few minutes we came to the Parral highway. We drove about thirty miles and reached an arroyo with a lot of scrub timber. Tex pulled off the road and behind some trees, where we couldn't be seen from the highway. While Tex and I filled the cars with gas, Jim had his first look at the gold. Removing a bar from under the seat and taking a good look, he whistled and said, "Goddamn, Mark, if this ain't the prettiest stuff I ever saw."

"How much do you think a bar will weigh?" I asked him.

"I'd say between twenty-two and twenty-five pounds," he said.

Jim stroked the bar affectionately and put it back with the others. "Before we get back to Parral," he said, "let Tex and me take the lead. I have a good friend who runs a filling station and cafe there. While the cars are being serviced and we have something to eat, he can be trusted to drive through town to see if a road block has been set up or an alarm sent out.

About sixty miles before we got to Paral, we passed the big ranch that the Mexican government had given to Pancho Villa in order to stop him from fighting. In passing, I gave him a wave and a "*Gracias,*" for he was the *hombre* who started it all some thirty or forty years ago. I was grateful to him and felt I owed him my respects.

Before entering Parral, I slowed down and let Jim and Tex take the lead. The service station attendant gave Jim a hearty welcome and said he'd be happy to get the information Jim sought. When the cars were serviced we drove back to the cafe and parked where we could keep an eye on the truck from inside the cafe. While we were waiting to be served, the service station man came back and announced that he hadn't been able to pick up any information whatever.

"What do you think, Jim?" I said.

"I'm afraid you broke that damn Mexican's neck," Jim replied comfortingly. "He sure fell with his neck twisted. If you did, they'll catch us somewhere between here and Chihuahua. I know an old road from here to Guantemeco that I've used in buying cattle. It's about one hundred and sixty miles, and there's no danger of our being stopped going that way. I don't think you can ever get the car over it, but we ought to try anyway, because I've got lots of rancher friends in that vicinity. If we had to leave the car, it would be better than losing all the gold; and if you did break Flores' neck, I can get the whole deal settled without too much trouble if we can make it back to Casas Grande or Chihuahua. If they catch us here, our goose is cooked."

The waitress brought our order of beans, potatoes, and meat, which was all the bill of fare offered, and we were so hungry that it tasted like manna from Heaven. Jim asked the waitress to fix a box supper to carry with us.

About three miles out of Parral, Jim stopped and turned the wheel over to Tex, telling us to stay on the old road until we came to a river, then to call him; that he was going to sleep in the back of the car. The road was as rough as they come. Most of the time we were traveling over rolling arroyos. Twice Tex had to back up and tow me out of sand beds.

Just before sundown, we passed over a small mountain, and I could see the river. When we stopped at the river, I had to shake Jim to wake him. He was surprised we had made as good time as we had; we were about half way, he said. We got out and ate our box supper. I walked up a short way to where the water was deeper, and asked Jim and Tex if they wanted to join me in a swim. Tex was all for it, but Jim said, "I only bathe on Saturday, and any damn fool ought to know this is Sunday."

Jim told Tex to ride with me, so we could alternate in driving. "I'm good for the night," he said. "There are several roads that cross the one we are on, and we damn sure don't want to get lost."

Tex offered to drive, but I insisted that he sleep a while; then he could relieve me. About 1:00 we crossed one of the most rugged mountains God ever created. How anyone could have slept with the car bumping over the rocks, and the grinding sound of iron as the frame skidded over high centers, is beyond my understanding. It was enough to make a corpse sit up and take notice. On top of the mountain was a rock ledge so high the car couldn't pull over it. I backed up and tried to cross at an angle. I got the front of the car over, but didn't have enough speed to clear the entire vehicle. The back wheels were at least six inches off the ground. I blew the horn, and Jim backed up, and towed me over.

"I don't see how in the hell you made it this far," he said, "I've been in four-wheel drive for the past six or seven miles. I would have bet all that gold against a lead peso that you couldn't do it! This is the last real rough place. From here on, it's sandy as hell, but open country. We've got her made."

We had gone only another mile or two when I had a flat tire. After I changed the tire, I looked into the back seat. Tex was sleeping the sleep of the just.

We finally arrived at Guantemeco about 9:00 in the morning. It had taken us eighteen and one half hours to drive the one hundred and sixty miles. It wasn't what you'd call establishing a speed record, but after all, we'd come over an obstacle course, not a speedway.

Chapter 5

EVERYBODY IN the village seemed to be on first name terms with Jim. He introduced Tex and me as artist friends of his who wanted to paint some desert scenes. Like most *gringos,* though, he told them, our rear systems were too soft to take to riding in a truck, so we had spent our time getting out of sandbeds instead of painting. All the natives agreed that, truly, *Americanos* were very thick-headed like the burro when it came to traveling in the sand and desert.

While we were having breakfast, Jim suggested that we could separate here if we wanted to. "There's a good road from here to Chihuahua," he said, "and it would save you from having to fight your way over another hundred miles of road as rough as the one we've just left behind us. I'm safe now, and I'm back here where I know everyone, so if you fellows want to take off for home, I'll head for Casas Grande." With a tongue-in-cheek grin, he added, "If you trust me with the gold?"

That was a pretty rhetorical question if I ever heard one. To say that I trusted him with my life would have been a gross understatement. I had known Jim Dunlap eleven years. He had practically adopted my two boys. The previous summer they had spent three weeks of their vacation with Jim at his ranch; and nearly every weekend, if Nita would let them, they would call Jim and lament that they didn't have anything to do. In about two hours, "Uncle Jim" would be knocking on the door, ready to fly them to the ranch for the weekend. When they returned from their summer vacation with him, he gave them a large sealed envelope with instructions to turn it over to Nita and me for safe-keeping and not to open it until after his death. Since Jim had no family of his own, I had a pretty good idea what the envelope contained.

"Are you sure you can fly the gold across the river without any trouble?" I asked Jim.

"Hell, yes," he said. "I have been flying the river for twenty years and I've never had any trouble; but I have to admit this is the first time I've ever flown any unlawful cargo across. Mark, do you remember that little abandoned airstrip about twenty miles from your place, where we practiced landing six years ago, when I was trying to teach you to fly?" I remembered it well, and told Jim he had done a good job teaching me; that I now had over five hundred hours of flying time.

"Damn, Mark, if you don't get cockier every day! I didn't ask you to tell me how many medals you'd won as the world's greatest pilot, I just asked you if you remembered the airstrip. Now, shut up a minute and listen to me. I'll leave the ranch at daybreak, stay on the same course I always fly, and identify myself at the check station at Columbus. You and Tex be at the old airstrip. I'll touch down just long enough to unload the gold, and then head straight for the airport; and if the authorities want to search the plane, let 'em."

I followed Jim out of the village to the point where he turned off to go to Bavicora, Buenaventura and Casas Grande. He pulled off the hard-surfaced road and stopped on a sponge-soft, sandy road that led to Bavicora. I was glad we didn't have to follow; I had had enough rough roads and sandy roads to last me a lifetime. Tex and I got out and walked over to say goodbye. Jim and Tex, who had become fast friends in that adventure-filled week, shook hands and said goodbye. Then Jim extended his hand to me and said, "I'll see you and the boys tomorrow, you ugly little . . ."

That's as far as he got. I couldn't resist giving him the same treatment I'd given Flores. To make sure I didn't hurt him, I held onto him until his feet touched the ground. As soon as I let go, I ran to the car and jumped behind the wheel. As I started off, I hollered to him, "That was the first lesson on the hold you asked me to teach you when I rocked Flores to sleep."

That brought Jim back to life. "Come back here, you cocky little bastard. I've got a few things I'd like to show *you*." In the rear-view mirror, I could see Jim standing there in the middle of the road, shaking his fist. I couldn't hear him, but I knew the words that were tumbling out of his mouth in rapid succession weren't the kind you'd hear at Sunday School.

Once we'd lost sight of Jim, I stopped. "Okay, Tex, it's all yours. This cat hasn't had any sleep in over fifty hours, and that back seat looks like it's just my size. Be sure to stop in Chihuahua, gas up, and have the flat tire fixed."

It seemed as if I had been asleep only a few minutes when Tex literally shook me awake. We were at the inspection station, only eighteen miles from Juarez. I had slept while Tex had driven over three hundred miles. We had no trouble clearing customs; and what's more, we were almost at journey's end. It was just a thirty minute drive from there to El Paso. Once arrived in that fair city, which looked fairer to me than it had ever looked before, I headed for a nice restaurant. Visions of a big, juicy steak, with all the trimmings, and all the cold milk I could drink, were dancing in my head.

We had been too preoccupied, physically and mentally, to give any thought to our appearance. We'd been two days without shaving or changing our clothes, and if I hadn't been well known by the management, I am sure we would never have made it inside the restaurant. A waitress brought us the menus and looked at us in surprise as she handed them to us. Then she took a second look and recognized me. "What in the world happened to you?" she asked, with an air of incredulity.

"You wouldn't believe me if I told you, honey. Just pretend you never saw us before and bring us two of the best steaks you've ever served, and with all the trimmings."

While we were waiting to be served, two beminked dowagers came in and started to sit at the table next to ours. One of them happened to glance at Tex and me. She almost swooned with horror, grabbed her companion by the arm, and with an air of outraged pride, said, "Come, Hortense, let's go elsewhere. What is this restaurant coming to—catering to such riff-raff?"

When Betty returned with the steaks, she said in a low meaningful voice, "I'm sorry, but I forgot to ask how the sheep were when you left them."

I was too tired to appreciate the joke, but not too tired to appreciate the sizzling steaks she served us. If I've ever eaten a more succulent, savory or scrumptious steak, I don't remember where or when.

It was only a three hour drive from El Paso to our town. When we drove up to my house, Tex's wife was there, having a waiting-and-wondering session with Nita, so we had a happy double homecoming. The returning prodigals looked like a brace of shaggy dogs, and our spouses would have been justified in holding us at arm's length, but they couldn't have given us a warmer greeting if we'd been decked out in white ties, tails, and boutonnieres.

Nita put on the coffee pot, and while the coffee was brewing, we told the girls that we'd had a close shave with disaster, but had accomplished our mission and the trip had been even more fruitful than we'd hoped for. Before they had time to pose any questions, the door flew open and my two sons bounded in, just home from the movies. They asked more questions about the trip in two minutes than I could have answered in two weeks.

While I was renewing acquaintance with the boys, I heard Nita introduce Tex to someone. I looked up from my position on the floor, where I was roughhousing with the boys, and there stood my wife's brother, Elbert. Seeing him was, to put it mildly, a surprise. He lived in the East and I'd seen him only twice, on vacation trips. I knew his family looked upon him as a black sheep, but personally, I'd always liked the guy. I got up and shook hands with him. All of us sat around for an hour or so drinking coffee and shooting the breeze. Then I hustled the boys off to bed. They were fairly foaming with excitement, delighted that Uncle Jim was coming the next day. Jim had them both spoiled rotten, and seldom failed to bring them a gift, no matter how often he came.

After we'd said goodnight to Tex and Jackie, I headed for the bathroom. A hot shower and shave restored my self respect and left me feeling like a new man. Nita had gone to bed, and I went in and joined Elbert in the kitchen and had another cup of coffee. Elbert told me he was looking for a job. That gave me a jolt since I knew he had fifteen years seniority with a major company.

"I've been fired," he said. "I let the bottle get the best of me, and went to work drunk once too often." I made no comment. "I've got no one to blame but myself," Elbert said.

At least, I admired him for being man enough to admit he was at fault.

"Mark, I wonder if you can help me find a job. I've learned my lesson, and I'm never going to touch another drop of the stuff as long as I live."

"Elbert, I've really had it this last week. I'm a spent force, and I've got to hit the hay and get some rest; but we'll talk about it tomorrow, and I'm sure we can work out something."

It was wonderful to lie down in a clean bed again. Never had clean sheets felt so smooth and cool. Gently I took Nita into my arms. I thought she was asleep, and gave her a little shake. "Wake up, darling," I said. "Your man is home and you've got a lot of loving to do, to make up for the week he's been gone."

"Yes, I know," she answered in a troubled voice, "but first I want to tell you how much we have worried about you, Mark; and I've got to tell you about Elbert, too. He came three days ago, and the day before he got here his wife called me, collect, and wanted to know if he was here. She said he had left home over three weeks ago. He was fired five months ago, and Mary said he had never tried to find another job, just stayed drunk until he had spent all their savings, and then borrowed money from friends until no one would lend him any more. Then he mortgaged all of their furniture, gave Mary five dollars and left. The Lord only knows where he's been during those three weeks."

Nita was visibly upset, and trying hard to keep from crying. "Mary called because the baby was sick and she didn't have the money to have the doctor's prescription filled. Elbert left town owing so many bills that the drug store refused to give her credit. I hope you understand, Mark, and don't be angry with me; I wired Mary one hundred dollars.''

"Of course I'm not angry, honey; it was the thing for you to do.''

"Mark, Elbert is my brother, and I love him, but my love doesn't blind me to the fact that he is no good. Please just buy him a tank of gas, give him a few dollars, and send him on his way. He all but broke dad; and he has hurt or messed up every member of his family he has been around. Please don't let him stay here and destroy us, too.''

"I know you're upset and unhappy, darling," I said, stroking her hair, "but Elbert can wait until tomorrow. Tonight, let's talk about us. Are you too sleepy to hear about our trip?''

"Of course not, sweetheart, I want to hear all about it. Tell me everything.''

I told her everything, just as it happened, and I didn't try to make any excuses or offer any alibis when I came to Maria. I didn't know it would be so hard to try to find words to explain three kisses. At the mention of Maria, Nita stiffened and became tense. She said nothing, but I knew what she was thinking.

"My darling," I said to her, holding her close, "We've been married eleven years, and please believe me when I tell you I have never been unfaithful to you—not even once. Maria was beautiful, the most beautiful woman I have ever seen, or ever hope to see, and she was unfaithful to you. I ask not fall in love with her, and I was not unfaithful to you. I ask you to believe that, Nita.'' Nita neither relaxed nor replied.

I got up to go to the bathroom, which was just across from our room, and as I reached for the light switch, I was startled by Elbert's voice. "I'll be right out," he said. "I didn turn the light on because I thought you and Nita were asleep and I was afraid the light might wake you." I wondered for an instant if he had been eavesdropping, but quickly dismissed the thought.

When I got back to bed, I drew Nita into the circle of my arms; but hurt and doubt had raised a wall between us. If I had been a thousand miles away, we could not have been farther apart. Nita soon went to sleep, but I lay awake for hours, cursing myself for going to Mexico, and cursing José for telling me about the gold. I would gladly have given all the gold in the world if I could remove all doubt from Nita's mind. I wondered if I would ever be able to convince her that I had withheld nothing from her, if she would ever believe in me again.

Early in the morning the ringing of the phone awakened me. It was Tex, calling to see if I was ready to go to meet Jim. I dressed and drove over to pick Tex up. After a fast cup of coffee, we headed for the old airstrip. We parked a short distance from the strip, so it wouldn't look as if we were waiting for a plane, should someone happen along. We rehashed our adventure, and before we realized it, it was 8:00. Jim should have arrived by that time. We started counting the minutes, and when he didn't show up by 9:30, we were really worried. I was trying to dredge up one reason or another to account for the delay when Tex tapped my arm and said, "Listen. Do you hear a plane?"

I grabbed the binoculars and heaved a sigh of relief when I saw Jim's black and white Cessna heading toward us. We drove to the edge of the strip. The plane was still rolling when we drove alongside. Jim opened the door. "The first goddamn time I have overslept in twenty years," was his greeting and his farewell. The bars were in three gunny sacks; he handed them out to us and started his run. He was on the ground about thirty seconds.

On the way home, I stopped at the bank. I walked up to Bill Bradford, the cashier, an old fishing crony of mine, and introduced myself. "Sir, my name is William P. Jones, and I'd like to rent three large safety deposit boxes."

"I'm too busy now," Bradford said, unimpressed. "Come back in an hour and we'll go out for a cup of coffee."

I finally convinced him that I really wanted the safety deposit boxes, and he gave me the keys and receipt made to William P. Jones.

"I'd like to borrow five money sacks," I said, "for good measure."

"If you intend to rob a bank," Bradford said, dryly, as he handed me the sacks, "get the one across the street. I don't like the competition."

When we reached the house, I found Jim there having breakfast. He'd landed at the airport and taken a cab to our place. "I'm not mad at you or the boys," he said to Nita, casting a murderous look in my direction, as I came into the kitchen. "The fact that I've eaten eight of your biscuits, plus two eggs and six strips of bacon, and drank four cups of the best coffee I ever tasted, proves that. But I'll be damned if I want to have anything to do with that no-good husband of yours after the low-down trick he pulled on me." I ignored the remark and sat down at the breakfast table beside Jim.

Tex and Elbert brought the gold in from the car while I was eating, and I told them to put it in the den. When I went into the room they had all the bars lying in a row. It was the first time I'd seen the gold in daylight, and it was as beautiful a sight as ever I have seen.

"Got a buyer?" Jim asked, softening at the sight of the gold.

Until that moment, I hadn't given a thought as to how we'd go about selling the stuff. "The reason I'm asking is tht I know a fellow in El Paso who buys gold around Chihuahua and Inda, and he ought to be interested in this since it is already in the States and he wouldn't have to worry about smuggling it across the border. If you want me to go down and see him, I'll be glad to do it."

I was all for it. The sooner we could sell the bars and go back for the rest of the treasure, the quicker we'd have a nice chunk of money in hand. "But in the meantime," I suggested, "let's get this gold into the bank." We put two bars in each of the sacks and carried them to the bank. No one paid the slightest attention to us. A number of rolls of coins would have made the bags look larger and fuller than the gold bars did. The difference, of course, was in weight.

The bars deposited, I drove Jim to the airport. He was going straight to El Paso and try to establish contact with the man he thought might buy the bars. "Let me have one of those gold coins, Mark," he said before he climbed into the plane. I handed him a coin and he opened his knife and cut a small gap in it. "If anyone offering to buy the gold doesn't give you this coin as an introduction, I didn't send him. If you do make the sale, call me as soon as the transaction is completed and I'll fly up and we can decide what to do about the rest of the treasure."

I took the boys fishing that afternoon after school, and Elbert went with us. When we were alone, Elbert asked, "Mark, are you going to need any help when you go back for the rest of the treasure? If you will give me a break, I promise you I won't drink a drop, and whatever you want to pay me will be all right. All I want is just a little start, so I can have my family with me."

I was sure we could use another man, so I made him a proposition. "I'll wire your wife three hundred dollars, pay all of your expenses, and give you five percent of the net profit, but you've got to understand that there's a chance of getting killed, or being caught and put in prison, and that it's possible we won't be able to get the rest of the treasure. If we're unsuccessful, then we're even, and you won't be obligated to me for the money I'll advance your family. And above all, you've got to give me your solemn promise that you won't take a single drink while we are in Mexico."

He swore he wouldn't touch a drop. "You'll never know," he said, "how much I appreciate this favor, when I'm on my last legs. Even more than the opportunity to make a lot of money, I appreciate the confidence you've got in me when all my family is down on me. Now that I've got the chance to make good, I'll show everyone I'm through with the juice for good."

I rounded the boys up, and we headed for home. When I arrived, Nita gave me a telephone number and room number I was to call the instant I got home. Before I had a chance to walk over to the phone, it rang again. It was the man I was supposed to call. "A Mr. Jim Dunlap has contacted me," he said, "and informed me you have ten mining claims you want to sell."

"That's right," I replied.

He was in town, and gave me the name of his motel and

asked me to come right on over if I could.

I hurried to the designated address and when I knocked on the door, a dapper-looking, middle-aged man opened it. "My name is Snider," he said, and he handed me the gold coin I had given Jim, and into which Jim had cut the gap.

We went into conference and Snider told me he wanted the gold, but $532 for an ounce, a thousand fine, was all he could pay. I finally raised him to $533 an ounce, but he made it plain that that was his ceiling. I agreed to let him have it at that figure. I was sure I could get a better price by shopping around, but I realized that being new in the game, I could also make a mistake and sell it to a treasury agent, lose all the gold, and get five years in Leavenworth, to boot.

We finally agreed that the pay-off would be made in the bank, after I convinced Snider that the cashier could be trusted. I called Bradford and he said he would let us in early the next morning before the bank opened. The following morning, Bradford let us in through the side door. I removed the bars from the safety deposit boxes, and once they were drilled to Snider's satisfaction, returned them to the boxes.

Then I borrowed a friend's plane and flew Snider to El Paso to have an assay made. The bars averaged eight hundred forty fine, or eighty-percent pure, which made the gold worth $447.72 per ounce. Snider said he would get in touch with me as soon as he could get the money. After buying a set of scales accurate enough to weigh the gold, I caught a cab to the airport, and was home within an hour.

After Nita and I had gone to bed that night, I told her about the proposition I had made Elbert. "I think he has learned his lesson," I said.

"I hope you're right," she sighed; "but I'm afraid you will regret giving him the chance. Please watch him, for I'm so afraid he will cause you trouble."

"Just have faith, Nita," I said, planting a kiss on her forehead, "and everything will be all right."

"I hope so," she said fervently. Then she asked, "Did you sell the gold?"

"The transaction ought to be closed in a day or two," I told her.

"Are you going back to Mexico then?" she asked anxiously.

"I have to go back and take José his money. After all the trust he's placed in me, I can't let him down."

"Oh, I know, darling, I know, and I want you to give José every penny it brings, but please have him meet you here where it's safe. Give him the money and forget the rest of the treasure."

"What about all the expenses I've incurred?" I asked.

"Forget the expenses, Mark; that's unimportant. Now that I know what a narrow escape you had, I can't bear for you to go back again."

"Nita, I promise you that if there is any risk involved, or we run into any danger, I will forget about the rest of the treasure and come on back without trying to move the gold." This was the first time I had ever lied to Nita, and I knew she knew I was lying, and that I would try for the rest of the treasure regardless of the danger involved.

The next morning, while I was at breakfast, Bradford called. "I've just had a call from Snider," he said. "He's in town and you and he are to meet at the bank in ten minutes, so we can complete the transaction before the employees arrive for work."

I wasn't expecting Snider so quickly. I got the scales and drove down to the bank. Bradford drove up as I was getting out of the car. As we opened the side door of the bank, Snider arrived. He was carrying a large briefcase, and he, too, had brought a set of scales. I asked him if he had any objection to Bradford's inspecting the money while we weighed the gold.

"Not at all," he replied.

We weighed one bar of gold on both sets of scales. They were so close on the weight that either set was acceptable. The ten bars weighed 2,892 ounces. The total value came to $1,294,806.00. Snider counted the money, I recounted it and put it in one of the safety deposit boxes. Snider walked to the door and signaled the driver of his car across the street. He rounded the block and parked by the door of the bank. I helped him carry the bars out to the car.

As the others were driving away, I shook hands with Bradford. ''Thanks, Bill.'' I said, ''Buy yourself a new suit and charge it to me.''

Chapter 6

JOSÉ'S ENTIRE lifetime had been spent in wretched poverty. from the time he and Juan, as small boys, had helped their papa bury the gold in their patio, he had dreamed of becoming rich. For forty years, the treasure that might be the means of fulfilling his dream had lain buried under eighteen inches of earth in his own backyard. Now that part of that treasure had been unearthed and converted into cash, his dream was soon to become a reality. In José's wildest dreams he could not conceive of being the possessor of such riches.

This consideration gave me far more satisfaction than did the thought of any possible profit to me if and when we were able to bring the balance of the treasure out. Like so many peons, José and his family had never had a chance, and had lived a hand-to-mouth existence, scarcely better than that of the burrows and goats they tended. Now, because of his trust in me, his *amigo,* they would be able to live a life of comparative ease, and have a chance to learn something about the dignity of human life.

I hurried home and called Jim. He was surprised to learn that the sale had been completed so quickly. "I'll leave at once," he said. "Pick me up at the airport in two hours."

I went to my office to meet Tex and take care of some paperwork that had accumulated during my absence in Mexico. Tex was pleased that the sale had gone through so smoothly. Then I briefly outlined to him a plan that should enable us to get the rest of the treasure. The scheme called for two more men we could trust. As I had previously asked Tex for his opinion of José, I now asked for his appraisal of two brothers, Carlos and Luis Trujillo, who had been working for me for over a year. "Tex, you gave them such a good recommendation that I let you hire both of them when we really needed only one. What do you think of them after a year's tryout?"

"They're just what I told you they were when I recommended them, Mark—trustworthy, honest and industrious. I've known those boys for a number of years, and worked them on several jobs before we put them on here. They are to me, as José is to you, *amigo.*"

"Do you think they'll be interested in going to Mexico on this treasure deal?"

"I'm reasonably sure they will. Another thing, Mark, Luis, the younger one is no dumbbell. He had two years of college at the University of New Mexico; then he and his girl friend had to get married, so he quit school and started mining."

"Can you have them at my office by the time Jim arrives?"

Tex was sure he could. I called Elbert and asked him to pick Jim up and bring him to my office. Tex was back with the Trujillo brothers before I'd finished my work. I explained to them the same compensation I'd offered Elbert. Without hesitation they said they were ready to go.

When Elbert and Jim arrived just before noon, I dismissed my secretary and told her to take two hours for lunch. When she'd gone I locked the door and said to Elbert and the Trujillo brothers, "I want you to know just what we are undertaking and what the risks are." I gave them a full account of everything that had happened on the first trip. "I'm sure you realize," I finished, "that the hazards we face on the return trip could be even greater. If any of you feel the risks are too great, you are at liberty to change your minds." Not one of them batted an eye.

"As Mark knows," Jim said, "I've got a ranch, well stocked with cattle. I've worked twenty-five years for what I have. I've got enough money to last me as long as I live. My greatest pleasure is in looking after my ranch, and hunting and fishing—and you can't beat Mexico for either of those sports. What I'm trying to say is this: I tried for twelve years to get my Mexican citizenship before I finally succeeded. If I had been as large a rancher then as I am now, I could never have gotten citizenship papers. You fellows are welcome to use my truck or my plane; and should you get caught or get into trouble, I have enough political pull to get you off the hook. If I were to get caught, the Mexican government would seize my ranch and deport me as an undesirable citizen. I tell you men that if you will listen to Mark and give him your complete cooperation, you can all make it big on this deal. That's all I have to say. Let's listen to his plan.''

''Now listen carefully,'' I began, ''and when I've finished I'll welcome any suggestions any of you have to make. First of all, we are at least ten days ahead of the time José expects us; and second, we don't know whether I killed Flores or not, and we have no way of knowing what kind of welcome we would receive in Loreto unless we send in a stranger to the people of the village. Now, this is my plan: Let Tex, Elbert, Luis and Carlos leave at once for Torreon. Once in Torreon, they can buy a good, serviceable pickup truck; then Carlos and Luis can take the truck and drive to Loreto, posing as cattle and goat buyers. Tex and Elbert can stay in Torreon until Carlos and Luis return. I don't think anyone will get wise to Luis and Carlos, since they will have the truck and it will have a Mexico license. Of course, José knows you, but he will realize that you are there because I sent you, and he won't make contact until you are alone. Then he can give you all the information we need.''

''If it isn't safe for us to go back to Loreto, you boys leave a deposit on a few cows and promise to be back in several days to complete the deal. Then leave Loreto and drive around to Aquelia, the little village on the Durango-Mexico City Highway. It's only ten miles from Aquelia to Loreto by pack horse or burro. When you get to the village, rent a corral; and make it a point to let everyone know you are buying cows in Loreto and that instead of hauling them by truck over the rough road, you are going to drive them the ten miles on horseback. Buy or rent four horses, and ride to Loreto and back by horse, so you'll know the trail. Then drive back to Torreon and report your findings. I'll fly down to Torreon in the meantime, and get the picture from you before I go on to San Luis to meet José. After I give José his money and pick up the key to his house, I'll fly to Fresnillo. In the meantime, you boys can drive the truck there and meet me. After dark, we go on to Aquelia in the truck, pick up the horses and slip into Loreto around midnight, dig up the treasure, pack it to the highway, load it in the truck and take off.''

All hands agreed the plan was workable. They had no suggestions and only one question: ''When do we start?''

Elbert offered to take his car. It was almost new, but needed two tires. They all agreed they could be ready by the time I had the two tires mounted and drove Jim to the airport. Tex called Jackie and told her to start packing his bag, and that he'd pick it up within the hour. He wanted to go along with me when I drove Jim to the airport, to discuss the plans and make sure he had every detail perfectly clear. Once we were in the car, Jim let me have it: ''As a judge of character, I've got no respect for you. That damned brother-in-law of yours is no good. I'm afraid you made a mistake on him, and I'll damned sure bet you a Stetson hat that you realize it before this deal is over.''

''I think you're wrong, Jim,'' I replied. ''Elbert's too glad to get this chance, and he can't afford to fail.''

''I sure as hell hope you're right,'' Jim said fervently.

At the airport Jim shook hands and said, ''Call me when you need the plane; I'll come and pick you up, and you can drop me off at the ranch and go wherever you need to go.''

I withdrew twenty-five hundred dollars from the bank for the boys' expenses. I loaded Luis and Carlos with last minute instructions: be sure to change their money into pesos; recognize José only when there was no one around; be sure that José left at once for San Luis Potosi; and make sure José understood that just as soon as he got his family to San Luis he had to come back for Juan and his family, because we wanted them all out of our way as soon as possible.

They all assured me they knew the plan by heart; and as they drove off, Tex promised to call me when they arrived in Torreon, so I would know where to contact them should there be an unexpected development at my end of the line.

When I went to the office early the next morning, I heard

the phone ringing as I was unlocking the door. It was Tex. They had driven all night and were in Torreon, and he gave me the name and telephone number of the motel at which they were staying. They weren't letting any grass grow under their feet. Through the motel manager, Luis had already bought a half-ton truck in good mechanical condition. Luis and Carlos were leaving for Loreto at once and would arrive there late that afternoon.

Nita wanted to go shopping in El Paso the next day. After the strain I'd been under, I hankered after a little recreation, so I agreed to drive her to El Paso if she'd let me take the boys to Sunland, the new race track, while she shopped. It's only three miles from the city to the track. My sons and I spent an exciting and profitable afternoon at the track. I was three hundred dollars ahead after the sixth and added another four hundred on the last race. The boys were bursting with excitement and pride, and could hardly wait to get back to the motel to report to their mother on how smart and how lucky their daddy was.

"Congratulations!" said Nita, giving me a kiss for good measure. Then she deflated me, "It's usually the other way around."

By way of celebrating the windfall, the four of us drove over to Juarez for dinner and then went to a movie. I told Nita that if she finished her shopping early enough the next morning, I'd take her to Sunland and show her a thing or two about scientific betting.

The next afternoon before we left for the track, I gave Nita all of my winnings except $200. "This is all I need to break the track," I assured her.

I was snakebit all afternoon. After the fourth race I had to borrow a ten-spot. I never got past the $2.00 window the rest of the afternoon. Nita decided to play one race because she felt sorry for the horse and the jockey since no one was betting on them.

"Come on, Mark," she cajoled, "buy a ticket on *my* horse."

I shook my head and stalked over to place my $2.00 on another horse, and she headed for the $10.00 "Win" window. My humiliation was complete when Nita's horse won, and paid $78.60. Her ticket paid $393.00! I had the boys lined up to leave when she came back from cashing her ticket. "Aren't we staying for the rest of the races?" she asked disappointedly.

The answer was "No." When you can't tell the difference between a race horse and a mule, you've got no business at a track.

About 11:00 Tuesday night, I had a call from Tex. He'd been trying to get through since Sunday night, but there'd been trouble on the line. "Get down here as quick as you can, Mark," he said with a note of urgency in his voice, "Elbert is in jail, and I don't have enough money to get him out."

"The best I can do is make it there by 2:00 or 3:00 tomorrow afternoon," I told him. "I can't leave until the bank opens. I'll meet you . . ." That was as far as I got. The connection was broken. I tried for an hour and never could get through to Torreon. I was worried about Elbert, and was sorry that I hadn't found out what he had done to land him in jail.

Nita was fit to be tied. "I just knew something would happen. If only you had listened to me! I tried to warn you."

"There's no need to get excited," I soothed, "for all we know, Elbert might not have been at fault."

"You don't know Elbert as well as I do," she said ruefully.

I called Jim around 6:00 in the morning and told him about the development and asked if he could get off for a day or two and fly me down.

"I can't possibly get away," he said. "I've committed myself to look at a herd of steers this afternoon; but if you'll be at the airport in two hours I'll pick you up. We can set down at Palomas just long enough to get your passport, and then you can drop me off at my ranch and fly down yourself."

I was waiting at the bank when it opened, and Bradford let me in the side door. I took all the money out of the safety deposit box, and withdrew another twenty-five hundred dollars from my account.

Nita had my clothes packed when I got back to the house. I had told her earlier in the day that I expected to stay in Mexico until we were able to get the rest of the treasure. She extracted a promise that if we ran into any danger we would forget the whole thing and come back to the States. "Be careful, Mark. Take care of yourself, and don't take any chances." She drove me to the airport. Jim was waiting, and after a quick goodbye to Nita, we took off.

We landed at Palomas just long enough to get my tourist visa. It was only a fifty minute flight to Jim's ranch. Jim suggested a cup of coffee while one of the ranch hands was servicing the plane. I carried the brief case containing the money from the gold into the house and put it in Jim's safe. "Can you get this money changed into pesos?" I asked him. "José could never explain having so much American money."

"Sure," Jim assured me. "It'll be no problem at all. When you take the money down, I'll fly as far as Chihuahua with you and take care of getting the pesos. I'll send Miguel down in the truck, ahead of us, so I'll have transportation home."

Jim told me he'd like the plane by noon Saturday, if at all possible. He said he had located a bunch of steers at Sahauripa, a small village just over in the State of Senora. "If you can make it back by noon Friday," he added, "and have the weekend free, we can take my lion dogs, and I'll look at the steers Friday evening and we can hunt until Sunday noon."

With Jim's assistance, I charted my course for Torreon, and promised to have the plane back before noon Saturday. Then I took off. In two hours and twenty minutes, I was circling the field at Torreon. Tex was waiting for me, and we went into the cafe at the airport to have lunch.

This was the first chance Tex had had to give me the scoop on Elbert. "Saturday night," he said, "we went to a night club. Elbert was determined to go, but said he'd made up his mind strictly to do no drinking—he just wanted to see what night life in Mexico was like. He did take a drink, though, and then another. I was afraid he was heading for trouble, so

I insisted we all leave and go back to the motel. Elbert and I undressed and went to bed, and as soon as I hit the bed, I was dead to the world. When I got up in the morning, Elbert's bed was empty. I figured he was having breakfast. I shaved and dressed and walked over to the cafe where we had been having our meals, and found no one had seen hide nor hair of Elbert since the day before. By the middle of the afternoon, I was really worried, so I hired a taxi to drive around and find some trace of him. When we passed the police station, there was Elbert's car, parked in front. I went in to find out what I could, and when they found out I was with Elbert, they almost threw me in jail."

It seemed that after Tex went to sleep, Elbert had gotten out of bed and dressed and gone back to the night club.

"Although he didn't speak a word of Spanish," Tex said, "he found a Mexican who could speak English. He took a few drinks and informed his companion that he was in Mexico to buy all the gold he could get. Well, his new-found English-speaking *amigo* quickly informed the others in the club as to what the *Americano's* mission was. Someone called the police, and in a few minutes a plainclothesman came down and got himself introduced to Elbert and told him he had a lot of gold for sale. Although he didn't have ten pesos to his name, Elbert bit, and they threw his carcass into jail. The damned idiot didn't know that the punishment for trying to do business in Mexico without a permit is punishable by a ten thousand peso fine, or six months in jail, or both. Anyway, they questioned me for about four hours before they let me go. It was the damndest ordeal I've ever been through."

After lunch Tex and I checked to see that the plane was tied down, paid the service charge, and took a cab to the police station. We talked with the chief for an hour and donated two thousand pesos to charity before he finally agreed to turn Elbert loose, provided I would pay the ten thousand peso fine.

"And to prove to you that I am a fair man and like the *Americanos*," he said, "there will be no jail sentence."

They brought Elbert in and I paid the fine. The chief didn't offer to give me a receipt. If he hadn't been so damned ugly, I would have asked the robbing bastard to kiss me; there was no doubt about it, I'd been taken for damn near one thousand dollars.

Elbert was happy to be out of jail. He apologized to Tex and me and begged like a child for another chance. He promised he would never take another drink under any circumstances. I talked it over with Tex and we agreed we'd take another chance on him since we would probably need him and his car.

After dinner, we all went to the night club the boys had gone to on Saturday night. Elbert insisted on going with us, but vowed he would stick to Cokes, that he was on the wagon for good. After we'd had a couple of drinks, a Mexican came over to our table. He had a bottle containing about three ounces of placer gold. He tried to sell it to us very cheap and told us he could get us all the gold we wanted. "Thanks," I said, "but we're here on vacation, and we're not interested in buying anything." The chief of police must have been a disappointed man. At least Elbert remained true to his promise.

Friday at 3:00, I started for the airport and then changed my mind. I had a hunch that Luis and Carlos would arrive before morning. I could leave early in the morning and have the plane at the ranch before noon. Sure enough, about 2:00 in the morning, Luis and Carlos showed up. They had driven all night and were worn out and sleepy. I managed to get hold of a pot of what was supposed to be coffee. It tasted like ground wood, but it was black and hot, and it had a stimulating effect. After two cups of it, Luis was able to tell his story.

They had been successful in passing themselves off as cattle buyers, and the first night in Loreto they had seen José in a *cantina*. José gave no sign of recognition, but when he had finished his beer and no one was looking, he motioned Luis to follow him outside. Once outside, he whispered to Luis that when the village was asleep, he would meet him in the arroyo above the arena where they fight the bulls.

Luis and Carlos had spent several hours in the *cantinas*—making themselves known as cattle buyers and keeping their eyes and ears open for all the news they could pick up about the *Americano's* visit there the previous week. It seemed that several people had a few cows and goats for sale. Everyone in the village was still talking about the big dance, and how the *Americano* had whipped Flores. I hadn't broken the son-of-a-bitch's neck, but his jawbone was broken and what teeth I hadn't knocked out on one side, he had to have pulled; and even now, he couldn't eat the *frijoles*—his mouth was too sore.

For once, psychology had paid off for me. Sure enough, Alfonso and Felipe were found drunk and passed out, lying close to Flores. It was around noon before they were sober enough to tell *el presidente* what had happened. At first they told the story I had told them to tell. But the next day, when Flores was able to talk a little, they changed their stories and backed Flores up, in order to keep their jobs, saying they'd been too drunk the first time they told the story to know what they were saying, and they were sure it happened as Flores claimed. They couldn't explain why they had the one hundred dollars I had given them. Most of the people were for the *Americanos*. A few of them felt we had something to hide; but knowing how jealous Flores was, the majority believed the first story that Alfonso told.

Flores was telling everyone that if I ever came back he would kill me because I had hit him in the face with a pistol when he was looking the other way. He couldn't explain why the skin on his face wasn't broken but tried to fortify his claim by bragging that everyone ought to know that, as tough as he was, no one could do so much damage to his face with a bare fist.

After Luis and Carlos had gotten all the info they could and made an appointment to go out and see some steers the next day, they went back to the hotel. At 1:00 in the morning Luis left for his rendezvous with José. He was careful in making his way to the arena and up the arroyo, so as to avoid being seen. José was waiting for him at the appointed place, and his first question was an anxious one, "How is my brother, and is he safe?"

Luis told him that we were safe and had had no trouble after we had disposed of Flores.

"And already *Señor* Mark he has sold the gold," he said,

"and you are now a very rich man. You are to leave for San Luis Potosi at once and take your family, and get your brother-in-law to bring his car and come quickly to get Juan and his family."

At first, José refused to go. "Luis," he said, "You go and tell *Señor* Mark to keep all the money and stay away from Loreto. *El pesidente*, with Flores and Alfonso, he come to my house and ask many questions and look in my patio. Of course, I didn't know nothing and they could not tell there had been any digging."

"And only this very day when I go to church to say the prayers for my brother, Maria wait and come in the church with me, and she ask me to write *Señor* Mark and warn him of the danger from Flores. Maria don't think her papa is angry at *Señor* Mark. She think he would try to protect him, for he is very greedy for the *dinero*. She say Flores came and ask her to marry him and she refused and told him her heart would always belong to *Señor* Mark if he ever came back. Even Maria knows that Flores would not have the nerve to face my brother, but he has many cousins and brothers. They would wait and kill him from the back, and if they were all afraid to kill him, they would watch him day and night. So you go back and tell my brother to keep all the money, for he can never get the rest of the treasure."

Luis finally got José to shut up long enough to give him a good talking-to. "Look, José, you call *Señor* Mark your brother. You are not the brother to him; he is the brother to you. Look at all the expense and danger he has gone to just to make you a rich man. Why does he not keep all the money and say, 'To hell with José!'? I tell you why! Because he is the brother to you. No expense and risk is too great for him to keep his word and promise to you. Do you, José, a peon, think you are as smart as *Señor* Mark? He has a plan and knows how he can easily get the rest of the gold. But only after you and Juan and your families are safe can he succeed."

"I'm sorry, Luis," José said humbly, "it is only that I do not want my brother to get hurt. I will do as *Señor* Mark wants me to do. Tomorrow my family and me we will leave if the *camione* she does not break down."

For once, the *camione* made it, and José and his family took their few earthly possessions and went to San Luis Potosí. Two days later José was back, with his brother-in-law. They borrowed all the money they could on their goats, and told everyone how sick their mother was and that Juan and his family were going to San Luis to see her.

After José and Juan had shaken the dust of Loreto from their heels forever, Luis paid a forfeit on 22 head of steers and took them to Aquelia. He leased some land about a mile from the village and had four peons build a rock and brush corral. Then he bought ten more horses and four old saddles and asked the men building the corral to take care of the horses until they drove the steers back from Loreto. He had decided it was better to drive back to Torreon promptly and report his findings, knowing that he and Carlos would still have time to scout the trail in advance of our going to bring out the treasure.

Carlos and Luis had accomplished their mission in Loreto, and gathered all the information we needed.

"If you boys are ready to move out," I said, "Tex and Elbert can drive the car and truck while Luis and Carlos catch some sleep. By leaving now, you can be in Durango before noon. Luis and Carlos can drive the truck on to Aquelia and get there before dark and get a good night's sleep. In the morning, they can pick up the horses at the corral and ride to Loreto and study the trail, so we won't make any mistakes after dark. Tex and Elbert will stay at the Mexico Courts in Durango, and I'll fly in Monday, around 1:00. Luis and Carlos will have to leave Aquelia early Monday morning to get back to Durango by the time I arrive. I'll have to go on to San Luis Potosí late Monday afternoon to carry José his money and get the key to unlock his door.

"Look, men, we have spent a lot of time and money on this treasure," I said, "Now it's ours for the taking, and I want each of you to give me your word of honor that you will stay in your rooms and steer clear of any night clubs or *cantinas*. One drink and one slip of the tongue could upset the apple cart and keep us from making a small fortune." All of them gave me their word that they'd stay as dry as the sands of the desert.

"If one of you will run me out to the airport, it will be light enough for me to see to take off by the time I check the plane out and warm it up," I said. Elbert offered to take me, and on the way to the field, he assured me he would stay in his room, and that I had nothing to fear from him. "I'll see you in Durango," he said, as I got out of the car.

There was no light in the control tower. I checked the plane out, and when I could see enough of the runway to know it was free of goats and burros, I took off. There was a little headwind, so I was two hours and forty minutes on the return flight. When I touched down at the ranch, Jim was waiting. "I figured you'd gotten lost and wound up in Mexico City," he said dryly as he came out to meet me when I stepped out of the plane.

While we had breakfast, I gave Jim a run-down on Luis' and Carlos' findings, and told him the plans I'd laid out. I also told him how Elbert happened to land in jail. "Why in the hell didn't you bring him back and leave him at the ranch until you moved the rest of the treasure?" he asked.

"Elbert has gone on to Durango with Tex," I told him.

"Have you gone plumb crazy?" he exploded. "How many times does a no-good son-of-a-bitch have to foul up before you run his carcass off?"

Jim howled with glee when he heard about the shape Flores was in; and he gave his stamp of approval to our plan of going to Aquelia and using horses to pack the gold from Loreto to the highway rather than going back to Loreto and taking a chance on the trouble that was lying in wait for us there.

Chapter 7

JIM LOOKED at his watch as we got up from the breakfast table. "It's still early, Mark," he said. "Why don't we take the dogs and leave right now for Sahauripa? I can look at the steers this afternoon; then we can hunt until 2:00 or 3:00 tomorrow afternoon. We might get lucky and bag a lion; there are a lot of them in that neck of the woods."

I thought it was a swell idea.

"I'll call the bank in Chihuahua before we leave," said Jim, "and ask them to have the pesos ready Monday morning. You change your clothes, and Lupe will get you the boots you left here last year; they're in the closet." He called Lupe, his housekeeper, who doubled as his mistress, and gave her more orders in a minute than she could have executed in a week. I'd changed clothes, found my boots and pulled them on before Lupe figured out what was going on. Jim came through the room loaded down with sleeping bags, rifles, and ammunition.

"If you can't do anything but stand there, Lupe, get the hell out of my way." Lupe got the hell out of his way. He turned to me and growled, "Damned if I wouldn't fire her if she wasn't the best bed partner I ever had." Lupe was an attractive young woman of about thirty. I couldn't resist telling Jim that an electric blanket would be more suitable for a man his age then Lupe was.

He stopped like he'd hit a brick wall. "Look, you little bastard! Let me tell *you* something. I have spent 25 years in Mexico and 35 years roaming over the U.S.A., and I have seen a lot of pretty women; but never have I seen a woman as beautiful as that señorita in Loreto. Maria topped them all. And what did *you* do? Not a goddamn thing! And let me tell you something else: I may be sixty years old, but if she had looked at me just once like she looked at you every time she set eyes on you, I wouldn't have given a goddamn if it had broken the plan of salvation—nine months and five minutes later she sure as hell would have had twins.''

I knew when I was fighting a losing battle, so I gave up, laughed, and turned around and headed for the pen where the dogs were kept. Jim had about fifteen dogs, half walker hound, and half Airedale. As I reached the side of the pen, they all started barking at once. I had to shout to make Jim hear me. ''What dogs do you want to take?''

''Damned if you ain't getting as bad about asking questions as Lupe is. You know Old Trailer and Lady are the only two that are any good; those pups ain't had enough training.''

The dogs knew a hunt was on and all of them wanted to get into the act. I finally managed to get the right two separated from the others and out of the pen. Jim had thrown the sleeping bags and the rifles in the back of the plane, and the dogs jumped into the luggage compartment like seasoned travelers.

I opened the door and stepped aside, expecting Jim to get in first and take the controls. As usual, he surprised me. ''Don't stand there all day like a damn fool. Get in. You know how to fly this machine don't you?'' It was Jim's way of telling me he was sorry if he'd been too rough on me, and made me mad.

It was only an hour's flight from the ranch to Sahauripa. When we came in sight of the village, Jim told me to circle the field two or three times while the *muchachos* ran the goats and burros off the strip. I was down to five thousand feet, and as I banked, I asked him where the strip was.

''Damn it,'' he said, ''you are looking at it there on the south side of the village, at the end of that corral.''

I had seen basketball courts that looked longer than that landing strip did. I lined up with the strip, but came in too fast on first approach. I pulled up and made another trip around. On the second pass, I got in and I almost hit a tree at the end of the runway before I could stop. Jim comforted me, "I've come a hell of a lot closer than that."

Everyone in the village knew Jim. It took about thirty minutes of handshaking, backslapping and passing the jug of mescal, before we could get down to business. The steers were in a pasture about five miles from the village. While a horse was being saddled for me, Jim asked if there were any pumas around close. Antonio, the *vaquero* who had ridden in from the camp to take us out to where the steers were, told us that only that morning he had seen fresh signs just a mile or so from where the herd was being held. Jim asked if there was enough food in the camp for us and his dogs, and the cowboy told us there was plenty of meat, beans and tortillas.

We arrived at the pasture about 3:00. On the way out Jim had suggested that we'd better spend the night in the camp, so we could get an early start in the morning. I browsed around the camp while Jim looked at the steers. The cook for the outfit was a man about sixty-five. Water was scarce, I know; but still, it was unpardonable for anyone to be as filthy as he was. He looked like a charter member of the Society of the Great Unwashed. I'd have bet my bottom dollar the old bastard hadn't had a bath since he was a baby, or washed his face and hands in a year. He was using an old adobe hut for a kitchen. I didn't dare go close to it because I knew that was where the food I'd be eating during the next three meals would be prepared, and a close-up of the kitchen would not serve to whet my appetite.

Evidently the old man didn't find me any more attractive than I found him. He answered my questions in mono-syllables, but other than that, he was as silent as the Sphinx. Since there was no one else around to talk to, or to ask questions of, I wandered around and found a clean spot and spread out our sleeping bags. When I unrolled them, out came the four packs of Luckies I had brought along. I took a pack over and gave it to the cook and told him that if the frijoles and meat were as good as they smelled, I wanted him to put my name in the pot for an extra helping. He reached for the cigarettes and, without a word, pulled off the greasy, filthy leather apron he was wearing, sat down and lighted a cigarette. He took a couple of deep pulls and if I ever saw anyone enjoy a cigarette, Old Filthy did. His eyes lit up like a Christmas tree, and he started talking. "All my life I've heard how good the *Americano cigarros* were, but never did I think they would be like this. I will see you get all the beans and meat you can eat, and the tortillas, they will be very hot." He damned near drove me loco, talking and asking questions. He even condescended to tell me his name was Rusty.

Finally Jim and the five *vaqueros* came back to camp. I have never seen five tougher, meaner-looking *hombres* in my life. They were too poor to own a pistol, but they all carried bowie knives on their hips. Once the cigarettes had set Rusty off on the talking binge, he spent so much time gabbing that he was late getting supper ready. While waiting for the grub, the *vaqueros* put on a knife-throwing exhibition. They were so damned good, I wouldn't want any one of them throwing at me if they were within two hundred feet of me when they made the pitch.

Rusty forgot and left his package of cigarettes lying on a bench just outside the kitchen door. One of the *vaqueros* spotted it and made a run for it. But Old Filthy was surprisingly fast for his age. He grabbed a stick of wood and stood his ground. If he could swing a baseball bat like he swung that stick of wood, he could have broken the Babe's record while Roger Maris was still in knee pants. I walked over to my sleeping bag and produced two packs of Luckies and laid them on the table and told the cowboys to help themselves; that I was sorry I hadn't brought along enough to give each of them a pack. They tore open a pack, started smoking, and waxed as lyrical over them as Rusty had.

Rusty filled Jim's and my plates almost to overflowing with beans and meat, and told the *vaqueros* that if they wanted any frijoles to get them themselves. They all made a run for the beans, and Old Filthy took advantage of the opportunity to steal all the cigarettes but one out of their pack. I've got to admit the meat and beans were good, so long as we didn't look toward the cookhouse or Old Filthy while we ate.

After supper, we sat up by the camp fire and talked for hours. The *vaqueros* and Rusty related some interesting experiences they had had. The averge Mexican is more superstitious than the old Southern darky, so some of their stories were pretty hair-raising. It was an unforgettable evening for me—like something you see in the movies but somehow never expect to experience yourself.

The next morning we had an early breakfast. The *vaqueros* asked me if they could come along on the hunt, since the steers were already corraled and they had nothing to do. It was still dark when we headed for the mountain about two miles away. Antonio, who had spotted the signs and kill of a lion the day before, led the way. At daylight we entered a large canyon, and after about an hour's ride up the canyon Antonio told us we had almost reached the point where he had seen the signs. He had no sooner spoken than the dogs started barking; they had run across a hot trail, and were only about five hundred yards below us and about half way up the side of the canyon.

We rode on to where we could see the head of the canyon. There were a lot of rocky cliffs and scrub timber on both sides of the canyon. I handed the bridle reins to one of the *vaqueros* and started to dismount when the *vaquero* behind me shouted, "Look! Look! The puma!" Sure enough, the cat was crossing a rocky ledge to my left. I threw the .270 to my shoulder and as I started to snap off a fast running shot, the lion stopped on the ledge for a split second. I drew a quick bead and fired. When the gun fired, my horse jumped out from under me, and the next thing I knew, I was sitting flat on my fanny in the rockiest spot of the whole damned mountain. Jim and the *vaqueros* sure had a good laugh at my expense and kidded me the rest of the day. The dogs crossed over the rim at least a quarter of a mile from where I shot at the lion, and went out of hearing. I picked up Jim's .270. The fall hadn't hurt the gun half as much as it had my pride.

Even though the dogs had gone off in another direction, I decided to climb up to the ledge where the lion was standing when I shot at it. Two of the *vaqueros* went along. We reached the place where I had spotted the lion, and about twenty feet beyond it, found a little blood. I had hit it, after all. While the *vaqueros* waited, I made sure I had a shell in the chamber of the rifle; then I walked very cautiously over the ledge and saw the lion lying about a hundred feet ahead of me in a crevice in the rocks. It was dead as the proverbial doornail. I called the *vaqueros,* and they congratulated me on making such a long shot. Actually the range was less than two hundred yards. They carried the cat back to where Jim and the others were waiting and when the horses saw it, they tried to spook.

Until Jim called my attention to it, I hadn't noticed that the lion was only about two-thirds grown. "Mark," he said, "those dogs are running the old cat; and if this was her kitten, she'll circle back after she figures she has given the kitten time to reach safety." Sure enough, in about an hour the dogs came back in hearing distance.

Jim said what we were all thinking: "Listen to those dogs push that damn lion. Ain't that the prettiest music you ever heard? That old lion won't run much longer if those puppies keep pushing her that hard."

The lion came around the head of the canyon, down the slope behind us, and crossed the canyon and started back over the rim—the same way she had gone when the dogs first jumped her. She was trying to confuse the dogs and throw them off her trail. We could hardly hear the race because of Jim. He would stand up in his stirrups and shout encouragement to the dogs at the top of his voice: "Whoa! Get 'er boy! Catch the old bitch! Run her up a tree." Then while he was getting his wind back, he'd repeat, "Ain't that the purtiest damn music you ever heard?"

The dogs were over the rim, out of hearing distance for about twenty minutes. Then they came back over the rim and crossed at the head of the canyon, as they had done before, and down the same ridge, crossing the canyon to where they had first jumped their prey. The lion made a circle and started back the way she had just come. The trick didn't work. Old Trailer and Lady didn't lose the trail even for a second. They were really pushing that lion. Almost half way up the ridge they stopped barking for a minute, then barked treed.

"If this doesn't beat all!" Jim said. "I have hunted for a lion a week at a stretch and never even got a bark; and here you kill one slipping out, and we sit on our horses and hear the purtiest goddamn race that ever was run; and then the dogs run the old she-cat up a tree not a quarter from the horses. Leave that .270 here, and let's get the other lion."

Jim wouldn't let anyone shoot a treed lion with a high powered rifle. He claimed that the knock-down power, even if a head or heart shot, would knock the lion out of the tree and it would still be able to rip or kill a dog, even if the cat was dying. He had an old Remington bolt action .22 that he had carried for years, and it was still as accurate as the day he bought it. This is what he used to shoot a treed lion. A heart shot, and the cat would lie on the limp or cling to the tree and die before relaxing its muscles and falling out.

When we came in sight of the dogs, they had the lion up a dead tree. It was lying on a limb about 30 feet above the ground, looking down at the dogs. Jim handed me the .22 and told me to get on the cat's left side and shoot it low and close behind the shoulder. I tried to get Jim to shoot it, but he said, "Hell, no; shoot it yourself. I'll have the hides tanned and give them to your boys. Then they can tell everyone how their daddy killed two lions in one morning of hunting. Chances are they will turn out to be gabby and windy as hell like their old man, and this will give them something to talk about."

I walked up to within a hundred feet of the tree and stopped. Jim told me to get up closer—that the cat wouldn't jump. I stopped about fifty feet from the tree. Bracing myself against a large bush, to be sure I didn't pull off, I drew a bead and fired. The lion didn't move, just quivered slightly, and in a minute or so relaxed its hold and fell to the ground, dead.

Jim had both cats skinned, and we were back at the village by 3:00. While I loaded the plane, he proceeded to tell everyone he saw about the hunt. We turned the plane around and backed it against the tree at the end of the strip. I opened the door, and was damned glad when Jim took the controls. The more I looked at that short strip, the smaller it became. "Watch closely," Jim said, "there's nothing to it." He held the brakes and fire-walled all throttles. He released the brakes. When we were about three-fourths of the way down the strip and three hunded feet from the corral, which was full of goats, Jim started easing back on the stick. We cleared the corral by all of three feet.

While we were gaining altitude, Jim laughed and said, "Seven years ago I came over here to look at a herd of steers and we all got drunk and decided to go to a rodeo in Chihuahua. I clambered into the 170 I owned at that time, along with four Mexicans, complete with saddles. I knew that with such a load I could never get off the ground on such a short strip, so I took a pole about six inches thick and laid it across the runway about 100 feet from the corral; then I wound the plane up as tight as I could, and just as I touched the pole, pulled back on the stick. We bounced about thirty feet into the air, but the plane didn't have enough power to pull up, so we landed in the corral, killing nine goats. Well, we didn't get to Chihuahua, but we barbecued the goats and had our own rodeo. The plane was a total loss, but you know, not one of us got more than a mild shake-up."

The hunt had left Jim so excited that he was in high spirits all the way back to the ranch, and didn't gripe or swear even once. The minute we landed, he started hollering for everyone to come and see what we had. Jim's ranch was pretty well populated, since the families of twelve ranch hands lived in the vicinity of the ranch house. While he was showing the cat hides and telling everyone about the hunt and how the dogs had performed, I went into the house and had a shower and shave and changed into clean clothes. We had a good dinner, and then Jim challenged me to a game of dominoes. By 10:00 we agreed it was time to hit the sack. We'd had a long and eventful day.

Jim awoke me the next morning, pounding like mad on my door and charging into my room: "Do you want some breakfast, or don't you? If you do, get that carcass of yours out of bed and let's eat before I starve to death."

While we were eating, he told me he had already started

Miguel to Chihuahua with the truck, and that we would have to hurry to get there by the time the bank opened. He went to his safe and brought in the briefcase containing the money. Then he asked Lupe to get the big leather suitcase out of the bedroom. She brought the suitcase and put it down by Jim's chair and gently started to message his neck and shoulders.

"Have you decided to go with me, Jim?" I asked.

"Hell, no," he said, "and damned if you ain't getting as bad as Lupe—can't see one goddamn inch in front of your nose. How in the hell could I put a million pesos in that little brief case? I wouldn't be a damned bit surprised if you don't turn out to be a damned cotton picker." I noticed he gave Lupe an affectionate little pat on the behind. She winked at me. She hadn't been his mistress ever since she was sixteen without learning that he was all bark and very little bite.

I thanked Lupe for her hospitality, and Jim and I were off to Chihuahua. When we arrived there after an uneventful flight, Jim suggested that while he went to the bank, I stay at the airport, have the plane serviced; and file my flight plan to Durango, so I would be ready to take off when he returned from the bank with the money.

I was ready to take off, and waiting at the plane when Jim got back about two hours later. He walked out to where I was standing. I never saw so damn much money in small bills before. He said it had taken forty-five minutes for them to count the money and change it into pesos. He put the suitcase in the baggage compartment and locked it. Then he turned to say goodbye, and put his arm around me. I couldn't have been more surprised. In all the years I had known Jim, I had never seen him show any affection or outward emotion that would indicate that he valued any man's friendship. He had always pretended to be as hard as you would expect to find old ranchers who had to fight for everything they got, and then had to fight to hold onto their gains.

Jim told me the .270 rifle, automatic shotgun, and .38 pistol, with plenty of ammunition, were under the lining in the baggage compartment. I didn't tell him that we had guns in Elbert's car.

"Now, let me give you some advice," Jim said in parting. "You be damned careful in Loreto; and if Flores should surprise you, or find out you are there, don't hesitate to kill the son of a bitch. A Mexican's hate is as deep as his friendship, and he's already sworn to kill you if he gets a chance. You know that. If you kill Flores, the others will back off; they haven't got anything against you. Then get the Hell out; and under no circumstances get careless and let yourself get captured, 'cause if Flores ever gets the drop on you, you're a dead man. Since Maria has refused to marry him and he knows she would jump at the chance to be with you, he is crazy jealous, and as dangerous as a rattlesnake, and don't you forget it. Don't relax or let your guard down for a single second."

Then he asked me if I wanted him to fly the gold across the river when we brought it back, or if I intended to fly it myself.

"I can handle it," I said. "I'll land at Delicias. There won't be any danger of the police searching the plane while it is being refueled, and if they become suspicious there'll only be one or two of them. If we can't buy them off, we can easily take care of them. Then I'll go straight to the airstrip where you landed when you flew the first gold across. This way there shouldn't be any trouble, and you won't be involved." I told him we were making our move Tuesday night, and I would have his plane home not later than Thursday morning. Jim agreed that landing at Delicias, a small town about sixty miles south of Chihuahua, was better than stopping at a larger airport. I thanked him for his cooperation, told him he was a grouchy old man, and assured him that he and I had an equal share in the treasure.

"I don't care about the money; but if I just had my clothes packed, damned if I wouldn't go along at the last minute to see that you don't get hurt." I started the engine and as I reached over to close the door, I gave him a parting shot I knew would make his hackles rise: "What good would an old man like you be? You'd only be in the way."

He started shaking his fist and shouting to try to make himself heard above the roar of the engine. "Let me tell you something, you cocky little bastard . . .'' I didn't stop to hear him out.

I turned on the Number 2 Runway, checked out, and got the green light from the control tower. As I started my takeoff, I looked at Jim as he walked toward the taxi and watched me take off. When he saw I was looking toward him, he stood still and waved to me. Until that goodbye at the airport, it had never dawned on me that under all that tough armor, Jim Dunlap was the loneliest man I had ever known; and his few close friends would probably never know that his most treasured possessions was their friendship.

Chapter 8

IT IS approximately four hundred and twenty airline miles from Chihuahua to Durango. I climbed to eight thousand feet. The air was rough, so I took it up to ten thousand and smoothed out. After double checking to make sure I was on course, I relaxed and lit a cigarette. I looked at the clock; it was 11:30. In less than three hours, I should be in Durango. Visibility was exceptionally good.

At 2:10, Durango came up on my right. I was about four miles off course, which wasn't surprising. The plane had a high frequency radio and all the smaller towns in Mexico are on low frequency, so I wouldn't have been able to reach the control towers if the towns along the route had had them. I circled the field, came in, and taxied over to have the plane refueled. I saw Carlos get out of the truck and start toward me. I signaled him to wait, paid for the fuel, and taking the suitcase of pesos with me, checked with the control tower and filed a flight plan for San Luis Potosi. Then I walked out to the truck. I shook hands with Carlos and asked him where the others were. His answer all but floored me. "You not going to like this," he said. "Elbert is drunker than the hooty owl."

I was so damn mad I couldn't see straight. I asked Carlos if everything was going as planned. He thought so, but he didn't know for sure.

When we stopped at the motel, while I was getting the money out of the truck, I could hear Elbert talking loud and cussing like a trooper. When I opened the door he was standing about six feet in front of me. He was wearing a beautiful black eye that somebody had donated to his cause. Seeing me, he bellowed to the others: "Stand up! Don't you know peons are supposed to rise when the big boss comes into a room?" Then he turned to me with a poisonous look. "I guess, by God, you will say I'm drunk too, huh?"

"Yes, you are, and I . . ." That's as far as I got before he broke in: "You are a lying son of a bitch."

I dropped the suitcase, grabbed him by the collar and tried to drive my fist through his stomach. He went out cold. I finally cooled down enough for Tex to tell me what had happened. "We arrived in Durango Saturday at 11:00," he said, "had lunch and went to our room. About 3:00, I decided to take a nap. Elbert asked me for money to take the car across the street for gas and a grease job and oil change. That was the last I saw of him until 7:00 Sunday morning, when he came in drunk as a lord. Someone had beaten the hell out of him. He laid across the bed and went to sleep. I went out to the car and got the keys and his bottle. I poured all the stuff out except one drink to give him when he started sobering up."

"I thought he was asleep so I went to the cafe for breakfast. Just as I started to eat, Elbert staggered in. As you know, these waiters here all speak pretty good English. Elbert started telling me in a loud voice how he would kill every damn Mexican that got in our way while we were bringing out the gold. I couldn't get him to shut up, so I dragged the drunken bastard back to the room and stayed there with him, even had my meals served in there. He slept all day. When he woke up about 10:00 last night, I gave him the drink I'd saved to bring him through, and he went back to sleep. He woke up when Carlos and Luis came in this morning from Aquelia, and we thought he was sober since he began begging us not to tell you.

"Luis and Carlos hadn't had breakfast and neither had I. Elbert got up and started to shave. He seemed to be in pretty good shape and asked us to order for him when we ordered, so we could all eat together. He said he'd be down to the cafe as soon as he had a bath and dressed. So we three went to the cafe and ordered breakfast. Those cooks are as slow as molasses in January, but they finally served our orders, and Elbert still hadn't made it. I hurried back to the room and told him his breakfast was on the table and would be stone cold if he didn't get down there quick. He answered from the bathroom: "I'll be down in just a minute; you don't need to wait for me!"

"I went back and ate my breakfast. We all finished eating, had a second cup of coffee, and still Elbert hadn't shown up. We came back to the room. I don't know whether I overlooked a bottle he might have hidden in the car, or whether he sent someone after another bottle. Anyway, when we walked in, he had a bottle of tequila and had drunk almost all of it and was drunker than hell, just like he is now. I don't know how a man could get drunk so fast. Well, that's the story on Elbert."

I looked at Elbert and saw he was coming to and was trying to get up. I told Carlos to drag him in and throw him under a cold shower, and if he stuck his head out, to knock it back inside. "It would be a pleasure to knock his head inside out," Carlos said, meaning every word of it.

I remarked that I didn't know what to do with Elbert; that we'd put so much into the venture and were too far along now to change our plans. Luis knew exactly what to do. He wanted me to let Elbert go with him and Carlos. There were many deep, sandy arroyos between Durango and Aquelia that would provide the perfect and final answer to the problem. I was tempted to let them have him, but decided that we couldn't kill him just because he was no damn good and in our way. I could think of only one thing to do and that was to put him in the car and let Carlos drive him back to El Paso.

If the others were willing to try, we would go ahead as planned. Being short-handed would increase the danger, I told Tex and Luis, and they were free to say so if they felt the risk was too great. They both said they were ready, to hell with the danger, and that if we made it there would be a bigger cut for everyone, with Elbert out of the picture. I called Carlos in from the bathroom and told him what we had decided on. I've never seen anyone more disappointed over

93

anything, but he agreed to do anything that would contribute to the success of our mission.

Thirty minutes under the cold shower did wonders for Elbert. He was almost sober when he emerged from the bathroom. "So you're cutting me out, are you?" he snarled savagely.

I told him that he had cut himself out, and if he didn't want to ride to El Paso in wet clothes, he had just two minutes to change. While he was changing clothes, I asked Carlos if he had enough pesos to make it to El Paso. He had more than enough and gave me what he wouldn't need. I gave him two hundred dollars and told him to give Elbert one hundred after they crossed the river and were in El Paso, and he was to keep the other hundred. I made Elbert give me all the money he had. He reluctantly shelled it out. Then I searched him to make sure he wasn't holding out. He was. I told Carlos to feed him whatever he wanted to eat, and see that he had cigarettes, but not to give him a penny until they were in the States; that I had paid for his last drink; that if Elbert gave him any trouble, to use his pistol on him; and that under no circumstances should he let Elbert drive.

Luis carried their luggage out and put it in the car. Carlos was all broken up about having to turn back. He shook hands with Tex and me, embraced Luis, and got behind the wheel and drove off. There is a stop sign about half a block from the motel, and when Carlos stopped at the sign, Elbert stuck his head out of the window and shouted back to me, "I'll get even with you, you son-of-a-bitch."

I shouted as loud as I could. Carlos heard me and looked back, and I motioned for him to circle back. When the car stopped, Elbert jumped out and struck at me with a wrench he had picked up in the car. I ducked and punched him in the stomach with my right. He almost sunk to his knees. I grabbed his shirt collar and forced him back against the car. I was so mad I guess I went completely loco. How long I punched his face and head, I don't know; but I was holding him up with one hand, to keep him from falling, and just kept punching with the other.

Tex and Luis grabbed me by the arms and gave me a damn

good shaking. When Tex saw I had gained control of myself, he told me that if I wanted to kill Elbert they would turn me loose; if I didn't want to kill him, he had taken all a man could take. Only then did I notice that blood was running out of Elbert's nose, mouth, eyes and ears. I asked them to throw him in the car and told Carlos to take off.

While Tex paid the motel bill, I washed; but there was so much blood on my shirt and trousers I had to change clothes. My luggage was in the plane and I couldn't wear Tex's clothes; he was 6'2'' and weighed over 200 pounds, I weigh only 165. We drove to the airport, Tex brought my luggage from the plane, and I changed in the truck.

With Elbert out of the way, we were ready to take up where we had left off. After calling José at San Luis Potosi and asking him to meet us at the airport there in two hours, Tex and I threw our luggage and the suitcase of money into the back of the plane and took off.

Two hours later we flew over a large mountain, and there, in a beautiful green valley, was San Luis Potosi. At the west end of the runway there is a large cemetary, with a number of almost life-size white statues. The evening shadows gave the statutes the appearance of soldiers guarding the resting place of their loved ones, daring anyone to break the silence. As we taxied up to the terminal, out came José and Juan, grinning from ear to ear. When I caught sight of José, the ugly little devil, I realized once again, as I had when I had said goodbye to him at Loreto ten days before, that I had actually come to love him as a brother.

José had rented a hangar, or rather shed space, for us. We taxied about four blocks to an old shed that could accommodate two small planes. Juan followed the plane in a borrowed car. We tied the plane down, and taking our luggage and the suitcase full of pesos, drove to José's mother's house. The treasure and the pesos weren't mentioned during the drive. José's and Juan's mother met us at the door. She was very old and very gray and her face and hands and stooped body bore witness to many years of toil and hardship. She opened her arms to me and said, ''José has told me much about you, *señor,* and since you and he are the brothers, I will be your mama and love you as my son."

I gave José some coins and asked him to send all of his and Juan's kids to a movie. The kids were tickled pink and nearly fell over themselves hurrying off before their parents changed their minds and took back the money. Some of them had never seen a movie; money was too hard to come by to be spent on such frivolous pastimes. When the kids were gone, I asked José and Juan to bring their wives and their mother in. When they were all gathered in the room, I asked José and Juan how much money they thought I had received from the sale of the gold. Since neither of them had had any education, they wouldn't even venture a guess. When I told them what it had brought, they couldn't believe it: Sixteen million pesos and fifty centavos.

I opened the suitcase and dumped all the money on the bed, and counted it for them as quickly as possible. They were overjoyed and all of them cried a little. There was no evidence of greed—just sheer joy that the burden of the poverty under which they had staggered all of their lives was going to be lifted from their shoulders. After counting all the pesos I looked into the suitcase but couldn't find the fifty centavos, which is the equivalent of four cents in American money. I told José the banker had robbed him of the fifty centavos.

"Aw, Mama, just listen to my brother," José laughed merrily, as he slapped his knee, "he brings us all this money and then makes the joke over the centavos. Never will we have to watch the centavos again so the *niños* can have beans and tortillas."

Mama left the room and came back with a bottle of very old wine. "This wine," she said, "we have for many, many years; and now, all of you, my sons, will celebrate."

After a round of drinks, I asked Mama for permission to speak. "Speak, my son," she said, "this is your home."

"*Gracias*, Mama," I bowed. "I want all of you to listen very closely to what I have to say. José, if you and Juan go to Mexico City and buy the two big cars like you say, and a nice home each, almost half of your money will be spent; and then all both of you will do is stay in the big *cantinas* and stay drunk. This you will do until all of the money is gone. Then, how are you going to buy gas for the big cars and pay the taxes on the big house? For one year, you will live like rich people. Then your money will be gone and your rich friends will no longer be seen with you; and they will stop their children from playing with your children, or courting or marrying your children. Then, what can either of you do to make enough money to support yourselves and your families in the fashion to which you will have become accustomed during that year? What can you do? Sell hot tamales?

"You know how to do nothing but mine and raise the cows and goats. So why don't you take my advice and go buy a large *rancho*, and stock it with good cows and horses? Then you can always go to the big cities and have a good time. Both of you know how to raise and tend cattle, and with the big *rancho*, you will always be respected and be known as the big ranchers, and each year, only by seeing that the *vaqueros* do their work, you will become a little richer and can buy more land and more cattle. Take your mama with you, so her last years will be happy ones."

"Now I know why José respects you," Mama said approvingly. "You are my smartest and wisest son."

José and Juan agreed that they would do as I had suggested. Already, Juan remembered having heard of just such a ranch. I turned to the wives and said to them, "Don't let José and Juan waste the money. All of your lives you have worked hard and have had nothing. Now you are entitled to have an easier life, and get some new and pretty clothes, and even go to the beauty parlor. You are both young, and very attractive, and many men would desire you." They were pleased over the compliment and blushed like school girls.

"What can we do with all this money?" José asked.

"No one knows you have it, so it is perfectly safe to keep it in the house," I told him.

They insisted that Tex and I spend the night in their home. After dinner all of us went for a walk around the town. San Luis is a picturesque and beautiful old town, and they proudly showed us some of the points of interest.

When we got back to the house and were finishing the

wine, Tex asked me what I intended to do with the truck, a matter to which I had given no thought. I told José that if he and Juan would fly over to Fresnillo with us the next day, I would give them the truck after we came back from Loreto. At first they were afraid we might want them to go to Loreto with us, but I explained that they would stay in the hotel in Fresnillo, and when we came back and loaded the gold on the plane, the truck was theirs. If that was the way it was to be, they were all for it, if I would permit them to pay for the truck. "You keep forgetting, my brother," José said proudly, "that now we are also wealthy men."

"You know that we left more gold than we took out," I reminded José by way of saving his pride, "so by giving you the truck we will be just about even."

We had a good night's sleep and as good a breakfast as Mama could stir up for us. After thanking Mama for her hospitality and receiving her blessing, we went to the hangar and had the plane refueled. There were no gas pumps; they carried the gas in five gallon cans and strained it through a chamois cloth.

On the runway, as I was checking out and waiting for the green light, Juan became highly nervous, and decided he had better stay home and protect the women until José came back. José gave him a good cussing, and then crossed himself. Neither of them had ever been up in a plane, and deep down in his heart, he was as scared as Juan was. He put up a nice show of courage, though, and told Juan that if it wasn't safe his brother would never have let either of them get in the plane in the first place. Tex showed them how to fasten their safety belts. Juan still wanted out. I got the green light and told him to make up his mind, as I had to take off or get off the runway. "Take off, *Señor* Mark," José commanded. As I started to pull back on the stick to raise the plane off the ground, Juan said, "I need to go to the toilet; my waterworks she is not holding too good, I don't think."

I circled over the town to gain enough altitude to clear the mountain. Once we leveled off, both José and Juan relaxed and even enjoyed the ride. "The airplane, is she very hard to learn to fly?" Juan asked me. I told him that it was easier than riding a horse.

"I think maybe José and me will buy us a plane after we make a lot of *dinero* off our *rancho*. I am sure José could fly it, since he has been in the States for two years."

The airport at Fresnillo is close to the town, and Luis was waiting when we landed. After making sure the plane was properly serviced, and paying the bill, I went to what was supposed to be the control tower. The radio operator was only on duty in the daytime, from 8:00 to 6:00. He explained that they had not had time to put lights up for night landings, and since no planes could land after dark, there was no need for him to stay at night. I gave him fifty pesos and told him to have a drink when he got off work; that I planned to leave very early in the morning for Mexico City, and if I had already taken off when he came to work, he would know everything was all right.

"Thank you, *señor*," he said, "That is all right with me. You can leave any time you want to."

We went to the hotel, had lunch, and then went to our rooms. I asked José if he and Juan could go to the saddle maker and buy or have made three sets of saddlebags, and regardless of how strong they looked, to have them resewed at least twice, and also to find seven or eight gunny sacks. I also asked Luis what kind of title or proof of ownership they had given him when he bought the truck, and told him to go with José and transfer the truck legally to him. José protested when I tried to give him some money for the saddlebags. "No, my brother," he said with the dignity and importance befitting his newly attained station in life, "you forget that now, I am a rich man, too."

Tex and I decided a little sleep wouldn't do any harm, and asked Luis to be sure and wake us at 4:00. I have a great talent for sleeping, and would probably have slept all night if Luis hadn't called me. José was on hand, too, and for once he had done something right. The saddlebags were very strong and the gunny sacks almost new.

We ate dinner, then changed into comfortable clothes and boots and sat around shooting the bull as we waited for it to get dark. I told José that when we got back from Loreto, we would park the truck close to the airport and leave the keys under the floor mat. "And, José," I said, "after you leave

99

San Luis I won't know where to find you. Here is my mother's phone number. She can always tell you where I am."

We decided to get underway, and not wait until it was dark; all of us were too restless to sit for two hours. A sad feeling came over me as the hour of parting came, and I realized this could easily be the last time I would ever see José. I am sure he shared my feelings. When he said goodbye, he thanked me for all I had done for him, and said, "This night, I will pray all goes well with you, and always all of my family will bless and remember you, my *hermano*."

I told José to be damn sure he bought the *rancho* and didn't spent the money on the *muchachas*. He promised, and crossed his heart. At least, at that moment, his intentions were good.

We drove the truck as close to the plane as we could, loaded our luggage aboard, and slipped the guns from the plane into the truck. Then we filled the truck with gas; and Tex, Luis and I were on our way to Aquelia and Loreto, for better or for worse. About three miles from Aquelia, the highway followed a little valley. About two thousand feet of the highway were very straight and almost level. I remarked that if only we could have hidden the plane, we could have landed and taken off from the highway.

Luis stopped the truck at the end of the straight strip. A large arroyo crossed the highway. He explained to us that we were just a mile from Aquelia, even though we couldn't see the village from where we were. Once we crossed the bridge over the arroyo and reached a small plateau, we would be almost to the village. He also told us that this arroyo curved and ran by the corral where the horses were. "It is about a mile and a quarter from here to the corral," he said. "We can go on to the village and drive to the corral."

"How would it suit you guys to walk from here to the corral, and not be seen in the village?" I asked.

They subscribed to the idea. Tex told Luis to back up and get off the road while he checked to see if we could get the truck under the bridge and out of sight. We were in luck. The last rains had washed all the sand away and down to solid bedrock. We drove the truck under the bridge and Tex and I sat in it while Luis stood watch until it was too dark to tell us from Mexicans. We didn't have to wait long. Taking a saddlebag each and putting the gunny sacks inside the bags, we loaded the guns and started for the corral.

It got dark in a hurry, and the moon wouldn't rise until almost 1:00. We didn't dare use the flashlight we had brought with us, so we had to feel our way along. We finally reached the corral, and had one hell of a time catching the horses. We finally caught and saddled three of them and decided we didn't need the fourth. The saddles were old and had wood hulls, with just enough leather to hold them together. When we reached the old pack trail a half mile from the corral and a mile below Aquelia we had easy riding for two or three miles. Then we started through the gap of a mountain. It was so dark I could barely see the bulk of the horse in front of me. We came down into the large canyon of arroyo through which ran the little river that circled down from Loreto.

We stopped and had a smoke while the horses drank and rested. I asked Luis if this was half-way. "Yes," he said, "And from here on the trail is wider, and the mountain ahead of us isn't half as steep and rough as the one we have just come over. It's only a mile from here to the pass, a mile from the pass to the little valley, and another mile across the valley to the arroyo that comes by the arena and circles within five blocks of José's house." Luis had done a perfect job of scouting the route for us.

It hadn't taken long to reach the divide. From there we would see Loreto. We counted only nine lights in the whole village, but we were still too early, so we stopped for another smoke. When we came to the arroyo, Luis said we were to leave the pack trail and follow the arroyo to the spot where we would leave the horses, and the horses shouldn't be discovered in the arroyo, especially at this late hour. He suggested that we walk, and lead our horses. The river had water in it the year round. Although it was low now, during the rainy season it would wash big holes in the ground and deposit large rocks in the old stream bed. As dark as it was, the horses could fall or stumble in the hole.

Luis stopped, and then walked ahead and up out of the arroyo. When he came back, he said we should leave the horses right where we were. Small mesquite was all there was to tie the horses to. Luis took off his belt and asked for our belts, explaining that the horses had been hobbled ever since they were colts and that was why he had so much trouble catching them at the corral. We tied the bridle reins to the stoutest mesquite branches we could find, and Luis hobbled the horses' front legs with our belts.

An old wagon road crossed the arroyo about a hundred feet from where we left the horses. We walked up out of the arroyo and couldn't see a single light. It was almost 11:00. We decided to wait until midnight before starting for José's house. There were three or four houses on each side of the alley before we came to José's and we wanted to make sure their occupants were asleep. We took turns standing watch, while the other two stayed in the arroyo and had a smoke.

At a quarter to 12:00, Luis checked the horses and brought the saddlebags. I gave Tex the .38 and I kept the rifle. We hadn't been able to find any shells for the shotgun, so we'd left it in the plane. I wanted the rifle; in case of trouble I knew what I could and would do with it. At last we were ready to go. The full cycle had been completed; once again the zero hour was at hand.

Chapter 9

AS WE quietly made our way up the street, there was no sign of life until we had almost reached our destination. Then a dog started barking. When we reached José's house I pulled off my boot and took the key out—I hadn't taken any chances on losing that all-important key. José had padlocked the door from the outside. We agreed that once Tex and I were inside, Luis would lock the door, then climb up on the roof to stand watch while we dug up the gold. Should anyone come within sight, Luis was to toss a pebble into the patio and we would stop work.

I unlocked the door, gave Luis the key, took his saddlebag, and Tex and I stepped inside. Luis locked the door and we heard him climb onto the roof. Then I shined the flashlight and found the lantern, shovel, and tarp.

"How could human beings live in such poverty," Tex pondered aloud, "knowing all the time that they had a fortune buried in the patio?"

We went into the patio and lit the lantern. There were no windows in the house; the only light anyone could possibly see would be through the crack around the door. José and I had done such a careful job of replacing the rock that in order to be sure which rock the gold was buried under, I had to do as he had done—go to the southwest corner of the patio and count the rocks.

We removed the rock and I could see that the dirt had recently been disturbed. Tex spread the tarp and reached for the shovel. I knew the excitement he was experiencing. As for myself, I wasn't too excited, because I knew what we were going to find. I asked Tex to let me handle the shovel since I knew just how I had re-covered the treasure, and suggested that he hold the lantern. I had all the dirt thrown out and could just see the old cowhide, when Luis tossed a pebble which hit almost at Tex's feet. I set the lantern down in the hole, reached for the rifle and motioned for Tex to follow me.

Stealthily we crept through the hallway and to the door. We heard approaching footsteps, and I recognized the voice of my old buddy, Flores, the chief of police. The footsteps ceased as they reached the door, and Alfonso, the fat cop, spoke up, "Just because the dog she barked does not mean nothing. Always they bark at nothing, and we have not seen nothing." Then Alfonso blew his nose like a bird dog and asked Flores if he too, could smell the smoke from a cigarette. I had a cigarette in my mouth when Luis gave the alarm and had forgotten to throw it down. I removed it at once, dropped it behind me, and ground it out with my foot.

Flores came to the door and rattled the chain. I was thankful I had insisted the Luis lock the door after we came inside. Alfonso insisted that he smelled smoke. Flores gave the chain another hard pull and said, "I cannot smell nothing, but if you are so sure, maybe we should break the lock and investigate." He struck the lock and then, unknowingly, made a decision that saved his life. "The lock is very strong, and it is as José left it. There is no need to break it. I can smell nothing. Always when we do not have the *cigarros* you can smell the smoke."

"But *compadre*," Alfonso persisted, "I know I smell the smoke; you have not smelled so good since the *Americano* hit you so hard."

Flores blew his top. "Why, Alfonso," he barked, "are you so thick-headed like the burro that you cannot remember never to mention the damn *gringo* in my presence? And never to anyone are you to admit, as you once did, what truly happened that night? If only the *gringo* will come back, I will kill him and cut off his ugly head and place it in the plaza so everyone can see that I am a braver and tougher man than the damn *gringo*."

Poor Alfonso, he was a glutton for punishment. "But what

of *el presidente* and Maria?'' he asked.

If I ever heard a man fly off the handle, Flores did. ''To hell with *el presidente,*'' he snorted, ''and in short time, Maria will forget and then we can make the marry. But why do I work with a man so stupid as you? All the time you make me remember the *gringo* and how Maria wants him instead of me, and all the time you know this makes me very angry. I warn you for the last time: never mention again in my presence the *gringo*. And you do not smell smoke. I am going to my house and go to bed. What you do, I do not care.''

Flores almost ran up the street. Alfonso stuck his nose into the crack of the door and sniffed like a bloodhound, then turned and followed his chief up the street.

''Damn! That was close!'' Tex exclaimed, as he and I started back to the patio. For a minute, I wished that Flores had broken the lock.

We waited about five minutes before we resumed our work; then Luis whispered that all was clear. It took only a few minutes to remove the rest of the dirt. I jerked the cowhide back, and Tex's eyes popped out. I asked him to get down into the hole and hold the gunny sack for me so I could take the gold coins from the rotten leather bag. When I had transferred all the coins to the gunny sack, Tex lifted the sack out of the way. ''These weigh at least fifty pounds,'' he said.

I removed the nine gold bars, and while Tex was packing them in the saddlebag, I pointed out the spot where the silver was buried, just two or three feet from where we had removed the gold.

''Mark,'' Tex said, ''I can easily carry two of these saddlebags, and Luis can carry the other, so let's take just enough silver to make us all a good load.''

I didn't want to take time to remove the silver, and told Tex that silver was only worth nine dollars an ounce. ''I know,'' he persisted, ''but let's take enough of it to keep as souvenirs.'' I reluctantly agreed.

We carefully refilled the hole from which we had taken the gold, and replaced the rock. I spread the tarp and handed Tex the shovel and told him to go to it, I was going to rest and have a smoke. He quickly dug down to the old hide and removed the dirt. When he folded the hide back, he grabbed me by the leg and turned over the lantern; he was so excited he was absolutely speechless. I recovered the lantern and when I could see what he was pointing at, I damn near fainted. There, stacked by the silver, was another stack of gold bars. Tex began taking them out and laying them down by the side of the lantern.

When the two of us finally calmed down enough to count them, we found there were twenty of the bars, and they were as large as the other nine bars. We knew the other bars weighed approximately twenty-five pounds each. We now had twenty-nine gold bars, plus the fifty pounds of gold coins. "What in hell are we going to do with all this gold?" Tex asked. It was a good question. Gold is troy weight twelve ounces to the pound, but we still had over five hundred pounds of gold. In one trip we couldn't possibly carry all the gold from José's place to the spot where the horses were. I asked Tex if he could carry one load to the horses while I refilled the hole and packed the other saddlebags, leaving Luis on guard until he came back. "Hell, yes, I don't mind. I believe I could carry a ton of that yellow stuff." He put eight bars in a saddlebag.

I asked Luis to come down and open the door for Tex, and when Tex was gone, to lock the door and then get back on the roof and keep a close watch until he got back. As Tex went through the door, I noticed he also had the sack of gold coins. It made a big load for a man even as strong as he was. I refilled the hole and put the rock back in place, then carried the shovel and tarp inside the house, and came back and started packing the saddlebags. I put seven bars in one and six in another. Luis only weighed around 115 pounds, and I didn't want to give him more than he could carry. I put the remaining eight bars in a gunny sack for I knew Tex could carry them without any trouble. I looked around and tried to conceal what little signs of disturbance we had made, so that it would not look as if there had been any digging. Then I sat down to rest.

It seemed like an eternity before I finally heard Tex tell

Luis to get down and open the door. "I damn sure had a load," he said as he came in, "but I didn't see or hear anyone, and the horses are as we left them."

I helped Luis get the saddlebags over his shoulder and asked if he could carry that much. "I think so," he said. Tex helped me load and handed me the rifle; then, without any effort, he picked up his load. I stopped at the door and looked around. There was no one in sight. Tex told us to go ahead and he would lock the door and catch up with us in a minute. When we were about two blocks from the arroyo, I noticed Luis had almost given out; he made it another block, then staggered and fell. I told him to leave it, and while they were putting the packs on the horses, I would come back for it. He didn't reply, and made no attempt to pick it up again; the little guy had done his best.

When we reached our horses and dropped our loads, Luis learned for the first time about Tex's finding the second cache of gold. Both of us thanked Tex for going for the silver; we had almost passed up a fair-sized fortune. We couldn't understand why José hadn't known there was gold buried in both places, unless, because he was just a kid, his father had neglected to tell him.

I told Tex that since he knew more about packing than I did, he and Luis could start loading the horses and I would go and bring the saddlebags that Luis had dropped. As I came out of the arroyo, I noticed it was getting lighter. In a few minutes the moon would be over the mountain. We had completed our work just in time.

I had no trouble finding the saddlebags where Luis had dropped them. I bent over to pick up the bags, and as I started to straighten up, I saw legs moving behind a mesquite bush about four feet from where I was. Without moving, I looked again to make sure. I had left the rifle in the arroyo, and forgotten to get the pistol from Tex. I had been careless and now I was going to pay a bitter price for it. For there, behind the mesquite bush, I could just see my old enemy, Flores, with a cruel, self-satisfied leer on his face. Once again the son of a bitch had me by the tail. I knew he wouldn't harm me until I raised up with my load; then I would be completely at his mercy and have no chance whatever to defend myself. I also knew he wouldn't deprive himself of the satisfaction of giving me a good look at him so as to make sure I knew it was he who finished me off.

I glanced around and saw a rock about the size of a softball just beside my foot. Very slowly, I reached down and got a good grip on the rock. After bracing my feet, I moved my head just enough to look up and estimate the distance to and over the mesquite bush. I had one very slim chance, but I was damned sure going to try. I sprang up and dived head first over the bush. As I started the dive, I reached out with my left hand and got a handful of hair, while I tried to strike down with the rock in my right. I never completed the swing. I was thrown at least eight feet high; before I hit the ground, I realized I had made a mistake and let my imagination get the best of me. Never in my life, will I ever see anything more clearly than I thought I saw Flores' face.

When I made my high drive, I came down and landed flat on my stomach, across the back of a small burro. Don't ever think a burro can't explode like a stick of dynamite when scared. I hit the ground flat on my back and before I could get up on my knees that little burro had set a new track record for a two-block dash; then it turned around and looked at me. I never heard a burro bray as loud as he did. If I could have understood donkey dialect, I am sure I'd have heard the darndest cussing out I ever had.

I don't usually appreciate a joke when it's on me, and undoubtedly I had just pulled the biggest boner of my whole life. I don't know why it struck me as being so funny. Maybe it was the relief of knowing I was still alive, or the release of tension. Anyway, I started laughing and I laughed so hard the tears ran down my cheeks. Tex had heard the commotion, and he and Luis came running. They were calling to me but I couldn't stop laughing long enough to answer them. When they came within a hundred feet of where I was trying to get to my feet, they could see me on my knees, laughing like the proverbial hyena. I was so weak I couldn't stand. I just pointed toward the spot where the little burro was standing, still trying his best to bray. The poor little beast was as spent as I was.

Tex dropped down on his knees, jerked the rifle to his shoulder and looked around in all directions. Finding neither man nor beast to shoot, he handed the rifle to Luis. Then he laid me down on the ground and gave me an examination. I was shaking with paroxysms of laughter, and couldn't stop long enough to say a word. "He's not bleeding anywhere," Tex told Luis solicitously, "and I don't find any broken bones. I don't know what the hell could have happened to him. You lead him back to where the horses are, and be damned sure you don't let him get away from you. The way he's acting, if he gets loose, we will probably have to chase him down to catch him."

"I've always heard," said Luis, "that strange things happen around where the gold is buried."

"I don't know about that," Tex said, "but be damn sure to hang onto him."

As Luis and I walked ahead, Luis kept his arm around me and talked to me in a maternal tone, as if I were a sick child unable to understand the language of full fledged men. This set me off on a fresh laughing spree. When we reached the arroyo, I regained my power of speech and told Luis to turn me loose. I walked over to the edge of the water and washed my face and drank a few swallows. Tex came along with the saddlebags and as he dropped them he reprimanded Luis: "Why in hell didn't you hold onto him like you were told to do?"

"I'm watching him carefully," Luis reassured Tex, and then added, "I've got an idea about this thing. I've always heard that the bite of a coral snake paralyzes the nerves . . ."

"Why, hell, yes," Tex interrupted, "I don't know why in the hell I didn't think of that. Jerk that gold off those horses while I go get poor old Mark; maybe we can still get him to a doctor before it's too late."

"Leave the gold alone," I spoke up, "and hurry and finish the packing. I'm all right. I'll explain later; there's no time for it now."

Neither of them questioned me further, and in a few minutes Tex asked if I was ready to go. I looked at my watch. It was 1:35. The past hour and fifty minutes had seemed like a lifetime to me. I told them I was ready, and it was getting late and we had to hurry.

As we led the horses down the arroyo to the pack trail I explained my strange behavior. Tex and Luis had a good laugh and Tex told me I would never know how happy he was when he realized I was all right and hadn't really flipped my lid. When we came to the pack trail, we all mounted and rode across the valley at a fast walk. We dismounted when we reached the mountain, and led the horses to the divide; then we remounted and rode down to the river.

At the river we stopped to water the horses and let them rest. If we'd only realized that carrying all that weight was tiring the horses so, we would have walked all the way. It had taken us two hours to come from Loreto to the river. We were only half-way, the roughest and steepest part of the trip was the next two and one half miles, and the horses were almost given out by the time we reached the divide. Before starting down the mountain, we let them rest for a few minutes. We were just down the mountain and starting across the plateau when it began to get light. In another fifteen minutes we could see the highway, and we were still about two miles from the corral and a mile and a quarter on to the truck. With the horses as worn out as they were, it would take at least an hour and a half to reach the truck.

I asked Luis if it was possible to leave the trail, so we wouldn't meet anyone. The people of Aquelia could have seen us approaching the village a mile before we turned to go across to the corral.

"I was just fixing to make the same suggestion," Luis said. "I am sure we can turn to the right and stay in small arroyos. Behind the low hills the ground would be very sandy and as tired as the horses are, they will have to take more time."

"We've got plenty of time," I told him, "because we can't get to the truck and drive to Fresnillo and load the plane before the customs officer and the radio operator come on duty."

Tex turned to me and asked, "Can you land and take off from the highway on that straight strip that runs through the little valley?"

"I probably can," I said.

"Then why don't you head for the corral, catch the horse we left there, and ride to the truck? Then you can drive to the airport like a bat out of hell, leave the truck there as we planned, and take off before the radio operator comes on duty. You can land right at the end of the straight strip, near the bridge, and we'll meet you there. You can be there with the plane almost as quickly as we can make it with the horses, as spent as they are."

The thought had occurred to me before Tex suggested it. Luis agreed it was our only chance.

"All right, you guys. I believe I can take off from the highway with all the weight we will be carrying, but I can't be sure."

I gave Tex the rifle and box of shells, and the pistol, for they were the ones who needed protection now. I hadn't forgotten that at the arroyo in Loreto, their first concern was for me, even if it meant leaving the gold. "Keep a sharp watch," I cautioned them, "and if there's trouble, take care of yourselves and fight your way to the bridge where we parked the truck."

Walking as fast as I could, I stayed on the pack trail until I was even with the corral. When I reached the corral I was completely exhausted. I had no trouble catching the horse, and as I put the saddle on, I could tell how poor he was. I hadn't seen the other horses in daylight. If they were in the same condition as this one, it is no wonder that their burdens tired them. It felt good to be riding instead of walking, and it took me only a short time to cover the distance to the truck. I used a mesquite branch on the horse all the way. When I rode under the bridge, I removed the saddle and bridle and turned the horse loose; his job was finished. As I pulled onto the highway, I looked at my watch. It was 6:52. I kept the old truck wide open all the way to Fresnillo.

I parked within two hundred feet of the runway, boarded the plane, and started the engine. When I looked back toward the control tower, I saw the radio operator and another guy running toward the plane. I pulled onto the runway, and without looking back, took off, circled, and headed toward Mexico City.

When I was out of sight of the airport, I banked sharply to the right and headed for Aquelia, following the highway. It was free of traffic except for one bus going toward Aquelia. When the village came into sight, I came down to five hundred feet and hedge-hopped until I came into the valley where I was to land. I sat down on the straight strip of highway and had taxied almost to the bridge before I caught sight of Luis resting on a pile of gunny sacks, with his legs crossed as if he didn't have a care in the world. And why not? He was using between three and four million dollars worth of gold for his pillow; what the hell did he have to worry about? Tex came up from under the bridge, and I motioned for him to grab the tail of the plane and help me turn. I didn't want to race the engine and alert anyone; as low as I had come in, I was sure no one had heard the plane.

I jumped out and unlocked the luggage compartment. It was essential to distribute the weight as evenly as possible, with three passengers, luggage, full gas tanks plus six hundred pounds of gold to get airborne.

As Tex started to the plane with the last saddlebag, a car came over the mesa, and of course it had to stop, since the plane blocked the highway. Luis and I walked around to talk to its occupants and give Tex time to load and lock the baggage compartment. There were five Mexicans in the car and they were pretty well oiled. They wanted to know what had happened. Luis told them he had been out looking for his horse when we landed, and he thought the engine had been giving us trouble, but it was running all right now.

All of them got out of the car, and before I could get away from them they wanted to borrow a "leetle" money. I should have given it to them to get rid of them, for before I could persuade them to leave, the bus I had passed came along and stopped. All of the passengers piled out, and damn near wrecked the plane, running their hands all over it, and trying to lift a wheel off the ground by the wing.

I pushed three of them back and told them to keep their damn hands off the plane. Then I grabbed the bus driver, gave him a hearty handshake and told him what a lucky man he was; that I was on my way to Mexico City when I had to

112

land for minor engine repairs; and that I was about to sell the bus line he was driving for six new streamlined buses that had air conditioning, two big radios and the loudest air horns in the world.

I knew he wouldn't give a damn about a new bus, but the radio and air horn and air conditioning he couldn't resist. I asked him to give me his name and told him I would recommend him for the first bus and hold out until his boss promised it to him, and to please load very fast, drive to the top of the mesa and park across the road so no one could get by until I was off the ground.

He gave me his name and thanked me, ordered everyone to get back into the bus, and in a couple of minutes he was ready to roll. Two of the passengers had gotten into the Mexican's car to take a drink; he didn't wait for them.

I rechecked to make sure the luggage compartment was locked, and removed the key. Three of the Mexicans ran to the door asking for money when they saw we were ready to take off. While Luis was arguing with them, I noticed the wind was out of the west, and about six to ten miles per hour. Luis and Tex told the beggars to go to hell, and I started my run to take off. The highway was slightly elevated down to the arroyo, and what with trying to take off a little up-grade, and the wind blowing the same way we were taking off, I had used almost half my distance and over eighty percent of the power. Realizing that I couldn't make it, I cut the throttle and taxied to the end of the straight stretch of road, so that I could turn around and take off into the wind.

When I turned the plane, I saw that the carload of Mexicans had followed us part of the way, then stopped in the middle of the highway. Tex jumped out of the plane and signaled them to come on. They sat there like Stoughton bottles. Tex reached into his pocket and waved his wallet. That did it. They shot toward him so fast they had a hard time bringing the car to a stop when they reached the plane. Tex walked out to the car. I could see he was arguing with them, and I signalled him to get them on their way. He reached under his shirt and pulled out the pistol. I couldn't hear what he said, but I could see he was getting results. He pointed the gun at the driver, who promptly got the idea. The jalopy shot around the plane like a space rocket on its way to a rendezvous with the moon.

I started my take-off and by the time I had gone eight hundred feet, I knew I could get off. I held it to the ground for another seven hundred feet, eased back on the stick and we were airborne. The little 182 came off the ground like a bird. We cleared the bridge with about three feet to spare.

"I didn't know whether we'd make it or not," Luis said with a sigh of relief. I was too busy to take verbal notice of his comment. At ten thousand feet I leveled off. "Well, men, it looks like we've made it."

"Yeah," Tex replied, "and Mexico sure does look pretty from up here."

I asked if they had had any trouble after I left them. Luis told me they saw no one, but that he horses had a hard time making it, and they had been at the highway only about ten minutes when I landed.

Tex wanted to know if I planned to land at Durango. I said we were headed straight for Delicias. We had some high mountain country to cross, but allowing for the landing and two attempted take-offs from Aquelia, we would still have a minimum reserve of an hour's fuel when we reached Delicias.

We congratulated ourselves on our good fortune in having found the extra twenty gold bars and on our luck in having succeeded up to that point without running into any trouble. Tex told us what he intended to do with his share and how he was going to invest it.

"I am going to buy houses and lots with my share," Luis contributed. "Cat houses and lots of them."

That started a general bull session.

"I was very scared to get into the plane," Luis teased, "for everyone knows that even a small child can ride a burro, and in my opinion it ought to be easier to ride a burro than fly an airplane."

He and Tex really gave me the works, razzing me unmercifully until I finally asked them how they would like to get out and walk.

Visibility was good and it was a perfect day for flying. Tex called my attention to a large village that had just loomed into view some thirty miles northeast and to our right. I checked the map and looked at the clock; it was 11:20. It had been two hours and thirty minutes since we had taken off from Aquelia. The town was Jimenez. Soon we sighted Parral off to our left. "Well, boys," I said, "we are on the last lap. It's only forty miles to Camargo, and another sixty to Delicias." In eighteen minutes we were directly over Camargo, and in a few minutes Delicias came in, dead ahead. I didn't even circle the field, just lined up on the runway and came in for a landing.

Chapter 10

I TAXIED to the far end of the strip to have the plane refueled. Tex opened the door, and I looked out and could not believe my eyes when I saw Jim running toward us at a fast clip. He shouted to Tex to get in the back; then he leaped into the plane.

"What the hell is wrong, Jim?" I asked.

"Goddamn it, don't ask questions. Just turn the controls loose." The plane had dual controls. Jim swept the tail of the plane around and headed down the runway for take-off. About nine hundred feet down the runway he eased back on the controls, realized he couldn't get off, then sucked the plane back to the ground and used every foot of the strip. He barely cleared a power line at the end of the runway.

"Damn it, what's up, Jim? We've got less than a fourth of a tank of gas."

"I know you're low on gas, but that's comparatively unimportant," Jim said. Then he turned to me accusingly, "What the hell have you done?" He didn't wait for an answer. "Yesterday evening about 7:00, *Señor* Gomez called at the ranch and asked where my plane was." I knew that Gomez was a high-ranking politician at Chihuahua and a friend of Jim's. Jim continued, "He told me that at the request of the American as well as the Mexican authorities, a description of the plane was sent to all airports in Mexico, with orders to hold all passengers until the proper officials could arrive and search the plane and question everybody aboard. Now, tell me what happened?"

I told him we'd been successful in getting all the gold out

116

of Loreta, that no one knew we had been there and that we had definitely had no trouble with anybody. I also told him about finding the twenty gold bars buried with the silver. That bit of information seemed to offset his agitation.

"That explains my trouble in taking off," he said. "We were overloaded." Then he asked again, "Are you sure there wasn't any trouble and that no suspicion was aroused anywhere along the line?"

"I'd stake my life on it," I assured him.

"Where are Elbert and Carlos?" he asked suddenly.

I told him about the incident at Durango and that I'd had Charles drive Elbert back to El Paso to get him out of the way.

"By God, Mark, that's it! That son of a bitch turned twenty percenter and put the finger on us, sure as hell. Why didn't you have enough sense to leave him down there, at least until you had the gold safely across the river?"

I knew what Jim meant by that. Anyone having knowledge of a shipment of gold, or anything of value being smuggled across the river can report it to the authorities and the informer will be paid twenty percent of the value of the contraband captured. After our experience with Elbert the past few days, I knew that the bastard was custom-made for that kind of a deal.

"If the alarm was sent out last night," I asked Jim, "Why didn't the officials arrest us at Delicias?"

"I'll tell you why," he said. "I piled Miguel into the truck and drove all night to be on hand when they came on duty this morning, and no one can ever say I ever wasted good whiskey for nothing. By the time you landed, they were all so drunk a submarine could have passed by and they wouldn't have known it. Any more stupid questions you want to ask me?"

"Just one more, Jim: Where are we going and will you let me off just before you run out of gas?"

"You remember that little ranch southeast of Casas Grande that I bought last year?" Jim asked.

I remembered, and 11,000 acres didn't seem small to me.

"We'll try to make it there. I built a small landing strip several months ago. You three can stay there and I'll go to

Chihuahua and find out what this is all about. I have two women there to keep the house open, and there's plenty of food in the larder.''

I couldn't keep my eyes off the fuel gauge; it had been registering empty for over five minutes. At last we sighted the ranch. ''Hope we don't bust a tire,'' Jim said as he lined up on the small dirt strip for a perfect landing.

When we stopped, Jim gave us a little advice. ''When I bought the ranch, I kept all the help and the same ranch boss. I don't know how far any of them can be trusted. Let Luis do all the talking. Pretend you are friends of mine and will be staying here a few days until I have time to take you lion hunting. And the saddlebags contain ammunition.''

The old ranch house was built almost like a fort; in years past, ranchers needed all the protection they could get. Jim suggested that since Tex was the only one strong enough to carry such a load without showing too much effort, he'd better unload all the gold. He told me to come inside and he'd show me to our rooms. As we walked toward the house Jim said to me, ''You're the luckiest man alive; if you had set down anywhere except where you did, our hide would have been nailed to the fence.''

Jim gave Tex and Luis a room next to his bedroom. I was to have his room, which contained a huge old wall safe that could probably have been opened with a can cutter.

After all the gold was locked in the safe, we went outside to see if we could help Jim service the plane. He had two barrels of gas stored for emergency. He put in just enough gas to reach Chihauhua and promised to be back before dark. We returned to the house and locked the door.

To kill time and to satisfy my curiosity, we checked out the gold coins. There were five, ten, twenty, fifty and hundred peso coins, and at least half of them were minted before 1900. We spent an interesting hour examining them before we returned them to the safe.

It was almost dark when Jim landed. We walked out to meet him. He was cussing like a sailor.

''By God, Mark, I told you you would regret taking that no-account brother-in-law of yours. The sorry drunken bastard turned twenty percenter just as I suspected. My friend in Chihuahua who tipped me off the other night didn't know the guy's name, of course; but he did know this much—and if it doesn't make you so damn mad you can't see straight, I will kiss the behind of the first burro we see. Yesterday, the American authorities came to Chihuahua and asked assistance from the Mexican officials, to help them locate and seize the plane and all aboard; and this is the story they told the men at Mexican Federal:

"Yesterday morning around 10:00, a guy called and asked about the reward for reporting contraband. Since the officials receive several such calls a day from people who don't know a damn thing, they insisted this guy come to the office if he wanted any information. Mark, I think you'll remember that in Elbert's presence we remarked that the officials were not too hard on anyone smuggling gold in. So when the bastard gets down to the office, he dresses the story up to make sure there wouldn't be any leniency and that he'd get his cut. He spouted off all our names. But this is the shot that killed Cock Robin: He swore you had hired him to go to Mexico and didn't tell him what the deal was about; that once he got down there he found out we had four hundred pounds of gold and were buying dope and paying for it with the gold. But he said that when delivery was made, you only got half as much dope as you were expecting, and exacted a promise from the sellers to have the rest of the stuff on hand within twenty four hours.

"Elbert swore that once he knew what was going on, he refused to have any part of the deal, that he was a law-abiding citizen and had no intention of becoming involved in any criminal dealings. He said you had tried to kill him when he told you he was washing his hands of the deal and pulling out, but that he managed to get away and came straight to the officials. They probably wouldn't have believed his story if he hadn't been almost beaten to death. They checked and found he had obtained a tourist passport. When they tried to get him to go to the hospital, he balked, so they had a doctor patch him up. From their description of the beating you gave him, why in damnation didn't you go on and finish the job?"

"I wish to hell I had," I said heartily. Then I added, "What do we do now?"

"Hell, there ain't but one thing you can do. I called Snider in El Paso. He already knew we were hot, and the finger is on him, too. He wouldn't buy the stuff down here now at any price. They are checking all the flight plans you filed, and the way you have been traveling for the past week, the authorities will be more convinced than ever that you are guilty. Of course, there's nothing they can do but keep a close watch on you, but they damn sure will do that. My advice will be hard to take, but believe me, it's the only way. Bury the gold and forget it for at least a year. Any of us that tries to move anything across the river until they stop watching us is sure to be caught.

"I told the officials that I loaned my plane to you to fly to San Luis Potosi on business, and you were now a guest here at my ranch and they were all welcome to come and see for themselves that we were hiding nothing. So we had better clean up, quick; if they come, they will be here in two hours."

"What shall we do?" I asked Tex and Luis.

The decision was up to me, they said, and whatever I wanted to do was fine with them. I asked Jim where we could safely hide the gold.

"The best place I know is about eight miles from here, where the old ranch headquarters used to be until the water all dried up. They dug two wells and never did get any water. You know how superstititious some of the Mexicans are. They think the place is devil-possessed and avoid it like the plague. I wish to hell Miguel would get back with the truck so we can start moving the stuff. I saw the truck five or six miles from here when I flew back. The son of a bitch can't pass a skirt without stopping and trying his luck. He's been all day coming from Delicias."

While we waited for the errant Miguel, we had ten minutes to cuss Elbert in three different languages.

When Miguel finally showed up he started telling Jim he'd had a lot of trouble with the truck. Jim listened for a minute to his tale of woe and then said, "I'll bet you a beer that not one of the *senoritas* said 'yes'."

"This time you lose, *jefe*," he gloated, "two did, and one of them was young and pretty."

Jim cussed him from here to yonder and told him to get in the bunkhouse and if for any reason he came out before he was called in the morning, he'd put him back on a horse and never let him drive the truck again. Miguel took off for the bunkhouse like a jet.

"We haven't got any time to lose," said Jim. "Let's get going." We loaded the gold into the truck in nothing flat, while Jim kept up a steady stream of cussing.

"Hey, you blind old devil," I broke in, "Do you want me to drive?"

That stopped him long enough to catch his breath.

"No," he said. "I don't trust you; you might decide to drive off and find Elbert and give him another chance, you're such a damn do-gooder."

When we reached the deserted ranch house, I had to agree with the Mexicans; it did look spooky. There had been eight small houses built close to the big house. The walls had partly fallen down. Not one of the houses still had four walls except the old ranch house. Jim pointed out that one well had been dug in the patio of the big house and the other about three hundred feet away.

I decided to take a look at the well in the patio and concluded that was the right spot, since we would have walls to work behind when we came back for the gold and no one could see us while we were digging it out.

We carried the saddlebags to the edge of the well.

"Always," Luis muttered, "men have risked their lives for the gold in the ground; then they have it for so short a time; and always it goes back to the ground from which it came."

I told Luis to quit his philosophizing and bring Jim's lariat from the truck. I aimed a light into the well and judged it to be twenty feet deep.

When Luis came with the rope, we held both ends and in the center laid a saddlebag across it and lowered it into the well. If we had thrown the bags in, they would have burst. When the saddlebag reached the bottom, I released my end of the rope and Tex pulled the rope under the saddlebag and out. As we started to lower the last saddlebag, I decided to remove five of the gold bars and bury them separately, where they would be easy to get to, for we might need a stake before we could recover the gold in the wall. Everybody agreed it was a good idea.

After we'd buried all the bags, we pushed one of the inside adobe walls over and piled the debris in over the bags. Within thirty minutes we had the well filled even with the top of the ground. Then we pushed another wall over, and it reached two or three feet above the ground and beyond the well, and covered the patio so as to obliterate all traces of the well. Anyone who gets that gold is surely going to have to work for it.

Tex put the five reserved bars in a gunny sack, Luis brought a shovel from the truck, and we went into one of the small houses and in one corner dug down a couple of feet and buried the five bars. It was almost like attending a funeral. We were a disappointed lot. We'd spent a lot of money, risked our lives, and now we were having to leave the gold behind. I tried to kid a little by saying that it would be just like Jim to die, if for no other reason than to inconvenience us to the point where we'd have to buy the property or give the new owner a cut.

"If I do," he said, "you will have to make arrangements with your sons."

Now I knew for sure what was in the envelope that Jim had given the boys.

After taking a mesquite bush and brushing away all the evidence of tampering, we returned to the ranch. The officials we expected never came. The next afternoon we flew over to Jim's other ranch and waited there three days, and still no one showed up. On the fourth morning we decided to go home and Jim said he'd fly us.

We had just crossed the river when the check station came in and asked us to identify ourselves and give our destination. Jim gave them the information they asked for. They instructed us to maintain a minimum of eight thousand feet altitude and change our course to the airport they named, and keep the required altitude until we received instructions to land. Jim started to bank and follow their instructions. Within two minutes we found we had company in the form of an escort. Two planes followed us all the way. Jim asked for landing instructions and they gave him the number of the runway to land on. He was told to taxi to the end of the runway and was cautioned not to open the door, and to remain inside the plane until further notice.

Within a minute after we landed, the plane was surrounded by a swarm of officials. Then we were told to get out of the plane. It would have been impossible for us to have concealed a pin in our persons or in the plane without their finding it, they gave us such a thorough shake-down. Upon finding nothing, they took us down to the station for questioning. Four hours later we were released and returned to the airport.

As we took off, Jim said, "Now, by God, you know what I mean: And just because they slipped today and found nothing, don't kid yourself into believing they were satisfied with our story. They'll keep a trail on us until they do catch us with the goods; so forget for at least a year what you have, and by that time, if you keep your noses clean, maybe you can move it across the river without getting caught." When we arrived at the airport, I called Nita to see if she could come and pick us up. No one answered the phone. I supposed she was out shopping, so we called a cab. When Jim and I arrived at my house, after dropping Tex and Luis by their places, I saw that my car was in the garage. In the living room I found a cryptic note: "I have gone to mother's. If you come back, call me."

When I looked into the closets, I found they had been stripped of Nita's and the boys' clothes. I called Jackie and asked her if she knew what he score was. Apparently she did.

"I'll be right over," she said.

I was fit to be tied. Jim tried to calm me and assure me that there was nothing to worry about. Tex and Jackie came over at once and I asked Jackie if she knew what had happened.

"I most certainly do," she said. "I was over here visiting Nita Tuesday afternoon, and about 5:00 Elbert walked in. I have never seen anyone beaten up so badly as he was. When he came in, he almost scared us to death; we thought all of you had been hurt or killed. He was drinking, but not drunk. This is the story he told:

"When Luis and Carlos came back from Loreto to meet you in Durango, they had found out that the police were watching for you day and night, and after that fight in Loreto the first time, the police became suspicious and made José confess that he had sold you the treasure. They had put José and Juan in jail, trying to make them tell where the rest of the treasure was, but they claimed you had taken it all. Elbert told us that, since it was impossible for you to get the rest of the treasure, you decided to keep all the money and let José stay in jail, or get out the best way he could. Then, he said, you sent a note to Maria by Luis and Carlos, and she slipped out of the house at 2:00 in the morning, met Luis and Carlos, and they brought her to you in Durango.

"He said that you then called them all together and explained what you intended to do. You were going over to the coast for a month to take a vacation and fish, and get a Mexican divorce. Once married to Maria, you would automatically become a Mexican citizen, and would then return to Loreto and start working the rich mines, and when the chance came, get the rest of the gold. Elbert said he had tried to talk you out of the idea, and when he couldn't, he had refused to go with you and told you he was going to tell Nita what a dirty deal you had given her. He claimed that all four of you carried him out of town and tried to beat him to death and, in fact, left him for dead. He said he finally came to and made it out of Mexico all by himself.

"We didn't want to believe his story, and the only reason Nita did believe it was that he knew all about Maria. After Elbert told his story, he went to bed. Nita then told me that you had told her everything that had happened on the first trip, including your meetings with Maria, but she was sure you hadn't mentioned it to Elbert, so he couldn't be making up the story he told them. She was pretty broken up about it.

"The next morning she called and told me she was going to visit her mother and would drive the car for Elbert since he wasn't able to drive."

My memory carried me back to the night we got home after the first trip to Mexico. I recalled that I had gone to the bathroom and found Elbert sitting there in the dark, and that he had claimed he didn't want to turn on the light for fear of waking Nita and me.

"If only I had mentioned it to Nita when I went back to bed," I lamented, "but at that time, it seemed unimportant. Now, I know he was eavesdropping. I never mentioned Maria's name in his presence."

Jim jumped up, banged his fist on the arm of his chair and said, "By God, in my whole life, I never have heard of any one man being such a damn liar and troublemaker." Then he told Jackie about our having been reported, and how lucky we had been not to have gotten caught. He also told her that we had brought back the treasure and were forced to bury it on his ranch. This got Tex off the hook, because Jackie was fixing to scalp the old boy.

Carlos and Luis came in, and Tex retold the story for their benefit. "I tried to get you to let Carlos and me take care of him when we had the chance," Luis reminded me, "but you wouldn't do it."

Carlos told us he had driven all night and arrived in El Paso Tuesday morning at 8:00, and given Elbert the $100. Elbert then told him to get his luggage out of the car;. he wasn't riding any further with him. Carlos rode the bus home.

Jackie asked us to come to their house for dinner, but I vetoed the suggestion. I was in no mood for food. She asked me if I minded if she called Nita. I gave her the telephone number and headed for a liquor store. In the eleven years I had been married, I had never been drunk, but there's a first time for everything, and this looked like the night. I'd had more than I could take standing up.

When I came back into the house, Jim was talking on the phone. I went into the kitchen for ice and glasses, and fixed myself a drink. Then I heard Jim call Nita's name, and could tell he was painstakingly explaining everything that had happened, and assuring her that Elbert had told her a bunch of lies. "You get ready to come home," he said. "We will be there tomorrow, and make sure Elbert stays until we come. I'm sure Mark wants to present him with another bouquet."

I fixed Jim and Tex a drink and gave the rest of the fifth to Jackie. It looked like good old Jim had applied the healing balm; getting drunk didn't hold any appeal for me after all.

Jim asked how far it was to Nita's folks' home, and I told him nine hundred miles. He wanted to take off at daylight so we could be there by 1:00 in the afternoon. Personally, I would have been willing to start at once. We left for the airport about 4:00 in the morning.

When we got to Nita's family's home the next day, I scarcely recognized her. It was easy to see she'd been through the wringer. She looked as if she had neither eaten nor slept since I had last seen her. My first question was, "Where is Elbert?"

"He decided to leave last night and go home," she said dispiritedly. I was disappointed; I had looked forward to seeing Elbert again.

After a demonstrative, joyous greeting from the boys, I got things straightened out with Nita, thanks to Jim's having laid the groundwork the night before. Within a few minutes, she packed all the clothes we could carry on the plane, and her mother promised to ship those we couldn't take along. Jim had to be back at his ranch the next day, so we decided to fly until dark. He insisted on my taking the controls, so that he could ride in back with the boys, and he kept them laughing during the entire flight. We landed and spent the night in Veron, Texas, and were home by 10:00 the next morning.

While the boys and I were transferring our belongings from the plane to our car, which I'd parked at the airport the previous morning, Nita asked Jim to drive out to the house and have lunch with us, but he shook his head.

"You kids have something to work out. It's no one's fault, and neither of you have anything to forgive. You are both grown, so goddamnit, act like it. One hell of a big lie came between you, that's all." He gave the boys an affectionate cuff on the shoulders, climbed into the plane and waved to us, as he started to take off.

"I'll see you in a few days," he said.

Chapter 11

ALL WINTER, Tex, Luis, Carlos and I mined a silver and lead property. I worked hard at the mine, and even harder at home, restoring the confidence and love of my family, which meant more to me than anything on God's green earth. In late summer, after losing money for six months, I was forced to close the mine. When I had sold my equipment and paid the debts I owed, I had less than $2,000 I could call my own. I called Tex, Luis and Carlos into my office and told them what I had done, and what my financial situation was.

"*Señor* Mark," Luis said, "I will appreciate if you and *Señor* Tex will listen to a deal that Carlos and I have been talking of for a long time. We know you have been losing the money, but we hoped the vein of the ore would swell instead of getting smaller as it has. I am sure that Carlos and I, being Mexicans, can slip into Mexico and make our way to *Señor* Jim's ranch and get the five bars of gold we buried in the house. Then *Señor* Jim he can drive us to Juarez and be waiting until there are lots of people crossing the bridge, we can cross with the bars; and then we will have at least enough money for a long time and to look around and find someone who will buy the rest of the gold and take the delivery in Mexico."

"How can you cross without being caught?" I asked him.

"We will buy a lot of wide adhesive tape and tape a bar to the inside of each leg between our knee and hips," Luis said. "I know what I am doing and how to do it," he assured me. "Eight years ago, I smuggled things across."

I asked for a little time to consider their suggestion. After they had gone, Tex and I went over their plan and concluded there was no reason why it would not work. It had been a year since we had buried the gold. We didn't believe we were still being watched, and as small as the bars were, if the tape would hold them in place, they wouldn't be noticeable. Tex and I drove to El Paso and contacted Snider and he agreed to buy the bars if delivered in El Paso. He still refused to buy anything in Mexico. The next day Luis and Carlos left to cross the border. I gave them a note to Jim, so he would know they were not operating on their own, and I asked him to please bring them to Juarez when they were ready to leave.

Once they were safely across with the gold, they were to register at a motel and call me collect, from a pay phone, using a name we had agreed on. I would refuse the call, with the excuse that I didn't know anyone by that name. If my phone was tapped, we wouldn't be giving out any information; and when I received the call, Tex and I would know we were to leave at once to meet them in El Paso.

Luis was to wait four hours and call the pay phone in the lobby of the hotel where Tex and I were to stay. That would give us time to reach El Paso and contact Snider. If we had any reason to believe we were being watched or followed, then we would try to get the officers to follow me, while the others made their escape with the gold.

The fifth day after Luis and Carlos had gone, I received the phone call we had been waiting for. Within three hours Tex and I were registered in the hotel in El Paso. On the way to the elevator, we passed the pay phone in the lobby. It was ringing, and something told me to answer it, although Luis wasn't to call for another hour. It was Carlos, and I could tell he was excited and badly frightened. I finally got him to calm down to where I could understand him. The authorities had caught Luis, he said, and once more his talk became incoherent.

"Look, Carlos," I said to him, trying to calm him, "it's very important for Luis and for you and for me that I understand every word you say. Now, light a cigarette, and then start from the beginning and tell me everything."

He was scared and nervous, but he made a brave try. "Me

128

and Luis we get the five bars. *Señor* Jim, he bring us to Juarez. We rent the room and wait. This day there is many people crossing the bridge, then we tape the bars to our legs like we tell you we will do. But we only have four legs and there is five bars, so Luis he hides the other bar in the room. We cross the bridge without any trouble; then we come here to this motel like you say, and rent the room. Luis he is afraid someone will find the bar he hides in the room in Juarez. He tells me to make the phone call to you and he will go back and get the other bar, so I hide these four bars, and go make the phone call to you.

"Then I have nothing to do, so I walk to where I can see the people crossing the bridge. Pretty quick like I see Luis. You know how the people line up to pass through the narrow gate? When Luis gets to this gate, I am too far to hear, but I see two men with the big pistols grab him by the arm and take him to the room where everyone is searched. Then they bring him out and put him in the car and drive by me. Luis, I know, see me, but he don't say or do nothing. I think he is in jail, and we must go at once to get him out."

"Listen to me, Carlos," I said, "and be damn sure you do only as I say. I am sure Luis is in jail, but he knows we know he is in jail, and the reason he didn't say or do anything when he passed by you in the car is that he is giving us time to sell the gold. None of us has enough money to help Luis now, but when we sell the four bars we will have a lot of money and can do something for Luis then. Don't leave your room under any conditions, and for God's sake, don't take a drink. I will get the buyer and be over to your room as quick as I can. I haven't called him yet, so I don't know when he will be ready. I will be there as soon as I can, and if it should be tomorrow, you be damn sure you stay in your room and don't open the door, or let anyone see you."

I called Snider and for once I was in luck. He was ready to do business and had enough money in his safe to pay for the four bars without having to wait for the bank to open the next day.

He and I went to the motel. Carlos had the bars hidden, but he was so scared he had forgotten where he had hidden them. He finally remembered they were in the bathroom. Snider drilled each bar and asked if I was willing to accept his estimate as to the purity of the gold. He was sure they would assay eight hundred fine. I knew he was underestimating their value, but I was more than glad to take the loss before he found out Luis had got caught and refused to make the purchase.

We settled for a total of five hundred thou plus. I told Carlos to go to the hotel, get Tex and the car, and start at once for home.

I would go with Snider, receive the money from the sale of the gold, and fly home with the cash. I would get my friend, Bradford, at our home bank, to open up long enough for me to put the money in one of the safety deposit boxes we had rented in the name of William P. Jones.

After I collected the cash, I flew home in the plane of a friend, as planned. Tex and Carlos came by the house soon after I arrived, and told me they had not been stopped or questioned as they came from El Paso.

The next morning, Luis called and asked me to get him an attorney when I was ready. I knew he meant when I had sold the gold, so I told him I was ready and his attorney's fee had been taken care of. From this, he knew we'd been successful in swinging the deal.

Luis had told me he had smuggled from Juarez to El Paso a few years past; what he didn't tell me and we didn't know until he came to trial was that he had been caught and served a year in prison. Actually, the first time he was sentenced on circumstantial evidence. I am sure no other attorney would have represented Luis more ably than the one we picked for him, but this time, he was caught with the goods on him and didn't stand a chance. The judge gave him three years. The prosecution tried their darndest to break Luis and get him to confess and implicate the rest of us, but they were unsuccessful.

After Luis' trial, on which we'd spent ten thousand dollars in attorney's fees and court costs, we divided the rest of the money equally so that Luis' wife would be well cared for until he was released. Then we decided to take one thousand dollars each and make a kitty for expense money to try and find someone who would buy the gold in Mexico. I flew all over the United States and even into Canada. I found several people interested in buying, until they found out they would have to take delivery in Mexico. Then they wouldn't touch it with a ten foot pole. We were disappointed, but agreed we would just have to wait until the heat was off, and then move the gold ourselves. We decided not to try to find another buyer for a while. The word was getting around, and we sure didn't want to sell to the wrong party and join poor old Luis.

I have a friend who owns a large uranium property in the Grants area. He had tried for two years to get me to come and take the Superintendent's job. I called and asked if the job was still open, and he told me it was, and that I was in luck, since his brother had just left for the coast and wanted to rent his house. "Can I bring two of my old crew who have been with me for a long time, if they want to come?" I asked.

My friend had no objections, so I went to Tex and Carlos and told them of my plans and that they had jobs if they wanted them. Both of them declined, with the same story. They were going to fish and take it easy and enjoy life until after their money was gone; then they would look me up. We agreed to stay in touch and if they found anyone interested in buying gold in Mexico, they promised to let me know so I could check it out.

My new job gave me more time at home with the family than I had had in years. We all spent a happy winter together. Jim came to visit at least twice a month, and tried to lend me money to start back in business on my own. I couldn't make him realize that even if I had all the money I needed, I still couldn't find a property to work. "Damned if I would follow such work as that," he said. "I can always buy a cow and find a little grass and sit in the shade until she gets fat enough to sell." I had to agree the old devil had something there.

In late March I received a telephone call from Snider in El Paso. He had gotten my address from Jim. He and another party were interested in buying all the gold we had and would take delivery in Mexico if we would bring it to Chihauhau, or any place they could get a plane down and take off from. I asked Snider if it would be convenient for them to meet me in El Paso on Sunday, the 26th. The date was set.

I called Tex and told him and Carlos to be ready Sunday morning, that I had heard from our old buddy in El Paso and he was prepared to do business again. Tex assured me they'd both be ready. I left Grants at 3:00 A.M., and arrived at Tex's at 7:30. Jackie fixed a good breakfast for me, and before I had finished my coffee, Carlos arrived, all set to go. We were in El Paso before noon.

I called Snider and he asked me if we would drop by his house. We drove out, and Snider introduced us to a Mr. Block, who he said was his partner. Block wanted to know how much gold we had, and when we told him, he agreed to buy all of it, and then upset the applecart by offering only four hundred dollars an ounce. We flatly refused the offer and started to leave. He asked us if we were aware of the danger in bringing it across. We told him we were, but we weren't going to sell for four hundred dollars.

After we'd haggled for more than an hour, Snider and Block suggested we stay and go to the races with them that afternoon. We agreed, but I told them I couldn't stay beyond the fifth race, since I had to be back at Grants and be ready to go to work at 7:00 the next morning. The first person I saw at the tracks was an old friend of mine, who had several horses entered, and one he was going to run that afternoon. He had held him back until the odds were right and he was sure he could win, he told me. I couldn't resist a try at it. His horse wasn't running until the eighth race, so I decided to stay on. I passed the tip on to Tex and Carlos and told them not to get hurt before the eighth and we stood a chance to make some money if the darned horse didn't fall and break his neck.

During the course of the afternoon, Block made several offers and finally got up to $450 per ounce. Once more, we refused the offer and told him that when he met the price we had named, we were ready to do business, and that so far as we were concerned, that was rock bottom.

I had lost $20.00 and only had $60.00 more with me when the eighth race came up. I passed the tip on to Snider and Block for what it was worth. They both went for the favorite, and I decided to go for broke. If I lost, I could get a check cashed when I took Tex home. So I put the $60 right on my dark horse's pretty nose. He won by five lengths going away, and paid $18.60. I collected my $558, said goodbye to Snider and Block, and set out to find Tex and Carlos. They were ready to leave and had won almost as much as I had. We had done all right by ourselves.

Carlos offered to drive. I climbed into the middle in order to give Tex room to stretch his long legs. We were just a few miles from Lac Cruces, discussing Block's offer. Whether Carlos went to sleep, or just took his eyes off the road for an instant, I don't know. But I felt the car swerve to the left, looked up and saw that we were about to hit the end of a bridge-head at a high rate of speed. I remember trying to brace myself for the impact.

The next thing I knew was when I regained consciousness the following afternoon in the hospital. I tried to ask where and how Tex and Carlos were. Before I could utter a word, the nurse gave me a shot and out I went. I came to again sometime during the night and was given another shot. When the pain became bearable, I asked for Tex and Carlos, or to be told how they were. "You are to rest and do no talking," the nurse said. I started raising so much hell she gave me another shot and I went out again.

When I came to the next morning Nita and Jim were sitting by my bed. They had been there all night, they told me. Nita couldn't keep from crying just a little as she tried to assure me I was fine. I tried to put my right arm around her and the thing wouldn't work. My right side was paralyzed. I cried out, half in pain and half in shock over the realization that I was paralyzed. The nurse asked Nita and Jim to step outside so she could give me another shot.

When they returned and before I slipped back into the nether world, Nita stepped aside to let Jim say hello. I looked up at him and tried to smile. His tanned and wrinkled face showed the hard years he had spent out in the open country, but his eyes were still as bright and alert as those of a young man. For just a second, though, as he looked down at me, they became moist. The tough old devil almost cried. I will never forget his greeting, and I am sure the nurse won't either: "Get your damn carcass out of that bed, you cocky little bastard. What the hell are you trying to do, get on welfare?"

I have never seen anyone so surprised and shocked as Miss Bush was. She grabbed Jim by the arm and ordered him out. He didn't budge, so she tightened her hold on his arm and tried to drag him to the door. "The very idea!" she exclaimed in horror. "Never in my life have I heard such a remark made to anyone, and especially to a man in his condition. What kind of a heartless friend are you, anyway?"

Jim tried to explain what kind of a heartless friend he was, but the harder he tried, the more confused he became. By the time Miss Bush had dragged him as far as the hall, he was swearing for all he was worth, and so mixed up he was talking gibberish. Miss Bush came back in the room and announced indignantly, "I didn't know there were men like that in the world."

Jim overheard the remark and decided to try to build up his damaged ego. Being a bachelor, he didn't know when he was well off. He stuck his head back in the doorway and issued a fighting challenge to his adversary. "I'll bet an old hell-cat like you could tell me some things that would curl my hair." The angel of mercy slammed the door in his face. As I drifted off to another world, I could hear Jim cussing to himself as he started down the hall.

Late that afternoon, I regained consciousness again. Nita was sitting beside the bed. Once more I asked about Tex and Carlos. Nita looked at the nurse and she nodded her head. Then Nita broke the news. Tex was in the next ward and had a leg broken in two places, a broken collar bone, and some fractured ribs. Carlos was dead on arrival at the hospital. Although I had feared the report would be bad, I didn't expect it to be that bad. I needed another shot, to ease the mental anguish; it was worse than the physical pain.

In a week I could work the fingers on my right hand, and in another five days, I could use my arm a little. I began to raise cain for them to move Tex into the room with me. They finally did, and the days passed a lot faster once Tex became my roommate.

134

In another week, Tex was able to go home. I was out of danger, but would have to remain in the hospital for a while longer. With Jim's backing, I finally persuaded Nita to agree to move me back east where we owned a home and a little farm to which we hoped to retire some day and which was within a few miles of where our parents lived. My doctor told her the transfer would be good for my morale, and said he'd make arrangements to have me transferred to a hospital in that locality as soon as I was able to make the trip. It would take only three hours by commercial airlines.

Three weeks later the doctor arranged for my transfer to a hospital near our home place. Jim and Tex made my reservations and came to drive me to the airport after they'd gotten Nita and the boys underway in our car. One of the floor nurses who had hovered over me like a guardian angel during my entire stay at the hospital, helped me dress and get into a wheel chair. Then she rolled me out to the car, and gave Jim and Tex minute instructions on how to drive and how to help me aboard the plane.

Jim secured permission to get me aboard before the other passengers started loading. He gave the stewardesses my medicine and instructed them how and when to give it, and made each of them promise at least ten times that they would keep a close watch over me during the flight. "Tex and I will come to see you, kid, as soon as Tex can make the trip," he smiled.

I thanked Jim and said goodbye. His concern over me was so great that for once, he had played the role of a perfect gentleman. I don't think a single cuss word even crossed his mind, much less his lips, while he was in the plane. I couldn't afford to take that kind of a memory of Jim with me. As he started to leave, I cautioned him, "Be careful going down the ramp. An old man like you could easily fall and break a leg." He didn't dignify my parting shot by making any reply to me, but I could hear him cussing and fuming to himself as he descended the ramp.

When we landed, my family was waiting at the airport, and had an ambulance standing by to take me to the hospital, where I was destined to spend three months. The day the doctor released me, I marked off as the happiest day of my life. I still had no use of my right leg, but Dr. Floyd told me he was sure I'd be able to use it in a short time. He spelled out a set of rigid rules on just what I was to do and was not to do. Being a lot wiser than the doctor, however, I didn't follow his advice; and within thirty days from the time I was released, I got just what I had coming to me; I had to be readmitted to the hospital.

The tenth day of my second tour of duty, brought me the surprise of my life when Jim and Tex walked into my room. I couldn't find words to tell them how glad I was to see them, and to know that Tex had improved so rapidly and was walking without the aid of a crutch. Jim said he'd called Nita from the airport and she was coming by to take him to the house for dinner and a visit with the boys.

"I bought each of them a new saddle," he told me, "and want to be at the house when they come home from school." Nita showed up in about thirty minutes, and she and Jim left at once so they would be home when the boys arrived.

Tex and I talked and played gin rummy all afternoon. He had been to visit Luis, and also Carlos' family. They were doing fine and had had no trouble collecting Carlos' insurance. Time went by so fast that it was hard to believe it was suppertime when the nurse brought in the tray. Tex apologized for staying after visiting hours, gave me an affectionate clap on the shoulder and told me he'd have dinner and be back at 7:00.

A few minutes past 7:00 there was a knock on the door, and when it opened, my eyes stood out on stems. There stood my old *amigo*, José, and another Mexican I had never seen.

José told me he had tried to call me in New Mexico, to find I had moved, he had no idea where. He had lost my mother's telephone number, so he had gone to Casas Grande and located Jim. Only then did he learn of the accident. "*Señor* Jim told me he would bring me at once to visit my sick brother."

There had been only a short delay while he and the other Mexican, Raul Grijalva, made their way to Las Cruces, but they had no passports and had to be very careful. I asked about Juan and about their families. "They are all well," José said, "and never does the day go by that we do not remember our brother. Juan and me, we bought the big *rancho* about half-way between Nieves and Torreon. We have many cows and goats and horses and we are making the *mucho dinero* as you said we would."

José looked at Raul and again turned to me. "My brother, I have something very big and good for us. Raul has been the *vaquero* on my *rancho* since the day we bought it. Always he has been the good worker and very truthful. We became very good friends and I make him what you call the ranch boss. She has only been the month ago that we were in Zacatecas and he get very drunk. After the muchachas had gone home, Raul he come into my room and tells me he knows where much gold, silver, and jewels are buried. I think he is loco from drinking so much of the *tequila.*

"But, no, my brother, the next day when we are very sober and on the way back to the ranch, I ask him of what he told me last night. He is very scared, like one time I was. Then, for the first time, I tell him of how I became a rich man, and of my brother, the *Americano* and it was you who make me rich and I will trust you with my life. Then he tells me everything. You remember, my brother, how in Mexico, many *Americanos* and even more Mexicans have hunted so long for the treasure that General Zaragoza steals and hides when Pancho Villa captures and robs Guadalajara?"

I remembered, and had read many stories on the raid. It is of record that Pancho's biggest and richest raid or robbery was at Guadalajara. They captured a train, loaded all their loot and horses aboard and made good their escape. One theory is that Pancho and a part of his troops got off the train somewhere near Durango. Another is that Pancho wasn't with his troops at Guadalajara, and trusted the general to carry out the complete operation. Anyway, it is a known fact that the general stopped the train about half-way between Durango and Torreon, loaded all the stolen wealth on wagons and hauled it about fifteen miles to a small village and hid all the loot.

The general wasn't too helpful and never would tell where he hid the treasure. It seems that Pancho was very simple minded about the general's stealing all the wealth, and didn't believe the story he was told, and had the general shot. The general took his secret with him, and no one has ever been able to find the cache.

"My brother, Raul," José continued, "he knows where the treasure she is buried and has known all these years, and this is why he knows . . ."

"José," I said, "how about letting Raul tell the story? You listen very closely to see if he tells it to me as he told it to you." Then I asked Raul to start at the very first and tell me all he knew, and to speak slowly since I hadn't spoken Spanish or heard it spoken for six months.

"*Bueno, señor,*" Raul began: "When I was very young, no more than fourteen or fifteen, the village where we live with mama, my brothers and sisters, we have but very little to eat. We have no pesos to buy food and there is no work. Almost everyone is like us. Each day, me, my big sister, and brother, we each go to the valley or the mountains and set the traps to catch the *conejo* and *codorniz.*" I recognized these as Mexican words for rabbit and quail. "These we can trade for maize to make the tortillas, and have a little meat to eat. This way there is a little food in our house and we do not starve.

"One day there comes to our village this General Zaragoza. All have heard of him or know him, for from this village a few years ago, he marries the prettiest and wealthiest *señorita.* This day he comes with maybe fifty soldiers, and they have four wagons and each wagon is pulled by four big strong mules. On each wagon there is a small stack of wooden boxes, such as the shells for the rifles and machine guns are packed in. Everyone thinks the wagons carry many shells. This general and the soldiers go to the stores and into our houses and take all the food they can find, and promise they will return and pay for it later; then they spend the night in our village.

"The next morning I leave my house just when the light of day I can see. The soldiers have taken all of our food, and until I go to the traps, the little ones cannot eat. I have a long way to go, for already the close quail and rabbits have been caught. But I know higher up the canyon is where I will find many quail in my other traps. I walk up this canyon or arroyo, and since I have nothing to eat, I am very tired and hungry, so I sit down to rest.

"When I am no longer tired, I start to get up and go to the other traps, and then, *señor*, I see many horses coming up the arroyo. This I do not understand, so I sit back down behind the rocks where I cannot be seen. Soon, I can see this general and three of the soldiers, and they are driving twelve mules and seven horses, and on these mules and horses are the boxes of shells for the guns. This I no understand, so I sit very still and they do not see me.

"When they get to an old mine, they take the horses, that I can see have four of the boxes on each side, and go up to the old mine. Then they take the boxes off the horses, get a shovel from a horse that one of the soldiers ride; then the soldiers carry the boxes inside. The general stands on the outside and looks back the way they have come from. In a little while, one of the soldiers, he comes and the general, he goes back in the old mine with him and then very quickly, they all come out, and they go to the mules and these they drive across the arroyo toward where I am hiding. Then they stop at a very large rock.

"I am so close I can hear them talking, but still I say nothing and stay hid behind the rocks. The soldiers they go and dig a hole this deep." Raul measured up under his arms, "and this hole they dig very close to the big rock; then they start taking the boxes from the backs of the mules. The mules look very tired. This I do not understand, for they only carry two boxes on each side, but when the soldiers start to carry the boxes to where they dig the hole, it is all they can do to carry one box each. I can tell they are very heavy. Then one soldier, he drops the box, and I am close enough to see the yellow bars that fall on the ground when the box busts. They put all the boxes in the hole and then put the dirt back, and take a mesquite bush and sweep all around on the ground.

"Then this general he tells one of the soldiers to go and bring the saddlebags from his horse. This he does; then they all take a drink from the large *cantaro*, and they drink all the mescal. Then one of the soldiers opens the saddlebags, and from each he takes out a cloth sack. Then they start putting something into the jug. Then the general tells the other soldier to help these two. So the soldier gets down on his knees. All this I see very plain, I am no farther than this," he pointed to a house less than a hundred and fifty feet from the hospital.

"When all three of the soldiers are down on their knees, this general pulls out his pistol and very fast he shoots two of them dead, through the head. The other soldier throws wide his arms and begs for his life and promises the general that never will he tell anyone nothing if only he will spare his life. Then the general tells him that he was the only one he could trust and never would he harm him. And now, he was to drag the other two soldiers over to where the water had washed a big hole out under the bank of the arroyo. This he does and then the general helps him put one of them back under the hole. And then, when the soldier reaches down to pick up the other one, this general, the lying son of a bitch, he shoots him also, very dead in the head. Then he pushes the soldiers under the hole and rolls some big rocks down so the water cannot wash them out, and then he caves the bank off on them, and they are very good buried.

"Then this general, he comes back and finishes taking everything out of the sack and puts it in the jug. Señor, this jug, she was no smaller than three litros, and when he picks this jug up, and when the sun shines on it, all the stars in heaven could not have shined and sparkled as bright. Then he takes this jug and buries it on the other side of the rock from where he bury the boxes. The general looks all around very carefully and then he gets on his horse and drives all the other horses and mules ahead of him down the arroyo and then I can see him no more.

"Never have I been so scared and frightened. I did not go to the other traps, for when I stood up I was very weak. I went back to my house but did not tell nothing. The next morning, I was too afraid to go to the traps and mama, she knows something she is wrong, and I will not tell her, and then she says she will go with me to the traps this day. After we come to the arroyo I do not wish to go near where the soldiers were killed, but my mama, she makes me tell her where the traps are set.

140

"When we are almost at the spot where the soldiers were shot dead in the head, I cannot keep from being afraid, and I start to cry. Mama makes me say what is wrong. Then I tell her everything I see here yesterday. Then mama she too, gets scared, but we have to go on to the traps or this day we do not eat.

"As we come to the place where the soldiers were filling the jug, I see something shining like the star, and this, *señor*, I pick up from the ground where one of the soldiers dropped it."

Raul reached into his pocket and handed me a large diamond ring. The stone was at least four carats and the ring handmade of solid gold. It was a beautiful diamond, although it needed recutting to bring out its full brilliance.

"Never, *señor*, did me or mama tell anyone, until I tell José. Even Pancho Villa comes back to our village and offers many pesos if anyone can tell him, or show him where the general buries all the treasure. But me and mama are too scared, so we say nothing, or we, too, might get killed like the soldiers were killed. It is still there, for me and José we go to look and make sure, before we come to see you. There has been no one doing the digging. It is still there like it was buried so many years ago."

"What do you say?" I asked, as I turned to José when Raul reached the end of his story.

"What he says is true, my brother," José replied. "It is far from this village, no one can see you when you dig it up, and this time you can take all of it and sell it at once and then bring half the money back to me and Raul."

"I don't know, José; let me mull this over until morning." Then I handed the ring to Raul, but he gave it back to me.

"No, *señor*, the ring, it is yours."

I thanked him, and before we could say anything, Nita, Jim, and Tex walked in. Within fifteen minutes, the floor nurse came to the door and announced that visiting hours were over. Jim, Tex, José and Raul said goodnight, and told me they would come to see me in the morning before they took off.

Nita lingered beside my bed for a few minutes. I told her why José had come, and repeated the story Raul had told me, and the deal he and José had offered me. Then I showed her the ring Raul had given me.

"It is a very beautiful ring," she said, "But Mark, please give it back to them and when they come in the morning, please tell them you aren't interested. Besides the danger, remember your family, and how hard we have all worked to rebuild what we almost lost. When something keeps being torn down, some of the pieces will get lost or be damaged beyond repair. Be honest with yourself, Mark. How much have any of you gained from the treasure you already have? Please tell them no."

I patted Nita's hand and she leaned over and kissed me goodnight, but I did not answer her. I lay awake for a long time after she had gone, and finally admitted to myself just how unprofitable the venture had been.

I had spent over nine thousand dollars and probably lost the use of my right leg for life. Luis was in prison. Carlos had lost his life. Tex was the lucky one; he would completely recover. And unless we could sell the gold in Mexico, all we had was the satisfaction of knowing where over a quarter of a million dollars in gold was buried. Until we could sell it, the gold wasn't worth its weight in styrofoam.

Until last night, I had not given much thought as to why some men have to climb forbidding mountains, others pit their strength against the forces of the mighty sea in frail sailboats, and still others risk their lives in high-speed racing cars. I've done a lot of pondering in the last twelve hours, and I know what my answer will be when José comes this morning. You may ask why men embark on such hazardous adventures, often knowing that even if they win, they have lost. As José would say, Quien sabe? Who knows?

Part II

LOVE AND GOLD

Chapter 12

I HAD just finished my breakfast when the door flew open and Miss Horner, the nurse, ran into my room and said, "There is the most awful-talking man I ever met, and two Mexicans wanting to see you. He said his name was Jim Dunlap and he claims to be an old friend. I can't imagine you knowing anyone as uncouth as he is, much less considering him a friend."

It was easy to see that dark storm clouds had already cast a shadow over what sunshine the day might have had in store for the good nurse.

Out of the corner of my eye, I saw Jim standing in the hall and decided it might just as well come a big thunder storm as a little sprinkle, so I told her that she was absolutely right; that I had never met any such person, and even if I had, I most certainly wouldn't associate with him.

A frog couldn't have jumped as far as Jim did. He landed in the middle of the room, ready for battle.

"That done it, by God, that done it!" he said. "I don't give a damn if you are a sick cripple, you tell this lady the truth, or I'll jerk you out of that bed and beat the hell out of you."

I pretended to be scared and asked Miss Horner if she was going to allow me to be talked to in such a manner. "Of course not," she replied, "I'll go right now and call the police."

Miss Horner started to leave the room, but José was standing in the door.

"Please, Señorita, you no call the police," he pleaded.

"You no understand. Few man have shared so many dangers together, they are closer than most fathers and sons."

Jim had laid his rope-burned and calloused hand on my forehead. "How are you feeling, you ornery little bastard?" he asked.

Miss Horner turned and looked. Her only comment as she left the room was: "Well, I'll be damned."

Jim, José, and Raul had just sat down after asking how I was, when Miss Horner re-entered the room with a tray containing cups and a pot of coffee. To say we were all surprised is putting it mildly.

We drank coffee and talked for about ten minutes. Finally, José couldn't stand the suspense any longer. He stood up and asked, "What you say, my brother, what you say? Will you help me and Raul with the other treasure?"

"Look, José, I don't know how long I will have to stay in the hospital, and after I get out, how long it will be before I could physically take on such a task."

"Is not important the time, my brother, we are only interested now in your recovery, but once you ees able, then will you help us?"

José translated to Raul what he had just told me, and Raul was in complete agreement and promised that he and José would light the candles and pray for my speedy recovery.

I was deeply touched by Raul's concern until he added: "I have been poor so long, and there is so much *cerveza* and *tequila* that needs drinking and so many beautiful muchachas that need loving, and this I cannot do without the money." Which was all right with me. He could have the beer and the girls. I would be satisfied with the money.

"Okay, José, it's a deal, as soon as I am physically able." José gave me a big embrace and, with tears of happiness running down his cheeks, turned to Raul and said, "You see, my brother will do anything for me. Now you know why me and my family love him so much."

Raul was pleased and happy, but he wasn't going to put his stamp of approval on me until I had fulfilled my promise.

We visited for another half hour. Then Jim announced they had to be going just as soon as Tex arrived. I gave Jim the

146

diamond ring Raul had given me the night before, and told him to keep it until we went for the other treasure. I didn't want Raul to sell it and get drunk and tell all he knew about the treasure.

Tex came in and announced that the plane was ready to go. Our goodbyes were strained, for we were four very dear and close friends.

Since I wouldn't have to listen to Jim cuss and complain on their journey home, I decided to liven up the trip for the other guys. Just as Jim started out the door, I asked him how Lupe was.

"Fine," he said, "I'll tell her you said 'hello'."

"Please do," I said, "And Jim, I was just wondering."

"What the hell are you wondering about?" he asked.

"Actually, Jim, it's none of my business, but is Lupe being properly taken care of?"

"Of course she is," he replied, "and why in the hell would you ask a damn fool question like that?"

"Well, Jim, you are getting up in years, and I figured you were like an old bull—only able to make love twice a year, once in the Spring and once in the Fall."

He knew I was putting him on, but I also accomplished what I had set out to do. His temper got he best of him. He slammed the door so hard it jarred open, and as they started down the hall, he was cussing a blue streak.

I heard Jim ask Tex, "Did you hear what that cocky little bastard asked me? I'll have him know, and you, too, by God, I am as good a man as either of you two dicks. Hell, I am still as fast as a rabbit and hornier than a stud bedbug."

He was still swearing something scandalous as they went out of hearing. I knew their trip home wouldn't be dull for it would take Jim hours to blow off enough steam to get back to normal.

The third week after their visit, I had a phone call from Jim and Tex. They were both excited. Snider had contacted them and wanted to buy the gold we had cached and would take delivery at the air strip at Jim's ranch in Mexico, where we had buried it.

Jim had to kid me a little that he was a better businessman

147

than I was. He had raised Snider's price and arranged for delivery at Jim's ranch in Mexico.

I couldn't understand why Snider was offering such a high price, but I certainly wasn't going to look a gift horse in the mouth.

I congratulated Jim and Tex and told them to sell by all means, before he backed out, and to have Luis present at the transaction. Luis had been out of prison only a short time, and I knew he needed the money. He could represent Carlos' family and receive their share. None of us would ever get over poor Carlos' death. At least now, his kids' education were secure.

They both agreed and said they would bring me my share as soon as the transaction was completed.

I was about half asleep on the afternoon of the eighth day after Jim and Tex had called, when Miss Horner rushed in to my room and informed me a car had just driven up outside and she had recognized a very refined and cultured gentleman by the name of Jim Dunlap, and since she was an angel of mercy, she felt it her duty to come and warn me in advance of his arrival.

Jim didn't bother to knock. The door flew open and when I looked at him, I thought he was either drunk or crazy. His greeting was, "Get out of that bed, you little bastard, I've been screwed."

In all the years I had known Jim, never had I heard him use vulgar language in the presence of a woman. To cuss, gripe and complain, yes. This was too much. So I reminded him that a lady was present.

His reply almost knocked me out of bed. "I don't give a god-damn if the Virgin Mary was here. I've sure as hell been screwed, and big, too."

When it dawned on him what he had just said in the nurse's presence, he hauled Tex, José and Luis into the room and practically shoved Miss Horner out the door. At least he tried to apologize: "I'm sorry, ma'am, but it's the honest to God's truth, I've really been screwed."

Jim closed the door and ran back to my bed. "Goddammit, Mark, don't just lay there, do something. Didn't you hear what I said?"

"How could I keep from hearing what you said, you've been braying like a jackass and told me at least four times that you had just been screwed. Congratulations, that's quite an accomplishment for a man of your age."

Jim threw up his arms in a gesture of helplessness and said, "That done it, by God, that done it." Turning to Tex, he said, "Don't just stand there like a bottle of stale piss, tell him. So help me, I'll strangle the bastard if I so much as look at him. I am going to find that nice nurse and apologize."

As soon as Jim left the room, José and Luis started talking a mile a minute. Tex interrupted and said, "Mark, what I have to say isn't easy, but Jim was right. We have all been taken. In other words, we were swindled out of all the gold. You were right. Forty dollars an ounce above market price was too high a price and we should have been on our guard. Anyway, Snider and Block arrived at the ranch right on schedule. We had the gold dug up and were waiting.

"They drilled all the bars and took off for Chihuahua to have an assay made. They came back the next day with the assay reports and it all averaged eight-forty fine, making the gold worth $512.56 an ounce."

Tex took a notebook out of his pocket to be sure of the facts and figures. Then he continued. "There were 7,656 ounces in the bars at $512.56 an ounce, making a total of $3,914,159.36.

"Then came the payoff. He had a cashier's check for $4,300,000.00. The cunning son-of-a-bitch made his move then. He suggested that Block fly their plane to Chihuahua and he would go with Jim and me in Jim's plane to Jim's bank in Chihuahua and have the banker verify the cashier's check which was issued on a bank in El Paso. We could then deposit the check, pay him the balance due him, and he would be on his way.

"He was sharp as hell. When we arrived in Chihuahua, he went with us to the bank, met the bank Manager, Señor Padilla, and presented him with the cashier's check. Of course, Señor Padilla wanted to verify the numbers on the check with the bank in El Paso. Snider was in complete agreement.

"We finally got the call through to El Paso, but the bank

didn't answer. Finally the operator told us all the banks were closed because it was a legal holiday. We hadn't even thought about it being a holiday, because it was not a holiday in Mexico.

"The bastard had it timed just perfect. Snider was very upset and we could understand why. All that illegal gold—he couldn't stay long at a large airport.

"We held a conference. Snider said they had extra wing tanks on their twin engine plane so they could fly non-stop to a brush strip in Canada and his buyers were expecting them that night around 10:00. But if he could not meet them, he would have to take the gold back to the ranch.

"We all went to the bank Manager's office, and Jim asked him if we could deposit the cashier's check. The manager said yes, and that he would notify us when the check cleared. Snider also told the bank manager to transfer the balance due him to his bank in El Paso.

"We then went back to Jim's ranch to take it easy for two or three days before going back to the bank, in order to give the check time to clear.

"The next morning, Señor Padilla called the bank in El Paso and the bank Manager there told him the cashier's check was counterfeit. Besides that, Snider had cashed over $200,000.00 worth of these same counterfeit checks before he left El Paso, and every lawman in the southwest was looking for him.

"In all my life, Mark, I've never seen a man throw such a fit as Jim did."

Before Tex could continue, Jim came back into the room. He took a cashier's check out of his wallet and stuck it so close to my face I couldn't have seen the letters and figures if they had been as big as a box car.

"Just look at that check you little bastard, just look at it. Counterfeit as hell. Worthless by God. I tell you, we've all been screwed."

"Okay, Jim, Okay, now, dammit. Sit down and listen for a change and cool off. All you are doing is repeating yourself. It's not as hopeless as it seems. I know where Snider is."

Jim jumped straight up. "Where? Where?" he asked.

"That dirty thieving, lying, conniving son-of-a-bitch won't live to see the sun come up in the morning."

"Please, Jim, if only you will shut up and listen. I know how mad we all are, but if we use our heads, we can get the biggest part of our money back."

"See!" José said. "I know and told you my brother was smart enough to get us out of what we're not smart enough to stay out of."

Jim made a grab for José's shirt collar and said, "José, I'll wring your scrawny little neck, dammit, that little cocky bastard didn't hang the moon."

"I know, Señor Jim," José agreed, as he crossed the room out of Jim's reach, then added, "but if my brother had been there, he would have."

I interrupted their sarcastic argument and told them both to shut up and listen for a change. Then I asked Jim and Tex to try and remember everything that Snider and Block had said when we met them in El Paso on the day of the accident.

My memory carried me back to that afternoon. While we were at the races, Snider had asked Block if the River Jalan was still at flood stage and if the banker had asked when he was going to bring him another shipment of gold.

At that time, I hadn't given it a thought, but when Tex told me they had wing tanks on their plane for a non-stop flight, they gave their destination away. I asked Jim if he was positive about the long-range fuel tanks.

"Hell, yes. I'm sure they had the extra tanks. All pilots take notice of every little detail about a plane. But, I don't see how knowing the name of a river, and a plane with long range tanks tells us where those damn thieves are."

"All right, I'll explain it. About three years ago, a guy from Alburquerque hired me to go with him to Honduras to make a geological report on a placer mine.

"We went to Tegucigalpa, the national capital, and then flew about 120 miles to a brush strip on the river Jalan. This guy told me that the strip we landed on was built by an American by the name of Block. Block had a small placer operation as a cover and he and another American bought gold in the States and flew it down to Honduras.

"The taxes were so cheap that they could afford to resmelt it, pay the taxes and operate legally, pretending that all the gold came from their placer mine. Also, a banker in Tegucigalpa has a direct sale on the world market.

"These guys were gone all the time we were there. I never had an opportunity to meet them. You guys think about this for a minute. Would you go to Canada after passing over four million dollars worth of counterfeit checks, besides being in possession of our four million in gold, and take the chance of being arrested and face extradition back to the United States, or would you go to Honduras and live like royalty where you had friends and connections, where there are no extradition laws and you are absolutely safe from the long arm of Uncle Sam?"

A big smile of relief appeared on all their faces. At least we now had a clue to go on. They all asked at the same time when we could take off and go get our money.

"Look, men, maybe my doctor will let me out of the hospital tonight to have dinner with you and we can discuss our plans with more privacy in the motel."

They gave me the name of the motel and took off.

Chapter 13

WHEN THE doctor made his evening call, I told him four friends had flown up from Mexico to visit me and I'd like to have dinner with them at their motel. To my surprise, the doctor agreed that it would be good for me to get out of the hospital for a few hours. Then, in his most professional tone, he instructed me as to what I could do and could not do, and to be back at the hospital no later than 10:00.

At 7:00 I called a cab and headed for the motel. I had given a lot of thought as to how we could go about collecting our money, and as to Snider and Block's possible weaknesses. Once more, I relived the afternoon at the race track in El Paso.

They both had tried to date two pretty young Spanish girls who were sitting in front of us. The girls finally got up and left, rather than telling the bastards they were too old for them to date.

When I arrived at the motel, all four of the guys were trying to help me out of the cab. They finally realized they were in each other's way, so Tex did his good deed for the day.

Once we were inside the room, I asked if they had any ideas as to how to go about collecting from our friends.

Jim jumped up and said, "You're damn right, just give me five minutes with them thieving sons-of-bitches and they will be glad to pay. I'll beat nine different kinds of hell out of them."

I interrupted Jim and told him if he could control himself by keeping his mouth shut for a change and listen, I thought

I had a plan that would work. He cast me an icy stare and sat down muttering to himself that he didn't know what this world was coming to. The younger generation was so damn cocky that they had no respect for their elders.

I began, "As much as we all would like to, we can't just go to Honduras and beat the hell out of these guys and get our money. First comes the money, then our revenge.

"As you all know, down there, if you have money, nobody questions where it comes from. Remember these guys can't return to the United States, and they will die, if necessary, to keep that money. If they know we are after them, they will hide out for as long as necessary, or they could hire someone to kill us. You can't protect yourself from someone if you don't know who is after you.

"Now, let me ask you a question. If you wanted to trap a man, what would you use for bait?" After a few minutes of thinking, Tex said, "Money!" Jim said, "I'd say money, too." This was Luis' reply also. "What about you, José?" "Aw, my brother, there is only one thing, a beautiful woman."

"You're right, José, come to the head of the class." Jim jumped up and said, "Dammit, Mark, this is no time for bullshitting around. What in the blue blazes of hell has a woman got to do with this?"

José interrupted. "*Quien sabe, Señor* Jim, but I am sure . . ." That was as far as José got before Jim told him to shut up, since he didn't know a damn thing about anything.

"Why you say that, *Señor* Jim, did I not know the answer to the question, and you three Tontos did not?"

Jim made a grab for José. I stuck my crutch between them and told them both to sit down and shut up. Then I continued, "Gentlemen, José was right."

José couldn't resist jumping up and pointing his finger at Jim. "See, see, I told you I was right. Am I not almost as smart as my brother?"

I grabbed my crutch again and waved it above Jim's head before he could get up, then turned to José and told him I was going to brain the next man who interrupted me. That restored peace and order.

Once more I continued, "We have to find a way to get these men out of Honduras and back to Mexico. This idea I have might work, but first, I have to know if Snider and Block know José."

"No, they don't," Tex replied. "José stayed in the bunk house with the two cowboys who were acting as guards."

"That's great, Tex, but before I continue, this is important. It will mean the success or failure of our attempt, if my theory is accepted by you guys."

I then told them about how Snider and Block had tried to date the two Spanish girls at the race track that afternoon. Judging by their conversations, a pretty woman was their weakness.

"This is my idea: I will go through it step-by-step. As soon as I am physically able, we will rent a twin-engine plane. The reason for waiting for me is, as we all know, a better bush pilot than Jim never lived, but he doesn't have a multi-engine or an instrument rating."

"Don't need one," he growled, "even the birds have enough damn sense to stay on the ground when they can't see to fly."

I ignored him and continued. "Also, in Central America, in order to fly a plane at night, you must have a twin-engine plane and be instrument rated. We may be forced to do some night flying and we must have a plane where we can fly non-stop from Tegucigalpa to Jim's ranch.

"Now, step-by-step: First, the right plane to do the job. Second, we must arrive at Tegucigalpa Airport just before dark so it's dark when we get into town. Third, Jim, Tex, Luis, and I will have to get rooms and stay inside and not be seen. Fourth, as we all know, José can mix with the peons so he will be dressed as one of them.

"José has seen both of these men and can easily find out where they are staying, where they take their meals, do their drinking and partying, then pass the information on to Jim and me. Now, Jim, you and Luis don't interrupt me until I have finished. Then I'll welcome your comments.

"What I am going to ask is more than any man has a right to ask of another man. A few minutes ago, I told you all I thought beautiful women were Snider and Block's weakness.

"If my theory is right, we have to have two pretty Mexican women we can trust. Gentlemen, nowhere on this green earth do I know of two such women except Luis' wife and Lupe."

They both had half risen out of their chairs. "Please, fellows, let me finish." They sat back down. "I know Mexican women—how honest, decent and loyal they are. Your two wives will appear to be respectable women alone on a vacation. Luis' wife, Carmen, speaks perfect English, but Lupe doesn't, so they would have to be cousins; one from California, and one from Mexico City."

"Once we know where these guys are doing their partying, the girls will go there for a drink and to eat. José will accompany them and wait outside. All the girls will have to do is go in and sit down, and wait for these men to make their play.

"The girls can play hard to get and appear that they are afraid of gossip and then invite the men up to their rooms for a drink. I will be waiting in one room while Jim is waiting in the other.

"We knock the bastards out, handcuff them, load them into the plane. Next stop—Mexico and Jim's ranch. Once we have these birds in Mexico, at the ranch, they will pay rather than spend ten years in a Mexican prison and then be extradited to the U.S.A. for another ten to twenty years.

"After they pay us, then we take them to Mexico City and they are on their own. If they won't pay, then Jim, they're yours to have arrested or do with as you please."

Jim jumped up and threw his arms around me and damn near squeezed me to death. "It will work, Mark. Sure as Hell, it will work."

"Just a minute, Jim, just a minute. Luis hasn't consented to using his wife as a decoy."

Luis spoke up and said he didn't like the idea, but was willing to go along if Jim was. He was very jealous, as most Mexican husbands are. I didn't blame him, for his wife, Carmen was a beauty.

We went over the plans for almost two hours. All agreed it would work, and once Luis understood that no petting would be necessary, he became excited and happy, too.

Then a thought occurred to me, and I asked whether Carmen and Lupe would go for the deal. Luis said I had very accurately described a good Mexican wife, but had neglected to add that the wife never questions a husband's action or decision.

This was music to my ears. I could already count the money. I then asked all present if they realized that to transport anyone across a national boundary or from one country to another against their will was kidnapping. Jim assured us there was no need to worry once we were in Mexico.

It was all settled. As soon as I was physically able, we would all meet in El Paso and go from there to Jim's ranch and on to Honduras.

They suggested we say goodbye at the motel so they could get an early start home. I asked Jim if he intended to visit my two sons. "No, Mark, much as I'd like to, I am ashamed to face them and Nita after the dumb stunt I pulled letting those boys swindle me out of all that money. Tell them hello and the next time I come, I'll bring them each a wild cat with a barb wire tail."

I told Jim not to worry, we would recover the money. Besides, I would have done the same thing if I had been there. Jim put his arm across my shoulders and said, "Thanks, Mark. I really appreciate those kind words. It makes my load a hell of a lot easier to carry."

Chapter 14

THE NEXT day, the doctor suggested that I transfer to another hospital where they had all types of whirlpool baths and advanced therapy available.

I kept Jim and Tex posted about my progress. At the end of four months, I was well enough to be discharged. After another three months at home, I had almost recovered completely.

The day of my departure finally arrived. I was very sorry to leave my sons, but relieved to be away from their mother, which is an awful thing to admit. There are some things a man has to do, and getting back that money was very important to all of us.

At the airport, Nita said, "Mark, this is the beginning of the end." I could find no words to answer her, except to assure her I would be careful and not get in any trouble and that everything would be all right when I came back.

They boys sensed something was wrong when she didn't kiss me goodbye, she replied that she had kissed me goodbye at home, but she failed to say when. It had been over three months since the last time she had kissed me.

When that 707 landed in El Paso, I felt like a poor lost soul that had been in hell and had unexpectedly arrived in heaven. Tex and Jackie were there to meet me. Tex was very happy that the time had finally arrived to make our move.

I could sense Jackie's concern for our safety. After lunch, Tex and I went to see about renting a plane. I had flown in and out of El Paso International for years, and the manager of one of the leading plane dealers there was a very good friend of mine.

I cautioned Tex not to mention my accident. I didn't want F.A.A. to check on me. If they did, and I had to take a physical, they would pull my license.

When we arrived at his office, my friend Walt luckily was on the ground. I told him I wanted to rent a plane and gave him the required specifications. He told me his company had come out with a new plane, a push-pull job, one motor in back and one in the front that was ideal for my purpose.

We went out and looked at the plane. I was very impressed. It was a five passenger plane and very roomy. What really sold me was that anyone who could fly a large single engine could fly this plane, even if they had never had any multi-engine time.

Jim had thousands of hours on a single engine, but no twin-engine time. In case of emergency, he could safely fly and land this plane with no trouble.

My friend told me I would have to have ten hours check-out time in this plane before F.A.A. would issue me a center thrust rating. I hated to delay the trip but thought it best to go ahead and get checked out.

I spent an hour in the cockpit getting familiar with the instruments. We then took off for my first official flight time. After an hour with the instructor, I was turned loose on my own.

The next two days, I spent three hours in the morning, and two hours in the evening shooting touch and go landings and off field landings. When I was absolutely positive I had mastered the plane, an F.A.A. instructor went with me for my check ride. I had no problem getting my center thrust rating, although I could tell my right leg was weak when I used the right rudder.

It took an extra day to put the long-range tanks on the plane which cost me an extra four thousand dollars. At last, all delays were over and we were finally ready to start our adventure.

The following morning, Tex, Luis and Carmen were at the airport waiting when I arrived. Carmen looked more beautiful then I had remembered her. She blushed when we said hello, for this job was strictly out of line for her.

We had no problems with customs at Juarez and had a nice

flight to Jim's ranch. He came out to meet us at the airstrip which was only five hundred feet from his house.

"I thought you would never get here, and what the hell is that damn thing?" he asked as he pointed toward the plane.

"That" I informed him, "is an airplane."

"Airplane, hell," he said, "it looks like a morphidite to me. Are you sure the damn thing will fly?"

I ignored him and his questions and headed for the house to say hello to Lupe. I was finishing my coffee when Jim and Tex came in.

"Damn it, Mark, you didn't answer my question. Does that thing actually fly?"

I took him by the arm, walked back to the plane, and told him to get in and close the door. I started the engines, taxied to the cement slab at the end of the dirt runway, checked out, and took off.

At about eight thousand feet, I eased the nose down, leveled off, and called Jim's attention to a mountain on his right. The second he looked off, I chopped the front engine. He looked back around as the front prop stopped dead straight up and down.

Jim almost tore the seat belt loose trying to rise. He grabbed the stick on his side and shouted. "You stupid little bastard, get her nose down. For God's sake, don't stall it out up here."

"Look, Jim, don't get excited, what do you think that rear engine is for? Relax and enjoy the ride." I knew he had forgotten about the rear engine, which was not visible from the cockpit.

We cruised around another five minutes on the rear engine before I started the front engine and cut the rear one. We flew another five minutes using only the front engine, then I started the rear engine again. All this time, Jim didn't say a word.

After I stared the rear engine again, his only comment was, "Well, I'll be damned." He finally asked me to turn the controls over to him and he flew the plane for about fifteen minutes and really wrung it out. He did a magnificent job of flying.

"Let's go shoot a few touch and go landings and see how I can do." After the first one that I made, while instructing him, he made five good landings.

When we landed, Tex asked Jim how he liked it. "Hmmm." was his only comment.

Lupe's call to lunch stopped any further discussion. As always, Tex and I were ready to eat. Lupe had a delicious ranch dinner of steak, gravy and potatoes, salad and sour dough biscuits. The way Tex and I put the food away, I am sure our hostess thought we were magicians.

After lunch, I got Jim and Tex alone. "Look boys, we have a problem. The plane will only carry five people and their luggage. It's imperative that Jim, Carmen, Lupe, José and I go together. What do we do with Luis? He's going to raise hell and not let Carmen go when he finds out there isn't room for him.

"You are right, Mark," Jim spoke up, "and I know how jealous a Mexican is of his wife."

"Yeah, I know, Jim, but I've been worrying about Luis throwing a jealous fit if the girls have to flirt a little to get those suckers to their rooms. I wish we could think of some way to keep Luis out of our way a day or two."

Tex came up with a wonderful idea. "If we are lucky enough to trap those birds, you two guys will have to fly them out alone. Why don't Luis and I fly down on a commercial airliner. After you and Jim take off with Snider and Block, then the five of us can fly back to Chihuahua on a commercial flight the next day.

"This way, if you two have any trouble, the girls will be in the clear. Also, if we break the news to Luis now, we can apply the healing balm to him.

"By leaving at once for Chihuahua, we can catch the evening flight to Mexico City. Once in Mexico City, I'll make sure we miss the first two flights out and they only have one flight a day. This will keep Luis out of your hair for two days and there won't be a darn thing he can do about it."

We agreed that this was the thing to do if we could get Luis to go for it. Tex went and got Luis and Jim explained it to him.

To our surprise, Luis was all for it, if they could be there when we arrived. I gave them the name of the motel I had stayed at when I was in Tegucigalapa three years before, and told him to be sure and rent six rooms on the ground floor.

All three of us were ashamed that it was necessary to deceive Luis, but as long as Jim and I were alive, no harm would ever come to his wife.

Tex took off to pack and Luis called Carmen. We knew he was giving her very strict orders as to what to do and what not to do. I asked Jim to go with me to take Tex and Luis to the airport in Chihuahua. We would take the push-pull and it would give him an opportunity to become more familiar with the plane.

Once in Chihuahua, we had an hour's wait for their flight. Luis was very nervous, so Jim and I decided to wait until they were on their way to Mexico City before we started back to the ranch.

As we were leaving the terminal, I asked Jim if he thought he could fly the plane back home. Without answering, he got into the left hand seat, then asked, "Who in the hell do you think invented the airplane?"

Neither of us said a word all the way to the ranch. Jim was too occupied with his flying, and I had time to do a little thinking to see if we had overlooked anything that might go wrong.

Back at the ranch, José and I gave the plane a complete check out and refilled the gas tanks. After dinner, Jim and I spread all our maps on the table and charted our course to Tegucigalpa. We spent an hour checking and familiarizing ourselves with all the alternate airports where we could land in case of an emergency.

We didn't want to refuel in Mexico unless it was absolutely necessary. We wanted to be absolutely sure of the amount of fuel needed on our return flight. We estimated five and one half hours flying time, at sixty-five percent power to San Salvador where we would get our visas to enter Honduras. From there, we would have one and one half hours flying time to Tegucigalap.

At 4:00 A.M., the next morning, Jim almost tore my

bedroom door down. "Get up, Mark," he shouted. "I don't see how in the hell you can sleep. I've waited nearly eight months to get my hands on those dirty sons of bitches, now, dammit, get up. Coffee's made."

I showered, dressed, and followed the fragrant aroma of fresh perked coffee into the kitchen. As usual, I was the last one to arrive at the table. Everyone else was already eating. After we had finished breakfast, I asked Lupe, Carmen and José to bring all their luggage to the plane so we could load and be ready to take off at daybreak.

Jim came in and announced that it was light enough to take off. We had a nice flight from the ranch to San Salvador, kidding Carmen and Lupe unmercifully about the duties they were to perform.

After five and one half hours, we arrived in San Salvador, obtained our plane permit and visas, had lunch and decided we had enough fuel to real our final destination—Tegucigalpa.

The sun was almost down when we sighted Tegucigalpa. In five more minutes, we were circling the airport. I was taxiing toward the control tower when Jim started shouting and cussing. "That's it, by God, let me out of here." I looked at him and when he saw I was looking, he said, "Can't you understand a damn thing? That's their plane."

I looked to where he was pointing and there, tied down, was a blue and white Aztec. I could tell from the letters and numbers it had an American registration.

"Are you sure?" I asked.

"Hell, yes, I'm sure. I could never forget that plane, besides I remember the registration number. Just wait until I get my hands on them two bastards."

I slapped him on the back of the neck, not too gently. "Look, Jim, you could cuss and throw a fit in Mexico or the States just as well as here. We didn't make this trip for you to throw a fit. Now damn you, shut up and listen. I am going to taxi behind this terminal and let José, Carmen and Lupe out, and Jim, you help them with their luggage.

"José, you three clear customs as fast as you can, and go directly to this motel and get three rooms on the ground floor. José, you register for one room, Lupe for one room, and Carmen for one room.

"Remember, if anyone asks, José, you are Lupe's papa from Mexico City. Carmen is your niece from Los Angeles. Jim and I will close our flight plan, clear customs and eat here at the airport. That way it will be after dark when we get to town. If those two guys should have someone watching for us, maybe they won't find out we are together.

"As soon as it gets dark, José, you go about half a block down the street toward the big church and wait until Jim and I get there. Then we will slip into the motel.

"If Snider and Block get suspicious and check the motel for Americans, we won't be registered so no one will know where we are staying. Jim and I will stay in the rooms and not venture outside."

José didn't understand. "But my brother, only three rooms is not enough." "Yes, it is, José. One room for Jim and Lupe, one for you and . . ." Before I could say "me," José interrupted. "Luis is going to be very mad if he finds out you stay with Carmen. Of course, my brother, I won't tell him nothing."

"Damn it, José, you and I stay together. Carmen has a room by herself." I looked at Carmen expecting her to be embarrassed and blushing. Instead she was smiling invitingly. As José always says, *"Quien sabe* about a woman?"

José and the girls headed for the terminal. Jim and I taxied down and had the plane refueled and tied down. Taking our luggage, we went to the control tower and closed our flight plan. I had to use my correct name, but where the number of passengers were listed, I put one and the guy never questioned me.

We cleared customs and had dinner, then took a cab to the church and walked toward the motel. We had only gone a short distance when José came running to meet us.

"You know something, my brother? You know who just passed and went in that big hotel across the street? Those two dirty bastards, Snider and Block."

Jim started cussing, dropped his luggage, doubled up his

164

fist and headed across the street. I grabbed him by the back of his shirt collar and shook him like a dog shakes a rabbit.

"Jim, remember what I told you in the plane. If you don't settle down and control yourself, you will ruin everything. And furthermore, I don't intend to spend every minute babysitting a grown man."

His reply almost floored me. "Sorry, Mark." Never had I heard Jim Dunlap apologize or say he was sorry to any man.

I asked José if there was a back entrance to the hotel. "Sí, Sí, my brother," he said. "Just like you, I look for everything. But we will have to go back to the church and around to the back."

We retraced our steps and made it inside José's room without seeing anyone or being seen. Once inside the motel, I told José to go and get the girls, but as he started out the door, I changed my mind. "Hold it, José, let's go to their rooms."

Lupe's room was the first we came to and Carmen's was only three doors down. Jim knocked on the door. Lupe answered that she was dressing. I told Jim to go in and I would get Carmen and bring her to their room.

José and I walked on down to Carmen's room and I knocked on the door.

"Quien es?" she asked.

"Me, Mark, quick let me in before someone sees me." My only thought was to keep my identity concealed. I don't know if what happened was as much a surprise to Carmen as it was to me, or if she had planned it that way.

Anyway, when I heard her release the lock, I opened the door and quickly stepped inside. I am sure she didn't expect me to make such a fast entrance. She didn't have time to step back and I bumped her, then threw my arms out to keep from knocking her down. She also threw her arms out wide to try and keep her balance. I caught her by the shoulders and we regained our balance.

I looked down at Carmen and started to apologize. To my surprise, she had on only a very thin robe. Nothing else. It was open from top to bottom. Instead of letting her arms down and closing her robe, she let them fall around my neck and pressed her large warm breasts against my chest.

As Jim says, "That done it, by God, that done it." I am sure it happened as I said, for I had gotten up and dressed and was standing by the door when I heard Jim ask José, "Where's Mark, what's taking them so damn long?"

"Ah, *señor* Jim, my brother is *muy macho,* is he not?"

"What the hell you talking about, José?" Jim asked.

"*Si, señor* Jim, it is true. My brother opens the door and very fast goes inside. He almost knocks the *Señora* Carmen down, her robe comes open. She has nothing underneath but titties, and such pretty ones. I have not seen their likes for years.

"They grab each other to keep from falling, then the *Señora* puts the titties on my brother. My brother puts the *Señora* on the bed. I close the door. I think my brother is, how you say in the English? Throwing the pecker to her?"

"José, if you aren't lying to me, that's a logical assumption."

"No, *Señor* Jim, I swear it is the truth, and I am worried."

"What the hell are you worried about?" he asked.

"Well, *Señor* Jim, if in nine months there comes a *guerita*—like you say a 'Blondie', then Luis is going to be suspicious, and again, how you say in the English? Then the sheet enters into the fan."

"Listen, José, go to your room. We will call you when we want you. If you ever tell anyone about this, I'll wring your neck."

"*Señor* Jim, you know never would I tell or cause my brother problems."

I asked Carmen how much longer before she would be ready.

"Only a minute," she answered.

"Okay, when you're ready, come to Jim and Lupe's room. I'll go get José and meet you there."

Once we were all together, I asked Jim what plan he had in mind. "None," he answered. "You're the gabby one, let's hear what you have to say."

I spoke slowly in Spanish so there couldn't be any misunderstanding. "All right, girls, it's now your show, the guys are across the street. When you're ready, go to the hotel and have your dinner.

"Be very ladylike, accept a drink if they offer to buy you one, but no more than one. Let them join you at your table if they want to. If they don't show any interest in you, give them the eye, but don't overdo it.

"Try to make a date for tomorrow night. Explain that you just flew in today and are very tired, but that tomorrow night things could be different.

"And, girls," I added, "don't let them get you in a car or taxi under any circumstances. And don't tell them where you are staying. Just promise to meet them at this same hotel. Then as quick as you can, come back to the motel.

"José, you follow at a safe distance behind the girls and wait at the bar while they are eating. Don't pay any attention to them, and two beers are all you drink—remember, only two, and then follow them back here to the motel."

The girls and José said they had everything straight and were ready to go.

Once Jim and I were alone, he asked me what was the deal between Carmen and I. I told him my version of it just as it happened. He leaned back in his chair and closed his eyes, then said, "That beats me. Usually Mexican women are the most faithful wives on earth. It just goes to show you, you never know when a woman will show her butt."

I lay back on the bed and went to sleep. Jim shook me awake and I was surprised to see that José and the girls were back. All three started talking at the same time. Jim finally got them to shut up, then asked Carmen to tell us what happened.

Carmen laughed and winked at me. "It was very easy. We had no more than sat down when they started undressing us with their eyes."

"The dirty sons of bitches," Jim broke in, then remembered himself, and told Carmen to continue.

"In just a minute the waiter brought over a bottle of cold wine, compliments of the two Americans."

"Lupe and I sent our thanks by the waiter. He came right back to our table and asked permission for the gentlemen to join us. We took about five minutes to talk it over and then accepted.

"They came right over and introduced themselves as Mr. Block and Mr. Young. Block speaks good Spanish. Young or Snider doesn't, so Block talked to Lupe and Snider talked to me.

"They sure thought they were ladies' men, and tried very hard to get us to stay and dance a while. Of course we have dates with them for 9:00 tomorrow night.

"Snider tried to caress my leg all through dinner. I whispered to him to be nice and maybe I would have a surprise for him tomorrow night when we were not so tired. I thought he was going to split his mouth grinning when I told him that."

Jim laughed and said we sure as hell would have a surprise for them.

José said he was going to bed. It sounded like a good idea to me, so I told all goodnight, congratulated the girls on a perfect job and stepped outside.

I was about halfway to my room when I heard someone very softly call my name. I turned around and there stood Carmen. I didn't need a brick wall to fall on me to get the message. I picked her up in my arms and carried her to her room.

Much later, I was smoking a cigarette with Carmen in my arms when she said, "Mark, I want to thank you for not asking me any questions. I am yours for as many times as you want me tonight, but in the morning, when you have had me for the last time and walk through the door, you will never touch me again so long as I am Luis' wife.

"You are the only man, except Luis that I have ever known. You remember Luis was in prison 14 months. I am only twenty-two years old, and very human. I needed love, and many men tried, but I remained true to Luis.

"Prison changed Luis, he now loves me like an animal, and he is crazy jealous. All this has made me cold toward him, for when we start to make love, he starts accusing me of having loved other men while he was in prison, and begs me to tell him, so he can forgive me. This kills all the desire in me. He will not believe the truth, then he tries to hurt me as we make love. You will never know how jealous and what a fool he is.

"No one will ever know how I have suffered so much for something I have never done. So, now I have done something to suffer for." Gently, I took her in my arms and told her she was a little fool and to leave him.

"No, I cannot. I married him in the church and he is my husband. But why do we talk of Luis? It has been over eighteen months since I could feel love and give myself so freely to a man."

She started biting on my ear and I was kissing her neck and caressing her with my hands. I didn't know a woman was capable of feeling such passion. I raised my head laughing and looked down into her lovely eyes and asked if she was not suffering.

Her answer was very appropriate for this particular instance. She locked her arms and both legs around me and pulled me closer to her. "Shut up, you fool, and do it to me right now. Suffering is my only pleasure."

We had too much to do even to think about sleeping. When it first started getting light, I got up, took a shower and started to dress. Carmen motioned for me to come to her. She was still in bed.

She sat up, exposing her beautiful large bare breasts, put her arms around my neck and said, "Mark, another night with you and I would forget all about decency." Then she pulled my head down, kissed me, and rubbed one of her breasts against my lips and said, "This is the last chance you will ever have to have me. Do you want me again?"

I did. But, like the monkey who made love to a skunk, I declined with regret: "I haven't had all I want, I've just had all I can stand."

Chapter 15

IT WAS daylight when I headed for my room. Luckily, no one else was up. José let me in with a knowing smile. Before he could say anything, I told him to dress, take Jim some breakfast and stay there until it was dark. This would give me all day to sleep and recuperate. I was a spent force.

"José, you had better wake me up at 7:00, have you got all that straight?"

"Si, my brother, don't worry. I do everything you say the way you say."

I fell across the bed fully clothed, and was asleep before José left the room.

Jim shook me awake and started cussing up a storm. "Damn if you ain't worse than some old tom cat. Howl all night and sleep all day. Get your fanny out of that bed. It's almost 8:00." I sat up on the bed and lit a cigarette.

"Boys, I have something to say. My conscience is bothering me. In my book, any man that will take liberties with a friend's wife is as sorry as a man can be, and I have done just that."

I told them what Carmen had told me about Luis, and his jealous accusations.

Jim spoke up, "Well, Mark, that explains everything. I couldn't understand until now. Your typical Mexican woman will live with you in a hut on beans and tortillas and be happy and faithful if you will only love and respect her."

"But don't ever accuse one of something she hasn't done, for rich or poor, they are very proud. Never question their loyalty without a reason."

"*Señor* Jim," José spoke up, "All you say is true. We are fools for husband." Then jealousy got the best of José's imagination. "Do you think my wife, Melinda would do such a thing as Carmen did?"

Melinda was very fat, half toothless, and looked like a reject from the human race.

Jim had to grin. "Hell, no, don't worry, José. Who would want to sleep with Melinda?"

José still wasn't convinced. "I admit, *Señor* Jim, she is *muy fayo* but in the bed—*mamma mia*, what a woman!"

"I'll take your word for it, José, and you take mine. You have nothing to worry about."

I quickly changed the subject and sent José out for our dinner. After we had eaten, I told José to go and get Carmen and meet us in Jim and Lupe's room.

The girls were waiting for us and really looked lovely. They had been to the beauty parlor getting prettied up for their dates. Jim even took a second look at Lupe.

I looked at Carmen and she blushed, knowing, of course, I was remembering last night. She pulled her dress down over her knees and looked away from me.

At 9:00 they asked if there were any last minute instructions. I told them to be sure they didn't get separated, to enter their rooms at the same time, and to be sure to lock their doors once they were inside.

"Now, girls, this is the most important thing of all. Be sure you clearly understand and do exactly as I say. Jim and I will be in the bathrooms. We can't see you, or know when to come into the room unless we have a cue. These guys will be carrying guns, and we don't want to have to kill them."

"Just speak for yourself," Jim said.

"Don't interrupt me," I told him, "and for once shut up."

The rooms in the motel were small, so the bed was no more than three feet from the bathroom door. I walked Carmen around the foot of the bed toward the bathroom door, and asked her to sit on the bed, facing the bathroom.

"Now, notice where Carmen is sitting. All right, when you come in with Snider and Block, go to your own room, and just as soon as you get inside, lock the door and go sit down on the bed as Carmen is sitting now, then get your date to come sit beside you. See, there is just enough room to sit down beside Carmen.''

I sat down. ''Now, Carmen, put your arms around my neck. Now, lie back on the bed and pull me back with you as if you were going to give me a kiss.

''Girls, you can see that my back is to the bathroom door, but Carmen can see the door. Also, notice the awkward position I am in. If Carmen tried to hold me, it would take a little while for me to break loose from her. Jim, you and Lupe run through this so there can't be any mistakes.''

When Lupe put her arms around Jim's neck, I told her to hold it a minute. ''Girls, this is the time for our cue. When you're in this position, say *vengasi mi amor* and lie back. Jim and I will enter the room and give them a kiss, before they can kiss you.''

We all laughed and the girls assured us they would do it exactly that way. At ten minutes after 9:00 they left to keep their dates. I went and got a bath towel and showed Jim how to wrap it around his pistol so he wouldn't bust Mr. Block's skull and have blood all over the room. I cautioned him to be sure and not hit him too hard and to put his hands behind his back when he handcuffed him.

I asked for a set of handcuffs and a gag that Jim had brought along in his suitcase. I went to my room for my pistol and back to Carmen's room. We didn't know how long it would take the girls to deliver the pigeons.

I was positive Snider would be with Carmen. I didn't want Jim to see him before I had administered the *coup de grace* for he might lose all control and beat his brains out. I rechecked the bathroom and made sure the door didn't squeak, then sat down on the bed. A lot of pleasant memories of last night came back to me.

Being by myself, the time passed very slowly. I chain smoked and tried to assure myself everything was going as planned. I thought about how Jim must feel, and was very thankful that my head wasn't going to be his target. Never had time passed so slowly. By midnight, I was really beginning to worry. Then I heard voices and recognized the girls' laughter. I could also hear men's voices.

I went into the bathroom and left the door open about one inch and checked my gun. I heard the door open and then the bolt slide into place as it was locked. Snider said, "At last baby, we are alone."

Carmen told him to take it easy and not to tear her clothes off, that he had plenty of time to come sit on the bed beside her. "No, baby, wait a minute," she told him, "Don't rush me. Here, sit down." Then those magic words, *Vengasi mi amor.*"

I eased the door open and laid the old 357 Magnum between his ears. He didn't make a sound. I reached down and helped Carmen to her feet. He had sure been in a hurry. He had unbuttoned Carmen's dress and had one of her breasts out.

I thought it might ease the tension to kid her a little, so I told her, "Carmen, your titty is prettier than it was last night."

Carmen gave me a smack that nearly dislocated my jaw and announced in any icy tone, "I told you this morning never to disrespect me again. Last night was all." The way my ears were ringing, I damn sure believed her.

I rolled the guy over and wasn't surprised to recognize *Señor* Snider. I took a .38 pistol out of a shoulder holster, handcuffed him and had just put the gag in his mouth when someone knocked on the door.

"Who is it?" Carmen asked.

"Who is it, hell, it's me." I recognized Jim's voice.

I opened the door and when he saw Snider, he pushed me over backwards and had Snider by the throat before I could get him stopped. I punched my thumbs in the hollow behind his ears and he turned loose of Snider. "What the hell did you do that for?" he asked innocently.

"Look, Jim, damn you, do you want to get our money back, or do you want to kill Snider? He's out cold. Like I told you before, I don't intend to babysit a grown man. There he is. If you want to kill him, go ahead."

I left the room and went to check on Block. He was all

right, breathing deep and regular, but still out, and properly handcuffed and gagged. I told José to guard him and to lock the door behind him. Then I took Lupe by the arm and went to check on Jim and Snider.

When we entered Carmen's room, Jim was still sitting there banging his fist on the floor and having a cussing seizure. He gave me a murderous stare, but for once, he didn't say a word.

I told him José and I were leaving for the airport. I would try to make a deal with the guard to let us take off before daylight, then come back and get him and these two birds.

"I'm ready," Jim replied.

José let me in and we moved Block into the room with Snider. José had rented an old car that I doubted would make it to the airport. It took forty dollars and thirty minutes of talking before the guard agreed to let us take off before the control tower opened. But, since it was an emergency, he was sure it would be all right.

When we got back to the room, both Snider and Block had regained consciousness. I walked up and extended my hand to Snider and asked if he wasn't going to shake hands with an old friend. Of course, he couldn't have even if he had wanted to. There was the most surprised and frightened look in their eyes.

We sent José to load the bags in the car, then drive around to the back of the motel and stop when we signaled. We would take our pigeons through the bathroom window.

We pushed Snider through the window. José was too small to hold him up and they both fell. The same happened with Block. Jim kissed Lupe goodbye. I thanked them both and we were off to the airport.

José drove us as close to the plane as possible. I told him to go and keep the guard busy so he wouldn't notice the handcuffs. As soon as we left, he was to go straight back to the motel room and stay with the girls until Tex and Luis arrived.

Snider didn't want to get in the plane. Jim never said a word. He slapped him in the face, and he got in. Block followed. We threw our luggage in and I started the engines. Once we were off the ground, Jim said, "Mark, we were lucky as hell."

I had to agree, we had been lucky. I replied, "Jim, why don't you take the gags out of their mouths?"

"Where are you taking us," they both asked. "Well, now, fellas," Jim said. "I need two extra cowboys at the ranch."

Snider squawked, "You're crazy! We aren't going."

Jim backhanded him across the mouth. "Shut up, you dirty, lying conniving son-of-a-bith, unless you want to wear that gag. When we get to the ranch, I have a check you can cash."

Block started trying to lay all the blame on Snider. It was easy to see that he wasn't enjoying the ride. They held a lengthy conference. All this time Jim had been clenching and unclenching his fists and cussing under his breath.

I had been able to overhear enough of their conversation to know that Snider thought we were bluffing and wouldn't dare take them out of Honduras, that we were only going to fly around a while and try to scare them into paying us.

Just after daylight we crossed into El Salvador, about 50 miles from where a large river forms a lake and then empties into the ocean. San Salvador, the capitol of El Salvador, is situated on the shores of this lake.

This is one of the best known check points from Mexico to Honduras. Being a pilot and having flown this course for many years, Block recognized it. He started cussing Snider.

Snider wanted to know what was wrong. "For your information" Block told him, "We have just passed over San Salvador, and we are less than one hour from the southern boundary of Mexico."

When Snider realized we were really taking them to Mexico, he started trying to make a deal. He promised he would pay us in full, plus our time and trouble. "You're damn right you will," Jim told him, "but at my ranch."

Then Block started laughing and sarcastically asked Snider if this was the dumb rancher who couldn't find his way from the house to the barn if he couldn't smell the cow shit.

Jim laughed, "Oh, he said that, did he? Well, my friend, I have a bunch of stalls in the barn that need cleaning out, and a new short handled shovel so you can get down close to your work.

"That will be your job while we are waiting for your check

to clear the bank. You have a choice—shovel that cow shit or you don't eat. Everybody at my place works or they don't eat. Of course, I am generous as hell. All the water you want to drink is free."

Block laughed and Snider started begging and blubbering like a kid. I had misjudged them, Block was the better man after all.

Jim turned around and told Snider to shut up. "There are three things I can't stand. Number one, a coward and a cry baby; number two, a damn thief and a liar; and number three, a no good son-of-a-bitch." Then Jim slapped him full in the face. "By God, you are all three."

I could tell Jim was getting worked up so I asked him to take the controls and let me rest awhile. I lit a smoke and Block spoke up. "Mark, if you had done to me what we did to you, I wouldn't give you the time of day, but you can't imagine how grateful I would be for a smoke."

I lit a cigarette, turned around and placed it in his mouth. He thanked me with his eyes. Snider said he wanted one. Jim put in his two cents worth and said, "That's tough, there's people in Hell wanting ice water," as he passed the controls back to me.

Everytime Jim or I smoked, we gave them cigarettes. Snider started complaining about their arms being behind them. Jim grabbed him by his hair, twisted his head around and put the gag back in his mouth. Then he looked at Block.

Block laughed and said, "I'm not complaining. I know when I am well off. I wish I knew I would live another fifty years in this position." He realized if we didn't get our money they were dead men, or had at least twenty years to serve in prison.

At 10:30, we flew directly over Durango, but we were too tired to make any comment, and we still had two and a half hours flying time to reach the ranch.

When I estimated we were about thirty minutes from the ranch, I started descending at one hundred feet a minute. When the ranch came into sight, Jim said, "I've never been so happy to get back home as I am right now."

"Why?" I asked.

"Hell," he replied, "look at those empty gas gauges, you

176

stupid bastard, and you'll know.''

It felt good to be on ground after seven hours of flying. I helped Snider and Block out, unlocked the cuffs, and re-handcuffed them with their hands in front. We put Snider and Block in the same room after searching them. They only had one hundred and eighty dollars between them, which we took.

The room had only one window, with iron bars over the outside. Jim left the room and came back with his two big German Shepherd dogs. They were the best trained and most vicious dogs I've ever seen.

Jim tied one on each side of the door and told Snider and Block to feel free to leave anytime they wanted to. He closed the door, but he didn't bother to lock it.

We were too hungry to talk while we were eating. After our appetites had been satisfied, Jim asked how we were going to go about getting our money.

I didn't know how a bank handled such a transaction from one country to another, so I suggested that Jim go to Chihuahua and bring his banker, *Señor* Padilla, to the ranch with all the papers that Snider would need to sign.

Jim left early the next morning for Chihuahua. I had the maid fix breakfast for our guests. After they had eaten, I told them where Jim had gone, and what his mission was.

I assured them that our money was all we wanted. If they cooperated with us, once we received the money, we would fly them to Mexico City and put them on a flight back to Tegucigalpa. If they refused, then whatever Jim wanted to do with them was all right with me.

When Jim and Padilla arrived, they signed the drafts on a Tegucigalpa bank without comment. The banker told us it would take at least eight days to clear and he would notify us. I was proud of Jim, for he didn't lose his temper a single time.

Jim asked me to fly Padilla back to Chihuahua and meet the flight bringing the others back from Honduras. This would give him some time to catch up on the neglected work around the ranch.

In Chihuahua I had about three hours to wait before the flight from Mexico City was due. I spent the time admiring the scenery. They certainly have a lot of beautiful *señoritas*.

When the plane landed from Mexico City, the first person off was José, grinning from ear to ear. When I shook hands with Luis, my conscience started bothering me. Carmen evidently didn't share my feelings. She held on to Luis' arm and acted as sweet and innocent as a virgin.

When we were all in the plane, I asked if there had been any trouble or anyone asking about our two guests. There hadn't been. We had pulled off a perfect job.

When we landed at the ranch, Jim was waiting. He was very relieved and happy that they were back home and safe. He gave Lupe a big hug. We were all surprised at his show of emotion.

That night we sat around the dinner table and talked for hours and finally decided that Tex and I would help Jim and his *vaqueros* start gathering the steers he was going to sell, while Luis and José kept an eye on our guests.

We were up early the next morning and I thought ready to go to work. Jim brought both of the dogs, called José and me, and asked us to go to the barn with him. Then he returned to the house and brought Snider back with him.

Jim took off the handcuffs and pointed to a stall. "My friend, inside you will find that short handled shovel I promised you. You don't have to work, of course, but damn you, you will if you eat.

"José, under no circumstances do you go within fifty feet of him, do you understand? When you get tired, call Luis to relieve you. If Snider tries to run off, just unchain the dogs. They ain't had no fresh meat to eat all week."

Snider asked Jim where he thought he could go without money, and besides it was ten miles to the closest house or public road. Jim didn't answer, just pointed to the stall. Snider went inside and sat down. Jim told José, no food until he worked.

I've never been as tired as I was when we arrived back at the ranch. While we were unsaddling, José told Jim that Snider hadn't even picked up the shovel all day. Jim stomped his foot and said, "God damn him, he will when he gets hungry enough."

I went and got Snider and we started to the house. Jim was just ahead of us. Lupe and Carmen came out to greet us. When Snider saw them he was surprised, and said: "There's the bitches that set us up." Jim turned and gently slapped him in the face. He was a fool, and did exactly what Jim wanted him to do—fight back.

He punched Jim in the ribs and the fight was on. In just a minute, Jim had him going but he wouldn't knock him out, just cuss and tantalize him until he came back for more. Jim was sure enjoying dishing out the punishment.

The fifth time Jim knocked Snider down, he landed on his side. Snider grabbed for a rock, jumped up, and threw it at Jim's head. Jim threw his arms up and the rock hit him hard on the arm. Jim really sailed on him, knocked him down, fell on him and locked both hands around his throat.

Tex and I started trying to get his hands loose. Snider was screaming at the top of his voice. Tex and I worked his arms free but Snider was still screaming. I couldn't imagine what was hurting him. I looked down to see one of Snider's ears in Jim's mouth, and before we could choke him loose, he completely chewed the upper half of Snider's ear off, and spat it on the ground.

Tex and I carried Snider to his room. I didn't have the heart to handcuff him in his condition. Even a healthy and strong man couldn't get past those two dogs.

Jim was still so mad he didn't show up at the dinner table. Lupe fixed a tray and carried it to his room. I was so stiff and sore the next morning, I didn't think I could get up. I finally limped to the breakfast table, everyone sure kidded me about how soft I was.

I managed to saddle up and follow the other guys. It was a long tiresome day. All that time in the hospital had taken its toll. This was just what I needed. After the fourth day, I could tell my muscles were hardening and strength was returning to my body.

Jim gave Snider a day off with food to recuperate, then he went back to the stable. The first day he didn't do any work, so he went to bed without eating. The second day he really put out a good day's work. Block asked if he could help, that he was tired of being confined to the room.

We really did a hard week's work gathering and bunching cattle. We were all scratched and bruised all over. On the ninth night back at the ranch, Lupe gave Jim a message that *Señor* Padilla had called. We were to be at the bank the following morning.

Chapter 16

JIM, TEX, Luis and I were waiting at the bank when *Señor* Padilla arrived. He waited until we were all inside his office, then he told us the check was no good.

Jim threw his hat on the floor and started cussing and stomping. We finally got him calmed down and *Señor* Padilla showed us the check. They didn't even have an account at the bank.

We persuaded *Señor* Padilla to go back to the ranch with us with additional bank drafts. When we shoved them the draft, Snider claimed we had misunderstood, and mentioned another bank with a similar name.

They both signed another draft and assured us this was the correct bank. When *Señor* Padilla started to write in the name of the bank, I shook my head at him and motioned him outside.

When we were alone, I suggested that he go in person to Tegucigalpa. Being a banker, he could transfer the money from there to his bank and save about a week's time. It took a lot of talking and persuading, but finally he agreed to go.

Tex and I flew the banker back to Chihuahua, gave him expense money and returned to the ranch. We continued the cattle roundup.

Four days later we received another call from *Señor* Padilla asking us to be at the bank the following morning. The news the banker gave us wasn't what we had wanted to hear.

Upon his arrival in Tegucigalpa, the bank was already closed for the day. He was at the bank next morning when it opened and the manager received him at once.

After *Señor* Padilla had explained his business, the manager advised him to keep his mission a secret, for the police were looking for our guests and knew something had happened to them.

The banker admitted he had bought the gold, and showed *Señor* Padilla a deposit slip where they had deposited the money from the sale of the gold in his bank.

On the day we had arrived in Tegucigalpa, Snider and Block had withdrawn every cent and closed their account. The banker there gave *Señor* Padilla photostatic copies of all the transactions.

To say Jim threw a cussing fit would be the understatement of the century. He raised hell all the way back to the ranch.

After I had Jim settled down and in the house, I told Luis to go bring Block to the house. They were still in the manure business. When Block entered the room, I motioned for him to sit down.

"All right, Block, the games are over. We know you guys withdrew every cent from the bank in Tegucigalpa. Now, where's the money?"

"I honestly don't know," he said. I grabbed Jim by the collar and pulled him back down in his chair.

Block continued. "What I am fixing to tell you is the honest truth. I knew that those checks were no good, but we were stalling for time so an alarm could be sent out for us. We had a deal with the police and were actually paying for protection. You guys will never know how lucky you were to get us out of Honduras.

"This is also the truth. I didn't want to swindle you in the first place, but Snider made me. A few years ago I did an awful thing. Snider knows about it, and could have me sent to the electric chair. I am his whipping dog as long as he is alive. I haven't got the guts to kill again and he knows it.

"Snider will offer to pay you if you will go back to Honduras, but don't go. Once there, you can't get out. If you won't go to Honduras with him, then he knows you will turn us over to the Mexican authorities for prosecution.

"This is all right with Snider, for he knows that within sixty days he can get extradited back to the States and once

182

there, get out on bond until trial. Then he and I, if I am lucky enough to still be with him, will jump bail, go back to Honduras for our money and then on to Brazil."

"But how?" I asked, "can he hope to do this when he is broke?"

Block grinned. "Snider has connections. Very key. His cousin is . . ." Block mentioned a name and I almost fainted. He was a very big politician in Washington. Now I understood.

Block continued, "When we withdrew the money from the bank, Snider bought a shovel and had me drive him about ten miles out of town. He got out of the car and told me to wait for him until he came back. I could show you where he parked if I was there, but I can't tell you, that high tropical country all looks alike.

"It's true, no one but Snider knows exactly where that money is. He had the money in a large tin suitcase. I timed him and he was gone only ten minutes, so it can't be more than three or four hundred feet from the road."

I told Luis to take Block back to the barn and bring Snider. When they had gone, I told Jim and Tex not to say anything in Snider's presence that would betray what Block had told us. I had another idea.

Snider sat right down and made himself at home. I told him we knew all about how he had closed his account in Tegucigalpa. He smiled, very sure of himself. "Okay, you guys, let's go back to Honduras and I'll dig up the money and pay you."

"We won't buy that. Padilla told us your friends were looking for all of us."

"Look Mark, you have been in the driver's seat for two weeks. Now, we do it my way or call the police and you can go straight to hell."

Jim and Tex pulled me loose from him. Then Luis and José carried him to his room.

I didn't get to finish my temper fit before Jim realized what Snider had said, then he threw one. I had to discontinue mine to get him settled down. After everyone was back to normal Tex asked, "What do we do now?"

"Look, Block told us the truth, Snider is ready to go to jail."

I sent José back to the barn to watch Block. Sometimes José drinks and talks too much. Once he was out of earshot I continued.

"We can recover that money by killing Snider, but is the money worth committing murder for?" This statement even had a sobering effect on Jim. "How would killing Snider get us our money?" he asked.

"As I said before, Block told us the truth. He is living in fear of Snider revealing his past. If we kill Snider with Block watching, he will know we wouldn't hesitate to kill him. He knows we will do what we say, and that we are honest. If Snider is dead, Block has nothing to fear.

"We will ask him if he would rather go to prison or do business with us. If he will show us where the money is, he will be free and alive, and can go on enjoying life."

"It might work," Jim replied. "I'll buy it except for one little thing. You said Block told the truth. Well, he claims he don't know where the money is hid."

"Not hid, Jim, buried. Remember Snider said 'dig it up'. Also, Block said the money was in a large tin suitcase. Even if Snider refused and we have to eliminate him, if Block will take me to the spot where they parked when Snider wasn't gone longer than ten minutes, I can take a metal detector and find that big tin suitcase in thirty minutes."

We spent another hour discussing every detail and angle. We finally agreed that this was the only thing to do. Snider would be given one last chance to tell us the exact location of the money.

If he agreed to cooperate with us, we would take the chance to go back to Honduras rather than kill him. If he told the truth, we would bring all the money back and take only our share. They could keep the rest and we would return them to Mexico City and see them aboard a plane to Honduras or Brazil.

Then came the big question. Who was going to do the job if Snider refused. Finally Jim spoke up and said, "Boys, I feel responsible for taking that damn phoney check in the first place. Also, Snider is more afraid of me. It's my place to do whatever has to be done. You guys all stay around the house in the morning until I get back."

One window in my room was facing toward the corral. Usually I can sleep through a Texas-sized tornado and never awaken, but just at daybreak, I awoke and looked out the window. I saw Jim, Snider and Block mounted on three horses and heading West. I went back to bed, but for once, I couldn't go back to sleep.

We all put in an anxious morning. When Jim hadn't returned by 11:00, we were really beginning to worry. It was almost noon when Jim slowly rode up to the corral, untied a shovel from behind his saddle and threw it as far as he could.

When he walked into the house, he was as pale as a ghost. He shouted for Lupe to bring him coffee. She did, then quickly left the room. Jim tried to hold the cup in both hands, but he was shaking so he spilled most of the coffee.

"I really played Hell." Jim said, as he began to tell us what happened. "I carried them out to this place I remembered, where there is a big tree with low limbs. Once out there, I put a rope around their necks and tied the ends to a large overhead limb. I only meant to scare Snider. If he wasn't such a tauntin', goadin' varmint, things woulda turned out different.

"I left about eight to ten feet of slack in the rope I had tied Block with. Anyway, after I had the noose around Snider's neck, I asked him where the money was buried, and offered him the deal we had agreed on.

"He laughed and told me I was a sorry actor, that this sort of thing went out with the third-rate movies thirty years ago. I assured him that if he didn't cooperate, that he was fixing to die.

"Then he started cussing me and said, 'You big mouthed son-of-a-bitch, you ain't got the guts.' Dammit all, I lost my temper! I kicked his horse in the flank and screamed at the top of my voice. His horse jumped out from under him, and I heard his neck pop as it broke. That was all for him.

"Then I saw Block's horse running away, and him being dragged. One foot was caught in the stirrup. I jumped on my horse and finally caught his horse. I had completely forgotten the rope around Block's neck.

"When that damn fool horse got scared and took off, he had about ten feet to run before he hit the end of the rope. It was awful. I caught the horse and started to take Block's foot out of the stirrup when I looked down and saw he didn't have any head. It was jerked off under the tree."

"Look, Jim," I tried to comfort him, "it's all my fault. It was my idea."

"No, it wasn't, Mark. Snider was a bastard and he asked for it. But my carelessness killed Block. He really wasn't such a bad guy after all."

Unnoticed, Lupe had entered the room. She dropped down on her knees and pulled Jim's head against her breasts. She kissed him and started rubbing his forehead and comforting him in Spanish. "Everything is all right, my husband, for all my life you have me and my love."

Never had I heard Lupe call Jim "husband." Although Lupe understood very little English, she knew Jim was in a desperate state and needed her now, more than he had ever needed anyone.

I told Lupe, in Spanish, to take Jim to their bedroom with a fifth of whiskey and stay with him until tomorrow. She took Jim's arm, and he followed her without a word. That was one of the longest and most lonesome days we had ever spent.

The next morning at 6:00, Jim started cussing and banging the door. "Get out of that bed, you lazy bastard. If you think you are going to lay up and sleep all day and eat my grub without working for it, you're crazy as hell. We got to finish gathering them steers."

For once the yell sounded wonderful. I knew Jim would in time be himself again.

We were all seated around the breakfast table when I told Jim I had a good excuse to get out of work. He reached for my plate. "It had better be good or you don't get your food back."

"Do we have any further use for the plane I rented? If not, I'll take it back to El Paso, and stop the rental."

"You'll come back, won't you?" he asked.

"Sure," I told him. "If you will meet me at the airport, I'll be back on the evening flight."

He started growling that I wasn't satisfied to get out of a day's work, now it would cost him two hours to come and get me. As I started to leave the room, I told him he should appreciate the excuse to get off work early. He was so damn old he could hardly mount a horse.

He turned red in the face and slammed his fist down on the table so hard it turned his cup over and spilled hot coffee in his lap. He jumped up and squalled like a scalded cat and started cussing worse than a marooned sailor.

I didn't stop to hear him out. I passed Lupe in the hall, she winked, smiled and said it was good to have her "Yemmy" back.

Chapter 17

I ARRIVED in El Paso, paid the plane rental and went to the snack bar. The first person I saw was Bill Williams. It had been two years since I last saw him. Bill was a cattle buyer and usually bought Jim's steers each year.

We talked for a few minutes and I told him I had just come from the ranch. He asked me if Jim had completed vaccinating her herd. I told him I didn't know but we had about three thousand steers bunched and would have the rest rounded up and ready to ship at the end of the week.

"Hasn't Jim heard?"

"Heard what?" I asked BIll.

"Good God," he said, "Mark, the whole states of Chihuahua and Sonora have been quarantined because of an outbreak of black leg."

"When did this quarantine go into effect?"

He reached into his coat and pulled out a paper and handed it to me. When I saw the date, I knew why we hadn't heard. We were in Tegucigalpa on that day.

I told Bill I was taking the evening flight back to Chihuahua and would give Jim the news.

"Hell, no," he told me. "Get in my plane while I call my wife. I'll take you back to the ranch. Jim has to know about this as soon as possible."

I walked out to his plane and realized how lucky old Bill was when he finally persuaded Eve to marry him. He was the ugliest damn man from Malaga, New Mexico to Bootstrap, Nevada.

In two hours we were at the ranch. It took us another hour

to drive out to where they were holding the herd. When we broke the news to Jim, he didn't bat an eye. His only comment was, "When bad luck hits a guy, it jumps on him with both feet."

Jim went back to the ranch with Bill and me. Bill headed for El Paso as Jim and I took off for Chihuahua for vaccine. After Jim had bought the vaccine and needles for the big job ahead, he called some rancher friends and told them what a spot he was in and he needed all the cowboys they could spare.

We went to the market and ordered enough food, it seemed to me, to feed an army. He gave them instructions where to deliver everything.

"Look, until we get this job done, we will all be living around the chuck wagon. We can't afford to lose two or three hours a day coming and going to the ranch. Before this job is over, I'll know how *macho* you are, and I don't mean you will be tested by loving Carmen.

"You ain't a very good cowboy, but cheer up. Hell, I'll even pay you the same as I do a top hand." That was very generous of Jim. I knew the cowboys made one hundred and fifty pesos a day, about seven dollars in American money.

We hadn't even gotten into the house before Jim started shouting. José and Luis came running. He told Lupe to get bed rolls ready for the four of us, then to help José and Luis load all of the cooking equipment into the two chuck wagons and not to forget the traps.

Jim asked Luis and José if they could drive the chuck wagons out to where the steers were corralled and hurry so the men wouldn't have to wait for their supper. He and I would go and get the job started.

Carmen came running after us and asked if she could go with Luis. Jim told her a roundup was no place for a woman. "Why not?" she asked. "Well, it's this way," Jim replied, "if a woman's housecoat was to fly open, it might cause a stampede." Carmen got the message, blushed, and ran for the house.

Jim laughed and said, "Let that be a lesson to you. There's more damn ways to kill a cat then smother it to death with

189

kisses.''

We vaccinated steers until it was too dark to see them, then headed for the chuck wagon. I didn't know beans, beef, potatoes, and tortillas could taste so good. As soon as I ate the last of my food, I got my bed roll and threw it under the chuck wagon.

The next thing I knew, the camp cook was beating on an iron wagon tire to come and get it or he would throw it out.

When we got back to camp that night, I was surprised to see about twenty extra cowboys. Jim came by and said, ''Now you know why we needed all the chuck.''

We would leave the chuck wagon before daylight, and it was always dark when we got back in the evenings. I did nine days of the hardest physical work I have ever done. It was just what I needed—hard work, fresh air, and no time to think.

On the eleventh day, about 3:00, we finished. When you gather over ten thousand head of cattle scattered over one hundred thousand acres, it's a man sized job, even if you have thirty or thirty-five hands.

We took the jeep and headed for the ranch. After sitting on a horse for eleven days, that jeep rode like a Rolls Royce.

I must have spent an hour in the shower. I had just finished dressing when Jim called to say dinner was ready. We three ate alone, and had just finished our coffee when Carmen came in and asked where Luis was. We told her not to get impatient. Luis would be here tomorrow.

Carmen made sure Lupe wasn't looking, then twisted out of the room. Jim's eyes popped out.

''Did you see that? Damned if she didn't shake it right in my face, just as much as to say, 'I got something you want, but I sure as hell ain't going to give it to you.' ''

I couldn't stop laughing. Jim turned on me with fire in his eyes. ''Laugh, you cocky little bastard, but you had better hope I don't make her; if I did and she found out, for once, what a real man was, I know of two little short dicked guys she'd start throwing rocks at.''

Jim jumped up from the table and high-tailed it out of the room. Tex and I laughed until tears ran down our cheeks. Jim finally returned and very casually sat down. We had another coffee and called it a day.

Luis and José arrived about 9:30 the following morning. After they had cleaned up and eaten, we all sat down for a conference to decide what we were going to do next. First, we took inventory of all the cash we had. I was surprised we had less than two thousand dollars between us.

"What about you, José, how much can you raise?" I asked.

Jim answered for him. "Mark, José doesn't have a cent. Ever since we came to visit you in the hospital, I have supported José and his family."

To say I was surprised was putting it mildly. I had an idea what had happened; Tequila and women. I grabbed José be his shirt collar and raised him to his feet.

"Talk, José, and you had better tell me the truth."

He started crying. "Go ahead, my brother, and beat me to death—is what I deserve after you and my other friends here go to so much danger and trouble to make me the rich man, and I am such a fool that I lost it all."

"For one year me and Juan work very hard on the ranch and make a lot of money. When we sell our cattle we go to Torreon for the celebration. There we meet *dos muchachas, muy bonita*. The girl ask us why we do not take them to Madero, the closest town to our ranch, and buy them a house so we can always be together. Me and Juan, we like the idea.

"My novia, was so young and *bonita*, and what a woman, *mama mia*. She had the prettiest tits, just like . . ." Jim elbowed José in the stomach so hard he knocked him over backwards.

José had almost unthinkingly let the cat out of the bag by saying his sweetheart's breasts were as pretty as Carmen's. José realized his near mistake and got up. All eyes were focused on Luis. Evidently Luis missed the point, for he didn't show any surprise or suspicion.

José continued, "We buy them a *casa* and pretty soon they want the *casa* next door. We think this is good, so we buy it. Now, we have a house each.

"Everyone knows we are big rich ranchers. Juan and me spend most of the time in Madero with our new women. They love us so much they don't want us to leave them solo. Soon it is necessary to mortgage the ranch until we sell our cattle.

"Then Raul, the el jefe (ranch boss) comes and says to us that someone is stealing our cows. We go back to the ranch. The police cannot find our cattle. Soon the bank wants their money. We have but a few cows and cannot pay, so they take our ranch.

"Then we go to sell our houses in Madero. We do not know this, but they are not our *casas*. Me and Juan cannot read the writing. The houses were in the names of our women.

"All this time me and Juan were mistaken. Once our *dinero* was gone, our lovers did not love us anymore. My brother, I think they were *putas*." I had to laugh and told José that I was in complete agreement with his opinion.

José said, "It's not as bad as it seems. We have almost three hundred goats that the bank cannot get. Also the truck you gave us. This we sell and hire the two big trucks to move all our families, mine, Juan's and Raul's and all the goats back to our old home in Loreto.

I was so surprised by this bit of information that for once I was completely speechless. Jim came to José's rescue.

"I know we should have told you this before, but José begged us not to, and we all thought José did right by keeping Raul and his family where he could watch him until you got out of the hospital and able to go for the other treasure."

I had to agree. José had used his head for something besides a place to hang his sombrero.

"All right, you guys, are there any more surprises you have for me that I don't know about?"

"No," they all answered at once.

It took about two hours for us to agree upon a plan to try for the other treasure. José would have to go to Loreto for Raul. I asked José if the people in Loreto would be suspicious when they returned after a two year absence.

"No," he replied, "we told everyone we got the good jobs and saved our money and that Raul was our cousin. When we all saved enough to buy so many goats, we were homesick and lonesome for our old home and friends and we decided to come home."

José went on to say he had told everyone he was returning to his job in San Luis Potosi so he could send money to support their families and let their goat herd increase. This way no one was curious about his absences.

We decided that we would take Jim's pickup and his car since we might need two vehicles to move the treasure. Luis and Tex would drive the car and pickup to Torreon, and meet us there. If Jim, José and I left at once for Durango in Jim's plane, we would get there in time for José to catch the evening bus to Loreto.

It was still about two hours before dark and only one hour's flying time to Torreon. Jim and I decided to fly on to Torreon rather than spend the night in Durango and take a chance on being recognized by someone we had met on our previous trips to this fair city.

Chapter 18

WE HAD a nice flight to Torreon and a quite peaceful evening. Jim had only two cussing fits from the time we left the ranch until bedtime. To the best of my recollection, only two fits in nine hours was a record. I was very proud of him.

José and Raul arrived about 5:00 the next afternoon. After getting them settled in their room, Jim asked me if I didn't think we should celebrate and have a beer since they had arrived on time and both of them were sober. We didn't have to break their arms to get them to go with us to a *cantina* which was just across the street.

We had just finished our first beer when Tex and Luis arrived. We were all very happy to be together again and all agreed a little celebrating was in order.

We had all been under one hell of a strain for almost a month, and now we were starting a new adventure, and it was a good time to bury the past.

Three beers is my limit. When I could see the others, especially José and Raul, were getting pretty well gassed up, I suggested we all go have a steak. To my surprise, they all subscribed to the idea. José, Raul and Luis had three tequilas while eating, and were well on their way to cloud nine.

Back at the motel, I suggested that José and I stay together in one room, Jim and Luis in one, and Tex and Raul in another. We had had some experience in the past with guys sneaking out and the cost involved in getting them out of the pokey. We didn't have any extra money to spare on this trip.

Once José and I were alone in the room, he started trying to tell me that he had seen Maria while in Loreto—that she was the most beautiful woman in all of Mexico and that she had sent me a message. José started talking about the treasure and got all mixed up and tried to talk about Maria and the treasure at the same time.

I lay down, since José couldn't discuss either subject clearly enough for me to understand him. I gave the beer and tequila the credit it was due and went to sleep.

There isn't any need for an alarm clock or a motel time call if Jim is present. As usual, he started cussing and banging on my door at 6:00.

After breakfast and four cups of coffee, José and Raul had perked up and decided life was worth living after all. At 8:00 we were ready to roll. Our next stop was Aldama, the village where Raul had been raised as a kid, and seven kilometers from this village was where Raul had watched General Zaragoza bury the big treasure.

I drove Jim's car. José and Raul accompanied me so Raul could give directions. The other three guys followed in the pickup.

Once under way, José told me, "You are very lucky and I fix everything real good for you."

"How's that?" I asked.

"As I say, you are the luckiest man in the world."

José was so proud of himself. He lost all control of his emotions and was trying to give me the glad tidings in both English and Spanish. I finally got him calmed down and told him to either speak in English or Spanish.

"*Bueno, mi hermano.*" He then switched back to English. "What you do not know is this. I had only been in my house not more than one hour when who comes to my house? None other than the beautiful *Señorita* Maria. She does not even ask me how I am. The first thing she says is 'Where is my Mark?'

"I tell her of the accident and how you are now a well man again. Then I say to Maria how much you love her and miss her, and even at this very time you are in Torreon and very soon you will send for her. That you cannot live without her love, and this you tell me to say to her while I am in Loreto. When I say this, she starts crying and thanks the Blessed Virgin for answering her prayers."

I was so shocked over José's speech that I almost ran off the road. He had fixed everything real good, for Maria was the one person in the world I didn't want to hurt, or even remember, for she had haunted my sleep more nights than I would even admit to myself.

I reached over and grabbed him by the throat. "José, you lying bastard, I am going to choke you to death for lying to such a good girl as Maria." He grabbed my arm with both hands and broke loose from me. "I don't do nothing wrong, my brother, and as you always say to us, don't interrupt me please, until I say all I know."

I told him to go ahead for anything else he had to say couldn't possibly make the situation any worse.

"What you do not know is that for more than one year now, Maria has gone to the Convent that makes the sisters. This is the only way she can save herself for you. Her Papa would force her to marry that son-of-a-bitch, Flores.

"Now the time has come that she must take her vows to stay in the Church. This she cannot do, for it is you she has loved, waited for and prayed for all this time. Her heart is not pure enough for the Sister."

"Look, José, I am married. I can't marry Maria. If I took her from her home, all I would do is hurt her and bring shame and dishonor upon her and her family."

"Look, *Señor* (it had been years since José had called me *Señor*—always 'my brother') always I think you are the smartest man in the world, but at this hour, I don't know. You speak the Spanish almost as good as I do, and all this time, I think you understand me and my people. But, no, you are the big damn fool. How you say in the English, you do not know your ass from the hole, and know nothing about our women.

"For your information, *Señor*, all Mexican girls, rich or poor, save and keep themselves pure for the man in their life. When this man comes into their life, of course, they want to get married in the Church. If it is not possible to make the marriage, he is still her man. She goes with him and does not have the regrets. He is always her man, wrong or right.

"This I know, so this is why I say what I say to Maria. It is you or that dirty bastard Flores. There is no more excuses or waiting time for Maria. With you, she asks nothing and is always happy. With Flores, she is in hell living all her life.

"If you do not take Maria, all my life I am so shamed and embarrassed. Always people will point to us and say 'there goes the Americano who is the brother to José Torres and who was loved by the most beautiful and desirable girl in all of Mexico and the *gringo no tiene heuvos.*' They will say my brother has not the balls!"

"Are you finished, José?"

"*Si, Señor,*" he replied.

"All right, then, dammit, shut up and keep quiet for awhile and let me think."

He gave me a big smile and the old confidence and respect was once more in his eyes. He slapped me on the back, then said, "To think is good; now that I fix everything, she is going to be all right, my brother."

In my life, I thought I had had problems and decisions to make, but this was the toughest nut I had ever had to crack.

I would not let myself think of how beautiful and desirable Maria was and how I had awakened so many nights remembering those soft lips which were sweet and pure as newborn life. Just remembering those kisses and the soft warmth of her young full body made my blood race.

I was so deep in thought that I didn't hear Raul telling me I was supposed to turn off the main highway. José shook me back to reality. I turned around and went back to where an old dirt road turned west between a one pump service station and a two table cafe.

I pulled off the highway and stopped. Jim and the other guys arrived in a couple of minutes and parked behind us. I looked at my watch. It was 11:30. I couldn't believe we had been on the road three and one half hours. I had been so deep in thought I had lost track of time.

We decided to gas up and eat. Raul said it was about fifteen miles to Aldama. From the looks of the road, and past experiences, I knew it could take anywhere from thirty minutes to twelve hours to travel the fifteen miles.

After lunch we started on the last leg of our journey. I could hardly believe our good luck; for once, the road was fairly good, and we were only one hour reaching Aldama.

Chapter 19

As IN so many of the smaller villages in Mexico, there was no employment in Aldama, and the people tried to earn a living by dry land farming. It must be an awful feeling for an able-bodied man to see his family in such a destitute condition when nowhere can he find a means to support them.

From the appearance of the village, this was certainly the situation in Aldama. I estimated the population to be four to five thousand.

Raul pointed out the way to the town's only hotel, which, like all the other buildings, was made of adobe. Inside the hotel, the patio was beautiful with flowers and orange trees and a large dug well in the center with rooms on both sides.

Raul and José left at once to visit his family. We had just checked in and washed up when El Presidente of Aldama and the Chief of Police, along with two other policemen came to our room. After the introductions, we invited them in and offered to send out for beer. They refused, putting us on our guard, for the Mexican people love a sociable drink.

The Chief of Police asked what our business was in Aldama. Jim looked at me and nodded his head. From his cue, I knew who had automatically been appointed spokesman for our group.

I used the same speech I had used in Loreto; that we were friends of Raul's and he had told us there was very old and rich Spanish mines in the Aldama region. That if they proved to be worthwhile after our inspection, we were interested in starting a mining operation which would benefit the town, as well as ourselves.

When I finished, the Chief of Police laughed and said, "*Señor,* we are not as big fools here as they were in Loreto."

I didn't bat an eye, but I could have fallen over. I have never been so surprised as when he mentioned the village of Loreto. I didn't look at Jim, Tex or Luis, for this was what he expected me to do.

Before I could reply, the Chief of Police told one of the policemen to go and get their friend. Evidently the guy was waiting outside the hotel entrance, for the policeman was back in less than a minute.

I took a second look at the man who followed the policeman into the room. I didn't recognize him. I asked Jim, Tex, and Luis if they had ever seen the man before, but neither of them knew him. I turned and told the Chief of Police he was mistaken, that none of us knew the man.

He smiled a cunning smile, then admitted that we did not know the man, but, the man knew us. He said that we all knew his cousin, *Señor* Tino Flores, who was Chief of Police in Loreto.

I realized we were no more than three hundred airline miles from Loreto, but finding a cousin of Flores here in Aldama was a million-to-one shot, because both villages were so isolated.

I admitted we had been to Loreto and had had some trouble with Flores, but if we had been able to return to Loreto without trouble, probably the mines there would be working and we would not be here in Aldama at this time. The Chief of Police asked, "How much money did you get for the treasure you stole from Loreto?"

"Look, my friend," Jim told him, "You or anyone who thinks we got a treasure in Loreto are very much mistaken. Our trouble with Flores was over the most beautiful *Señorita* in all of Mexico. He was not man enough to win her love and he was jealous over her attention to Mark. Flores is no better a fighter than he is a lover. Mark beat the hell out of him and that's it. He is lying."

For the first time, Flores' cousin spoke up. "My cousin does not lie, and he is a very brave and tough hombre. All the *señoritas* dream of him."

I laughed in his face and told him that he didn't know Flores, or, if he did know him, he was stupid to believe him, that I should know better than anyone that he was a gutless coward, a dirty, lying son-of-a-bitch, and that went for all of his relatives as far as I was concerned.

I should have known better than to insult this guy's relatives for the Mexican people love their relatives dearly and are a very proud race. In just a moment, I realized that I had made a mistake. He jerked a large switchblade out of his back pocket. Then he made a lunge at me, striking down with the knife. It happened so fast I didn't have time to think. All those hours of practice in Judo and two years of combat came back. Both my hands flew out as if they had been expecting and rehearsing for just such a move. My right hand, palm up, slipped under the knife and grasped the inside of his wrist and my left hand fastened firmly on the back of his elbow.

I threw my weight forward and fell on his arm. We both fell to the floor. He screamed like a wounded animal as his arm broke completely at the elbow joint.

I looked down to where the knife was, then realized why he screamed. The bone had come all the way through the skin at the back of his elbow, and at least two inches of bone were exposed. Everything had happened so fast, everyone was caught off base.

Jim shouted at me to lay flat on the floor. He had grabbed an automatic shotgun, and in Spanish, shouted he would blow to hell the first man that moved. I started to get up. If someone had run a red-hot iron rod through my chest, it couldn't have hurt more. Only then, did I realize that I had been cut with the knife.

I sat back on the bed and tore my short open. Starting two inches above my right breast, the guy had cut me all the way to the bottom of my rib cage—about a ten inch gash and the cut was very deep. You could see my ribs. I was lucky the knife hadn't punctured or entered the hollow of my chest.

When Jim saw what had happened, he started to knock the guy's brains out with the butt of the shotgun. The poor guy was passed out cold. I stopped Jim and told Luis to go and get the village doctor, and to send for Raul and José.

I told Jim to stand in the door and not let anyone in or out of the room, for if the news got out before the doctor came, we would all be lucky to get out of the village alive, especially if the guy had a bunch of relatives and they saw the condition he was in.

Luis took off for the doctor. I told the Chief of Police that once the doctor had me sewed up, we were leaving, El Presidente and the two policemen were to stay inside the hotel until we were out of town.

I told the Chief of Police that I wanted him to ride with us outside of the village. He could walk back. If he cooperated he had nothing to fear, but if he didn't . . . I didn't finish, but when Jim stuck the shotgun barrel under his nose, he got the message. Jim also told him if he ever reported this incident, that we would go to the Tourist Department in Mexico City and have him and the policemen fired from their jobs for not protecting tourists while on vacation in Mexico.

This we could probably have done, for Mexico welcomes the gringo dollar and the Tourist Department is very strict about their protection and welfare.

Luis and the doctor arrived just as Flores' cousin started to move and groan. I asked the doctor to give him a shot so he wouldn't be so much pain when he started coming to.

The doctor didn't ask a single question, of course, he could see what happened. He wanted me to go to his office. I refused and lay back on the bed and told him to start sewing me up.

José and Raul came in while the doctor was getting his instruments out of his bag. Tex wouldn't tell them what had happened or let them in the room. He just told them to pack all the luggage in the car and pickup and be ready to go in just a few minutes.

The doctor gave me a shot, sterilized the cut and started sewing. Nineteen stitches later, he was finished. I paid his fee of one hundred pesos, and for once I didn't feel like I had been overcharged.

My shirt was split wide open and soaked with blood, so I borrowed a fresh one from Jim.

Jim slipped the shotgun into a sleeping bag, put his arm

around the Chief of Police and put his hand into the pocket of the Chief's coat. In the hand was a cocked pistol. He then told the Chief to put his arm around his waist so they would look like old friends when they walked out onto the street.

Jim cautioned the other Mexicans to stay inside the room until the Chief came back if they ever wanted to see him alive again.

Luis, José and Raul took off in the pickup. Jim and the Chief of Police got in the back seat of the car. Tex drove. As we were getting into the car, several men started toward us asking what was wrong. Tex almost ran over two of them before they would get out of the way.

About two miles from the village, we stopped and let the Chief out. He hadn't said a word, and he was white as a ghost. He was afraid we were going to kill him. Before we reached the highway, I was almost out. The shot was really taking effect. I don't remember very much about the trip back to Torreon.

Chapter 20

ONCE WE were checked into the motel in Torreon, Jim called a doctor. It seemed like hours before he finally came. He wanted me to go to the hospital. When I refused, he gave me a shot and medicine for the pain.

The next afternoon I was feeling better and asked Tex to have the others come to my room. It was time for another conference. When everyone was seated, I asked them what we were going to do.

"I'll be damned if I know." Jim replied. "But one thing sure as hell, we can't go back to Aldama." We were all in agreement on this because the police and the people of the village would scalp us. If they didn't, they would cause a lot of trouble and would know why we came back. Everyone there knew the history of the treasure and we would be watched day and night.

Tex spoke up, "Mark, we know you are in bad shape to make any decisions, but we will look to you for planning any operations that we might undertake."

José put his arm around me and said, "It is true, my brother has more brains in his butt than we have in our heads." Jim jumped up and told José to speak for himself. "I just did," replied José.

I told both of them to shut up, that I didn't feel like hearing one of their childish arguments. Once again we pooled our money. We had less than fifteen hundred dollars.

"Well, we are about broke, so if anyone has any suggestions as to how we can raise some extra cash, let's hear it."

Jim spoke up and said, "As all of you know, I can't sell any cattle for at least a year due to the quarantine. I don't think the bank would even consider loaning me another cent. Tex and Luis have always worked for wages and been happy-go-lucky. They haven't saved a dime."

I was in the same boat as Jim. I had nothing else to sell or mortgage. I asked José if the silver bars were still buried in his patio in Loreto. As far as he knew, they were.

"You guys said you did a lot of talking last night. I did a lot of thinking. That treasure at Aldama can still be had. Don't ask me how at this time, but with time to think and plan, we can still get it and really be back in the money again. However, for the present, we have to have expense money to move around on.

"Tex, do you remember how much silver there was when we found the extra gold bars?"

"Not exactly," he replied, "but I do remember that the stack of silver bars was larger than the stack of gold bars."

"All right, here's the only way I know to raise enough operating capital for us to try for the big treasure. As Tex said, the stack of silver bars was larger than the stack of gold bars, so there must be about four hundred pounds there. Four hundred pounds of silver would sell for at least seventy-thousand dollars, and as far as I am concerned, that's all the money we will need for expenses to get the big treasure in Aldama."

When José realized we were actually going back to Loreto for the silver, he started shaking from head to toe. "No, my brother, is not possible. We cannot do it, for we will be caught and killed."

For once, Jim used a little psychology. He gave José a big drink of tequila and told him we were successful before with no trouble, and that all our futures were depending on that silver. "Let's listen to what that stupid Mark has to say. He probably doesn't know a damn thing or any way to go about this job."

José rose to my defense, stuck his finger under Jim's nose and told him, "*Señor* Jim, we will listen to my brother's plan. If he says we can get the silver, then, by God, we do it or we all die together."

Jim had set him up perfectly.

"Thanks, José. I am sure we can work this deal, but only with you agreeing to act as my number one boss can we succeed." I winked at Jim, Tex and Luis. They realized how important it was to have José's complete cooperation.

José's answer almost flooded all of us. Jim turned blue in the face from anger, but for once he didn't utter a sound when José turned and addressed me.

"I accept, Patron." Patron is a word the poor people use for a very respected boss. Of course, since José was number one to the Patron, he had to use his newly acquired position to let the peons know who their *jefe* was.

José stuck out his chest and in all sincerity said, "Shut up and listen well, you fools, to what me and the Patron have to say."

I thought Jim would have a stroke. The blood vessels in his throat were swelled up as large as my thumb. I have never seen a man's lips move as fast as his were. If José had been half smart he would have realized he was receiving the darndest cussing any man ever got. I looked at Tex and Luis. They were both bent double trying to keep from laughing at Jim.

I suggested a drink all around to give Jim a little time to cool off. In his present condition he wouldn't have heard a word I said.

After everyone was back to normal, I started outlining my plans.

"Time is the most important factor. We have to make our move before the people in Loreto know we are back in Mexico. We also know Flores' cousin and the Police in Aldama will notify Flores as quickly as they possibly can.

"If Jim, José, Raul and I leave at once in the plane, we can get to Durango in time for José and Raul to take the evening bus to Loreto. Tex and Luis can drive the car and pickup and meet Jim and me at the motel in Durango.

"Now, José, listen carefully and be absolutely sure you understand everything I say. This is an order. Do only what you are told to do—nothing else—savvy?

"When you are in Loreto, be sure to see Flores at once.

Make it appear your meeting is an accident. If he has heard of our trouble in Aldama, he will start asking you questions. Tell him nothing.

"If they haven't heard of our trouble in Aldama, be very nice to Flores and tell him that you all got drunk and spent too much time with the girls and lost your jobs, but in a few days, you and Raul are going to Mexico City to look for new jobs."

I asked Jim what time the moon went down.

"About 2:00 in the morning," he answered.

"All right, José, tomorrow night before the moon sets, you dig up the silver bars and be careful as you and I were when we dug up the gold. Don't scatter any fresh dirt and be sure to replace the rock."

As to how we were going to get the silver out of Loreto, we didn't have the time to go to Acquila and rent horses to pack it out.

My idea was to take a hell of a big gamble; wait until about 1:00 in the morning, and drive the pickup as close to Loreto as we dared without being seen or heard, hide the truck off the road and walk to José's house.

We could use the back way as we did the last time, carry the silver back to the truck and take off like a scalded cat. They agreed that this was our only chance and we probably would not be seen because of the late hour.

Jim said, "Damn it, Mark, you can't go in the shape you're in. You are too weak and have lost too much blood. You re-open your wound and we will have to carry you back."

I agreed and told him someone would have to stand guard at the pickup until they got back. This, they agreed, I could do, if I kept improving. I didn't argue the point and I certainly didn't relish the idea of making the trip in my present physical condition.

However, I knew I would have to go all the way regardless. There were six of us, and Juan, José's brother, made seven. I remembered how on our previous trip, Luis became so tired that he couldn't carry a hundred pounds for six blocks. We would have to leave the truck at least a mile outside of Loreto. If Luis, José and Juan each carried sixty pounds, Raul, who was large and strong, could carry eighty pounds; Tex, who was the jackass, was good for one hundred twenty-five pounds; and Jim carried a hundred pounds. It would total up to four hundred and eighty-five pounds.

What bothered me more was that I was the only one whom Jim would listen to. Tex was very capable of handling the job. Also, Jim was, if his temper didn't get the best of him. If they had any trouble, Jim would turn an automatic shotgun loose and to hell with the consequences. I had to go if only to keep the situation under control.

"José, this is very important. Raul and Juan will have to help us carry the silver to the truck. Tomorrow night, when the moon goes down, you guys have the silver dug up and be careful like I have already told you.

"Then, José, you come to the arroyo back of your house. You know where we told you we hid the horses when we came back for the gold. Meet us there, then we will climb over the back wall into the patio of your house. Even if the police should be watching the front of your house, they will never know we have climbed over the back wall into the patio, and escaped with the silver.

"If there is any trouble or suspicion, don't come to meet us. We will wait until we know you aren't coming, then go to the truck and back to Durango. The next night we will come back and try again."

"Now, José, repeat to me what you are going to do." He had it down pat. Tex drove us to the airport while Luis packed and checked out the motel. On the flight to Durango, I had José go over our complete plan twice more. He was word perfect. Then José asked what he was going to say to the *Señorita* Maria.

I told Jim about Maria, and José's conversation with her on his last trip to Loreto. I tried to repeat what José had told me and when I had finished, Jim said, "Damn it, Mark, I hate to say this as much as I think of you, Nita and the boys, but we both know it is finished between you two. José is right.

"The only thing you can do is get Maria away from that dirty bastard Flores. What you two do, I can't advise you— help her to get a job, send her away, or whatever you think best, but for Christ's sake, man, don't let her be ruined by a sorry son-of-a-bitch like Flores.''

"José, be very careful. Go to see Maria and tell her to be ready. That within ten days, sooner if possible, that someone will find a way to get her out of Loreto. Tell her that whoever comes to get her, if you or I can't, will give her an American penny for identification. That way she will know he is to be trusted and he will bring her safely to me.''

José shook my hand and congratulated me on having made the right decision. He assured me he had known all the time that I was too *macho* to let the beautiful *señorita* be taken by Flores.

When we landed in Durango, while Jim closed his flight plan and had the plane serviced, José, Raul, and I took a cab to the motel. The cab then took José and Raul to the bus station to catch the bus to Loreto.

I lay down and didn't even wake up when Jim came in. About three hours later, Tex and Luis arrived. I got up and went with them to have dinner.

I hadn't taken any pain medicine all day. I had a big shot of tequila which helped me to sleep all night. The next morning I woke up about 9:00. Believe it or not, Jim had let me sleep past 6:00.

I felt like a new man. After shaving, I invited Jim, Tex, and Luis for breakfast. "Breakfast, hell,'' Jim snorted, "I'll have you know, you lazy little bastard, we ate when men are supposed to eat breakfast. Damn, it's the middle of the day, but if you are buying, I'll have another coffee.''

We played penny ante poker until around 4:00 P.M., and then went to eat again. Back in the room, I lay down across the bed. Jim and Tex were playing rummy and after a few minutes, I realized I was getting sleepy.

Later, I heard a loud voice. I realized it was Jim shouting and throwing a fit. I didn't open my eyes. Jim was shouting to Tex, "Just look at that—asleep, dead to the world. Hell, we will be lucky if we don't get killed tonight, and that damn Mark is sleeping like he hasn't a care in the world.''

Tex interrupted and told Jim that sleep was what I needed.

"I know that,'' Jim said, "He is going to be all right, ain't he?''

Tex assured Jim I would be fine.

"Damn, that's good to hear," Jim grinned then added, "Mark is really a dick, ain't he?" I realized that very few men would ever have true friends like Jim and Tex. I turned over, took about two seconds to count my blessings, and went back to sleep.

Chapter 21

AT 8:00, Tex woke me up. I was surprised to see a well-dressed Mexican in the room. He spoke to me in perfect English. He introduced himself as Dr. Del Rio and informed me he had been called to examine and redress my wound. He informed me he had received his M.D. from John Hopkins in Baltimore. He did a nice job bandaging me up.

Dr. Del Rio assured Jim I had it made if I would take care of myself. He gave me some pain tablets in case I needed them. As soon as the doctor had gone, we started preparing for our little trip.

We decided to take two scoped rifles, four pistols and two automatic shotguns, with plenty of ammo. If we ran into trouble in Loreto, it would be very serious.

We had several leather saddlebags and gunny sacks which we had brought from the ranch and had expected to use in carrying out the treasure at Aldama.

Tex gave Luis two large thermos bottles and asked him to go to the cafe and have them filled with coffee. We drove slowly until we reached the turnoff road to Loreto, then stopped and had coffee. No one said a word. We were all too occupied with our thoughts and fears as to what lay ahead.

Finally, Tex broke the silence. He asked if we were ready to go. Once we were on our way, we accepted the fact that there was no turning back.

We all relaxed and even kidded each other. There wasn't anyone on the street of the little village as we passed through. From past experiences, we knew it was about a three hour drive from this small village to Loreto.

At twenty minutes after 10:00 we came to the little mountains and knew we were no more than a mile and one half from Loreto. Jim and Luis got out of the truck and walked down toward the river and arroyo that ran around the end of the mountain and curved back toward Loreto.

They motioned for Tex to follow them in the truck. About three hundred yards from the road was a small arroyo where we could park the truck and it couldn't be seen from the road above.

I handed Tex one of the shotguns and kept the other one. I told Luis to get seven saddle bags. Jim spoke up and reminded me there were only six of them. "Look, there is no need for anyone to watch the truck as well hidden as it is. Now, don't argue, I'm going and that's that."

Tex breathed a sigh of relief and Jim starting arguing. I started walking back to the road. When I reached the road, I waited for them to join me. They finally accepted the fact that I was going and no one protested. Luis asked what route we were going to take to the arroyo where we were to rendezvous with José.

"What do you think, Mark?" Jim asked me. "Well, I don't really know what's best. The way I see it, if no one is suspicious, and no guards have been posted watching for us, it doesn't make any difference. If they are watching for us, we are in trouble, regardless of how we go.

"If you guys are willing, we will walk down the road to the river, then cross the river to our rendezvous point.

"Fellows, this is hard to say, but if there is serious trouble and one of us gets hit, I don't care if it's me or who it is, if he is killed or so badly wounded he can't help himself, leave him. If possible, get the wounded or dead man's gun, if they can no longer use it.

"It would be very foolish for one or two of us to get killed trying to carry out a dead man. This I ask as a special favor. If I run out of luck this trip, whoever is closest to me, please finish me off, so Flores won't have the satisfaction." All three of the others asked the same favor.

"Now, listen carefully. If you smoke, be sure to tear the cigarette stub in such small pieces that it cannot be recognized as an American brand. Speak only in Spanish. I'll go ahead. When you can just see me, then, Jim you follow. Luis, the same with you. Tex will bring up the rear. This way we won't be bunched up. When we get to the meeting place, I'll go about fifty feet up out of the arroyo on the old road toward Loreto.

"I'll hide behind a cactus until José arrives. Luis, you go about the same distance down the arroyo. Jim will wait in the old road in the arroyo. Should anyone come along, whether it's a woman, man or child, they will have to be tied up and gagged. If it's a man, knock him out.

"Each of you get three or four small pebbles. If you see anyone, toss a pebble toward the man closest to you. One pebble, one person; two for two persons. Be damned sure you don't let anyone scream. Any questions or suggestions?"

They shook their heads. I turned and started to walk off. Jim stopped me. "Just a minute, Mark. I want to shake hands with the three best damned men I've ever known."

I was surprised and very deeply touched by Jim's show of emotion. I'm sure Tex and Luis shared my feelings. None of us spoke a word as we shook hands. I started down the road. I have never felt so lonely and afraid in all my life.

When I came around the end of the mountain and down to the river and arroyo, it looked just as I remembered it. I couldn't help thinking about the last time we were here, and how close a shave we had had. I wondered if we would be as lucky as before.

At the river, the people from Loreto had placed large rocks close together so they could walk across without getting their feet wet. I crossed on the rocks to the other side and started down the river. When I came to where the old road went to José's house, I waited until the other guys were all there. In a whisper, I warned them no talking, and motioned Tex and Luis to their lookout post.

Very carefully, I then eased up over the bank of the arroyo. The moon was shining bright enough that I could see the village. There wasn't a light to be seen or a sound to be heard. About seventy-five feet from the arroyo was a large cactus on the side of the old road.

Very cautiously, I walked to the cactus and sat down behind it. I re-checked the shotguns, then looked at my watch. It was 1:50. In about ten to twenty minutes the moon would be down.

I lit a cigarette, keeping it carefully cupped in my hands. Old memories of my previous visit came back to me. I had to smile to myself when I thought about how close I was to the place where I had jumped on the little burro.

I cautioned myself not to let my imagination play tricks on me again. I had always thought I was master over my mind and thoughts. But try as I would, I could not keep from thinking how close Maria was to me.

I just just finished my cigarette when I noticed it was getting darker. The buildings were not as visible as they had been a few minutes before. I looked at my watch. It was 2:14. I was wondering if José would come, or if he had had trouble. Everything had gone perfectly. But, just maybe our luck was changing.

Then I heard footsteps approaching from the village. I eased up on my knees and could see the bulk of two people. In just a minute more, I could tell one of them was a woman.

I started silently swearing to myself. Our luck had run out. I threw two pebbles one after another in the arroyo so Jim could signal the others to be prepared to receive company.

I would have to let them pass by me. They were walking about six feet apart. It would have been impossible for me to knock the man out before she could scream. When they were almost even with me, my heart stood still. I was sure the woman was Maria.

I cautioned myself about not letting my imagination make another mistake. Then, thank God, I heard José say, "Maybe my brother ees not here yet."

Very softly, I called, "José . . . Maria." They both stopped and looked toward me.

When I arose from behind the cactus, my legs were so weak I could hardly stand.

"Ah, my brother," José said.

Maria opened her arms and said, "Is it really you, Mark, *es mi amor?*"

"Yes, my love, I'm here." When those soft arms clasped my neck I pulled her to me and our lips touched. I have never felt such love and need for woman as I felt for Maria at that moment.

I wish I could find the words to describe how pure, sweet, and wonderful that kiss was. I don't know how long we stood there holding and kissing each other. I finally realized Jim had his hand on my shoulder and was shaking me.

"Hurry, Mark, you all go down in the arroyo. Tex will stand guard here." I pulled her arms from around my neck, put my arms around her, and pulled her head against my shoulder. "I don't give a damn who he is, Preacher, Priest, or Rabbi, no man could think with those arms around him."

I cooled down to the boiling point and told Jim I was as surprised to see Maria as he was.

"All right, José, let's hear what happened. Be damn sure you tell me the truth."

"Don't be angry sweetheart," Maria said, "I make José bring me."

"What did you say?" I asked her. She repeated herself. "But Maria, you are speaking English."

"It is true. Are you not surprised? I think you will never notice. For all this time all we say is in the English. You see, Mark, the eighteen months I stay in the convent, the Sisters teach me to talk and read in English. You are happy with me, No?"

"Yes, I am happy and proud of you Maria. Now, please, let José speak."

José was visibly shaken. As usual, he took the long way around before coming to the point. At last he got started.

"Yesterday, I see the son-of-a-bitch Flores. He knows nothing and is a little friendly. I buy the beers. We talk. He says nothing about the Americanos.

"This morning, I see Maria go to the Church. I go and say to her what you say to me to say to her. That, in no more than ten days you will send for her. Then she say many questions. I finally tell her that this very night you come to Loreto for the silver.

"I don't want to bring her here, but she say she will come

alone if I do not bring her. This I know she will do. So, I have to bring her."

I interrupted José.

"Maria, my darling, you will never know how happy I am to see you and how much love there is in my heart for you, but we are on a very dangerous mission. You know if we are discovered here, we will have to kill or be killed?

"How did you slip out of your home? Are you sure no one is looking for you?"

"I am ashamed for causing you the problems, please you will not be angry with me. For more than one year, all my prayers were to only see you once more and feel your arms. My love is so great I could not help myself. Marek, please, I had to see you.

"I received permission from my home to spend the night at the convent with my good friend, one of the Sisters. She alone know I am not asleep. She keeps the watch. All is well."

I could feel relief flooding through my body. I had been afraid she had slipped out of her house and a search would be made for her. I gave her a quick kiss and told her it was all right and I wasn't angry. I told her I would come for her or send for her as soon as possible.

"José, you go with her and see she gets safely inside the convent, then hurry back here."

As we kissed goodbye, I could see the tears in her eyes as she followed José out of the arroyo and up the old road toward the village. Maria's goodbye was, *Vaya con Dios, mi amor.*"

Jim said, "Mark, you are a lucky son-of-a-bitch."

It seemed like hours, but actually in less than fifteen minutes, José was back grinning from ear to ear. "My brother, she is safe inside the convent. You see, everything, she is all right. Nothing happened."

I asked José if the silver had been dug up. "*Quien sabe?* Maybe, maybe not. My brother, Juan and Raul will do this about now. Now that she is very dark."

We followed José in single file toward the house. We didn't see or hear anyone. When we came to the back of

José's house, we stopped and listened until we were sure no one had heard or was following us.

José couldn't find a ladder, but had a rope over the wall of the patio. I asked Jim and Luis to stand guard outside while Tex and I were inside.

Once inside the patio, it was darker than a sack full of black cats. Goats were everywhere. José called Juan and Raul.

Juan and Raul came out of the house carrying a shovel, lantern, and an old tarp. They shook hands with me, but it was plain to see that they were both scared and didn't like the idea of having to help move the silver.

Tex moved the large rock and started shoveling. I started worrying. Was it possible someone had found and removed the silver? My worries were wasted. In just a few minutes, I heard the shovel strike metal. Then I could see the old cowhide.

Tex started handing the bars out of the hole. I counted forty-nine bars, more than we had thought there would be. We estimated their weight at twelve to fourteen pounds each, making a total weight from six hundred to seven hundred pounds. I asked Tex if we should leave a few of them, or try to take them all.

"Take them all," he replied.

I put six bars in a saddle bag and asked Juan and José to lift the bag to see if they could carry that much weight. They were sure they could. I then put six bars in each of the saddle bags for José, Luis, Juan, Raul and myself. Eleven for Tex, and eight for Jim, making a total of forty-nine.

After carefully refilling the hole, we carried all of the saddlebags to the wall of the patio. José, Juan and I climbed over the wall. Tex straddled the wall, and Raul handed the bags up to Tex. He passed them down to us, and Tex placed each man's saddlebag over his shoulder.

Jim and I led the parade and walked slowly and quietly. We were in luck and made it to the arroyo without being observed. Jim dropped his load and told everyone we would take a five minute break.

Once again, Tex helped everyone load their saddlebags over their shoulders, and we were off. Before reaching the river, I could feel my strength giving way. I knew the other guys were also very tired, but we desperately needed to get across the river before we rested again.

After what seemed an eternity, we came to the river. I didn't think it in my physical power to walk the rocks across the river. The loss of blood was taking its toll. I finally made it across, staggered, and fell. As I fell, I felt some of the stitches pull loose in my chest. I dropped my load and rolled over to see if the other guys were coming. They had all made it across the river.

We had to rest four more times and we were forty minutes making the last mile and a half to the truck. I didn't say anything about re-opening my wound, but I could feel the warm blood gently running down my chest and stomach.

When we finally came in sight of the truck, I noticed it was getting light in the east. We had made it just in time. We waited while Tex went to bring the truck around. This gave me a chance to talk to José, Juan and Raul. I told José and Raul to come to a certain hotel in Mazatlan in two days. We were getting out of Durango as fast as possible.

I also cautioned them to make sure they were not followed when they came to Mazatlan. Once again, as I embraced José, I realized how much I loved the ugly little devil. I also realized that no man could ever be so loyal and completely devoted to me as he was.

As on our first trip to Loreto, his parting was, "Goodbye my brother, may God protect you until we meet again."

Tex stopped the truck and threw all the saddlebags behind the seat. We were on our way. With the four of us in the truck seat, we were crowded. Jim put his hand around my shoulders, and his hand came to rest on my chest. I felt him rub his hand over my chest. When he felt the warm, wet, sticky blood on my soaked shirt, he screamed at Tex, "Stop this truck!"

Tex didn't know what was happening. He applied the brakes. Jim opened the door, jumped out, and flashed a light on me. "You silly little bastard. Just sit there and bleed to death and not say a word."

"Look, you guys, just calm down. I am all right. We'll

soon be in Durango and Dr. Del Rio can sew me up again.''

Tex gave me fast first aid, and applied a bandage, consisting of two dirty, sweaty handkerchiefs.

Once again, we were on our way. "Let's go, and don't drive too fast, the jarring of the truck hurts me." I used this as an excuse to keep Tex from driving too fast and having an accident, or from hitting a hole and breaking a spring.

We had been too lucky to take any unnecessary risks now that we were in the clear. It was a long rough four hour drive back to Durango.

Jim had no trouble getting Dr. Del Rio back to the motal The good doctor insisted that I go to his office for a complete overhaul job. Jim and I started Tex and Luis on their way to Mazatlan before we went to the doctor's office. We were all in agreement, the faster we got out of Durango, the safer we were.

Mazatlan, being in another state, and on the Pacific coast, has a lot of American tourists all year round. We wouldn't arouse any suspicions.

Once again, Dr. Del Rio did a splendid job of resewing and re-bandaging my wound. Then he personally drove Jim and me to the airport. It was only an hour flight to Mazatlan.

Once in that beautiful city, we checked in at a hotel which was managed by two old friends of mine. Just across the street is the beach. Ever since Navy training I've loved the beach and the sea.

I didn't even take the time to unpack. I had a bellboy take a blanket and beach umbrella and we headed for the beach. I had just made myself comfortable and was enjoying the cool sand and ocean breeze, when Jim walked up. He was really upset.

"What the hell are you doing out here on the beach?" he blazed. "Why ain't you in bed? You know damn well the doctor told you to lay down and rest."

"Just take a close look at me, Jim," I replied. "I am not standing on my head. For your information, I am lying down, and very comfortable."

Jim became very upset. "Don't you get smart alecky with me, you cocky little bastard. I got eyes and can see you are laying down. But why in hell do you want to lay on the ground? I've been meaning to ask your daddy if he didn't drop you on your head when you were a baby.''

He turned around and headed for the hotel, then he gave me a farewell parting shot. ''I hope to hell a big shark chews off both of your damn legs.''

I fired up a good cigar, and was thinking over our past week's experiences, and how lucky we had been, especially on last night's trip to Loreto. Once the silver was sold, we had more than enough money to operate on. We could relax for as long as needed for me to recover without any financial worries.

I was so occupied in thought, I didn't realize anyone was within a mile of me. I heard Jim say, ''Just put it there on the blanket.'' I looked up and there stood my old friend, Juaneto who owns the Shrimp Bucket Cafe in the hotel.

He had brought two shrimp baskets and six cold beers. I sat up and made room on the blanket for Juaneto and Jim. Jim and I sure enjoyed the picnic. It had almost been twenty-four hours since we last ate.

After we had finished off the beer, Juaneto said he had to get back to work. He invited us for dinner that evening. I lay back down and was shocked to hear Jim say, ''Move over, you lazy little bastard, and make room on that blanket for me.''

Chapter 22

A DISTANT voice woke me. I laid perfectly still, then recognized Jim's voice. He was cussing like a marooned sailor. When I looked at him, he really opened up. "Beats me how any grown man can be such a sleepy-head. Hell's bells, Mark, you'd go through life never knowing you were born. Sleep your whole damn life away."

I ignored him and started to the hotel, then turned and said, "Be a good boy, and bring the umbrella and blanket. There's a peso tip in it for you."

That really put his cork to bobbing. He began shouting to himself, "A boy, he calls me! A peso tip! Come back here, you lazy little bastard, I don't give a big rat's ass if you are split wide open, I'll throw you in the ocean and feed you to the damn fish. I'll teach you to respect your elders."

I choked back a laugh and hurried across the street into the hotel and up to my room. I had just climbed into the tub when Jim opened the door. I heard the blanket and umbrella hit the far wall. He was still cussing as he slammed the door. I took about an hour to shave, bathe and dress, and to give Jim time to cool off. I had really fractured the old boy.

I walked down to his room and put my ear to the door before knocking. He had either cooled off or run down. I could hear him grumbling and complaining to himself like a sore tailed bear. I knocked and opened the door and greeted him as if nothing had happened.

"Say, Jim, how about having dinner with me?"

"You're damn right I will. If you think I'm going to starve to death, you're crazy as hell. And, I'll tell you something else. Put my peso tip with the rest of the bill, cause you're sure gonna buy my dinner!''

We walked down stairs to the hotel patio and almost ran over Tex and Luis. They had just arrived and were starved.

The four of us had just sat down at our table when Tex punched me with his elbow and asked if I recognized the guy who was sitting at the third table on my left.

I turned and immediately recognized Ray White. Ray had sold me mining supplies all the years I had mined in New Mexico. He looked up, recognized us and came over to our table.

''You are the last guys I ever expected to see in Mexico.'' I introduced him to Jim and asked him to join us.

''Ray, we might say the same for you. What in the world brings you this far from Albuquerque?''

''I've practically lived here for the past year,'' he told me.

I laughed and told him I knew at the time I was buying supplies from him that he was making a thousand percent profit, but I didn't realize he had made enough to retire in this fashion.

''Damned if I didn't,'' he replied, ''you know how competitive that business was. When the A.E.C. lifted the buying program on uranium, I held on for another two years, then had to close up. My wife went west with a customer, and I came to Mexico. Hell, I don't mind telling you guys, I've made more money here in Mexico in the last year buying gold and silver than I ever made in the States.''

When he said he was buying gold and silver, I almost jumped out of my chair. I looked at the other guys and they, too, had perked up. I shook my head. I asked Ray if he was kidding or was he really buying gold and silver. He assured me he was.

We finished our drinks and I tried to casually ask him what he was paying an ounce for silver. ''Whatever I have to pay, and it's getting high as hell. There are too many buyers. I usually have to pay from ten to fourteen dollars an ounce, depending on who has it and how hot it is.''

''Well, Ray, we aren't in the silver business, but I have a friend who only yesterday tried to sell me between six and seven hundred pounds of silver.'' He got interested in a hurry. "Where is the guy? Can you get in touch with him? Are you sure he has it?''

I assured him that he had the silver, that I personally saw it, and the guy wanted fourteen dollars an ounce. "He's too high, Mark, but I have a contract with a group and haven't been able to buy my monthly quota. Tell you what I'll do. If he will pay you your commission, I'll take it all at one time.''

I told Ray I didn't want any commission and would be happy to help with the sale since they were both my friends.

"This old guy will have to have cash,'' I added. "He won't accept a check.'' I wasn't about to take any chances. I remembered the last cashier's check we received.

Ray reached inside his coat and handed me a leather folder. When I opened it and looked inside, it was stuffed with one-hundred dollar bills. I still wasn't taking any chances. The bills looked authentic to me, but so had the counterfeit check.

I told him my friend didn't know how to count, or what the exchange was on American money. If he would change the dollars to pesos at the bank, I felt sure he had a deal. "If you guys will order for me, I'll go and try to call my friend and tell him I've found a buyer for his silver.''

I went to the room and called my sons. It had been three weeks since I had heard from them, and now that we were back in the chips, I could afford the call.

I waited another ten minutes and went back to the cafe. Ray couldn't wait for me to sit down before asking if I had made the deal. "That depends on you,'' I told him. "The old man wants his pay in pesos. Also, he is afraid to do business with a stranger. This is how he wants to handle the deal.

"He wants me to come and get the silver and sell it to you, and then bring him his money. This way you won't know who he is and you can't come back and rob him. He's a very cautious old cat.''

"That's perfect, Mark. Hell, you know there isn't a man alive I trust, and had rather do business with than you.''

"Okay, Ray, it's a deal. Where do we meet to weigh the silver and count the money?''

"I have a house with an enclosed garage if it is satisfactory with you."

I nodded that it was.

"Can you have the silver here by the time the bank opens in the morning?" he asked.

I assured him I could.

"All right, be parked in front of the hotel about 9:30 in the morning. When I pass by the hotel, just follow me home. Drive inside the garage, and don't reach for that dinner check. I'll make enough on this deal to pay several checks."

Back in the room we were all overjoyed with our turn of good luck and wondered what would happen to upset the applecart. We had been too lucky for the past three days.

This time our skepticism was unjustified. Tex and I were waiting in the pickup with the silver. Jim and Luis were parked around the block in the car and would follow us in case Ray should try a stick-up.

At 9:25, Ray passed and motioned us to follow. We drove inside the garage and closed the door. Tex started carrying the silver bars inside.

The bars averaged six kilos each, or thirteen and two-tenths pounds each. The forty-nine bars weighed a total of six hundred forty six and eight-tenths pounds. Silver being troy weight, twelve ounces to the pound, we had seven thousand seven hundred and sixty-one ounces at fourteen dollars an ounce, for a grand total of $108,654.00. With the peso at 22.5 to one U.S. Dollar, we had almost three and a half million pesos. We refused to drink with Ray, put the pesos in two large shopping bags and went back to the hotel. Only then could we believe our good fortune. We were all so happy over our turn of good luck that we decided to spend the rest of the day celebrating.

We each took four thousand pesos or two hundred dollars for our celebration. The balance we put in the hotel safe.

"I don't know about you guys, but I am renting a boat and going deep sea fishing. Anyone interested?"

Jim decided to go with me, but Tex said he had seen a very pretty baby and was going to play with the baby's mama. Luis subscribed to Tex's idea in hopes the baby had an aunt.

We rented a two chair boat and got underway. I pulled off

my shirt and lay back and enjoyed the ride out to the fishing grounds. I was so relaxed I didn't want to have to move. As usual, when one is so carefree and lazy, that's when he gets all the action.

We caught three dolphins, two blue marlin, and a small shark. I caught both the marlins and two of the dolphins, while Jim caught only a dolphin and a shark. I kidded Jim unmercifully about being such a poor fisherman, and he took it like a good sport. He didn't have a single cussing seizure all afternoon.

Jim admitted the shark was very skinny and if I kept talking, he was going to fatten him up. He went on, "If you don't know what that means, just keep talking and I'll have the fattest shark ever caught in Mazatlan."

After having our pictures taken with our catch, we were ready for dinner. After dinner, we sat in the hotel patio and talked for hours. It was an ideal spot for relaxing.

The patio was long and spacious and planted with palm trees as well as bougainvillea and all types of tropical flowers. There were rooms on all four sides and tables scattered among the palms.

By 11:00 we had drunk so much coffee it was impossible to swallow another drop. We finished our cigars and decided to go to bed. Tex and Luis still hadn't come back.

As I started to enter my room, I asked Jim if he realized the dangerous condition I was in, and if he remembered the doctor advising me to get plenty of sleep and rest.

"All right, all right," he stormed, "I won't wake you in the morning. I would rather have my coffee and eat alone than to have the company of some people I know. What do you think about that, you lazy twerp?"

I didn't make any reply. I felt I was ahead and wanted to stay that way, at least until about 9:00 or 10:00 in the morning.

I awoke around 9:00 and went down to the cafe. Jim was there having coffee and talking to Juaneto.

"Did you hear Tex and Luis come in last night?" he asked. I shook my head and he said, "I don't see how you could keep from it, they made enough noise to arouse the dead.

Both drunker than hell. I never heard such a commotion."

We decided to let them sleep if off while we went for a long drive up the coast. It was about 3:00 when we returned to the hotel. Tex and Luis were out on the beach. Jim went into the hotel, and I joined Tex and Luis on the beach to tell them about all the fish Jim and I caught. Tex laughed and said that wasn't anything, that I should see a couple of *señoritas* and hear about the suckers they caught.

We spent about two hours talking and walking the beach, then decided to go check on Jim and have dinner. When we entered the hotel, I got the surprise of my life.

There is always a band playing in the patio and cafe area. There in the middle of the dance floor was Jim dancing with a very attractive American woman. They were sure cutting a mean rug and dancing as close together as two well chaperoned teenagers during a power failure.

When the music stopped, we went over to their table. I asked Jim if they wanted to join us for dinner. "Hell no," he said, "can't you see we're busy?" I suddenly realized that Jim was as tight as I had ever seen him. Never had I seen him pick up a woman before. We apologized and retreated.

We went about two blocks down the street to the *Copia de Leache* restaurant. I don't think we said a word on the way there, but after the initial shock wore off, we laughed and kidded about Jim and his date while we were waiting to be served.

Even though Jim was tight, there was no excuse for his rude manners, and I was not going to let him get the best of me. I decided to fix Jim's clock.

I quickly finished dinner, left money to pay the check and excused myself. I hurried back to the hotel, cornered the desk clerk and asked how he would like to make five hundred pesos. He was not reluctant and wanted to know what to do.

"Do you see my friend, *Señor* Dunlap, dancing with the American lady?"

He did.

"Bueno. I will walk across the street and onto the beach. You watch me very closely and when I wave my hand, you go tell *Señor* Dunlap that his wife and three kids have just arrived and to please come help them unpack the car. Be sure to tell him in English.''

I crossed the street and walked out onto the beach. In a few minutes, I saw Tex and Luis heading for the hotel. I waited until they were almost to the hotel entrance, then waved my hand to the desk clerk.

I couldn't have timed it more perfectly. Tex and Luis stopped at the hotel entrance for just a few seconds. Just long enough for Jim to come flying out the door. When he saw Tex and Luis, he thought they were the ones responsible for having the message delivered. When he saw them, he started shaking his fist in their faces. You could have heard him cussing and shouting nine blocks away.

''That's the dirtiest, low-down trick anybody has ever played on me, and you two bastards will damn sure live to regret it!'' Tex and Luis were so surprised they didn't even move. They had no idea what had happened.

Jim re-entered the hotel then came charging out again. The fit he threw will be remembered and talked about for years to come around the hotel. His lady friend had flown the coop. She wasn't about to get involved in any family affairs.

Luis saw me standing on the sand. They all three came flying to the beach where Jim grabbed me by the arm and started telling me what a low-down, dirty trick Tex and Luis had played on him.

Not until then did they know what had brought on this seizure. Tex interrupted Jim and told him that was all he intended to take. Furthermore, he didn't even intend to be cussed out again for something he didn't do.

I got between them and told Jim that I personally had watched Tex and Luis walk up to the hotel, and they never went inside. Someone else was responsible (I didn't say who), or else the clerk had made a mistake. I told him that Tex was right, he shouldn't fly off the handle until he knew what really happened, because someday, his temper fits were going to get him in trouble.

I could see the crisis had passed. I asked Luis to go take a walk with me and maybe Jim and Tex would beat each other to death and there would be a bigger cut of the treasure for the two of us.

We were gone about an hour. When we got back to the hotel, Jim and Tex were sitting in the patio having coffee. Nobody said a word, but they both looked like a couple of kids who got caught swiping cookies. Luis and I sat down at an adjoining table.

Jim looked over and saw us. He told Tex he guessed we were too conceited to sit at their table. "So let's join them," Jim said. Jim picked up their coffee cups and came over to our table. From this gesture, I knew they had settled their little argument.

Luis asked if José and Raul were not supposed to arrive today or tonight. They were. I was surprised they hadn't already arrived.

Jim suggested a game of penny-ante poker. We really enjoyed the game. Before we realized it, it was midnight.

Chapter 23

THE FOLLOWING morning, I went to a doctor and had my chest re-bandaged and the stitches removed. The other guys started worrying about José and Raul. They were one day late. Knowing José, I wasn't too concerned, for one day didn't mean anything to him.

We sweated out another two days. They were now four days late. We really had something to worry about, but all we could do was to wait. After another three days had passed, we knew something was definitely wrong.

We all met in Jim's room to decide what to do. Once again, they asked for my opinion.

"Well, I don't know what to say. We all know something has happened. But what? That's the sixty-four thousand dollar question. Someway, somehow, we have to get someone into Loreto and find out what is wrong. None of us can go. Do any of you know anyone we can trust to go to Loreto?"

Jim had the answer. "I can go get my ranch foreman, Ramon. He is completely trustworthy and tougher than a recapped cob. He can take the damn village apart if he has to. He isn't afraid of the devil himself."

We all agreed Ramon was the man for the job. "When do you want to leave?" I asked Jim, then added, "I should stay here in case José and Raul should show up."

"Hell, I'm ready now," Jim said. "I can be back before noon tomorrow."

Luis asked if he could go with Jim to see his wife. It would be necessary for them to spend the night at the ranch. I kidded Luis and asked him if he was going to tell Carmen about the little party he and Tex had.

"Of course not," he said, "What she don't know won't hurt her."

I winked at Jim and thought to myself that works both ways, my friend.

Tex and I drove them out to the airport. After they took off, we came back to the hotel to wait and worry.

About 2:00 A.M., the phone rang. The desk clerk started to apologize for waking me up. He said there was a very poor, and dirty man who insisted on seeing me. "He claims that it is very important. Should I give him your room number or run him off? He says his name is Raul."

"Let him come to my room at once," I replied. Before I could dress, there was a knock at the door. I opened the door and almost failed to recognize Raul. He was so dirty, unshaven and unkept that he didn't look like himself.

Raul threw his arms around me and started crying like a baby. I led him to the bed. He was so exhausted, he couldn't sit up.

"What is it, Raul? What has happened?"

He didn't break the news to me gently.

"Already Tino Flores has killed Juan, and maybe José is dead by this time." I shook Raul until he regained control of himself. "Please, Senor Mark, is there no food here? I walked almost all the way. I have no money, and I beg for what little food that I eat. For two days, I have nothing at all."

I grabbed the phone and called the restaurant to send up four soft scrambled eggs, toast and milk, and to be fast about it. I then called Tex and told him Raul had arrived and to come at once to my room.

Tex didn't say a word when he saw the exhausted condition Raul was in. He looked at me. Before I could reply, the waiter brought the food.

A starved animal couldn't have wolfed down the food as fast as Raul did. I told Raul we knew he was still hungry, but to please rest and sleep. Then he could have all the food he wanted. I handed him a pack of cigarettes. "Now do you feel like telling us what happened?"

"Si, Senor, now I talk. What you do not know is the Chief of Police from Aldama was coming to Loreto to tell Flores of your trouble in that village, and how you broke the arm of his cousin.

"Somewhere on the highway as you were going to Durango after you left with the silver, you meet this policeman and he sees and knows you. This he says to Flores once he gets to Loreto.

"The police start to investigate. They find our tracks in the road and river arroyo. These they follow to where we hid the pickup. Then they back-track to where José and Maria meet you. They could not tell and still do not know who the woman was. They think she was not with you all, but was by herself.

"Then they come to José's house and look everywhere. But we were too careful digging up the silver. The goats have walked over the place many times. They cannot see anything. Still they know you are in Loreto. They take José and Juan to the jailhouse. Once there, they start to beat José and make him say why you come back to Loreto.

"I follow them and see everything from the street through the window. First they hit José in the mouth so hard that three of his teeth fall to the floor. He faints. They throw the water on his face, and he sits up. They start hitting him again, but he won't say nothing. He passes out again. They put more water on him, and he sits up again. They start beating him some more.

"Juan cannot stand to see José beat to death in front of his face, so he grabs a chair and knocks the son-of-a-bitch Flores over the head, and is fighting with the policeman from Aldama.

"Then Flores gets up and hits Juan very hard on the head with his pistol and keeps hitting him after he is on the floor. When the policeman realizes there are people watching them, they carry Juan and José back to their house.

"I go get the doctor, but still this night, Juan, he dies. The doctor cannot do nothing for Juan, and he helps José all he can. One day later we bury Juan. That night, José tells me to slip out of Loreto and come here to tell you everything. So, I am here."

I looked at Tex. His eyes were moist. I couldn't say a word. There was the most awful pain in my throat, like someone was choking me.

Poor little, loyal, pitiful José. They could have cut his heart out, and he would never have told them anything about his brother.

Juan, I did not know very well, but José was his older brother and could do nothing wrong as far as Juan was concerned. Who would be next to die, and where was it going to end?

Carlos, Luis' brother was killed in an automobile accident over the first half of the treasure. I had been crippled, but recovered, and now poor Juan—murdered. He had eight or nine children. I would personally see to it that his wife and children were cared for and his children educated.

It's a terrible thing to kill a man. It doesn't take much nerve to pull the trigger on a gun, or drive a knife in someone's heart, but to stand and watch them die, knowing you are responsible, and in the last seconds before death, having to watch them struggle trying to live, you are sorry you cannot give back the life you have just taken. Even if killing was necessary to save your own life, it is the most awful thing a man ever could experience.

Poor little José. He couldn't have whipped a third grade school boy. I didn't know whether José was dead, or might die from the awful beating he received on my behalf.

I knew at this moment that nothing on this earth could stop me from seeing Tino Flores one more time. And when we met, he would die.

When I realized this, may God forgive me for the satisfaction that I felt, for I knew I would enjoy seeing him draw his last breath.

How long I had stood there in meditation, I don't know, but when I came back to reality, Raul was lying across the bed, exhausted. He was already asleep, dead to the world. I pulled his shoes off, raised his feet on the bed, spread a blanket over him and followed Tex out of the room.

I went out to the beach. How long I walked, I don't know. I realized the sun was shining when Tex came to where I was sitting and asked me to join him for coffee and breakfast.

When I entered the room, Raul was still asleep. I tiptoed out and motioned Tex to follow me. I thought it best to order our breakfast before awaking him. If he was as hungry as he had been last night, he couldn't wait for the orders to be prepared. After we had ordered, I asked Tex to go wake Raul and bring him to the restaurant.

Raul and the food arrived at the same time. The poor guy was starved. He ate his bacon and eggs before I even got started on mine. I could tell he was still hungry, so I gave him my plate.

After he finished, I asked him if he could eat another order. "Si, *Señor* Mark, two more! You don't know how hungry I have been for the past five days. I walked so far."

I looked at Tex, "What do you think?"

"Hell, feed him all he wants. If it kills him, at least he will die full and happy."

After we finished, I could tell Raul was getting sleepy again. I told him to go to my room, take a hot shower, and go back to sleep. He was in complete agreement, if I would show him how to turn on and regulate the water. Once Raul was in the shower, I rejoined Tex for another cup of coffee.

At 9:00, Tex asked if we shouldn't go to the airport and wait for Jim. We left at once and were just getting out of the car when we saw Jim land. His first question was, "Have you heard from José or Raul?"

I couldn't keep my voice from quivering as I related to Jim what had happened.

"Look, Jim, I want to ask a favor. I want to borrow your plane as quick as it can be serviced. I am headed for Loreto." Jim grabbed me by the shoulders and started shaking me.

"Have you gone plumb crazy? I know how much you love José. We all do, but don't be a damn fool. You can't go to Loreto."

I jerked loose from Jim and told him, "Look, I don't intend to do anything foolish. Nothing or no one can stop me from avenging Juan and José. Flores had better give his heart and soul to God; his ass is mine."

Jim put his arms around me and said, "You didn't have to tell me that. From the look in your eyes, I know Flores is living on borrowed time."

"Jim, here's what I am going to do. Fly to Loreto and keep circling the village. This will draw a lot of attention. José is the only one who will recognize the plane. I'll keep circling lower and lower. With binoculars, maybe I can spot him.

"If José is able to get out of bed, he'll come outside and watch the show like everyone else. If he doesn't come out of his house after about ten minuts, I am going to Durango, rent an ambulance, and drive to Loreto and get him. He'll die if he doesn't have the proper medical care.

"After all, he could have talked and saved himself and Juan. But he wouldn't betray his brother. Now, his brother sure as hell ain't fixing to let him down.

"I'll drive and park the ambulance at José's door. Of course Flores will come to investigate, and when he does, I'll blow that son-of-a-bitch in half, put José in the ambulance, and head for Durango, and to hell with the hereafter."

Jim told Luis to go with Tex back to the hotel and get all the guns and ammunition and hurry back. "We're leaving for Loreto as quick as we can get the plane serviced."

Tex grabbed Jim and spun him around. "Where in the hell do you get that 'we' stuff? I am damn sure going too!" Luis and Ramon informed us they, too, were going.

When Tex and Luis went for the guns, Jim and I decided to take Ramon, who was big and strong and more able to protect himself in a fight than Luis. With Jim, Tex, and Ramon, I knew we could handle the police in Loreto.

Luis was disappointed when I told him he was to stay with Raul. The plane could only carry four people. I don't remember anyone saying a word on the two hour flight to Loreto. I was flying and Jim was on my right. He cussed to himself the entire flight.

I came around the mountain and dropped down to about one thousand feet and at full power, made a dive on Loreto. Then I pulled back to forty percent power and circled back over the village.

I circled as close a pattern as I could fly in order to attract attention. Jim had the binoculars and could easily recognize José's house on the third pass over the village. He started laughing and said, "Mark, I see him. José just came out of his house."

"Are you sure it's José?"

233

"Hell, yes, I'm sure," Jim replied, "with these binoculars, I could see a freckle on a tomcat's balls three miles away."

I banked and flew down the street where José lived. I dropped down to less than one hundred feet above the housetops. Sure enough, there stood José. I turned the plane on its side. It looked like I could almost reach out and touch him.

We have a sign we use in the mines when everything is all right. When I turned the plane on its side and passed José, he recognized me, and gave me the miner's sign for O.K.

I looked at Jim. He started cussing me for trying to kill them all. "Hell, Mark, you wasn't more than fifty feet above the roof tops."

"Shut up, you old bastard," I told him, "and take the controls. I'm tired."

We were all so relieved to see José alive and walking around that we were four happy men on the return flight to Mazatlan. Raul and Luis were as happy as we were when we told them we had seen José.

At last we were ready to try for the big treasure at Aldama. We spent all afternoon and until midnight planning our next move.

We decided first we should fly to Aldama and circle over the area to see whether Raul could recognize the exact location from the air. If he could identify the spot, we could then decide what our next move would be.

Chapter 24

EARLY THE next morning, Jim, Tex, Raul and I took off from the airport just at daylight. In less than three hours, we sighted Aldama. I asked Raul in what direction from Aldama the treasure was buried.

"North," he replied. After changing course, I dropped down to one thousand feet. In just a few minutes, Raul thought he recognized the canyon. I circled over the area until he was absolutely sure.

After he had pointed out the entrance to the old mine and the large rock where the treasure was buried, there could be no doubt that this was the right place. I went up to five thousand feet so we could get a better view of the surrounding terrain.

After circling for about fifteen minutes, we saw a small village to the north, and checking the maps, we identified the village as San Miguel. There was a small valley between the mountains all the way from San Miguel to the treasure site.

I dropped down and we flew the valley. There was one small ranch consisting of five buildings in the valley. No other houses. It was really a dry, hot, sandy, and uninhabited place.

I asked Jim and Tex how they would like to make a little pack from San Miguel to the treasure location. Both agreed this was our best chance to remove the treasure.

We flew the valley one more time and checked the mileage. Forty-seven miles. "That's a hell of a long way in such a hot, dry desert." Raul couldn't speak or understand English, so I turned the controls over to Jim and related our plans to Raul in Spanish.

When he realized what our intentions were, he became excited. "No, no, *Señor,* it is not possible. This valley is called the Jornado Del Muerto, the Journey of Death. In this valley are found more rattlesnakes and scorpions than in any other place in all Mexico. Not even the bandits will travel this valley.

"There is only one spring for water. A man lives there with his four sons who are more deadly than the snakes and scorpions. They raise and sell the dope, and put the cactus back to hide the airport when they do not need it."

I winked at Jim and motioned him to give the controls back to me. I circled and headed for the ranch. Sure enough, less than a mile from the house, on a small mesa, I could see the dirt strip. I estimated it to be three thousand feet long.

There were dead cactus and mesquite bushes placed all over the strip about forty to fifty feet apart. A very neat job of camouflage. Jim grinned and said, "Mark, someone above is looking out for you. I have never seen a man so lucky in all my life."

All the way back to Mazatlan, I was trying to think of some way to get José and Maria out of Loreto.

After lunch we gathered in my room to plan our next move. Everyone, except Raul, agreed we should go to San Miguel, buy enough camping equipment, mules and horses and take our chances on a pack trip through the Jornado Del Muerto. If we were lucky enough to find the treasure, Jim and I could go alone to San Miguel, hire a car to take us to Torreon, which is the closest airport to San Miguel, fly back to the landing strip there in the valley and pick up everyone and the gold.

I asked Raul if he had any idea how many pounds of gold there would be. He didn't know. From the number of mules and horses, we estimated each animal carried 200 pounds and there would be more than a ton and a half.

"Let's get it all in one trip. Jim and I will fly back for the men and give the mules, horses, and camping equipment to the old dope farmer, if we succeed."

Jim informed me his plane was a 182, not a DC-3 cargo. With full tanks, about one thousand pounds was all he could possibly get off the ground with.

"I know, Jim, but I can always rent the twin engine push-pull plane that we flew to Honduras. Also my friend in El Paso can be trusted and we can get him to fly another twin engine. This way, we can get it all at once."

"But first things first. My number one concern is getting José and Maria out of Loreto. Here's my plan. In the morning, Jim, you and Ramon will go and have a bill of sale for your truck made to Ramon."

"What the hell." That's as far as Jim got before I interrupted him and told him to shut up, that it was impolite to interrupt anyone. Jim turned red in the face, but didn't say a word.

"Look, Ramon is going to be a fish peddler." Jim jumped up. I pointed my finger at him and he sat back down. "The reason for the title transfer is no one in Loreto but José knows Ramon. Also, there are no fish available on Friday in Loreto except what they can catch in the river, and they are too small to eat.

"I will have two large tanks built on the pickup and have it repainted. No one will be suspicious, even if they should check the title. If Jim's name isn't on the title, Ramon is in the clear. With no communication system in Loreto, they couldn't check on us if they wanted to.

"Ramon goes to Loreto. The first thing he will do there is to find Flores and El Presidente, give them two or three big fish each and let them know he will be in Loreto early every Friday and would appreciate their help to get his business started. If they will help him, they will be given all the free fish they want.

"By peddling door to door, Raman can pass a couple of fish to José. Inside these two fish there will be money and a message.

"Now, I am going to take the truck in. How would you like fire engine red?" I asked Jim.

"I don't give a damn if it's purple," he replied. He grinned and said he thought my idea might work, but wanted to know how many of my hair-brained schemes it would take to get us all killed.

I picked up the truck keys and motioned Tex to follow me. Jim hadn't had a cussing seizure all day. I knew he was overdue. I stuck my head around the door facing and asked Jim, "What are you worried about? At your age, you're been a fugitive from the undertaker for years."

I jerked the door closed just as the ashtray landed. He was really upset. I didn't waste time getting down the stairs and on my way.

We talked the shop foreman at the garage into having two welders work overtime so the truck would be ready the following afternoon.

The next morning, Jim and Ramon went to have the title on the pickup truck transferred to Ramon.

They came back at 2:00 and we carried the new license plates down to the garage. While they were painting Ramon's name and address on the truck door, Jim and I went down to the fish market and made arrangements to buy three hundred pounds of red snapper.

We called Ramon at the garage and told him where to pick us up. Two hours later, he drove up in the reddest truck in all of Mexico. The sign on the truck doors made his occupation abundantly clear.

While Ramon was getting the fish iced down, Jim and I went back to the hotel. I got ten thousand pesos in tens and twenties and wrapped them in plastic. I wanted José, Raul and Juan's families to have enough money to live on comfortably until we could get them out of Loreto. I knew that, poor as they were, if they cashed a bill larger than twenty pesos, they would arouse suspicion.

I wrote José a note, put it in with the money, telling him where we were and to come to us as soon as he could, leaving the money with his wife, and Raul's and Juan's wives.

When Ramon came back, I selected two fish and put the money and note inside. I sewed them up with clear fishing leader and tied the two fish together so Ramon wouldn't make a mistake and give the wrong fish to José.

I gave Ramon an American penny. "Show it to Maria and tell her to expect a delivery of fish next week. There will be a message inside the fish."

"But how will I know Maria?" he asked.

"Look, Ramon, you will know her, for she is the most beautiful girl in all Mexico." I asked Luis to go with Ramon. By driving all night, Ramon could be in Loreto by 10:00 A.M. the following day which was Friday. Luis would stop at a hotel in Durango until Ramon came back from Loreto. I gave them money for expenses and they were on their way.

Jim, Tex and I spent the next day planning our trip from San Miguel to where the treasure was supposed to be. We decided to take Ramon, Raul, Luis and one other cowboy from Jim's ranch, for we would need twenty pack animals, plus the horses we rode. If we had any trouble there would be enough of us to take care of the pack animals and have a fighting force to protect the treasure.

We would leave José in San Miguel to watch the car. We decided to fly to El Paso and buy our supplies. Two tents with a zip-in canvas bottom should keep the snakes and scorpions out while we slept.

We would also take along four five-gallon cans of white gas for the lanterns and camp stoves. By digging a small trench around the tents, pouring the gas in the trench and setting it on fire, the sand would become hot. The hot sand along with the gas fumes would help keep the scorpions and snakes from crossing the trenches. With a little luck, we would only have to camp out three or four nights.

We decided to go to a leather shop and have leather leggings made for each animal. The leggings would cover them from their hoofs to their knees, protecting them against bites. It would be one big job to put the leggings on that many mules, but we couldn't afford to lose our pack animals.

We spent all day Friday and Saturday making out our list of supplies.

Chapter 25

ABOUT 11:00 Saturday night, someone knocked on my door. When I opened up there stood Luis and Ramon, tired, but very happy. I ordered food and coffee as Ramon began reporting on his trip.

When he arrived in Loreto, he drove directly to the jail and introduced himself to Flores. Flores went with him to *El Presidente's* office. After viewing his identification and truck title, they agreed to let him sell his fish.

He asked where *El Presidente* lived and promised to take to his home, the three biggest and best fish. Since very few people had any money, business wasn't very good.

Ramon finally came to José's house. They recognized each other, of course, and he gave José the two fish, but since Flores was watching Ramon, they had no chance to talk.

Ramon again asked directions to *El Presidente's* house. Flores got into the truck to show him personally. Once there, Ramon asked to meet the wife of *El Presidente* to ask what kind of fish she might prefer him to bring on his next trip.

Ramon sighed and continued. "You were so right. When the beautiful *Señorita* Maria came into the room, there could be no doubt who she was.

"I had the penny in my hand and when we were introduced by Flores, I forced her to shake hands. She was embarrassed to shake the hand of a fish peddler. My hand was so large and hers was so small and soft.

"Once the penny was in her hand, I stepped between her and Flores and closed her fingers over the penny. Flores was getting jealous of my attention to Maria and informed me that in only one month more the *señorita* would be his wife.

"All this time I stand between Flores and the *señorita*, for I am afraid she will drop the penny. I turn to congratulate Flores, and out of the corner of my eye, I see the *señorita* very slowly open her hand. Then she see the penny inside.

"Never have I seen such happiness in anyone's eyes. If only before I die, one woman will have the look of love for me that the *Señorita* Maria had for you, then God, I die happy. Then the *Señorita* excuse herself and said, *"Gracia por todo."* I knew she knew what my mission was.

"I was worried how to get the rest of the message to her. I went to the truck to get the three fish for her mama. Maria is the smart one. She comes running to the truck. 'Who are you, *Señor?*' she asked. 'And why you give me the American centavo? Does it mean what I think?'

"I am here for *Señor* Mark, I told her, and the American centavoes only you and the *señor* understand. Senor Mark says you are to be the one next Friday to receive the fish. For inside the fish will be a letter of love and instructions.

"Just then that son-of-a-bitch Flores comes running out of the house shouting, 'Why do you come out here to talk to a strange man? And, only a fish peddler?' The *señorita* is the smart one, she pretended to be very hurt and embarrassed.

"Look, you jealous man, what do we eat in Loreto? Beef, beef, beef, *todo tiempo* we eat beef. I was asking this man as a surprise, if for next Sunday dinner he could supply us with fresh shrimp. oysters, and fish. But now you have spoiled my surprise. I never want to see you again, and I hate you.'

"The *señorita* turned and ran into the house and slammed the door. Flores grinned a cruel smile and said, 'Have your little fits, my love, for after we are married, I show you who is the boss.'

"Almost I hit him in the face with a fish, and I want very much to say to him, 'Flores, you cruel son-of-a-bitch, you are living on borrowed time.' Never, *Señor*, have I seen such a cruel man."

I was very pleased over the perfect job Ramon had done. When I thought of Flores, anger got the best of me. I went for a walk on the beach to cool off.

Around 6:00 the next evening, I was reading a magazine in my room, when from the open door someone said, *"Mi hermano."* I looked up, there in the doorway stood little José. I took him in my arms like a mother does her small child.

Poor little guy. His front teeth had been knocked out and his face was still black from the beating he had taken. I gently rubbed my hand over his face. "Does it hurt very much, my brother?"

"No, my brother," he replied. "All the pain is in my heart, for when I see the small children of Juan, and his wife with no man to support them, I know they will go hungry. Then the pain is worse."

"José, you have known me for many years. Have I ever lied to you, or made you a promise I didn't keep?"

"No, my brother, never."

"All right, José, I now, before God, make you three promises. Number One: Never will Juan's wife and children want for food, clothes or medicine. Number Two: Every one of Juans' kids will get a college education, or I'll beat their little butts off if they even think of not going to school. And, Number Three: After we get the big treasure out and sell it, I will personally kill that son-of-a-bitch Flores. He will not die fast and easy."

Poor little José got down on his knees and kissed my hand. I'll never forget his prayer. "Thank you, God, for having give me two brothers. You were very wise when you needed one of my brothers, you left me the strong one to care for and protect our families." If it kills me, I'll be worthy of that prayer.

I helped José to his feet and called Jim's room to tell him José had arrived. "We know that he is here," Jim replied, then added, "We'll see him tomorrow. You guys need tonight alone."

While we were eating our dinner, a thought occurred to me. There were two things José loved above everything on this earth. A drink and a young woman. I had never partied with José in all the years I had known him.

I excused myself and went to find my friend, the desk

clerk, rented two adjoining rooms and asked him if he knew of any beautiful and available women. This was a very respectable hotel and didn't allow any women, but after ten minutes and fifteen hundred pesos he remembered knowing the two most beautiful women in all Mazatlan.

For another thousand pesos, he was sure he could slip them into the hotel if we were very quiet and careful. But, they were young and very expensive. Few men could afford them. I assured him we could, and asked him to have plenty of champagne and the girls in our room within one hour. I told him the party would be over about midnight, and for him to be sure to let the girls know that José was the big shot, not me.

I went back to the cafe, got José and we went for a walk on the beach. An hour and a half later, I guided the old boy back to the hotel. "Are you sad, José?"

"Yes, my brother." As we walked through the lobby, the clerk nodded his head. I knew all was ready.

As we started up to our rooms, I said, "José, tonight we will have a little party; good old champagne, and pretty girls." He grinned.

"*Quein sabe,* for never, my brother, do we make the party together."

When we reached the room, I opened the door. Both of the girls, and they were beauties, threw themselves around José's neck. He recovered from his surprise. "Aw, my brother, always you say to me the truth, and tonight we have no worries and really live."

"I'll go for that, José. Which of these girls do you want? The choice is yours."

He looked them over very carefully, like a rancher choosing between two thoroughbred horses, then made his choice. We had a fast drink, and José told his date to come with him to the next room. "So soon?" she asked. He was in his hour of glory and wasn't fixing to be denied.

"Look, woman, I am José Torres, the brother to Senor Mark. You go when I say, or for you, there will be no dinero for this night."

"Si, Senor," she replied. José stuck his chest out and

followed her into the bedroom.

The other girl and I had a good laugh. We were really having a good time. About every hour José would take his girl back to the bedroom for fifteen or twenty minutes.

The fourth time they went to their room, the girl came out first. I could see she was mad. "What's wrong?" I asked her.

"I don't mind undressing," she said, "if I am going to be loved, but to undress just to hear a dirty joke is too much."

"Look," I told her, "José has just lost a brother. This is his party, do what he wants. I'll see you are well paid for your trouble."

José, the ugly little bastard, was trying to impress me. At his age, I was surprised he could go three times in three hours. At eleven o'clock, José was really drunk. They retired once again to their room. When the girl came back, I could tell it had been another joke, and from her looks, she hadn't appreciated this one either.

By one o'clock, José was so drunk he could hardly stand. He finally managed to get on his feet and told his girlfriend he was ready to take her to the room again. She asked him if he wanted to make love or tell jokes.

José picked up a bottle of champagne, drank about half of it, and said, "Look, woman, I will show you I am a man, and muy macho." He took two steps, fell flat on his back and passed out.

"Well, girls," I said, "You can go home now. Looks like the party's over." I picked José up, put him on the bed, removed his shoes and then went to my room.

I woke up early the next morning, had a shower, and went to the cafe for coffee, and like always, I was the last one to get up. Everyone else, including José, was already having breakfast.

I sat down beside José. He looked like a dead man that had been warmed over. "How do you feel, José?"

"No bueno (no good), my brother. No bueno. Besides being sick in the head and stomach, I am sick everywhere."

I winked at Jim and said, "We really had a party last night, eh, José?"

"Please, my brother, I am at this time trying to never think again of women and wine." Everyone laughed. José had had it.

Now that we were all together, I asked everyone to please be in my room at three o'clock so we could make our final plan for finding the big treasure.

Jim spoke up and said, "I done a lot of thinking last night. Legally, the government has a claim on that gold. If we have trouble, or the officials get suspicious, my ranch is the first place they would look. We have all agreed that under no circumstances do we attempt to sell any part of this treasure in the States, or violate any U.S. Laws.

"If we try to find a market in Honduras, like we talked about, and we know our two ex-friends had a market there, why go north to my ranch in the first place? I have an American friend who is a rancher in the State of Guerrero, about eighty miles from Acapulco. He has a large house about five miles from this little village on a river, and only about six miles from the beach. He bought this place for his friends to use because of the good fishing and hunting.

"He even has a nice grass landing strip in the pasture adjoining the house. He has invited me down, many times."

We all agreed this was a great idea. If we went to Honduras to sell the treasure, we would be seven to eight hundred miles closer and could fly non-stop with no fear of running low on gas.

Each man was assigned his duty. Early tomorrow morning, Jim, Tex and I would leave for Guerrero to see if we could rent this rancher's house for two months. We would then go to Jim's ranch and on into El Paso to buy our supplies.

I would rent the plane we had used before and get my friend Russ Taylor to fly another twin-engine plane down. Luis, José, and Raul would take the car and go to Torreon and have the leather leggings made for the horses and mules. They also would have ten new saddlebags made.

While this order was being made, the three of them would go on to San Miguel and buy twenty mules and several horses. Raul would stay with the animals and make sure they had all the corn they could eat. We wanted the mules to be as strong as possible.

Ramon would remain in Mazatlan until Thursday, then buy another load of fish and be in Loreto Friday, deliver the message to Maria, drive back to Mazatlan and leave the truck and catch the Saturday night flight to Torreon. We would all meet at the hotel in Torreon, sometime late Saturday night.

Luis asked me why we didn't bring his wife, Carmen, Tex's wife, Jackie, and Lupe. There would be less suspicion if the women were there. Besides they could cook and we wouldn't have strange maids snooping around. We agreed this was the best idea of the day.

We gave Luis, José and Raul expense money to buy the horses and mules. They started at once for Torreon and San Miguel. They had a full week's work ahead of them.

We sat for hours trying to decide the best and safest way to get Maria out of Loreto. I wrote Maria a letter giving her these instructions.

"Next Friday, when the fish peddler comes to Loreto, at exactly 2:00, you try to slip out of your home. Go to the river and follow it to a point where you cannot be seen from the village. Then go to the road. At ten minutes after 2:00 the fish peddler will leave Loreto.

"When he sees you on the road, he will stop and you will get into the truck. I will be wiaiting no more than three miles from Loreto. He will bring you to me.

"It may be impossible next week for the fish peddler to come to Loreto. If he does not come next week, the next week he is sure to be there. Do not try to bring anything with you. If you are seen return to your home and pretend you were out for a walk. Then wait.

"On the fourth night, get permission to spend the night in the convent with your friend the Sister. At 3:00 in the morning, come to the arroyo where we met before. I will be there waiting."

We were all very nervous and afraid that we might make a slip. If we did, we would have one hell of a time getting Maria out of Loreto. Flores was very smart, and we couldn't fool him a second time.

The next morning, Ramon gave us a ride to the airport in the fish wagon. From the smell, no one could doubt that he was a fish peddler.

We were in luck when we landed at Agua Blanca, the little village in the State of Guerrero. Jim's friend, Sanford Parks, was at the house, and he was very happy to see Jim. I liked the guy on first sight. He was strictly a rancher, and the ugliest man I have seen since the last time I was at the Pike County Fair.

The place was perfect for our purpose. Sanford assured us the river was full of fish, and only six miles from a nice beach.

We accepted his invitation to lunch then took off for Jim's ranch. We had a head wind and were almost five hours in arriving at the ranch.

Lupe was overjoyed to see Jim. Carmen was disappointed that Luis hadn't come, but when Jim explained about the vacation in Agua Blanca, they were both very pleased and happy.

Tex called his wife, Jackie, and told her to meet him in El Paso tomorrow.

We were up early and arrived in El Paso at 9:00. Jim and Tex started shopping. I went to see my friend, Russ, and rented the same plane we had flown to Honduras. It wasn't as easy as I had thought to get him to fly another plane to Mexico; however, he loved fishing as much as I did. It was Tuesday, and we would be in Agua Blanca by 3:00 P.M. tomorrow. This would give us Wednesday afternoon, Thursday, Friday and until noon Saturday to fish.

We went together downtown to a sporting goods store. We really stocked up on lures and tackle. Russ took the tackle back to the airport. I finally found Jim and Tex. One thing we had forgotten was a metal detector to locate the treasure. It would be doubtful after all these years if Raul could pinpoint the exact spot where he saw them bury the gold.

By 2:00 we had all our supplies bought. We completely loaded four taxies and headed for the airport.

A few of the items were restricted and prohibited entry into Mexico. We decided to put everything that was restricted in my plane, and I would try to get through customs at Juarez. So Jim and Russ wouldn't be involved, and in order for us not to be at customs at the same time, we loaded my plane, and I took off.

Chapter 26

I HAD one hell of a time getting my visa and plane permits. I finally bought my way through. I was taxiing to the runway for take-off when Russ called the control tower for landing instructions.

In a matter of minutes, Jim made his request. The control tower told me to hold until the two approaching planes landed, then I would be cleared for take-off.

When I landed at Jim's ranch, Lupe had coffee ready. She and Carmen were very excited over the vacation trip which was to start tomorrow, and asked more questions than two kids could have.

I looked at Carmen's knee, her skirt was about six inches above it. She caught me and her eyes flashed like daggers. As much as if to say, remember when I slapped your face and told you no more.

The warning wasn't necessary. I sure as hell hadn't forgotten. Just remembering made my ears start ringing again. I decided then and there that I had been lucky and to forget the past. A man can't win all the time.

In a short time, Jim landed, while Russ circled the field to give Jim time to clear the runway. Then he came in.

Jackie, Lupe and Carmen were chattering like three magpies. We men went out, packed and serviced the planes. We took two pump shotguns, two 30-30 rifles and a new 243 rifle with a 2 1/2 by 9 power variable scope and plenty of ammo for each gun.

Jim, Tex, Luis, Ramon and the other cowboys, Pepe, who was coming to help with the pack mules, and I each had our own pistol. Jim carried an extra 357 Magnum pistol for Raul. We were armed well enough to start a revolution.

We were up at 6:00 the next morning and on our way to Agua Blanca. Before I realized it, we were over Acapulco. The four hours had passed very fast. In fifteen minutes, we reached our destination. I landed and taxied behind the house, I got out and saw Russ was on short final. I had our fishing gear out when he taxied beside my plane and stopped. We grabbed our stuff and headed for the river.

On my fourth cast, I got results. I really landed about a four pound bass. I have never seen such fishing. I lost all track of time. Jim and Tex joined the fun and we caught fish until our arms ached from reeling them in.

Pepe came to tell us dinner was ready. After we ate, Russ, Tex, and I fished until it was too dark to see our lures. We fished all day Thursday and until noon Friday.

We decided it might be better if Russ flew to Torreon that afternoon. This way, all three of us would not be arriving on the same day.

After Russ had left, I found I was the only fisherman left. I got my reel and rod and headed back to the river. I staggered back to the house after dark, tired and hungry, but happy, and smelling so fishy that all the cats in the neighborhood were squalling and following me.

Jim, Tex, and I were relaxing after dinner, when I happened to think about the metal detector and a few other items that we were not supposed to have in Mexico.

I suggested that Pepe and I leave about 3:30 the following morning and arrive in Torreon at least an hour before the custom officials would be on duty. We couldn't take a chance on losing these necessary items.

I called the hotel in Torreon where we always stayed. Sure enough, Luis and José had just checked in. Luis promised to meet us at the airport by daylight.

It seemed like I had only been asleep a few minutes when Jim started knocking at the door. I looked at my watch. It was 3:00 A.M. Poor Lupe had, at this ungodly hour, gotten up and fixed our breakfast.

We didn't have a thermos bottle, but Lupe found a large

tin cup and filled it with coffee, then gave it to Pepe to carry and hold for me to drink after we took off.

She cautioned Pepe to be sure and not spill it, for without the coffee, I would go to sleep and boom. As she said "boom", she made the sign of the cross.

Poor Pepe carried that coffee like it was nitroglycerin. Pepe didn't say a word during take-off, but when I had reached cruising altitude, I set the auto-pilot and lit a cigarette. He offered me my coffee and told me if I got sleepy to tell him and he would be happy to sing for me.

He kept watching me to see if I was getting sleepy. After finishing my coffee, I pretended to be very drowsy. He started to sing for me. After the first verse, I knew why he was a cowboy. He definitely wasn't in Sinatra's class.

I got him to stop singing and steered the conversation back to his life as a cowboy. He could tell a very interesting story. We reached Torreon before it was light enough to land.

I circled the field for ten minutes before I could see the runway clear enough to land, then taxied up to the terminal. Luis and José were waiting. Everything was going perfectly. We got all the restricted items out of the plane and into the car as quickly as possible. Luis and José took the items to the hotel to hide them.

Pepe and I stayed with the plane so we could close our flight plan. In another thirty minutes, the control tower opened. The customs inspector was very nosy and looked into the plane. It happened that he knew Jim and when he found out we had just come from Jim's ranch, he cooled it. I told him we were going on a hunting trip and Jim would be arriving later today.

It took Luis, and Pepe and José two more trips by car to carry everything from the plane to the hotel. I hired a taxi and we loaded the car and started moving our gear to San Miguel, which was a two-hour drive from Torreon. It took Luis and the taxi all day to accomplish this feat.

Pepe, José, and Raul were sorting out and making up packs in San Miguel. Around noon, Russ and I went to the airport to wait for Jim and Tex. They arrived at 2:30. We went back to the hotel. Luis and the taxi were on their third and final trip.

We decided to wait until morning before leaving for San Miguel. We asked Luis to return to Torreon so we would have transportation in the morning to San Miguel.

At 11:00, someone knocked on my door. Ramon had just arrived from Mazatlan. He spent an hour telling me about his trip to Loreto.

He had personally given Maria the fish with the message inside. Flores, of course, was present, but he didn't suspect a thing and Ramon was sure our plan would work. Furthermore, Ramon, Flores and *El Presidente* had had a few drinks together and were now good friends.

Maria was going to the church with her two younger sisters as Ramon was leaving Loreto. She had timed it just right as the girls walked in front of the truck. She had smiled and nodded her head, so the message had been received and understood.

God, I couldn't sleep for thinking about Maria. Just remembering her beauty, the warmth of her body, and those sweet lips made sleep impossible.

I wasn't too proud of myself when I had to answer my conscience these questions: Was I saving her from Flores because I was a gentleman and doing the right thing? Or, was I doing it for my own need for her? Did I love her enough to give up everything and marry her?

I knew I would never, never, never give up or put anyone ahead of my two sons. Once again I thought of her warmth and love and beauty. There was no right or wrong. Only my love and need for her. I finally drifted off in a restless sleep.

We left Torreon at 5:00 A.M. and arrived in San Miguel at 7:00. José, Raul and Pepe had all the minor details completed, but putting the leather leggings on the horses and mules proved to be one hell of a job.

All the village was present to see the gringos. They were not disappointed, for it took four hours to put the leggings on the animals.

José was very sad that he wasn't coming, but he admitted that in his present physical condition, it was best for him to stay in San Miguel and guard the car.

We didn't take time to eat lunch. We rode very hard. We wanted to be sure to arrive at the old dope raiser's house before dark.

About eight miles from San Miguel, we started seeing the first rattlesnakes. The farther we went, the more snakes we saw. We dismounted to let the horses rest for a few minutes. I kicked over a rock, and beneath it was a big poisonous scorpion.

The other guys started kicking over rocks and under ninety percent of the rocks were scorpions. Raul hadn't exaggerated. It really made cold chills run up a guy's back.

We came within sight of the ranch about 5:30. We knew we were being watched, but we didn't see a soul until we rode up to the largest house.

An old woman and a very pretty girl came out. We said we were looking for an old lost Spanish mine and could we spend the night close to the spring and water our horses and mules.

Luis told her we would be happy to pay for any inconveniences we caused them. The old woman didn't know if her husband would let us stay or not. We rode on down to the spring and under a large mesquite tree. We threw up our tents and put our folding cots inside.

In just a few minutes two men rode up. One was about sixty years old. the other no more than twenty-five. I knew we were about to meet the old dope raiser and one of his sons.

He was the dirtiest and meanest looking bastard I ever saw. We used Luis for an interpreter as if Jim, Tex, and I didn't speak Spanish. The old man was very nasty and impolite. He told us we were on private property and he had not give permission for us to stay.

The old man couldn't keep his eyes off our guns. The old man and his son had guns strapped to their hips also. Their guns, however, were very old. I guessed them to be single action 44's. My pistol was a new 357 Magnum Python. I told Luis to tell the old man I would like to show him my pistol. That softened him up. I extended the pistol to him, butt first.

The old man really warmed up and started looking at the rifles and shotguns. I am sure he had never seen a shotgun or a rifle with a scope before.

He asked Luis if the gringos could shoot, as if we didn't

understand. Luis interpreted the message. Across the valley was a dead mesquite with seven vultures sitting in the branches.

I told Luis to ask permission for me to kill the vultures.

The old man grinned and said, "If the gringo wants to make a fool of himself, tell him to kill them all, for at that distance, it isn't possible."

The old man's name was Rito Moya. We nicknamed him Dopey. Anyway, old Dopey wasn't aware of the latest improvements in Mr. Winchester's product.

With a nine power scope and range finder, I didn't have to guess; those vultures were almost sitting on the end of my rifle barrel. Even though they were almost two hundred and fifty yards away, I sat down in a canvas chair and laid the rifle across a camp table.

I looked up at old Dopey. He was really amused. I told Luis to ask him if he would like a little wager; one hundred pesos for each shot.

"*Si, si,*" he agreed.

I squeezed off the first shot. When that eighty grain bullet hit the vulture, it looked like a feather pillow exploding. I killed two more in two more shots before the other four flew away.

As luck would have it, they flew toward our camp. I looked at old Dopey, his eyes and mouth were wide open in disbelief. I set the rifle down and grabbed one of the pump shotguns. He didn't notice me change guns, or he probably didn't know the difference.

Anyway, when the vultures were about fifty yards away, I opened up on them with the shotgun. I was lucky and killed the other four in four shots.

I thought Old Dopey was going to pass out. He ran his hand over his face and in Spanish said, "I swear before the Blessed Virgin, what I have just seen is not possible." Then he turned to his son and said, "Let's go. We have to tell your brothers what we have just witnessed."

I stepped in front of Old Dopey, held out my hand, and in Spanish, told him to pay up. That I had killed seven of his vultures in seven shots, so he owed me seven hundred pesos.

It seemed he was financially embarrassed and out of ready cash. In that case, I told him we wouldn't pay for the water and camp site.

"Muy bien, *Señor*. You are my friend. My house is your house. For nothing, you may stay as long as you and your friends like."

He started to mount his horse, then came back and shook hands. He said he would like to bring his other three sons to meet me.

We had more food than we could possibly use on the trip, so I invited him and all his family to have dinner with us in two hours. He thanked me and assured me they would be on time. Tex, Luis, and I got busy preparing supper.

We had two gasoline camp stoves and four gas lanterns. We took all three camp tables and placed them end-to-end. We would serve buffet style and started opening cans of pork and beans, frying ham, and potatoes and opening cans of peaches and apricots. I heard Jim say, "Holy hell, here comes Cox's Army."

I looked and here came Old Dopey, leading his clan. Only three of his sons were married, which was enough. Between the three, they had seventeen kids. I counted a total of twenty-seven people. That was more than I had bargained for. I was thankful we had the extra food. Tex said, "I've never seen so many kids!"

He turned and asked Jim, "Why do you reckon they raise such large families?"

"Hell's fire, Tex," Jim replied. "They don't have television to watch at night, and they have to do something until bedtime."

Old Dopey introduced all of his family. When he came to his other sons, he really laid it on. "My sons, I want you to meet *Señor* Mark, the best shot and pistolero that has ever come to Mexico."

Jim gave me a go to hell look. Before he could reply, Old Dopey took over, showing his sons the tree where the vultures had been and how high and fast they were flying. He really did me proud.

The women were very fascinated and impressed with the

gas stoves and lanterns. We were all hungry and really put away the food. About half of our supply, in fact.

After dinner, we sat around, drank coffee and talked for hours. I finally asked Dopey, if we successfully located the old Spanish mine, could we use his airstrip to fly our samples out and not have to pack them all the way to San Miguel.

He agreed that they would move the cactus and mesquite from the runway anytime. Just buzz the house and flash the landing lights four times so they would know we were friends.

I told him if we were successful in finding the old mine, we would like to make a deal with him. If they would let us keep our tents here and watch the horses and mules, we would give them half of the animals. Their eyes really popped open. They didn't hesitate to accept our proposition.

We knew that if we were successful in bringing back the treasure, we would never return and they would inherit everything, which was fine with us.

Finally, Old Dopey mustered all his clan and announced it was bed time. It still took thirty minutes to shake hands with all of them and receive their thanks. We took the lanterns and made a careful search for scorpions and snakes. Then we poured gas in the trench around the tents and set it on fire.

Chapter 27

WE WERE up early the next morning, had a good breakfast, and were packed and ready to move out by 6:00. We knew we had approximately thirty miles to go before reaching the treasure location.

Within an hour after leaving Old Dopey's place, we knew why the natives called this the Jornado del Muerto. Even the animals were afraid, and walked behind each other. I was riding lead, and killed seventeen big rattlesnakes which were directly in our way. I saw many more, from fifty to one hundred feet away from the trail.

The sun was very hot and the fine dust kicked up by the horses' hoofs choked us until we could hardly breathe.

Scorpions were everywhere. I don't see how the horses and mules kept from getting stung. The ground was fairly level and we rode as fast as we could. At noon I motioned Jim to ride along side of me.

"How far have we come?" I asked him.

"I can't be sure," he answered, "but I guess between eighteen and twenty miles. I am sure we have averaged more than three miles an hour."

We rode side by side for another mile or so, then we came to a few scrub mesquite that offered a little shade. We decided to let our horses rest.

We all refilled our canteens from the five-gallon cans of water we were packing and had a good hot drink.

Pepe and Ramon started to get the two mules that were packing our food. Ramon caught his mule without any trouble. But the other mule wouldn't let Pepe get close enough to catch him. The darn mule started to trot and was trying to circle back the way he had come from.

Pepe started running to head it off. He finally got in front of the animal. The mule stopped by an old dead mesquite tree. Pepe reached down and grabbed a dead limp off the ground, drew his arm back to throw at the mule, then started screaming. We all broke and ran toward him.

A scorpion, nesting on the dead wood, had fallen down his shirt collar.

He tore his shirt off and just above his left shoulder I could see the ugly deadly scorpion. It was balled up and stinging him.

It was the biggest scorpion I had ever seen, at least five inches long. Pepe pulled it off, and it stung him again on his hand. He finally slung it loose. Jim stomped it. We carried Pepe back to the shade of the mesquite trees where I set up one of the cots and laid Pepe down.

By this time Tex had the first-aid kit. Tex had been a Navy Medic in World War II.

While in El Paso, we had consulted a doctor on how to handle an emergency like this. I know that within five minutes from the time Pepe was stung, Tex was giving him first aid.

In ten minutes, Pepe's eyes were swollen closed. His tongue was so swollen we could hardly understanding anything he said. The palms of his hands and the bottoms of his feet were swollen round. The poor guy was dying.

He started begging for a priest for confession. This we could not give him. I told him that he and Ramon had been cowboys and compadres for years, and to tell Ramon and let Ramon confess to the priest.

We all stepped back to give him privacy. Ramon bent over him. In just a minute he raised up, his eyes filled with tears. I've had to watch many men die, but never have I seen a man suffer as Pepe did, or any man that fought harder to live. It took four of us to hold him on the cot. Tex was doing his best as a doctor.

I am satisfied that the best specialist in the world could not have saved Pepe. In another ten minutes Pepe stopped breathing. He was fighting so hard to live that his heart actually beat another five minutes after he stopped breathing.

"Well men, what do we do now?" I asked. Jim spoke up and said that Pepe had worked fifteen years for him, and that he had no known family.

"Jim, he was your ranch hand. Ramon, he was your friend and *compadre*. You two decide what we do."

Ramon said, "*Señor* Mark, I do not know what we can do."

Jim said, "We all know how a *compadre* is here in Mexico —like a brother and the closest and dearest friend a man can have. The decision is entirely up to Ramon."

Once again I put it to Ramon. "Well, Ramon, in a circumstance like this, a decision is always hard to make. We are alive and have our future to look forward to. We can do one of two things.

"Take Pepe back to San Miguel for a decent burial, but the way he is swollen, I am afraid fourteen hours tied across a horse would make him burst. Or, we can bury him here in his sleeping bag, and next spring, during the rainy season, when it is cooler, fly to the airstrip at Dopey's place, bring a casket and take him wherever you want him to be buried and have his funeral mass."

Ramon thought for a minute and then said, "Since my *compadre*, Pepe has no family, you are right. We will bury him here."

It didn't take long to dig a grave in the sandy soil. We put Pepe in his sleeping bag and gently laid him to rest. I asked if anyone knew any scripture.

No one spoke up, so I started the Lord's Prayer. They joined in, some in English and others in Spanish, which was all right. I am sure the good man upstairs understood both languages.

As we stood by the newly made grave, I could read everyone's thoughts. First, Carlos, Luis' brother, had been killed in the car wreck when Tex and I were injured. Then Juan, José's brother was murdered by Flores. And now, Pepe. The question now in everyone's mind was who would be next.

"Men, I would like your attention. Each of us has lost loved ones. We have had more dangerous experiences in the past two years than a million men will have in all of their lifetimes. Is gold and a fast dollar worth it? Do we go ahead, or do we turn back?

"I speak for myself only. If Raul will show me where this treasure is, I have no choice but to go ahead."

Raul said, "*Señor*, I show you and I am your servant. Without this treasure, it would be better for me and my family to be there with Pepe. Is awful to see your family cold and hungry. I'll go all the way."

Everyone agreed we would go on and find the treasure. Jim said, "We are a closer group and now we stay together, come hell or high water."

We mounted up and started on our journey. In about three hours Raul rode up beside me, "There, *Señor*," he pointed to a canyon and a peak about three miles ahead of us, "is where the treasure is."

I asked if there was water in this canyon. Raul replied, "I am not sure, but I believe I remember a spring in the next canyon."

We rode on for about a mile to where I could see up this canyon. I saw a few green trees and my horse smelled water. When we got there, it was a nice spring and several cows were there drinking. I cautioned everyone before dismounting to watch for snakes and scorpions. The warning was needless—we wouldn't forget Pepe's fate so soon.

Tex, Luis and I gave the ground a careful inspection. We killed two big rattlesnakes, but didn't find a single scorpion.

I took a five gallon can of gas and burned the ground where we were to pitch our tents. I wasn't taking any chances.

We decided that Raul, Jim and I would take the metal detector and try to locate the treasure caches. While Luis and Tex made camp, Ramon hobbled the horses and mules. I cautioned Tex and Luis that we were no more than three or four miles from Aldama. If anyone came by, they should capture him, and we would do likewise. If word got to Aldama, we were in for a warm reception.

I unpacked the metal detector and checked to make sure it

was working. If we were lucky enough to locate the treasure, we would return and dig it up after dark.

I took a shotgun, the 243 scope rifle, and we took off. First, we went to the entrance to the old mine. Jim volunteered to stand guard outside.

I turned on and calibrated the metal detector. With flashlights in hand, Raul and I entered the old mine. About twenty feet back, one of the side walls had caved in, but the overhead looked solid. We climbed over the cave-in.

About forty feet farther back, the metal detector started working. I made a very strong location, then marked the spot with a stick. It was about three hundred feet to the back of the tunnel, and the metal detector wouldn't work any other place in the mine. I carefully rechecked on the way out.

The only place the metal detector would work was where I had made the first location. I was satisfied. Raul was beaming with happiness. "Si, *señor*, it is as I said." I gave him a nod and a smile, but until I saw the gold, I would not be one hundred percent convinced. A metal detector will work on any metal.

Jim was like a kid. "What did you find? What did you find?" he asked.

"We found something of a metallic substance. If we can make a location close to where Raul is taking us, and where the large cache is supposed to be, then I am completely sold."

Raul pointed across the canyon over the arroyo to a large rock. The rock looked to be about thirty feet long and at least eight feet high. Before we reached the big rock, Raul became excited, remembering having seen the three soldiers shot and killed.

I stopped and dismounted before we reached the rock and recalibrated the detector. "Now, Raul, show me where they buried the boxes of gold."

He rode about fifty feet and pointed beside his horse. "It is very close to here," he said.

The machine started working twenty feet before I got to where Raul was pointing. He was off about ten feet. There was such a large amount buried, I could block it to within six inches of the center of the cache. Once again, I drove a stick in the ground in the center of the location.

"Now, Raul, where did the General bury the jar of jewels?"

"About right there, *Señor*," he pointed. I could get only a very little reading in the machine. Actually a few little clicks in the earphones. I would check all around. Nothing, then at this one certain spot, a very weak reading.

"Jim, if you will keep a close watch, and if you think it's all right, Raul and I will see what's here."

"Go ahead," he replied. "I'll ride down the arroyo and keep both eyes peeled."

All we had to dig with was my Bowie knife and Raul's machete. We would drive our knives in the ground, loosen the soil, and clean out the dirt with our hands. It was a slow go.

We were down about eighteen inches deep. I was ready to stop until we could get a pick and shovel. Raul drove the machete about six inches deep into the ground and I heard the jar break. Raul heard it too, and started scratching the dirt faster than a cat covering up crap on a hot stove. I laid my hand on his shoulder and gently shook him.

"Look, Raul, the jar is broken. We must work very carefully and slowly, or we will cut our hands. Here, take a cigarette. We will calm down and then finish digging it out."

"*Bueno, Señor*," was his only reply.

We had taken only about four puffs each when we threw the cigaretts away. I stepped back and let Raul work by himself. I didn't want to be bent over looking in that hole when he saw the jewels. A lot of good men will go loco when they see a treasure uncovered.

"Look, *Señor*, look," he shouted. The old boy was really excited, but showed no signs of greed or violence. I couldn't believe my eyes. It looked like all the stars in the heavens had fallen in that little hole. I pulled my shirt off, laid it down on the ground by the hole, and told Raul to put all the jewels on the shirt.

I couldn't believe it—diamond rings, bracelets, necklaces, rubies and emeralds. There were enough jewels to fill a gallon jug. They were sparkling like stars.

I finally came back to life and checked to make sure Raul hadn't overlooking anything. I then very carefully wrapped them in my shirt. I helped Raul refill the hole. We then rode down to where Jim was standing.

When he saw me carefully carrying my folded shirt, he knew we had found something. He grinned and asked, "How much was there?"

I didn't want to unroll my shirt for fear of losing part of the jewels, so I told him enough to pay the expenses and would he wait until we reached camp to take a look.

"Sure, sure," he replied. I knew he was disappointed. We hurried on to camp.

They had the tents up and lanterns lit by the time we rode into camp. I went inside one of the tents. No one had said a word when we rode up. I didn't have to ask anyone to come inside. They almost ran over me getting in. I laid my shirt down on the tent floor and got down on my knees.

Not a word was spoken. They all got down on their knees in a circle. We looked like a bunch of crap shooters.

I got to my feet and stopped in the tent entrance. I wasn't fixing to be caught off guard. I looked outside, then back in the tent. Everyone was still down on their knees and staring at the unopened shirt. No one had spoken.

"Well, are you guys going to pray or open the shirt?" Tex unrolled the shirt. I've never heard grown men give out with so many oooh's and ahh's as they did. They all reached at the same time.

I said, "Aw, aw." They jerked their hands back like small children caught trying to snitch cookies. I laughed and that broke the tension. They all started talking at once and looking at the jewels.

"God, Mark, there's a fortune here, ain't there?" Tex asked.

They all chimed in. "How much are the jewels worth?"

"I don't know," I replied. "After you guys are through looking, let's eat!"

"After supper we will try to appraise it all."

Jim said, "You are right and the only one that didn't go crazy as hell. We were sitting ducks."

It didn't take us long to eat, we were all too anxious to get back to the jewels. Raul volunteered to stand guard. The rest of us hurried back inside the tent.

There were twelve beautiful diamond bracelets, about fifty carats each, over two hundred rings, and eighteen necklaces.

I had a twenty power magnifying glass. The stones I looked at were of quality. The rings ran from one up to five carats each. The bracelets were the most beautiful workmanship I had ever seen. They were large diamonds, not chips.

We estimated two thousand and two hundred carats of diamonds, eight hundred carats of beautiful large green emeralds, and three hundred carats of blood red rubies.

I estimated all the jewels to be worth over a million dollars.

Ramon picked up one of the smaller ruby rings and said, "Please, *señor,* may I have this ring?"

"Look, Ramon, when we get out of here, we will keep a few piece of this jewelry for our families and sell the rest."

"Please let me explain, *Señor* Mark. One night Pepe and I were in the house of prostitutes in Chihuahua. This one high-priced girl that we could not afford had a ruby ring smaller than this one. Pepe admired the ring.

"This whore laughed and told Pepe he couldn't even afford to look at such a ring, much less own one. From that day on, Pepe's only wish in life was to own such a ring. He wanted to own a much larger ring than the prostitute had, so he could show her and make her envious."

I handed Ramon the ring and told him. "Tomorrow, or whenever we pass by Pepe's grave, we will re-open the grave and put the ring on his finger."

He started crying. He was so happy, and thanked us over and over.

We decided to cut the cards to see who would stand watch. Since there were six of us, the two drawing high cards wouldn't have to stand watch. The other four would stand two hour watches.

We would leave camp at 4:00 A.M. This would give us time to dig up both treasure locations and pack it on the mules before daylight, while one man stayed at the camp site to take down the tents and have breakfast ready. When we returned, we would eat and be on our way.

Luis and I were the lucky ones. We drew an ace each and wouldn't have to stand watch. Tex woke us at 4:00 A.M. He had a pot of coffee made which we really appreciated.

We drank our coffee and went to round up the mules.

We decided to leave Luis in camp. He would take down and pack the tents and have breakfast ready when we returned.

We mounted and followed Raul. When we came to the old mine entrance, Jim stopped, checked his shotgun and said he would wait and stand guard.

We carefully made our way past the cave-in and to the spot where the metal detector had worked at yesterday. Then Tex and Raul went to work. They had dug down about two feet when they uncovered the first wooden box. We pried off the lid.

Lady Luck was with us again. The gold bars were a welcome sight to our eyes. We all did a little dance of happiness. The third box Tex handed out was lighter than the first two. I opened it. Silver! We opened each box and stacked the gold bars in one pile and the silver bars in another.

We estimated there were between eight and nine hundred pounds of gold and even more silver.

I started packing the saddlebags and tried to put between ninety and one hundred pounds in one side leaving the other side empty. Tex was carrying outside while Ramon and Raul packed the gold on the mules.

They would put the saddlebags on the mules and fill the empty side making each side as uniform in weight as possible. Each mule could carry two hundred pounds.

I followed Tex outside. When he had the last of the gold, I said, ''Let's go.''

''But what about the silver?'' they all asked.

''Look, we only have thirteen more pack mules. Remember, we left three mules in camp to pack our food and water and camping equipment.''

''If Raul remembers right the next cache is the large one. We are leaving the silver so someone will find it. This I want, for whoever finds it will be too afraid to talk. With all the jewels and gold, we don't need it.

"Furthermore, I don't ever want us to be tempted into coming back here. If we leave the silver uncovered, we know it will be found. If there isn't enough gold in the next cache to make a load for all the mules, then we will come back for the silver."

We crossed the arroyo over to the big rock. Ramon and I started digging. We worked very hard and fast. Every five minutes, Tex and Raul would relieve us. We were down about four feet when we hit the first box. The boxes had begun to rot.

I thought we had been lucky before, but this cache was something else. The bars were a different size. There wasn't any silver in the cache. There were three skeletons—those of the soldiers murdered by the General.

When the last bar was out, we divided the gold into thirteen stacks so the weight would be equally divided between the thirteen remaining pack mules.

While Tex, Ramon and Raul packed the mules, I gently placed the three skeletons back in the hole and refilled it. We made a small mound on top of the refilled hole, a marker for the three murdered soldiers.

I did a fast estimate of the gold. From the first cache, we had at least eight hundred pounds of gold. From this one, a minimum of two thousand pounds. Holy Smoke! That came to over a ton and a half. I was figuring avoirdupois, sixteen ounces to the pound, not troy. That made a minimum of fifty thousand ounces.

I knew we could easily get four hundred dollars an ounce. That was easy to figure. We had a minimum of twenty million dollars worth of gold, not counting the jewels. I looked up. Tex grinned and asked how much it all came to. When I answered, all three did a jig for joy.

Ramon and Raul were expert packers and mule drivers. They ran a lead rope through the halters and we were ready to go. The sun was just coming up when we rode up to where Jim was still standing lookout.

He looked first at the heavily-laden mules, then grinned. I grinned back and told him, "Well, Jim, old buddy, we hit the jackpot. There's at least twenty million dollars in gold on those mules."

"Damn, Mark, that's good to hear. I don't mind admitting that I was worried about the damn black leg disease and having my cattle quarantined, and with that mortgage on my ranch, believe me, I am really relieved."

I looked at Tex and winked. I asked Tex if he thought Jim's share of the gold and jewels would come to sixty thousand dollars, the amount of the mortgage on his ranch. Jim turned purple.

"Why, you two." Then he thought of himself, grinned and said, "If it don't come to sixty thousand dollars, maybe you will loan me the balance."

I shook my head and told him, "I can only speak for myself, Jim. I am sorry, I can't. You see, I have a deal with my banker. He won't smuggle gold, and I won't loan money."

Jim spurred his horse. As he ran past me he shouted back over his shoulder. "Go to hell, you cocky little bastard. I smell ham and eggs. Looks like all I'll get out of this deal is the food I eat, and I'll be damned if I am going to get screwed out of that."

When we rode up to camp, Jim was eating. He didn't even look up. Luis had everything packed and ready to go except one table and the coffee pot.

We ate, finished packing and were ready to go by 8:00. I suggested that Jim and Tex take a 30-30 rifle each and scout ahead, leaving the shotguns for Ramon, Luis and Raul.

I would keep the 243 with the scope and stay behind, for if we had trouble it would come from the rear. In this flat level desert valley, and with the scoped rifle, I could estimate a lot of trouble before it could get to Ramon, Luis, and Raul, who would be in the center driving all the mules.

They were very wise, and didn't hurry the mules, for it was a long, hot and tiresome journey. We had no difficulty, but were nine hours getting to where we had buried poor Pepe.

They were all standing around Pepe's grave when I rode up. Jim suggested we make camp and spend the night. The pack mules had to rest.

Chapter 28

WE SPENT a lonesome, but uneventful night and at 6:00 the next morning we had the mules packed and ready to move out. Tex and I got two shovels from a pack. Jim rode on ahead. Ramon handed me the ring. We helped them get the mules started, then Tex and I began re-opening the grave.

It had been a wise decision to bury Pepe as we did. His hand was swollen so bad I could only get the ring to the first joint on his little finger.

It may sound silly, but I had the feeling he could hear me when I said, "Pepe, my friend, you won't lose the ring. I doubt if you and that prostitute are headed for the same place, but if your trails should cross, it is she who will be humiliated this time.

"You now have your life's wish. It's such a small price for your life, and for your share of the wealth we have found." We refilled the grave, broke the handles of the shovels and made a crude cross for Pepe's grave. It wasn't a very pretty cross, but the best we could do at this time.

We would be back and see that Pepe had a decent burial and a last mass. I was very sad to leave him in such a lonesome place all by himself.

Tex and I talked as we followed the pack string. The mules were very tired and our pace was slower than the day before. We decided that Tex, Luis and I should ride on ahead and select a place and put up the tents close to the airstrip where we could taxi a plane to the tent for loading the gold aboard. By camping at the airstrip, we would be farther from old Dopey's house.

At 2:00 we estimated we were about three hours away from the airstrip. The mules were very tired and had to stop and rest every fifteen to twenty minutes. Tex rode on ahead to catch up with Jim. When they were about two miles from the airstrip they would stop and wait for me. At 4:15 I caught up with them. The mules were sure tired.

"Look, men, here's our plan. Tex, Luis and I will take the four mules carrying the camp gear and go ahead. In thirty minutes, you guys follow. We will camp by the airstrip. While Tex and Luis throw up the tents, I'll go to Dopey's house and make sure they don't come to camp before we have the mules unpacked.

"We will erect one tent so it will block the view to the houses. When you all arrive, put the gold in the other tent. I'll explain to old Dopey and his clan that we are almost out of food, then invite them all up for a visit and coffee after supper.

"We will let them know we have a lot of samples. If we invite all of them for a visit, they won't be half as suspicious as they would be otherwise. Agreed?"

Everyone did. Thirty minutes later we arrived at the airstrip and found a good place to pitch the tents where we could taxi a plane up beside them.

I coiuld see old Dopey's clan outside their houses. I took off for my visit. They were all very happy to see me. For once, I took plenty of time and shook hands with everyone.

I informed them we had found a lot of good samples and they now owned half of all the horses and mules. This really put the smiles on their faces.

I noticed Old Dopey's daughter was trying to give me the eye. She was very pretty and about twenty years old. In a very respectful way, I started showing her a lot of attention. This I could see pleased Old Dopey and his wife.

He told one of the boys to bring out the Mescale. Mescale is made from cactus and it takes a real man to drink it. I finally managed to down my drink without gagging. I stepped outside and saw that Ramon had all the horses and mules unpacked and was driving them toward the spring.

I thanked Old Dopey for his hospitality and the drink, and

apologized for our shortage of food, and invited them to have coffee and visit in one hour.

Old Dopey assured me they would be there. I rode to the spring and gave my horse to Ramon. He was very pleased over the way we had so easily got camp set up and the gold concealed inside the tent. I walked back to the camp.

Luis handed me a cup of steaming hot coffee. It really hit the spot. We were all very tired. Everyone, including Jim, was so happy that a can of cold Spam tasted like manna from heaven.

Chapter 29

JUST AT dark, Old Dopey and his clan arrived. We talked for an hour. I finally asked him how far it was to San Miguel. "Well, *Señor,* we have four very tough and fast horses that we can ride from here to there in three and one-half hours in the night when the air is cool."

"Look, *Señor,*" I asked him, "would you rent us three of these horses and let one of your sons go with us to return your horses?" Jim and I would be all night reaching San Miguel on our horses, as tired as they are. I told him we would be happy to pay him four hundred fifty pesos.

He readily accepted our deal and wanted to know what day we wanted to leave. "Now, tonight at 10:00. You see, we have a car in San Miguel. We will drive to the airport in Torreon for our plane and be back here early in the morning."

Dopey didn't understand our hurry and wanted us to stay two or three days to rest and visit. "We would be very happy to, *Señor,* but let me explain. Then you can see the reason we are in such a hurry." I knew how superstitious these backward people were and how they believed in dreams and signs.

I had an idea I thought was funny and would give me the opportunity to pull the best joke on Jim of my entire life. I pointed to Jim. "Do you see the old one there?"

"Only last night he dreamed his wife gave him two beautiful baby blue rabbits. They were fighting each other." All eyes were on me and no one was making a sound. They were so interested in my story. They all nodded their heads in agreement.

"All right," I continued, "the old one there has the most beautiful young wife in all Chihuahua. They are expecting their first baby."

"Humm . . ." Jim said.

I continued, "So you see, two baby blue rabbits fighting each other. For a man of the old one's age, to father a son is quite an accomplishment, but, my friend, two rabbits, can there be any doubt that he has done the impossible. The old one is now the father of twin sons."

They all jumped to their feet and started shouting, "Olé, olé," and clapping their hands. Jim's face turned redder than a turkey gobbler's snout. He threw his hat on the ground. I knew he was about to throw the damdest fit of his entire life. Tex and Luis were laughing and rolling on the ground.

I grabbed Old Dopey's arm, jerked him to his feet and told him, "Look how happy the old one is," Jim was so mad he was jumping up and down. I shoved Old Dopey toward Jim and said, "Quickly, let's congratulate him."

Old Dopey grabbed Jim, gave him a big hug, and started shaking his hand. The rest of his clan jumped up and formed a line like a bunch of G.I. recruits when the C.O. blows his whistle. They were waiting their turn in line to shake Jim's hand and offer their congratulations.

I knew he had about thirty minutes of hand shaking and back slapping coming. I took advantage of the opportunity to head for the coffee pot. As I passed Jim, his arm was going up and down like a pump handle on a wind mill in a forty mile an hour gale. He said it all in one syllable. "Twinboysblue-rabbitsI'llgetyouyoulittlecockybastard."

After all the congratulations, Dopey agreed time was of the essence and sent two of his boys to corral, saddle and bring the three horses to our camp. This decision, I am sure, saved my life. Jim was ready to murder me, and probably would have, but his arm was so tired he couldn't raise it up.

When the horses arrived, I paid old Dopey the four hundred and fifty pesos. In English, I told Tex to play it safe and take turns standing guard all night and we would be back by 8:00 tomorrow morning. I reminded him to have the airstrip clear of the camouflage and cactus, mesquite and animals.

I took the sneaky way out, mounted my horse, and asked Jim if he was ready. "Hummmm . . ." was his only reply. But he got up. I thanked Old Dopey and his clan, said goodnight, and told them we would see them in the morning. I was too tired to shake hands with all twenty-seven of them and waste another thirty minutes.

We rode abreast until we passed the house. I told Jim to go ahead. "Why?" he asked.

"Well, to be honest with you, I am afraid you would shoot me in the back." I couldn't have been more surprised when he laughed. He turned in the saddle still laughing and said, "Mark, that's the funniest thing anybody ever pulled on me. Listen, if you ever tell it on me, so help me, I'll sure as hell murder you."

Old Dopey wasn't so dumb. It was cooler and better traveling at night. At least you couldn't see the snakes and scorpions. We were really exhausted when we reached San Miguel, but we had made good time. It took us three hours and forty minutes. I gave the boy twenty extra pesos to help us locate José. We were too tired to walk. We finally located José and for once, he was sober.

At 2:00 A.M. we were on our way to Torreon. José was driving and very happy over our good fortune. "Now, I am again a rich man, am I not my brother?" I assured him he was.

I then told him about Pepe. He was very sad and I am sure it made him remember his brother, Juan. "Go to sleep, my brother," José told me, "for in the light of day you will need your strength to fly the airplane."

"Look, José we should be in Torreon by 4:00. At 5:30 go and wake *Señor* Russ. Order coffee and food for all of us. Then, come and get me when the food arrives. No later than 6:00 okay?"

I looked in the back seat. Jim was already asleep. Then I passed out. I opened my eyes and realized José was laying me down in the front seat. "What's wrong, José?"

"Nothing, my brother, we are in Torreon, now. Sleep, I'll call you at 6:00."

Russ and José had quite a time waking us. I was so stiff and sore, I could hardly walk. So was Jim. We felt better after having coffee and decided to shave and shower. This really helped.

We went to the airport and decided to file a flight plan to Jim's ranch. We didn't think anyone was suspicious of us, but, if they were, we were going to go in the opposite direction from what they expected.

I took off with Russ following me, and Jim following him. Flying sure beat riding a horse. When I arrived at old Dopey's place, Tex had a big fire built up and the smoke was going straight up. No wind, that was good. I circled the strip real low. It looked all right. I landed and taxied up to the tent. The guys hadn't had any trouble at all. We started loading the plane. It took two men to carry one saddlebag.

In no more than ten minutes, I was loaded. I moved my plane and helped load Russ's plane. Jim landed just as we finished loading Russ's plane. We were lucky and had finished loading the last saddlebag into Jim's plane when Old Dopey and sons arrived.

They couldn't understand why we had brought three planes. I told Tex to tell them anything he wanted to and to be careful until I got back.

I told Russ I would take off and circle the strip until he was in the air. Then for him to circle with me until Jim was off the ground. Should any of us have trouble on take-off, we would land and try to carry all the gold in two planes.

We shouldn't have any trouble. Russ and I had twelve hundred pounds each and Jim eight hundred pounds. I taxied to the end of the dirt strip and looked closely for holes or big rocks. I didn't see either.

I started my take off about half way down the strip. I glanced at the speed indicator—forty eight miles an hour. I went about eight hundred feet further and looked at the speed indicator again—seventy miles an hour. I held it on the ground another three hundred feet and pulled the nose up. I came off the ground like a bird and there was at least three hundred feet of strip I didn't use. I knew the other guys would not have any problem, barring the unexpected.

I continued to climb out and started to circle the field. I

saw Russ start his take-off. He and Jim both got off without any trouble.

I got them both on the radio and asked if they were ready to head for Agua Blanca. They were. I headed south. In two hours and forty minutes I was at the ranch in Agua Blanca. Jackie, Lupe and Carmen literally swarmed all over the plane. I assured them their husbands were fine. I didn't mention poor Pepe. There would be time to explain later. I talked to the girls until Russ landed.

I told Russ to wait for Jim and they could unload his plane and Jim's, and hide the gold wherever they thought best. I was in a hurry to get back to Old Dopey's and get the guys safely away from there as soon as possible.

Chapter 30

ON THE flight back to Old Dopey's I had a hard time staying awake. When I landed and taxied up to the tents, I could see Old Dopey and three of his sons were having an argument with Tex and the other guys. I got out and asked what was wrong.

Old Dopey was very suspicious over us bringing in three planes and wanted us to pay him fifty thousand pesos (over four thousand dollars) for the use of the airstrip. We all knew he was getting all the mules and horses and camping equipment, about thirty five hundred dollars worth, which wasn't hay.

"Look," I told him, "I thought we were friends and had made a deal. We are giving you half of the mules and horses. What more can you ask?"

Old Dopey wasn't any fool. "*Señor,*" he said, "this offer is too generous and three airplanes, I think you don't carry out the samples of the rocks, but something very valuable. Maybe gold and silver from a treasure, no? I think me and my sons have been made the fools. And now, we look in your camp."

I had left my pistol in the plane. All the shotguns and rifles were on a camp table about five feet away from me. I could see trouble coming. I asked Tex in English if the shotgun was loaded and a shell in the barrel.

"It sure is," he replied. Old Dopey and his sons had spent all their lives practicing with guns, and they were tough and not afraid of anything or anyone, or they wouldn't be in the business they were in and live in this tough God forsaken place. I had to get that shotgun in my hands.

"Sorry you feel that way my friend," I told him. "Go ahead and search the camp. I am going to have a cup of coffee."

He had expected me to refuse, and I was gambling my life that it would take two seconds for him to make up his mind. I turned and took two steps which put me even and beside the table.

I reached high and slow with my left hand like I was reaching across the table for a cup. I saw the old man's eyes follow my left hand. My right went around the shotgun stock, my finger pushed off the safety and was on the trigger when Dopey realized what was happening.

Very fast, with the shotgun in my right hand, I pushed it up and in his belly. He still made his move for his pistol and had his pistol out of the holster when the shotgun barrel punched him in his stomach.

I started to pull the trigger. He realized he was beat and dropped the pistol like it was red hot. He shouted, "No, no, my sons, this man is more dangerous than a scorpion."

The old man wasn't a coward. There was no fear in his eyes or face whatsoever. His only concern was for his sons.

I told Tex and Luis to get their pistols. Two of the boys had rifles. I told Old Dopey for him and his sons to sit down on the ground. He shook his head.

I faked him and made a half step, and pretended I was going to kick him in the balls. He dropped his hands to catch my foot. I popped him on the side of his head with the shotgun barrel. Not hard enough to knock him out, just enough to let him know we meant business.

I told Luis and Raul to load everything we had to carry into the plane, including Old Dopey's and his sons' guns. We couldn't afford to have them shooting at us while we were taking off.

Tex said he would throw everything we couldn't carry into the tents, and burn them. I agreed we should destroy everything we could because we didn't want to leave Old Dopey any more than we had to. I would have liked to have gotten the mules and horses out, for, the way Old Dopey had acted,

I hated to leave him anything.

Luis shouted that everything was in the plane and ready to go. I told Tex to get the 243 with the scope. I handed Luis the shotgun and told Tex that when Ramon, Raul and I were on the plane, and I had both engines started, to have the old man and his sons get up and run for their houses. When they were about half way between the airstrip and their house for Luis to throw a match on both tents and then run like hell for the plane.

I started both engines. Tex motioned for the old man and his boys to take off, which they did. Tex and Luis set fire to the tents. Luis came running, with Tex right behind him. I started taxiing to the strip while Tex closed the door.

I hit the runway. A rolling fire wailed it, and we got off the ground as fast as possible. Tex looked at me and grinned. "Lucky again, eh Mark?"

"We sure were, Tex, that's one of the most dangerous men I've ever met."

I headed for Torreon to let Ramon off. José was waiting for us at the airport.

I decided to take José with us to the ranch and let Raul go in the car with Ramon. They would go to Mazatlan so Ramon could get his truck and load of fish and go to Loreto.

This was Wednesday. They would have to hurry to make the entire round by Friday.

I cautioned both Ramon and Raul on how little time we had and reminded Raul to have the car at the airport in Durango and full of gas. At 10:00 Friday, I would take the car and be within three miles of Loreto for my rendezvous with Ramon at 2:00, if he was successful in getting Maria out of the village. We shook hands and took off.

When we landed at the ranch, Russ had already left for El Paso. I was sorry I didn't get to thank him and tell him goodbye.

As tired as we all were, no one wanted to sleep. We sat up and talked for hours over our good fortune.

We showed the girls the jewelry. Being women, they couldn't resist asking if they could each keep a part for themselves. We told them after all the waiting and worrying they had gone through, they were certainly entitled to select whatever they wanted.

I was surprised all three women selected a ring containing a diamond no larger than two carats.

Jim heaved a sigh of relief. "Damn, we got off lucky. I was afraid they would pick on one of those expensive bracelets."

We all slept late. I finally thought of all the good fishing I was missing. It was quite a decision—to get up or stay in bed. I decided to go fishing.

José was the only one who would go with me. When we reached the river, I wanted to instruct him on how to cast. He watched me make a cast, and I caught a fish on the third cast. Then I handed him the rod and reel and he wound it in.

"No more instructions are needed. I now know everything about this fishing, my brother." I started walking up the river and looked back as José attempted to make his first cast. Instead of snapping the lure out, he raised the rod high and above his head and bent his arm back until the tip of the rod almost touched the ground behind him.

José pressed the release on the reel and the lure fell on the ground. I don't know why, but he hesitated and removed his thumb from the release. Then he attempted to cast. He brought the rod over his head like a widow woman chopping wood.

He screamed, jumped straight up, and started doing a dance that would have made an Indian medicine man purple with envy. I could plainly see what had happened. The lure had come straight up and caught him in the seat of his pants.

I started to laugh. It wasn't funny to José. He screamed again, "Do not laugh, but come quickly, my brother. From where I feel the pain, I think I have caught my own ass."

I bent José over, but I couldn't hold him and remove the lure. I opened my knife and cut the entire seat of his pants out and could see three of the hooks were firmly fastened where José thought they were. Luckily, the barbs were just under the skin.

I told him to lie down on his stomach. I straddled him and finally got the hooks out. José made more noise than a stud horse in a tin barn.

The lure with the seat of José's pants still attached will always be mounted in my den. Regardless of how blue I may be, I am sure that I will only have to glance at this trophy to laugh.

We sat down and had a cigarette. I should have said, I sat. José smoked kneeling.

"Come, José, let me teach you to cast."

I demonstrated the reel and took his arm and showed him how to cast. He finally caught on. Once again, I started up the river. I looked back. José was holding the rod well away from his body. He wasn't taking any more chances. I had only gone a short distance when I heard José shout, but this time he had caught a fish.

Later, José came to where I was fishing. He had caught seven nice bass, each weighing from two to six pounds and he was very happy. He kept every one he caught. He couldn't understand my releasing every fish I caught.

I finally convinced him we kept only what we wanted to eat. The fish started hitting. We didn't take time off for lunch.

The time passed so fast, we didn't realize it was late evening. Jim and Tex finally came and told us that dinner was ready and we had missed lunch.

The girls had a very delicious meal waiting. After dinner, José and I went straight to bed. Serious fishing is the hardest day's work a man can do.

I had expected to lie awake and worry about tomorrow, for tomorrow, Friday, was "D" day. If everything went as we had planned, I had no worries. If Flores became suspicious and followed Maria, then this could be his last night on this earth—or mine.

I hadn't told Jim and the others, but I was going alone. This was a personal thing between me and Flores, and I didn't intend to jeopardize anyone else's life. I had no fear of Flores if only I had an even break. I knew he was cruel and tough, also a coward, so this made him even more dangerous.

I was willing, if necessary, to die tomorrow to get Maria away from Flores and the suffering she would have to endure all of her life. I didn't intend to fail. I was sure Flores was willing to die to keep her.

I guess Jim and Tex shared my feelings. They both came to my room and sat down on the side of my bed. Jim had a double shot of bourbon in a glass. "Here, drink this, you cocky little bastard and go to sleep."

"Thanks, Jim, I don't want it. Tomorrow I want my eyes to be more sure and my hands more steady than they have ever been."

I went right to sleep and didn't get up until 7:00. As always, everyone else had eaten breakfast, but they joined me for coffee. I would have to hurry to be in Durango by 10:00.

"I want to say something before I take off," I began. "Now listen and don't argue. This is my personal affair. I am not going to have someone killed over my private life. This is it. I am going alone.

"I don't anticipate any trouble. We have all suffered many hardships for the fortune we have. If I don't return, promise me you won't under any circumstances come looking for me. I will be beyond help. Just see that my two sons have my share. Also, don't forget Carlos' family.

"Get a good lawyer to set up a trust fund for Raul and Juan's families, so they will be well cared for each month, so the children's education will be secure and be sure you do the same for my brother José." I wanted to be sure the whores didn't get to José again.

"Be careful selling the gold. Now, José, go get me one pump shotgun and the rifle with the scope, and four boxes of shells for each gun."

They all started arguing and protesting that I wasn't going alone.

I walked out to the plane. Everyone followed me. José put the guns and ammunition into the plane, then embraced me. He was shaking from fright. Tears were running down his cheeks. "Be careful, my brother, I go now to the church and light the candle and pray for your safe return.

"And if you see that son-of-a-bitch Flores, kill him fast and tell him nothing."

"Don't worry, José, I'll be all right. Remember what I promised you."

"Yes, my brother, may God grant you the favors you asked."

I shook hands with Luis and Tex. Instead of shaking Jim's hand, I embraced him. He put both arms around me. Lupe understood Jim's feelings toward me. She started crying.

Jim asked Lupe what the hell she was crying about, then he realized we were embracing each other. He gave me a little push back and said, "What the hell is the matter with you, Mark? Turn me loose. The very idea of us hugging each other. People will think we're too damn queers."

I got in the plane and started both engines. Jim came running over to the plane, jerked the door open, and shouted. "You be careful or I'll stomp your skinny butt when you get back."

"Get out of the way you old helpless bastard." I told him. He threw his hat on the ground and started stomping it. I knew he was cussing up a storm.

As I took off, I looked at everyone and waved. Jim stopped and waved, then started stomping his hat again. No one could say Jim Dunlap was soft.

Chapter 31

AT 9:58, I was over Durango. Five minutes later on the ground, I headed for the control tower. Raul came running from the parking lot to meet me. He assured me everything was going as planned. The car was serviced and ready to go.

I told him to sneak the guns and ammunition out of the plane and into the car while I closed my flight plan.

I went back to the car and cautioned Raul to be very careful on his return trip to Agua Blanca and to go back over the mountain to Mazatlan and down the coast.

"Remember, Raul, when I get back, if I have the *Señorita* Maria, you drive slowly toward Mazatlan until Ramon catches up with you. Then you all stay together and come straight on to the ranch at Agua Blanca. While I am gone, don't admit to anyone that you know me or know the pilot of this plane. If I am not back here by 10:00 tomorrow morning, you go to the bus station and take the 10:30 bus to Mazatlan and go on alone to Agua Blanca. Do not wait for me or Ramon. Understand?"

As we shook hands, Raul said, "*Señor* Mark, on this day may God give you the eyes, ears, nose and cunning of the coyote."

I headed for the rendezvous with Ramon. I wouldn't let myself think. I had to drive very fast to keep from being late. When I came to the old road where I turned off to go to the small village and on to Loreto, I stopped, checked, and made sure both the rifle and shotgun were loaded and put all the shells on the seat beside me.

As I passed through the little village, I looked very close to see if I recognized anyone. Very few people were on the streets. I looked at my watch. It was 11:50. I would sure have to hurry to be on time if I was to meet Ramon at 2:00.

At 1:45 I was within five miles of the little mountain that you had to go around to reach Loreto. I drove on another three miles and knew I was less than two miles from Loreto.

I turned the car around, got out, and laid the rifle over the top of the car. Watching the road toward Loreto, I could see all the way to the mountain through the high powered scope. There wasn't anyone on the road. At 2:15, I was really getting worried. Ramon was late. Another ten minutes slowly passed. I had really started sweating. Five more minutes passed and the red pickup came around the end of the mountain.

When the truck was within a mile of me, I could see the driver, but no one was on the other side. I watched until the truck was within three hundred yards of me. I could recognize Ramon. He was all alone.

He stopped about ten feet from the back of the car. I ran toward the truck as he started getting out. "What happened, Ramon? Where is Maria?"

Before he could answer, I saw Maria raise her lovely head up. She had been lying flat on the seat in case they met anyone. I ran around the truck. Maria flew into my arms. She was so frightened she couldn't speak.

I picked her up in my arms and carried her to the car. "Everything all right?" I asked Ramon.

"*Si, Señor*, as far as I know, no one is suspicious. I had to have an extra drink with Flores before I could leave. That is the reason I am late."

"That's good, Ramon. We have at least a fifteen minute start and we probably have longer. Now listen carefully. They can't overtake us with the start we have. You take the rifle and shells. If you have any trouble, shoot first and then ask questions.

"If I reach Durango safely, Raul will take the car and start driving toward Mazatlan. He will drive slow. When you overtake him, both of you come on to the ranch at Agua Blanca.

"Check by the airport in Durango. If my plane isn't there,

you will know I have safely reached the airport and taken off.''

Once we were in the car, Maria was still so scared she was shaking. I didn't know if she really was scared or what was wrong.

"Maria, darling, are you sure you want to go with me, or do you want to return to your home?"

"Please, Marek, let's go quickly. We are so close to escape. Of course, I am sad to leave my family, but I had rather be dead than have to marry Flores, when it is you I love."

She crossed the seat and put both arms around my neck. "Oh, my Marek, I have waited so long. Now we have each other. Please hurry before they come and take me back." I took off like a turpentined dog.

We had gone only about four miles when we crossed an arroyo. The road was full of pack burros. I had to stop until the two men got the burros out of the road. Both men were from Loreto. Of course, they recognized Maria and me.

It would take the two men at least two hours to reach Loreteo. Then all the village would know I had eloped with Maria, and her parents would know that she was safe with me.

I made sure the shotgun was close at hand before we reached the highway. We both breathed a sigh of relief when we reached the highway and no one was in sight. Once on the highway and headed toward Durango, Maria got over her fright and realized we were safe. She became excited and started planning our life together.

I have never seen a woman so happy, and I've never had a woman to show me so much tenderness, love, and affection. It was very hard to keep my mind on driving with all the love and kisses I was receiving.

At 5:30, we arrived at the airport in Durango. Raul came running to meet us. He was so excited over our successful trip to Loreto that he was talking gibberish. I gave him the shot gun and told him to stay at the car and make certain that no one tried to stop us from taking off. Once we were off the ground, he was to leave at once for Mazatlan and drive slowly. Ramon should catch up with him in about an hour.

I took Maria's hand and we ran toward the plane. I didn't intend to file a flight plan for Flores would probably check the airport.

I got in and helped Maria into the plane. This was her first ride. I helped her fasten the seatbelt and started the engines. Then looked toward the control tower. No one was in sight.

I didn't turn on the radio or try to contact the tower. I ran up and checked out. As I taxied to the runway, I looked up and both ways. I couldn't see any other planes approaching for a landing. I didn't slow down when I reached the runway, just kicked the left rudder enough to get the plane headed straight down the runway, and fire-walled all throttles.

After easing the plane off the ground and raising the gear, I looked at Maria. She smiled, pulled my head toward her, kissed me and laughed. She wasn't the least bit afraid, and was actually enjoying the ride.

I held the nose up until I reached eleven thousand and five hundred feet and then pulled back to seventy-five percent power, trimmed out and set the auto pilot.

I reached over and unfastened Maria's seatbelt and took her in my arms. This was one flight I didn't get sleepy on.

It seemed only minutes until I saw the ocean which was probably a good thing, for I couldn't take many more of Maria's kisses. I was wondering if a woman had ever lost her virginity in an airplane.

The sun was just setting when I sighted the ranch. We were about three miles from touch down when I saw several small objects leave the house and hurry toward the landing strip. I knew all my friends had put in a very anxious and waiting day.

When we landed, Jim, Tex, Luis and José helped Maria out of the plane. She and José were overjoyed to see each other. Jim took Maria by the arm and escorted her over to meet Lupe, Jackie, and Carmen. "Any trouble?" Tex asked.

"None," I replied.

José was disappointed and said, "I am happy and my prayers have been heard, that you are safe. But my brother, I had hoped you could tell me that son-of-a-bitch who murdered my other brother was now dead and in hell where he belongs.''

"Easy, José, he will be. Just a little while longer, Okay?''

"As you say, my brother. I know the promise you made, and I know always you keep the promise.''

The girls took charge of Maria and headed for the house. Jim came over but didn't say a word. I knew he was dying of curiosity over what had happened. Luis spoke up and said, "Let's all go in the house.''

When we entered the dining room, everyone shouted, "Surprise!'' They had a beautiful table set and a nice selection of liquor. I also noticed the candles that were almost burned down to the holder.

I realized a lot of prayers had been prayed for our safe return. Jackie started pouring drinks. "A toast to our new friend, Maria, and to Mark.''

Jim came over and started talking to Maria. Finally he couldn't stand the suspense any longer. He grabbed me by the shoulder, "What happened Mark? What happened?''

"None of your damn business, Jim,'' I replied, "and if I didn't like you, I wouldn't even tell you that much.''

Fortunately, Jackie was standing beside Jim. She handed him another drink. He tossed it down and told Maria they were all happy to have her, but be damned if he would have anything to do with the cocky little bastard. He pointed at me and crossed to the other side of the table. We all sat down for dinner.

I looked across the table and asked Jim to give the blessing. The surprise of my life was when the bowed his head. I am sure it's the first time in his life he ever said the blessing, and I don't know how high a mark his prayer got since he kind of spoiled it at the end. Maybe the good Lord was so surprised he didn't hear, anyway. Jim bowed his head and cleared his throat.

"I thank you Lord for bringing our loved ones back safe so we can enjoy this food together. Amen.'' And in the same breath he added, "What in the hell is the matter with you, Lupe? Pass me one of them God damn tortillas.''

After dinner, the men went to Jim's room for another conference. Once again, we were almost broke. This time it was different. We had a fortune in gold and jewels, but we had to raise expense money to sell our treasure.

Tex came up with a good idea. "Why don't we call your old friend, Ray White, in Mazatlan, who bought the silver. He might be interested in buying the gold."

An hour later I finally got a call through to him. We visited for a few minutes on the phone, then I told him that the old gentleman who had the silver also had some gold to sell.

"Are you interested?" I asked.

"Sure thing," he replied. But ten thousand pesos or four hundred dollars was his top price.

"How much has he got?" he asked. He whistled when I told him two hundred ounces.

"Look," I told him, "I can't fly to Mazatlan and land at the airport and take the gold out of my plane in broad daylight."

"I know, Mark," he replied. "How do you want your money?" he asked.

"In pesos, the same as when you bought the silver," I replied.

"All right, where are you?"

"In Torreon," I told him, for we didn't want anyone to know where our hideaway was.

"All right," he agreed, "let's do it this way. There is a little dirt strip that I use on the river Paxlia, below the little village of San Ignacio. San Ignacio is only forty miles north of Mazatlan. You can't miss it." He gave me directions to San Ignacia.

"I'll be at the bank when it opens in the morning, get the money, and go straight to this little airstrip. I should be on the ground no later than 10:00. You can see my plane easily. Okay?"

"Okay," I agreed, "and be sure to bring your scales. I will be there at 10:00."

I hung up and told the guys that we were back in business. Although we were taking a beating for the gold was worth more than four hundred dollars an ounce.

We went to the garage where Jim had buried the gold about twelve inches deep. We dug down and tried to take out as close to twenty pounds as we could estimate. Tex laughed and said, "Just look, you can't even miss what we took."

"How are we going to go about selling the rest of this?" Tex asked. We finally agreed our best bet was to go back to Tegucigalpa, Honduras to the bank where Snider had sold the gold that he stole from us. We knew this market existed, and best of all, we were not violating the U.S. laws.

Jim had an idea and asked why we didn't call his banker, *Señor* Padilla in Chihuahua City and get him to help us with the transaction, and meet us in Tegucigalpa the following Monday. Today was Friday. Since we had nine days delay, he suggested that half of us go to Acapulco for four days.

The other half would remain at the ranch and guard the treasure. Then we would return to the ranch and take our turn guarding the treasure while they spent their four days in Acapulco. We all went for this idea.

We went back into the house. The girls had been so busy talking and hovering over Maria I don't think we had even been missed. I took Maria's hand and led her out in the patio. "Which of all the girls do you like best, Maria?"

"Oh, Marek, they are all so wonderful to me, but Lupe, the wife of Jimmy is my favorite."

"Well, the reason I asked you, Maria, is that early in the morning Jim and I have to fly for awhile. But, we should be back here by 1:00. Then Jim, Lupe, you and I are going to Acapulco for four days vacation. You will have to buy yourself a lot of pretty new clothes."

She threw her soft, warm, lovely arms around my neck, pressing her firm breasts hard against my chest.

I had never held her so close before. I didn't dare kiss her. "Look, Maria, there are many people here. We have to keep their respect. We cannot torture ourselves this way. Let's go back where the others are. Tonight you sleep here in my room. José and I will go to the little hotel in the village. Tomorrow is another day in Acapulco."

Before entering the room, I put my hand in my pocket like a little school boy on his first date. After all, I couldn't afford to pop all the buttons off the front of my trousers in public.

I helped Maria into her chair and told Lupe that José and I

were going to the village hotel to spend the night, but we would be back for breakfast at 6:30, and please show Maria to my room. I bent over and gave Maria a goodnight kiss, and then told everyone else goodnight. "Let's go, José." He didn't understand.

"But, my brother, we go to such danger to get *Señorita* Maria here from Loreto and you are not going to . . ." I got my hand over José's mouth before he could finish, raised him up and walked him out of the room. Once outside, I released him.

"I don't understand, my brother." Then José smiled and said, "I do understand. You are the coyote and will sneak in the senorita's room later."

"Wrong, José. We are going straight to the hotel."

José smiled again, put his arm around me and said, "Now, I understand. We are going to have another party, music, tequila and women. What a surprise."

"Wrong again, José. We are going to the hotel and go to sleep. I have to fly tomorrow. When the right time comes, I'll know what to do about the señorita."

"*Quien sabe?*" was his only reply.

I rented a room with two beds. The clerk promised he would be sure and call us at 6:00 A.M. I had been under so much tension and strain the past week that I was afraid I would sleep so soundly that José might decide to sneak out for a bottle and a girl.

I decided to play it safe and made sure that José saw me put my pistol under my pillow. Then I told him, "Look, José, whatever you do, don't go near the door tonight. You know how nervous I have been for the past week. If I hear a noise at the door, I would probably start shooting. I would be so sad if I made a mistake and shot you while I was still half asleep."

"But my brother, what if I need to go to the bathroom?" José's bed was by the window. Almost all the houses in Mexico have large iron bars over the windows just like a jail to keep people out. This window also had bars. I knew José couldn't get out through the window.

"Look," I told him, "play it safe and use the window, okay?"

I will always believe the little ugly bastard had planned on sneaking out. "But, my brother, the hotel man will be very mad if I pee into the window."

"I know, José, but which is better—the hotel owner to be mad or you full of holes?" This convinced him. "Goodnight, my brother, don't worry, I use the window." I told José goodnight and assured him he had made a wise decision. In five minutes the old boy was snoring up a storm.

For once, I couldn't go to sleep and I couldn't keep from rubbing my hands over the dents in my chest where Maria's beautiful firm breasts had been. I was panting like a fresh sheared sheep in a wool basket.

I would smoke a cigarette and get back to the boiling point, then I would forget and rub my hand across my chest and there I would go again. It seemed I went through this ritual all night.

I guess I finally dozed off for José awoke me telling me not to shoot, that it was the desk clerk at the door and already it was 6:00 and time to get up.

When José and I arrived at the ranch, Lupe, Carmen and Jackie were very busy. For once, they had overslept. While Lupe finished preparing our breakfast, we went and loaded the gold into the plane.

I asked Lupe where Maria was. "She is still asleep. Do you want to see her before you go?" I did, but thought it best to let her sleep.

Luis and Tex volunteered to stay at the ranch and watch the treasure, while Jim and I delivered the gold. As we were getting into the plane, José asked if he could go.

I told him to get in for we had plenty of room and no weight problem. Jim called Lupe and told her to be sure that she and Maria had everything packed and ready to leave for Acapulco the minute we got back.

On the flight to Mazatlan, Jim and José kidded me umercifully. I ignored them, so they started arguing like two kids.

At 9:50, I was over San Ignacio and spotted a small plane about five miles in the direction Ray had said the airstrip was. When this plane started descending, I followed it down.

Before it landed, I passed on the right side. It was Ray, for he dipped his wings and continued his descent. I circled and landed right behind him.

We didn't waste any time. We estimated the gold to be eight hundred fine, then weighed and transferred all of the gold to his plane.

The gold came to one million eight hundred forty-four thousand and eight hundred pesos. I didn't take time to count the money, just the packs containing fifty thousand pesos each, for one million eight hundred forty-four thousand and eight hundred pesos is a lot of pesos.

We shook hands and took off for Agua Blanca. We had been on the ground only ten minutes.

Chapter 32

AT 11:50, we were back at the ranch. Lupe and Maria came running to meet us. Maria put her arms around my neck and gave me a big kiss. With one arm around Maria and my other hand in my pocket, we went in the house.

The girls had lunch ready and wanted to eat before we left for Acapulco, so they could start shopping as soon as they arrived there. After lunch, I asked Jim, Tex, Luis and José to come with me to my room. We had to divide the money.

We decided to put fifty thousand dollars in a kitty for expenses. Tex, Luis and José only wanted eight hundred dollars each and wanted to credit the balance of their shares on the books. I asked permission to take six thousand dollars.

I had to buy Maria some clothes and send my sons some money. Jim spoke up and said, "Let's fly up in my plane. I need a hundred hour check, and I can get this done in the next four days."

We told José to drive the car to Acapulco and gave him the name of the motel where we would be staying. Tex told us not to worry, and he would call us if we were needed. He would also give us a call as soon as Ramon and Raul arrived.

When we landed in Acapulco, Jim taxied down to the Cessna dealer to have the plane serviced. The girls and I took a cab for downtown. I would drop them off for their shopping and go on to the motel and register.

I gave Maria one thousand dollars. She didn't want to take it. "Is too much money, Marek. I only need very little clothes."

"Look," I told her. "you buy anything you want." Jim

had forgotten to give Lupe any money so I gave her four hundred dollars.

I had the cab take me by Western Union, wired my sons one thousand dollars and went to the motel. This was a very nice motel and it was right on a beautiful beach.

I got four rooms, one for Jim and Lupe, and one each for José, Maria, and myself. I wanted Maria so much I would have sold this soul of mine to the devil to have her. But, I also would have to live with my conscience afterward.

She was too beautiful, young and innocent for me to have until I got tired of Mexico and had to return to the States, only to cast her aside.

I decided to go for a swim while waiting for Jim and José to arrive. I had been at the beach about an hour when Jim came.

In another thirty minutes, José arrived. He had met Ramon and Raul on the highway. They were on their way to the ranch. José announced he was ready to start his vacation.

"All right," I told him, "but listen, if you get drunk, do so in your room. And if you want a muchacha, take her to your room and register her at the desk as your wife.

"José, if you don't do exactly as I say, I'll send you back to the ranch and see to it that you never have another drink, or woman as long as you live. Furthermore, if you bring a girl to your room, don't try to impress her and tell her where you are from, and above all, don't mention the treasure and pretend you don't know *Señor* Jim and me if we meet. Savvy?"

"Si, savvy, my brother. It will be as you say."

José took off. He would have a never-to-be-forgotten drunken party, and some lucky prostitute would hit the jackpot.

Jim and I went back to the hotel, dressed and got ready to take Maria and Lupe to dinner when they returned from shopping.

We waited for awhile, then decided to play rummy to pass the time until the girls came. By 5:00, Jim had started worrying and growling. I am not an authority on women, but I know that when two women with money go shopping, they lose all track of time. An hour later, the girls walked in.

From all the packages they had, they hadn't wasted a

minute on their shopping spree. We helped them into their room. Jim started complaining that he was hungry and he was ready to go eat.

Naturally, the girls would have to have time to dress and put on their new outfits. "Come on, Mark," Jim said, "let's go to your room and finish our rummy game."

"Just a moment, Yemmey," Lupe said. She counted out two hundred dollars and told Jim to give me two hundred dollars more. Jim wanted to know what for.

Lupe told him. "You forget to give me money to shop, and Mark gave me four hundred dollars. I am sorry, but I spent two hundred dollars."

Jim really threw a fit. "Damn it, Lupe, at this rate in another thirty years, and in my old age, I'll be broke and we'll have to beg for a living."

"Stop your griping," I told Jim. "If you can't afford new clothes for Lupe, I'll be happy to forget about the two hundred dollars."

Jim really blew up, stuck his finger in my face and shouted. "Let me tell you something, you cocky little bastard, I am quite capable of supporting myself and Lupe."

"Well, Jim, I was hoping you felt that way," I held out my hand and told him. "Since you are such a gentleman, and insist on meeting your obligations, pay up or shut up."

He started growling and muttering, but counted out the money. He then asked me if I expected interest on the money. "Well, Jim I think that five pesos would be reasonable." He jerked a five peso bill out of his pocket, slapped it in my hand, and told Lupe to hurry and get dressed before he starved to death.

Jim and I went to my room. As we sat down at the table, he asked me if I knew how to play pitch. "I should," I told him. "I invented the game."

"We'll see about that. How about playing for fifty pesos a game, and fifty pesos every time you are set on your bid?"

"That's fine with me, Jim, but I always hate taking candy from a child."

"Is that so?" he said. "Here, let me deal those damn cards."

I got lucky and won three straight games and set his bid four times for a total of three hundred fifty pesos or fifteen dollars. "Had enough?" I asked.

"Hell, no," Jim replied. "Any damn fool can get lucky. Shuffle 'em up and we'll play another game."

Before I could deal, Lupe came in, ready for dinner. She certainly looked swell in her new outfit. "Doesn't Lupe look lovely?" I asked Jim.

"She shore as hell does," he replied.

Jim pulled Lupe down on his lap and actually gave her a kiss. If you call touching lips a kiss. Lupe blushed. I guess I did too, for I had never seen Jim show Lupe this kind of affection before.

Lupe was so happy she threw both arms around Jim's neck and really gave the old boy a big long kiss. He seemed to like it. When Lupe raised her lips from his, he pushed her off his lap and said, "Now, Lupe, stop that damn foolishness. This ain't no time to get romantic, as hungry as I am."

I had to laugh. Jim's face turned red, but before he could have a fit, there was a knock on the door. When I opened the door, there stood Maria in a light green dress.

I've been a few places and seen a few women in my life, but Maria was the most beautiful woman I've ever seen. King Solomon's reign was a few years before my time, but if the Queen of Sheba was as beautiful as the legend claims she was, I don't blame the good king. Hell's fire, I wasn't a king, prince, or even a potentate, just an average man. But no queen or princess was ever as beautiful or desirable as Maria. I would have given up any throne in the world for her love.

My arms were aching to hold the warmth and beauty of Maria. I guess Jim read my thoughts. He took Lupe by the arm, pushed me aside and reached for Maria's arm. "Stop this nonsense and let's go eat. Damned if a man wouldn't starve to death waiting for all of you to get over your romantic ideas."

Jim wasn't a king, but he will never know how close he came to getting crowned. I almost lowered the boom on him before I caught myself. I took Maria's hand and opened the front door of the car. I wanted to drive because I didn't trust myself to touch or hold her.

We went to a very nice restaurant, had a cocktail, and while our orders were being prepared, Lupe and Maria excused themselves and went to the powder room.

Jim said, "Mark, I've never told you this before, but Maria is the most beautiful woman I've ever seen in my entire life."

"I agree with you, Jim, but I can't take advantage of her beauty and innocence and then just discard her like an old shoe. I am going to send her to school or buy her a little business. I couldn't ever live with myself if I hurt her.

"I want to ask a favor, Jim, will you sleep in the room with me tonight, and let Lupe and Maria stay together. I don't trust myself, and I don't want to hurt Maria. But I will hurt her, I'm afraid, if you don't stay with me."

Jim banged his fist down on the table and shouted, "Mark, you are the biggest goddamn idiot I ever saw. You stupid bastard, that woman worships you. I've never seen so much love in any woman's eyes for a man as she has for you.

"Mark, I took Lupe when she was fifteen years old and a virgin. She loves and respects me, and no man could ask for a better woman than Lupe, but she isn't capable of loving and worshipping me as Maria does you. Hell's bells, man, marry the girl, a Mexican woman is the finest wife in the world."

"All right, Jim, why don't you practice what you preach? There is nothing to keep you from marrying Lupe?"

"Why, I never thought of it that way. Besides, that ain't none of your damn business. We were talking about you and Maria."

The girls came back before we could finish our discussion. We had a very delicious dinner and stayed for another hour of dancing and listening to the music.

When we reached our hotel, Jim practically jerked Lupe out of the car, said a fast goodnight, and led her to their room. I could see I wasn't going to get any help from Jim. I asked Maria to come for a walk on the beach.

Maria was very proud that she had learned to speak English and insisted we speak in English. She didn't speak English very well, but I could understand almost everything she said.

We walked down to the beach hand in hand. I started to

roll my pant legs up so we could walk in the surf. "No, Marek," Maria said, "first we talk."

Maria asked three questions before I could answer. "What is it? What is wrong? What have I done?

"You haven't done anything, Maria. It's only . . . this, I know how much a girl's reputation means to her, especially here in Mexico. I cannot ruin your life and leave you to suffer. All I would do is hurt and dishonor you."

That's as far as I got before Maria threw herself in my arms. When she started kissing me, I could feel her tears on my face. She forgot her English, or could express herself better in Spanish.

"My darling, you are such a fool. You risk your life to save me from a cruel man. Where most men would demand me to be theirs, you are such a kind and wonderful man. That is why I love and need you so much." I felt her body grow stiff in my arms.

"Marek, please tell me, am I not beautiful and desirable enough for you?" She slipped out of my arms and stepped back about two steps. With the moonlight shining on her, she was so beautiful that I was completely hypnotized. Since I couldn't answer, Maria thought she wasn't desirable to me.

She pulled her dress off, and very quickly stepped out of her slip and then stood in the moonlight with only her panties and bra on. "Look to me, Marek, am I not woman?"

A goddess or an angel couldn't have been more a woman than Maria. I didn't recognize my own voice when I spoke.

"Maria, you are the most perfect and beautiful woman I've ever seen. I want you so much, I would give anything for your love. Please put your clothes on. I cannot stand to look upon your beauty. I am going out of my mind."

She came back into my arms. "Why, my love you stand here like a fool and hold me? Why we do not go to our room?"

I gently picked her up in my arms. "Please, Marek, my dress." I reached down and picked up her clothes. I had only taken a few steps when Maria started crying. I asked her what was wrong.

"Oh, Marek, I am so sad for my beautiful new dress.

Maybe I tear it."

As José always says, *Quien sabe?* or will ever understand a woman worrying about a dress at a time like this.

I held Maria a little closer to me and kissed her sweet lips. "Why think about a dress now?"

"You are right, Marek. Now is not time to think. Please carry me to my room." Once in the room, I sat Maria down on the bed.

She was very embarrassed when she realized how she was dressed. She pulled the bedspread around her.

"Marek, one little kiss, then you will please go to the bathroom until I dress. I am ashamed. I spend so much money for the gown, but always I dream of wearing on my wedding night such a gown as I bought today."

"Now, Marek, you please go to the bathroom and stay until I call you." She didn't have to tell me twice. It seemed like hours before Maria called me. When I entered the room, Maria was in bed with the blanket pulled up to her chin. She smiled very sweetly and said, "I close the eyes while you undress."

I jumped straight up, came out of my boots, pants, shirt and shorts. It seemed my clothes and bare feet all hit the floor at the same time.

I turned out the lamp and got into bed. I gently took Maria in my arms. I had never felt so much love and tenderness as I did when Maria came into my arms. She tried to be very brave, but I felt a quiver run through her warm desirable body.

She raised herself on her elbow, took my face in her hands, gave me a kiss and siad, "*Mi amor* I am yours. Do what you want. Only, many women tell of how great the pain was the first time. Almost like having a baby.

"My only request, please, Marek, make me feel so much passion before you love me so I cannot feel the pain. As you will soon know, I have never known the love of any man."

I gently kissed her neck.

"Don't be afraid, darling. I am not an animal and will try very hard not to hurt you." She came back into my arms and with confidence, but still a little afraid.

I folded the blanket down to our waists. She had on the most beautiful light blue negligee I ever saw. I gently kissed her full red lips. When I started to caress her breasts, they were as smooth as satin, and more than a handful for my large hands.

As I kissed her soft neck, she said, "Now, Marek, I can wait no longer." The moon was shining through the windows and the room was almost as bright as day. I kicked the blankets off the bed and unbuttoned her gown while still kissing her sweet warm lips.

I ran my hands down her back, which was smooth as silk, and gently laid the negligee to the side. When I saw Maria's lovely body, I couldn't believe any woman could have such a beautiful figure.

Maria asked me, "Marek, am I as desirable as you wanted me to be?"

"Yes, darling," I told her. As I gazed at her I knew no angel, complete with a halo, could be more innocent and pure than Maria.

I never knew a woman could be so tight and close. It wasn't easy to control myself until I saw the pain on her face. Then my love was greater than the passion I felt.

I looked into her lovely eyes and although I was being as careful and gentle as a man could be, I could still see the pain in her beautiful face. Later, I took Maria in my arms and gently kissed her.

"Forgive me, my love. Did I hurt you very much?"

She started crying. I felt like a heel. "Please don't cry, Maria. I am sorry I was so rough."

Once again she took my face in her hands.

"Oh, Marek, you are so fool, of course it hurt, but you were so very careful. How anything could hurt and still be so beautiful, I do not understand. Already I forget the pain.

"I cry because I am so happy that you love me so much to be gentle and kind, but most of all, I am very happy and cry because I save myself for you and you will never know how hard it was for me to keep stalling my papa when he wanted me to marry Flores."

Maria came back into my arms. "But, you see, my love, I do it. As you know now, I've never been loved by another man. I will always thank the Virgin Mary for keeping me pure for you. One question, Marek. Will you always respect me? And here in Mexico, introduce me as your wife, if you are not ashamed of me?''

"Of course, darling," I told her. I started kissing her lovely neck and then her smooth firm breasts.

She raised her head up and said, "As you know, I have no experience, and I am ashamed to ask, but how often does a man and wife make love?''

"Once a month," I kidded her.

"I did not know," was the disappointed reply.

Then I told her, "As often as they feel the need and love for each other.'' In just a few minutes, I couldn't stand to kiss her anymore without having her again. "Do you feel like making love again?''

"I am yours to have and love when you want me. Never ask me again. If I don't feel like love, I tell you.''

This time, I was really careful. I talked and tried to get Maria relaxed and went a little farther. She did relax a little and it wasn't as painful as the first time. When we were through she smiled and kissed me, and said, "See, I wasn't afraid. Does it always hurt?'' she asked.

"No, darling, just a few more times, then no more pain and you will enjoy it as much as I.'' I tried to find the words to tell Maria how much love and complete satisfaction she gave me. She pulled my head down between her breasts. I couldn't stand to feel those soft pink lucious nipples on my face. I started kissing her again. In a short time, I was ready for more loving.

The third time I was able to control myself and gently instruct Maria on how to hold her shapely legs. We were doing fine. No longer was she afraid. Then she asked, "Marek, would you be ashamed if I felt us with my hand, for I know nothing of what we are doing.''

"Of course not," I told her. I gently took her hand and ran it down her tummy. She felt herself and then very shyly touched me.

"What that is?" she asked me.

"Look, honey," I told her. "It will be a long time before I

can put all of it inside you."

Maria said, "I am a fool woman, I thought already you had. Now, Marek, even if I scream, you put all inside me."

"No, Maria, I will not."

"Yes, you will," she insisted, "for the quicker you do is better for you and we have to sometime. So, please now."

"All right," I told her. "If you will relax and put your legs up and wide and spread, we will try." Very gently and a little at a time, then I let her rest, and then just a little more. She was very brave and unafraid. She did everything I asked. I felt so mean and cruel. When a tear ran down her cheek, I lay very still and kissed her.

"Is now all inside me, Marek?" Maria asked.

"Yes, darling." I told her.

She put both lovely arms, which had been clenched at her side around my neck and pulled my face down to hers and kissed me. "Is true, all is inside me?"

"Yes, darling."

She smiled and said, "Now, I am woman, am I not?"

I assured her she was the most desirable and most beautiful woman in the world.

She said, "Marek, I feel so full and funny inside."

"Maria, which do you feel, more pain or passion?"

She replied, "If you do not move very little pain and very much passion."

"All right, darling, I will not move. I am going to kiss your pretty breasts. You move any way you want. But slowly, until you see if it hurts or not. This way you will reach your first climax."

She tried very bravely and failed twice, but on the third attempt, she succeeded and was completed exhausted.

"Now I know, Marek, why I have loved and waited so long for you. It was wonderful and beautiful. I am not ashamed like I thought I would be."

Once again, I took her in my arms and told her in a few days when there was no pain, she would then know how a woman was supposed to feel and understand why God made woman to be loved, cherished, appreciated and protected. Even if men do sometimes forget.

We talked and loved each other all night. Each time we made love, it was easier and less painful for Maria. At 8:00 A.M., we hadn't been to sleep. I picked up the phone, ordered breakfast, and had a shower. Maria was taking her shower when the waiter brought our breakfast. We ate and went back to bed.

"Why you don't hold me, my Marek?" she asked.

I assured her it would be a pleasure. "Let's sleep a while," I told her.

Maria smiled and pulled my head down on her breasts. "Why you don't kiss my titty and make me a woman again before we sleep?" It was a pleasure to conform to her request.

After we finished, she snuggled up in my arms like a little kitten. "Is the best one of all night, Marek. Now, please we sleep, I'm so satisfied and tired."

"Yes, darling, now we sleep."

"Now, please, kiss me quick and hold me tight while we sleep, for never do I want to be out of your arms." In just a minute, she was asleep. The most radiant and lovely glow was on her face. No woman could have been happier.

As I looked at her adorable face, I knew I was the luckiest man who ever lived.

Chapter 33

THE PHONE started ringing. It was Jim, inviting us to have dinner with him and Lupe. I was surprised when I looked at my watch. It was 5:00. We had slept all day.

"It's a date, Jim. Just give us thirty minutes to get dressed."

I went to my room to shave and dress. I hadn't finished dressing when José came in. He smiled, shook my hand and started talking up a storm.

"You don't know this, my brother, but I, too, am lucky and have the most beautiful woman in my room. We are happy together. I go back to her. Maybe she is lonesome for me."

I was glad José was leaving and a little surprised that he wasn't completely drunk.

Jim opened the door, stuck his head in the room and said, "I've decided to stay with you tonight."

I didn't feel like being kidded. He jerked his head back and disappeared, just as my boot hit the door.

We spent a very relaxing evening together, at the same restaurant where we had dined the evening before. Lupe and Maria chattered like old married women. At 11:00 we went back to the hotel.

Maria and I had a very beautiful night. It seemed the moon was shining just for us. Our love grew. We were more satisfied with each other. Before the night was over, we knew complete love and fulfillment beyond our dreams and expectations. We were up and dressed at noon and went to the cafe for breakfast.

Jim and Lupe were there having their lunch so we joined them. While we were eating, I asked how everyone would like to go for a swim after lunch. Maria and Lupe said they didn't have a bathing suit, and even if they did have one, they had never worn one in public and would be embarrassed. They admitted it would be fun to play in the surf and lie on the beach.

Jim said he had to go to the airport and check on his plane.

"Look," I told them, "You girls go downtown with Jim, buy your bathing suits, and Jim can pick you up when he comes back from the airport. While you all are gone, I'll check on José."

The girls took about ten minutes to talk the idea over and decided they would go swimming. After lunch, Jim and the girls took off.

I went to José's room and knocked. When he opened the door, I saw the back of a naked girl running for the bathroom.

José was almost drunk, but very happy, and beginning to feel rich again. He pulled two chairs out and tried to help me sit down. He then completely missed his own chair and branded his tailbone when he hit the floor. The small incident didn't dampen his spirits in the least.

From his sitting position on the floor, he started telling me how much his new girl loved him and how he would buy her a house so they could always be together.

"Look, José, have you forgotten about buying the houses in Madero for the two girls from Torreon? And, remember how much they loved you and Juan until you spent all your money on them. Let me tell you something, José, it isn't going to happen again, believe me. You are staying out of the real estate business.

"And if you get any drunker, and if you so much as think about the treasure, I'll wring your skinny, little neck and ship your body back to the ranch and throw the little muchacha out on her behind."

The poor little humble guy smiled and said, "I do as you say, my brother."

"That's good, José. Now, I am going to my room, and I

304

will see you tomorrow.''

I went to my room, put on my bathing suit, left a note for Maria telling her to join me on the beach. At the beach, I met a couple of nice young boys from Idaho. We talked for a while, then I went swimming.

I came out of the water and was lying on the beach having a cigarette, when I heard a couple of wolf whistles. I looked and there came Maria in her new white bathing suit. She had bought the most modest suit she could get, but it still didn't hide her beautiful figure.

The boys from Idaho were really goggle-eyed and had whistled when she passed by them. Maria turned around and went back to where they were sitting.

They both got up. I could see she was very upset. Although I couldn't hear what she was saying, I started toward them. Maria saw me and came running. I have never seen a woman so mad. She thought she had been insulted.

The two boys came and started to apologize and assured Maria they didn't mean to be disrespectful. Maria was still angry and asked them, ''Why you whistle to me then? In Mexico, never do the men whistle to a woman if she does nothing to be whistled at. And I do nothing.''

I wanted to laugh, but didn't dare. This was very serious to Maria. I winked at the boys and hoped they would get the message and told them if they ever whistled at my wife again, I would beat the hell out of them. If they didn't get the message, they were too surprised to take up the challenge.

Jim and Lupe joined us and we all went into the water. I was surprised Maria was such a good swimmer. She immediately took a liking to the ocean. We really had fun. After an hour, Jim and Lupe announced they had had enough.

Maria and I played on the beach and finally found a place where the sea wall curved and we couldn't be seen.

We lay in the sun and smoked a cigarette. Maria carefully looked around and could not see anyone. She then said, ''Why you don't hold me?'' In just a few minutes, I was panting like a hound dog chasing a rabbit on a hot day.

''Maria, why don't we go to our room, and I'll make you a woman?''

She kissed me and said, "I am lucky to have such a smart husband who has the good ideas at the right time." Hand in hand we ran to our room.

Once inside the room, Maria spread the blanket on the couch, lay back and motioned to me. We didn't think about taking a shower, and her smooth skin was salty to my tongue.

After we made love, I showered and dressed. She was still in the shower. I started kidding her that her lovely pink breasts had been sweet to kiss even though they had been salty.

Maria came out of the bathroom with a towel wrapped around her from her neck to her knees. I was sitting on the edge of the bed. She gently pushed me back on the bed and let the towel fall to her waist. This was the first time I had ever seen her lovely breasts while she was standing up.

They were firm and stuck straight out and the ripe pink nipples turned up. She lay down beside me and put her breast against my lips. "Now, it is clean and sweet. Why you don't kiss my titty to see which is the best—salty, or clean?"

I could have kissed that smooth pink breast even if I had had lock jaw. Later, Maria put her hands behind my head and looked up into my eyes and asked, "How am I better, salty and sandy, or clean?"

"You are perfect both ways," I told her, "but to be absolutely sure, let's try both ways again tomorrow."

"Is another good idea," Maria agreed. "We will do it. But now, we get up and dress again so we are not late for dinner with Lupe and Jim."

"There's no object in dressing again," I told Maria, "if you want me to conduct another test on how sweet your titties are."

"Is all, Marek, until tonight."

That was good news, for I was almost out of ammo. I needed a rest. "In that case," I told her, "I'll get up and dress again."

The next two days and nights passed very fast, almost like a beautiful dream. We spent our time on the beach or making love. We couldn't get enough of each other.

On the fifth morning, while we were having breakfast with

Jim and Lupe, Jim said, "Mark, I've talked to Tex and Luis today. They want to spend only two days each here in Acapulco. Why don't you fly Lupe, José and me to the ranch and bring Tex and Jackie back. In two days, take them back and bring back Luis and Carmen."

This would give me an opportunity to get Maria a ring from the treasure cache, for she had been admiring Lupe's ring. I knew it would make Maria very proud and happy to have an engagement and wedding ring. I didn't want to buy an engagement ring with all the diamonds we had.

I got José awake and dressed. He couldn't remember what had happened to his girl or when she left. He had only a few pesos left. I had to pay his room rent.

I kissed Maria goodbye and asked her to move all my clothes into her room while I was gone.

When we landed at the ranch, I asked Jackie to please bring me the saddlebag of jewels. I carried it to my room, and with the aid of my twenty-power glass, started selecting Maria's ring, I finally settled on a two carat blue-white that was flawless. The ring looked like new. It was beautiful. My only concern was whether it would fit Maria's finger.

Tex, Jackie and I took off. When we landed in Acapulco, after having the plane hangared, we got a taxi and drove through town. I stopped at a jewelry store and bought a beautiful diamond wedding band to match Maria's engagement ring.

When we arrived at the hotel, Jackie and Maria hugged and kissed each other like long lost sisters. While Tex and Jackie unpacked, I told Maria to come to our room. I wanted to talk to her.

Once inside the room, I asked her to close her eyes. I held her hand and slipped the rings on her finger. They were a perfect fit. When Maria saw the rings, she was so happy she cried. "They are so big and expensive. I do not deserve such beautiful rings. Now everyone will know we are really married when they see my rings. And, they are so large no one can keep from seeing them. Why don't you hold me and I show you how happy and thankful I really am?"

The phone rang before I could comply with Maria's

request. I was surprised when the party told me he was the hotel manager and asked me to come at once to the office.

When I entered the office, he introduced himself and asked me if I knew my wife, or the woman registered as my wife had brought a known prostitute in our room after I had left with my friends. I didn't know what to say and thought he was trying to blackmail me into a payoff to let us continue staying at the hotel.

I started seeing red. "Do not get angry, *Señor*. If you and your friends register as man and wife and conduct yourselves as such, it is all the law requires. My only interest is in keeping this motel full of guests and a clean, quiet and respectable place. But, what I tell you is true.

"Your wife calls a taxi as soon as you and your other friends leave and goes downtown. In thirty minutes she was back and with her was this prostitute. They go to your room. The prostitute had just left when you come back. If this woman returns, I will be forced to ask you to leave at once."

"All right," I told him. "I still don't know whether to believe what you are telling me. If it is true, I'll find out why. If you are lying to me, I'll be back and beat the hell out of you, and that's a promise."

I slammed the door and headed back to our room. When I entered the room, I guess Maria could see I was angry. "Come sit beside me, Maria. I want to ask you a question, and be sure you tell me the truth."

Tears came into her big lovely blue-black eyes. "Of course, my Marek, and always you can be sure I only say the truth to you."

"Did you go to town in a taxi and bring a woman here while I was gone?"

"Yes, Marek, I did."

"Maria, did you know that woman is known all over Acapulco as a prostitute?"

"Yes, Marek, I know this."

"Then why in the hell did you bring her here and why were you associating with her? Give me your reason for this, and be quick about it. Why?"

Maria started crying and tried to put her arms around me. I

308

caught her arms and pushed her away. Once more, I demanded to know why she had done this. Maria tried again to put her arms around me, but I pushed her back.

She fell across the bed crying and unable to talk. Tears were streaming down her lovely face.

"Oh, Marek, you no understand. Now I can take all of you inside me if you are gentle. And you so satisfy me and I feel so much, but I have no practice or experience, and I know not how to please you.

"So, I go get this prostitute and pay her eight hundred pesos to come here, and lay on her back and show me how to do the wiggles that please a man, so I can learn how to keep you satisfied."

I was so taken by surprise that I couldn't say a word. Then it dawned on me that Maria was actually telling the truth.

I knew how proud the Mexican women were and how they try so hard to please their men. "Is what you say true, Maria? There was no other reason?"

"Of course it is true, my Marek. Never will I lie to you." There could be no other reason.

Knowing Maria, I realized this was true. I gently took her in my arms and kissed the tears from her lovely eyes. "Maria, you are a little fool. No woman on this earth could ever love and satisfy me as you do.

"Forget what the prostitute said. Please forgive me darling, you are the most beautiful and desirable woman for me in the whole world. I want you as you are. No one can tell or show you how to make love. Do what you feel, nothing else. Then it is natural and wonderful and you will always satisfy me. I promise you darling, I will never want or have another woman as long as we are worthy of each other's love."

Maria asked me, "You promise and kiss and cross that you say is true, my Marek, about me satisfying you? And I will learn with practice?"

"I can show you better than I can tell you," I told her.

We lay back on the bed. Her beautiful body was like a coiled spring. She was so passionate I kept on kissing her breasts and caressing her body.

When she could no longer stand the desire, she pulled me down and locked her shapely legs around me. For the first time, with her hand, took hold of me and guided me into her. Never will any woman more completely satisfy my desire than Maria did at this time.

Later, Maria said, "Is true, my Marek, all you say. And, I am so ashamed."

"It's all right, darling, but you really had me worried until I knew why you did what you did."

Maria still insisted that she was ashamed. "It's all right now that I understand," I assured her.

"It's not that, my Marek, you don't understand, I am ashamed that I so fool to pay that prostitute eight hundred pesos and she can teach me nothing. Is not good to waste eight hundred pesos."

I got up and went to the bathroom, for I had to laugh. This was very serious to Maria. While Maria dressed, I went back to the hotel manager's office. When I entered, I extended my hand and said, "*Señor,* my apologies. You were right.

"You know my wife is Mexican, so maybe you can understand what I am telling you. You see, we were just married, and are on our honeymoon. She was afraid she wasn't satisfying me, so she goes and hires this prostitute to show her how . . ."

That's as far as I got. The manager grabbed my hand and said, "*Nombre de Dios,* How could I be so stupid and cause the beautiful young *señora* so much pain and embarrassment on her honeymoon. Please forgive me, Señor Mark. I am more stupid than the burro."

He bent over and said, "I will feel better if you treat me as a burro. You see, always we kick the burro for being stupid, and no burro could be as dumb as I."

I couldn't resist, and put every ounce I had behind the kick. When my number ten boot connected with his rear end, he sailed across the floor on his belly. His head hit the far wall with a thump.

He pulled himself up in a sitting position and tried to look at me, but couldn't focus his glassy eyes. Then he said, "*Por favor, Señor.*"

I reached down, shook his hand, and told him no thanks was necessary, that I was always ready and happy to accommodate a friend.

He was so shook up, and confused, he actually started pulling his hair. As I went out the door, I heard him say in Spanish, ''Mother of God, it is not possible even for your son to understand the gringos.''

As I passed by Tex's room, he asked if Maria and I wanted to join Jackie and him for a swim.

We spent all afternoon on the beach, then dressed and went dancing. While we were having dinner, Maria and Jackie decided they would go shopping the next day. This gave Tex and me a chance to go fishing.

We were up early and rented a boat. We caught fish until we were tired and we got back to the motel at 7:00. The girls were still downtown.

I put on my bathing suit and went to the beach, lay down on the cool sand and went to sleep. I awoke with my face being cupped in two soft warm hands and full lips searching for mine. I kept my eyes closed and pretended I was asleep. Maria really put herself into those kisses.

In just a minute my tool was so hard a cat couldn't have scratched it. Maria noticed and said, ''Marek, you should be ashamed, and you are not asleep. Put this towel around you and we go to the room, for we have to dress for dinner. If you and Tex invite me and Jackie, we will accept the invitation to dance with you again this night.''

I opened my eyes and told Maria we would be very honored to have their company for dinner and dancing afterwards, except for one thing.

''What?'' she wanted to know.

''Well, darling, you can see what your kisses did to me. I can't go out in this condition.''

Maria laughed and said, ''It is true and since I am responsible put the towel around you and let's hurry to our room. I can take care of that better than I can tell you.''

Twenty minutes later, I had to agree with the old proverb, ''Actions speak louder than words.''

Chapter 34

I HAD started to the bathroom to take a shower when the phone rang. It was Jim calling to tell us that his banker, *Señor* Padilla, had just called and we had a change of plans. He wanted us to be in Tegucigalpa before the banks closed tomorrow afternoon, if at all possible.

I told Jim we couldn't possibly fly to the ranch before it was too dark to land. Jim told me to leave his plane here and drive down. He would have the twin-engine plane serviced and ready for us to take off at dawn.

Jim said if we would hurry, they would wait dinner. I hung up the phone and told Maria to start packing. Our wonderful honeymoon was going to be interrupted for a week or two.

Maria came and once again put those soft arms around my neck and said, "Marek, I am so sad it has to end. This I want you to know and always remember. Should I die tonight, never feel sad for me, Because this one week, I have had more love and happiness than most women will have in all their lives. Even if they live to be very old."

I gently kissed her and told her, "Darling, this is just the beginning. We have a long and wonderful life ahead of us, together." (At this time, I had no way of knowing, but I couldn't have been more wrong.)

Maria kissed me and said, "I do the packing while you go tell Jackie and Tex."

I playfully spanked her bottom, then jumped out the door. I knocked on Tex's door and told him of Jim's phone call. I was sorry for Jackie's sake. She had already dressed for a big night on the town. She was a very good sport and told me not

312

to worry, that after we sold all the gold and jewels, there would be many more nights.

Tex and I went to the office and paid our bill. We then helped the girls pack and in fifteen minutes, we were on our way.

It was a beautiful drive down the coast to Aqua Blanca and the ranch. The moon was shining on the beach and ocean.

When we arrived at the ranch, Lupe and Carmen had a delicious shrimp dinner waiting. After dinner, we went out to the patio for a meeting.

We decided that it would be better for Tex, Luis, José and Raul to stay at the ranch and guard the treasure while Jim, Ramon and I went to Honduras.

We talked for a long time, for we had no way of knowing how the police down there would receive us. Of course, they couldn't prove anything about Snider and Block. Since our banker could vouch for us, we didn't expect any problem. If we landed in jail, *Señor* Padilla would notify Tex.

Jim spoke up, "Hell, there's nothng for me to worry about. Tight as my banker is, he will see that I am well protected until I pay off my note." He stood up, stretched and said, "Let's all go to bed. We have to get up very early in the morning."

Later, with Maria in my arms, I tried to quiet her fears and told her not to worry. "Is all right if I worry just a little?"

"O.K.," I agreed, "but just a little, and I will sneak out of bed in the morning and not wake you."

Maria didn't like the idea. As a matter of fact, she wouldn't have it. "Look, Marek, am I not a good wife?"

"Yes, you are, darling," I assured her. Maria had sat up and was leaning over me as she talked.

I lifted Maria's lovely firm breasts and tried to make them bounce. Even though they were large and pointed, there was no sag. When I released them, they would jump back to attention like springs and stick straight out.

Maria got really angry, with fire in her beautiful eyes. She shouted, "Don't do that, Marek, don't play with my titties."

"I thought you liked for me to play with them."

313

"I do," she replied, "when we are not talking serious. I do not know if I am good wife or not."

I locked both arms around her. She started struggling and protesting. I started kissing those gorgeous smooth breasts. In just a minute, I could feel the delicious, ripe nipple in my mouth getting hard, as I gently ran my tongue over and around it. Maria wasn't trying too hard anymore to get away from me. As a matter of fact, she was easy to hold. In another minute, she ceased trying to get away.

I turned my head enough to get her breast out of my mouth, and said, "Look, woman, am I not your husband? In the morning, you will get up early and fix my breakfast and coffee. Understand?"

With happiness in her eyes, she replied, "Yes, my husband."

I awoke the next morning with Maria bending over me and kissing my eyes. "Is now time to get up and do the work you have to do. Your breakfast is waiting, my husband."

I'll have to admit that Maria's way of waking a guy up was far better than the way Jim did it. It made the day start off right. Maria insisted that I hurry down to breakfast.

"Aren't you coming with me?" I asked.

"As soon as I pack your suitcase, I be there."

As usual, everyone else was seated at the table having coffee. Very little was said while we ate.

José and Raul carried our luggage out and put it in the plane. With our arms around each other, Maria and I walked to the plane.

Maria made a sign of the cross on me with her hands and then pressed her thumb to my lips. "Please, Marek, kiss the cross, even though you don't believe my faith, it will do you no harm."

Lupe had been watching, for she then made the sign of the cross on Jim and put her thumb on his lips. He hadn't paid any attention to Lupe. When she asked Jim to kiss her thumb, he said, "What the hell is the matter with you, Lupe? You know damn well I ain't no hand kissing French lover?"

Lupe explained that this was her and Maria's prayer for our

safety. Lupe put her thumb back to his lips. I don't know if Jim kissed her hand or not. I guess he did, for I saw her nose twitch and Lupe moved her hand.

I hate goodbyes. I drew Marie to me, gave her a quick kiss, and got into the plane. Marie started crying. Then Lupe started to cry. Jim practically jumped into the plane. "Get this damn thing off the ground before those silly women get the strip all wet with their tears."

I started both engines, taxied up the dirt strip and turned. As we took off past the girls, I pulled the plane off the ground, waved and turned the nose up and hung it on the prop until I reached my altitude.

In three hours and thirty minutes, we were at San Salvador, where we had stopped on our first trip to Honduras. We had coffee, got our visa and plane permit to enter Honduras, and at 11:20, we took off. An hour and twenty five minutes later, we were circling the airport in Tegucigalpa.

I closed my flight plan and we headed for the bank. *Señor* Padilla was waiting for us. He introduced us to *Señor* Perez, who was the president of the bank.

Señor Perez was very hospitable. He invited us to have lunch with him at the Hotel Prado, where we were staying. At lunch *Señor* Padilla asked *Señor* Perez, as a favor to him, if he would buy our gold.

"Certainly," *Señor* Perez replied, "If you will permit me to charge ten dollars an ounce brokerage fee."

"How much an ounce net profit can we expect?" I asked. I damn near fell through the floor when *Señor* Perez answered that Honduras had no restriction on gold, just his fee as stated, ten dollars an ounce.

He offered us five hundred and twenty-six dollars an ounce. None of us had ever thought of receiving more than four hundred dollars an ounce net profit. "One other question, *Señor* Perez, can we land safely there at the airport in Tegucigalpa?"

"But, of course, *Señor* Mark, if you are asked, the gold is from your mine somewhere in Honduras.

"But do not worry, once they know you are selling the gold to me, there will be no questions. Just call the control tower thirty minutes before you land, and I will have an armored truck and police protection waiting to escort the gold directly to my bank. How many ounces do you have?"

When I answered between fifty and sixty thousand ounces, his eyes got really big and he started stammering. Once I convinced him we really had that amount, he became very excited and wanted to know how we wanted our money.

"We would like sixty percent in one hundred dollar bills, and the other forty percent in one thousand peso notes."

"It is good, for I have these bills already in my bank." From the greedy look on his face, I tried a shot in the dark.

"*Señor* Perez, we will shop around a little tomorrow, and see if we can get a better offer. If not, we will be happy to do business with you."

"Oh, no, *Señor* Mark. If you are sure that you have this large amount, I can pay a little more for such a large amount.'

We haggled back and forth over the price. Finally, *Señor* Padilla said, "*Señors,* there is a stopping point, and I have stopped. I will pay you a net price of five hundred thirty dollars an ounce, one thousand fine. It is my last offer. Take it or leave it."

"We will take it," I told him.

Jim breathed a sigh of relief. We shook hands all around. The deal was closed. *Señor* Perez asked if we could be at the airport for delivery to the bank before 7:30 A.M., Monday morning.

"I'll have you approximately twenty-seven thousand ounces here at that time."

Perez was overwhelmed. He started rubbing his hands together and the dollar signs started flashing in his eyes.

"How long will it take to have the gold assayed?" Jim asked. Perez told him if we were here by 7:30 A.M., he would have a chemist standing by and we would have the assay results late the same afternoon.

Jim insisted on splitting each assay three times. One third for the Banker's chemist to assay here, one third we would take to our own chemist, and one third we keep in case there is a difference of opinion. And, a bonded umpire assayer's report would be accepted by both parties. Perez agreed, but assured us there wouldn't be one-hundredth of an ounce difference between his assayer's report and ours.

I knew Jim didn't intend to have an assay made, but as long as *Señor* Perez thought we were checking his chemist, we would get a fair assay.

Señor Padilla agreed to stay in Tegucigalpa until the entire transaction was completed, then fly back with us.

Before the evening was over, I asked the banker if he would buy diamonds, emeralds, and rubies. "Si, Señor, just like gold. I buy them."

"Well, *Señor* Perez, this gold is from a very old treasure. Also, there is a fortune in diamonds and precious stones."

Once again, the dollar signs started flashing. "Please, will you also give me the chance to buy these stones?"

I tried to play it cagey, since none of us knew what they were really worth. I told him there was a jeweler appraising them now, and we would probably accept his offer.

Perez asked how many diamonds we had and when I described the jewelry and the amount, he really got shook up. "Please, *Señor*,, give me a chance to bid on this jewelry before you sell it."

"All right," I agreed, "after this man makes his bid, we will bring the jewels down on our second trip. If your offer is higher, fine. If not, we will take them back."

At 9:00 Perez excused himself and told us he would be at the airport Monday morning at 7:30 and ready to receive the gold. Since this was Friday, we decided to spend Saturday in Tegucigalpa and look the city over and fly back early Sunday morning.

We all slept late, had breakfast, and went out to look the city over. Tegucigalpa is a beautiful city. *Señor* Padilla called our attention to Senor Perez's bank. We decided to go in and look around.

Señor Perez saw us enter and came to show us around. I remarked that as big and grand as the bank was, he shouldn't have any trouble paying for our gold.

He smiled and led the way to the vault. The good banker was trying to impress us.

I hadn't realized there was as much money in the world as was stacked inside the vault. Jim and I were completely speechless.

As we left the bank, Jim said, "Now, I know how Jesse James must have felt. If I had had a gun, I would have damned sure been tempted."

I went to the airport and had the plane serviced, then to the control tower and told the guy on duty that we were leaving early in the morning to go look at a mine on the Jalan River, but that we would be back Monday morning.

We spent a very enjoyable afternoon shopping, and bought gifts and souvenirs to take back for everyone. After dinner, I got Jim in a pitch game. At 9:30, he informed me that he was going to bed.

True to habit, at 6:00 that next morning, Jim started trying to beat my door in. "I am up, Jim. Now, go order breakfast while I shave and shower."

While having breakfast, we decided Ramon should stay in Tegucigalpa until we had delivered and sold all the gold and jewels.

Chapter 35

WE FLEW from Tegucigalpa to the ranch at Agua Blanca. This way we had visa and plane permits to show that we were legal in either Mexico or Honduras, if we didn't get our wires crossed and show the wrong permits. To be sure, I kept he Honduras vias and permits for both Jim and me and he kept the Mexico permits.

In five hours and eight minutes after taking off from Tegucigalpa, I dropped the gear and landed at Agua Blanca. Everyone came running to meet the plane.

I had spent enough time with Maria that I should have become accustomed to her beauty, but as she came running to the plane, my heart stood still.

Everyone started asking questions. We went in the house and over coffee, Jim told everyone how successful our trip had been, and of the fabulous deal we had made.

Luis asked why we didn't all drive to Acapulco for dinner. I suggested he and Carmen go, and bring back twenty-four flashlights to mark the runway. We would take off at 12:30 tonight.

José and Raul stood guard while Tex, Jim and I dug up the gold. At first we divided the gold in two equal piles. Then decided to try and carry sixty-five to seventy percent of the gold on the first trip and the balance of gold and jewels on the second and final trip.

We estimated the total weight of the gold at three thousand pounds. If we carried seventy-five percent of three thousand pounds, plus full gas tanks, we would be at least five hundred pounds overweight, but we would burn off gasoline in flight and reduce the weight.

I suggested in order to reduce the weight at least two hundred pounds, that we only carry a two hour's fuel reserve. We gassed the plane and Tex and Raul started carrying the gold to the plane while José stood guard.

Jim and I very carefully started loading the plane and distributing the weight as uniformly as possible from the luggage compartment to the cockpit. Before we were finished, Maria came to tell us our steaks were ready.

José and Raul reburied the gold we were not taking. After dinner Tex and I checked to make sure they had done a good job. They had, and had even taken a broom and swept away all visible traces.

We asked José and Raul to keep a close watch on the plane. Jim and I were going to bed and get some sleep before we had to take-off.

José winked at me, and said, "Maybe my brother, you do not get sleepy." At times José was smarter than he looked.

I didn't answer, turned and went in the house. Maria met me in the patio. I picked her up in my arms and carried her to our room. Once in the room, she gave me a kiss and said, "Oh, Marek, I have worried so much for you. I could not live if something should happen to you. And how you say in English, I have the woman's tuition and I have been so afraid."

I gently took her in my arms and kissed away her fears and assured her nothing was going to happen to me and I wasn't about to leave her. For no man had ever been so happy and completely satisfied with a woman as I. "Maria," I asked, "are you my woman?"

"Yes, Marek, I am."

"Then why don't you love your man? Don't you know no man ever needed a woman's love as much as I need yours?"

"Yes, I know, my Marek, now why you don't undress us and let me love you the way a woman should love her husband."

As Maria always said, she had no experience. This I knew was true, but she sure learned fast.

I couldn't get enough of her love. At 9:30, Maria told me

no more love, for I must sleep at least two hours before our flight time at 12:30.

I gently took her in my arms and laid my head between her breasts. Maria was rubbing her smooth finger tips over my face.

I kissed her until she could no longer control her passion. She started moaning, "Why you don't love me, Marek?"

At 11:30, Jim knocked on the door. "Are you awake?" he asked. I answered in the affirmative. For once, I was awake and I hadn't been asleep.

This had been one of the most wonderful and beautiful nights of my life. We dressed and joined everyone in the dining room. Luis and Carmen had just returned from Acapulco, and joined us.

While Maria packed my suitcase, Tex and I took the flashlights that Luis bought in Acapulco and went out to the runway.

I knew that it was three thousand feet long. We walked to the far end and every two hundred long steps, we turned on a flashlight and placed it in on the ground facing the way we had come from.

Tex and I were about thirty feet apart. We had lights on each side of the runway, and at the end. We placed the remaining two flashlights in the center of the runway. A rather crude arrangement, but I had taken off under worse conditions.

Tex and I walked back to the plane, and again, Maria made the sign of the cross. This time she didn't have to ask me to kiss her thumb. Lupe did the same with Jim. We were ready to go. I taxied to the end of the strip and checked out.

I released the brakes, pushing both power and mixture wide open. At the sixth light, I glanced at the speed indicator —only thirty-seven miles an hour. We sure had a load.

I saw Jim also looking at our speed. "Shall I cut it?"

"I believe we can make it," was Jim's reply. When I estimated we were one hundred and fifty feet from the last two flashlights placed in the center of the runway, I eased the nose wheel off the ground and glanced at the speed indicator again—sixty-five miles per hour. It was going to be very close.

When the nose of the plane blocked out the light from the flashlights, I pulled the plane up about fifty feet off the ground then slightly lowered the nose, hoping we would pick up flying speed.

I was very thankful there were no high obstacles in our path. In about two minutes, I knew we had it made. At ninety miles an hour, I released ten degrees flaps and picked up an extra ten miles on the speed indicator. I gently released all flaps and circled out over the ocean.

I started a very slow climb out and circled back over the house so Maria and everyone would know we were okay. Our take-off was a rough one. It had really been close. When I completed my circle, I was up to two thousand feet. I made four more circles before I reached our cruising altitude of twelve thousand and five hundred feet.

I slapped Jim on the knee and told him we were on our way. These were the first words we had spoken.

Jim said, "Damn, Mark, that was as close as a man can get. For at least three miles, we were no more than twenty-five feet above the ground."

I checked the clock, 12:49, and made a note of it on the pad strapped to my leg. It was a beautiful moonlit night for flying. The heavens were sparkling with all the stars.

In three hours and thirty-five minutes, we could see the lights of San Salvador, which was our last and only check point on the way to Tegicigalpa.

I was only about two miles off course. I corrected and told Jim to take the controls while I grabbed forty winks. It seemed like I hadn't closed my eyes when Jim woke me.

"Mark, we have a small build-up or storm ahead of us." I looked at the clock in the plane. I had been asleep only thirty minutes. I thought I could see a hole in the clouds where we could slip through between the layers.

The air started getting rough. I pulled both engines back to fifty percent power and flew through the hole in the clouds. Any pilot who has flown Central America will know what I mean when I say it was like flying into a funnel. I don't have words to describe it, but in ten minutes, I was completely socked in.

It was a dark and scary situation to be in. Then came the wind, building in velocity, from the Pacific on our right side. I had never been in such a storm. Rain in sheets and wind at least sixty miles per hour. Our plane was so small and helpless, and the wind so strong. We bucked the storm for another ten minutes before the rear engine started heating.

I cut the power on the rear engine back to thirty percent and opened the cowl flaps full. But the engine kept getting hotter. I told Jim that I was going to have to feather the engine.

We had so much weight that I couldn't maintain twelve thousand five hundred feet altitude on just the front engine. In eight minutes, we were down to ten thousand feet. We were also over the Sierra Madre. Some of these mountain peaks reached heights of eleven thousand feet. They were so rough, an eagle couldn't have lit on them, much less a plane, even in daylight.

I told Jim that we couldn't maintain our altitude on one engine, and to start throwing the gold out. We had to lighten the plane. The plane was being tossed up and down like a kite. The velocity of the wind increased. I expected every second for the wind to tear the wings off the plane.

We found it impossible to get the door of the plane open to throw out the gold. We could only trust in the Lord and ride the storm out. The front engine started heating. We were down to nine thousand feet.

I looked at Jim and told him I thought our only chance was to make a ninety degree turn, so we had a tail wind, restart the rear engine and try to maintain our altitude until we were sure we were out over the Caribbean or Atlantic Ocean, and then descend to one thousand feet, get under the storm, and head back to the mainland.

Jim agreed this was our only chance. I turned ninety-five degrees and made a note of the change of direction. I finally got the rear engine started, climbed six thousand feet, and maintained ten thousand feet for thirty minutes. All this time we were being tossed around like a ball on a roulette wheel.

How any plane could take the beating this one did, I will

never know. I looked at Jim and told him, "I believe we should be over the ocean, but, as you know, trying to maintain a heading in this storm, we could be anywhere. If we go any farther off course, we won't have enough gasoline to make it to Tegucigalpa, even if we're lucky enough to get our bearings and get back on course."

I looked at the temperature gauge on the rear engine. It was all the way over in the red, or danger zone—as far as it could go. I would have to feather the rear engine again, for it was ready to blow. All this time we had been in complete darkness. The rain was falling like sheets of water. I couldn't even see the nose of the plane, only my instruments.

Jim looked at the temperature gauge and calmly commented, "We don't have any other choice except to take her down." I cut the rear engine, and with the loss of power, the wind really started tossing us around.

"You know, Jim, to most people, the most romantic words in the world are 'love' and 'gold.' You and I and our loved ones know better. We have been very lucky up to this point.

"But, Jim, old friend, you are looking at a mighty scared man. I'd give all the gold that we have in this plane to hear Randy and Rickey once more call their Daddy's name."

Jim gently patted me on the back of the head and said, "So would I, son, so would I."

I realized Jim Dunlap had never called another man son before in his life. I knew I was loved and regarded as the son Jim would never have.

I started down at three hundred feet a minute. It was still so dark, I couldn't see anything outside the plane. With every heartbeat, I expected to crash into a mountain. It seemed like a lifetime before the altimeter showed twenty-seven hundred feet.

I had begun to think my instruments had gone haywire. The plane was tossed violently to one side. I reduced power, my eyes glued to the instrument panel. The altimeter showed eighteen hundred feet above sea level when Jim's shout almost scared me to death.

I looked up from the instrument panel and there, before

324

my eyes, was the beautiful Caribbean Sea. We had broken through the storm. I have never seen a more welcome sight in my life, than the first light of day shining on that sparkling blue water.

On the third try the rear engine finally started, and I began a one hundred eighty degree turn. At about ninety degrees, Jim shouted, "Look, Mark."

I saw that we were no more than fifteen miles off shore. I couldn't have been luckier on my navigation if I had had a radar control tower bring us in on the beam.

Jim very quickly got out our maps. There was nothing recognizable that we could use for a check point to get our bearings.

"Jim, we can't be more than eight miles from the Putuca River, it runs all the way from Juticalpa to the Caribbean. Let's fly inland to the river and up the river until we know where we are."

Jim started growling and cursing. He said he would never go anywhere else with me, because I had gotten lost and tried to kill him. He was really complaining to himself. I didn't mind. I knew how thankful he was that we were still alive and this was his way of easing the tension and letting off steam.

In fifteen minutes, I spotted a river dead ahead and reached it in only eight minutes. We flew up the river another twenty minutes, then I recognized the little village of Juticalpa, where the Jalan and Yapia Rivers entered into the Putuca River.

Once I was sure, I told Jim to look to his left. He did and asked if that was the village of Juticalpa.

"Well, it sure as hell ain't El Paso, Texas."

The old boy really had a cussing seizure. "Go to hell!" he shouted. Then he started muttering to himself that the world was in one hell of a mess when the younger generation wouldn't even give a civil answer to their elders' questions.

I ignored him, smoked a cigarette, then started calling the control tower in Tegucigalpa. The tower answered me right away and informed me I was expected and the armored car was awaiting our arrival.

At 8:28, we flew over a beautiful green tropical mountain,

and there, dead ahead, was Tegucigalpa. In just a minute, Jim looked down and recognized the city. He didn't say a word.

I waited a couple of minutes, picked up the radio mike and shouted, "Ladies and gentlemen, this is your pilot speaking. Please check your bras, pantyhose, girdles, and seat belts, and babies. In three more minutes, we will be landing at El Paso International Airport."

I glanced at Jim, he was about to swallow his tongue, trying to keep from laughing out loud. "Hmmmm . . ." was the only reply I got.

Once on the ground, I turned and taxied toward the control tower. *Señor* Padilla and Ramon were waving to us. I taxied to the control tower and stopped.

Señor Padilla opened the door. He asked how the flight was and if we had any trouble, since we were an hour late. Before Jim could say anything, I assured *Señor* Padilla we didn't have any trouble and it had been a nice smooth flight down.

Jim almost choked, for never would we have a closer call or a more dangerous experience.

Señor Perez, the banker, came over, followed by six policemen carrying Tommy guns. After shaking hands all around, he asked if we were ready to load the gold. Jim assured him we were. The banker motioned for the armored car and it drove alongside the plane.

Once the gold was safely in the bank, the chemist started drilling each bar for assaying.

Jim, Ramon and I headed for the hotel Prado for breakfast. I ordered a double shot of bourbon. After the flight and beating we had taken, we needed a drink.

The waiter thought he had misunderstood. "A double shot of bourbon for breakfast, *señors?*" he asked.

"You heard right," Jim told him. "And don't get smart with us. What the hell's the matter with you, didn't you ever hear of people drinking their breakfast?"

The waiter was very polite. He didn't bat an eye. He then apologized, bowed, and said, "Of course, *señors,* as you wish."

The expression in the waiter's eyes plainly questioned the gringos' sanity. We ate and went to our rooms. I didn't even undress, just fell across the bed. I was exhausted.

The knocking at my door awakened me. I glanced at my watch. It was 3:30. I had slept all day. When I opened the door, there stood Jim, Padilla, and Perez. They had the assay results and it averaged eight hundred forty fine, or eighty-four percent pure. Jim and I were satisfied with the assay.

The gold was eight-four percent pure and contained sixteen percent impurities, which was the usual case in old gold that was smelted years ago. By deducting sixteen percent from five hundred and thirty dollars, our gold was worth four hundred forty-five dollars and twenty cents per ounce.

Señor Perez wanted to know what time to expect us tomorrow morning. I asked, as a favor, if he could see us at 8:00 A.M., one hour before the bank opened so we could weigh the gold and count the money before all the bank employees arrived. This he agreed to do.

Ramon and I went to the airport and had the plane refueled, and the rear engine repaired. I was surprised, for we had less than a thirty minute fuel reserve when we landed. I had all tanks filled to capacity.

We were at the bank at 8:00 the next morning and *Señor* Perez received us at once. When we finished weighing the gold, I couldn't believe there were thirty one thousand ounces—only eleven pounds short of a ton. No wonder I had trouble on take-off from the ranch. We re-weighed, just to make sure, and there had been no mistake.

Thirty-one thousand, eight hundred and twenty-four ounces at four hundred forty-five dollars and twenty cents an ounce, came to fourteen million, one hundred sixty-eight thousand, forty four dollars and eighty cents.

We watched *Señor* Padilla and *Señor* Perez count out that long green in good old U.S. one hundred dollar Williams.

I never realized that a foreign bank could have so much U.S. money. We had four large suitcases full of the lovely stuff. We shook hands and assured the bankers we would be back in the morning with the rest of the gold and the jewels.

Señor Perez insisted we ride to the airport in the armored car. This we did. Jim remained inside the armored car for protection, until I very carefully checked the plane over.

When I had both engines started, Jim came running to the plane and very carefully placed the suitcases of money on the back seat. He locked and closed the door.

"Let's go, Mark. If we can get off the ground, we have a fortune."

I hit the runway rolling. We really kept a sharp lookout for any squalls or thunderstorms, but it was a nice smooth, sunny flight all the way back to the ranch.

Chapter 36

IF JIM and I had been prodigal sons, we couldn't have received a more warm and loving welcome. Maria came into my arms. Tears of relief and happiness were streaming down her cheeks. Everyone was trying to talk at once. It seemed we had given everyone quite a scare when we took off yesterday morning.

Jackie told us the coffee was made and waiting. I asked José to bring the suitcase from the plane.

After we were seated around the table, I opened the suitcases and set them on top of the table. Everyone's eyes really popped out. Tex finally regained his speech and asked how much money was there. When I told him more than fourteen million, no one could believe our good fortune.

José did a little dance of joy and said, "*Esta muy bueno.* That will buy a lot of beer and *señoritas.* Why we don't have a big party and celebrate?"

"Easy, José," I replied. "Until our fortunes are secure, there will be no party, beer, or women. Understand?"

He didn't. "*Por qué*, my brother? What good is the money if you do not make the dance and party and enjoy it?"

I decided to ignore his question, for I couldn't explain and make him understand.

After lunch, Jim, Tex, Luis and I went to service the plane. Tex stooped down and was inspecting one of the tires when he called my attention to several large dents under the bottom of the plane.

Jim and I crawled under the plane for a better look. To our surprise, there were three dents where the weight of the gold had almost broken through the bottom of the plane. We told Tex and Luis about the terrible storm, and how close we had come to death, and how the good Lord had His protecting arms around us. Otherwise, we wouldn't be here, now.

Unnoticed, Maria and Lupe had come out to the plane and overheard our conversation. I turned around and Maria was as white as a ghost. She had understood everything we had said and was translating in Spanish to Lupe.

In just a minute, I had Maria's soft, warm and demanding arms around my neck. She was so shocked and scared, she couldn't say a word. I gently led her back into the house and up to our room. Once inside, she asked me to tell her all about our experience.

I tried to laugh and pass the incident off as if it never happened. Maria wasn't buying. So, I told her we had run into a storm and had had a very narrow escape. "That's it, Marek," she replied, "You are not going back, for I have nothing to live for if I should lose you."

"Look, Maria, I have been flying for over ten years. This is the first time I have ever had such an experience, and it will probably be the last. I have to go back, so let's not discuss it, okay?" I gently laid her back on the bed and started to nibble along her collar bone.

In just a minute, those soft arms that I loved so dearly came around my neck. I asked Maria if she was a student of Chinese philosophy. "Why?" she asked.

"Well, my darling, the Chinese say the best ideas are found in bed."

"Maybe," she replied. "Marek, why you don't undress us and we make sure." This sounded like a sure winner to me.

A short time later, Maria pulled my head down to her luscious breast. "Why you don't kiss my titty and make me a woman? The Chinos are very smart people, are they not?" I had to agree.

My blood had passed the boiling point and Maria's soft, warm body was quivering with passion. It seemed as if I had never needed a woman so much.

After we satisfied our desire for each other, we were too exhausted to talk. We lay in each other's arms completely contented.

We had a cigarette. Then Maria reached across me to the ashtray. One of her soft, warm breasts brushed across my face. I couldn't resist kissing it. In just a few minutes, we had forgotten all about being exhausted and, all the world ceased to exist. We were in a beautiful heaven all alone.

Later, there was a knock on the door. Jim asked if I wanted to load the plane before dark. Maria started to get up to dress. I took her in my arms and laid her back on the bed. "Stay in bed, darling. I'll be as quick as I can."

She stuck her chest out. Both beautiful breasts stood at attention. I started to kiss those pink upturned nipples, but Maria pulled the blanket up over her head and said, "No kisses until you come back. Remember what is waiting for you, and please hurry home."

I was surprised. When I reached the plane, the gold was there waiting for Jim and me to load and distribute as we thought best.

Once the job was finished, I asked Jim to wake me at 12:30 so we would have time to eat breakfast and put the flashlights out on the runway for markers, and be ready to take off no later than 1:15 A.M.

"What about dinner?" Jim asked.

"Forget it, old man," I replied. "I'll eat when I get old and cranky like some people I know. Right now, I have a very pleasant appointment." I made a run for the house.

As I entered the door, I looked back. Jim had thrown his hat on the ground and had jumped about two feet high before he landed. I turned and entered the house. I knew he was fixing to have a cussing seizure and now he could afford a new hat. Furthermore, the bigger the fit and more steam he let off today, the more bearable tomorrow's flight would be.

I entered our room, bowed, and introduced myself. "*Señorita,* I am looking for the most desirable and beautiful woman in all Mexico and the whole world, in fact. Maybe you can help me. She has the most beautiful blue-black eyes and hair like a lovely goddess. A figure that has never before been seen on this earth and the most perfect breasts that no man can resist kissing. Do you know of such a lovely creature?"

"No, *Señor*," Maria answered, "only from pity and sympathy do I speak. Would you consider a poor, ugly and undesirable Mexican girl who has none of the beauty you have just spoken of? But, *Señor*, this girl loves with all her heart and soul, and she lives only for an Americano who has completely won her heart and love."

"*Señorita*, I am an American, but don't get the wrong ideas. I can be had, but I am no pushover, and I do not sleep with strange women unless I have been formally introduced to them.

At this time, Maria was completely covered, with only one beautiful eye peeking out. "*Perdone, Señor,* I only wish I could be of help."

Maria pulled the blanket down and exposed her beautiful bosom. "From your conversation, I see you are a man of good judgment and good taste. Would you please look and see if in your opinion this would be nice enough for a man to want to kiss."

"*Señorita*, they are very beautiful breasts. As a matter of fact, the loveliest I have ever seen. But, only by kissing them can I be sure. Do you give me permission?"

"Very well, *Señor*, since we have been formally introduced, I know I am safe. So you may proceed."

I dropped to my knees and gathered Maria, blanket and all, in my arms and gently started kissing her breast. I took that pink, ripe, tasty nipple in my mouth and it got as hard in my mouth as fresh strawberry.

Once again, those loving arms came around my neck and pulled my lips down to hers and our bodies seemed to melt together and become one. She muttered between kisses. "I love an ugly Americano with all my heart and soul. He is smart enough to love and make me a woman when I need his love so much. If you are the one of my heart, why you don't stop this wahoo?"

I had previously told Maria a joke about a President who was campaigning through New Mexico. The President had stopped at the Apache Indian Reservation and was making a speech to the Indians, telling them of all the many and wonderful things he was going to do for them if they supported him.

After each promise he made, all the Indians would jump up and shout, "Wahoo." The President was very impressed with his speech and himself. After his speech, the Indian Chief invited the President down to the corral to see his prize bull.

As they entered the corral, the bull manure was everywhere. The Indian Chief pointed to a fresh pile of bull shit, and said, "Be careful, Mr. President, you don't step in that pile of wahoo."

"What did you say," I asked Maria. I wanted to hear her say 'wahoo' again. Her accent was like a very soft bell.

"Why you don't stop this wahoo and make me a woman?"

At 10:00, I got up, shaved, and showered and went back to bed. Maria put those velvet arms around me, arms that any man would die for. Then she rolled on top of me and gently brushed my face with her warm firm breasts. Even though I was a tired, spent force, I rose to the occasion.

She gave me a long, sweet passionate kiss, then looked down into my eyes and said, as she pressed her breasts in my face, "Marek, do you want me to make you a man?"

Maria had a wonderful sense of humor. For, always, my way of asking her if she was ready to be loved was, do you want me to make you a woman? She had very clearly informed me she was ready to be loved again.

After having those full, ripe breasts rubbed across my face, I was all for being made a man. It seemed a wonderful idea.

At 11:00 Maria got up and started to dress. "Where are you going?" I asked her.

She touched her lips to mine and said, "I go now, my husband to fix your breakfast."

I turned over and went to sleep. It seemed I had only closed my eyes when I was awakened by Maria calling me, kissing my eyes and lips.

When she saw I was awake, she kissed me again and I felt the warm salty tears on my face.

"Marek, it is time for you to go to work. I will never again ask you to not do what you must do. I will only pray for your success and safe return."

I washed up, dressed, and with my arm around Maria, went down to breakfast. Everyone was present except Raul, who was guarding the plane and gold.

After we had eaten, Tex and I collected all the flashlights and went out to mark the runway. We did exactly as we had before. After all the flashlights were in the desired position, we returned to the house, and, taking the saddlebags of jewels, we all walked out to the plane.

Once again, it was time for Jim and me to take off in a dark lonesome night with nothing to guide us. Only our experience would make the difference between success and death. No one said a word on our walk from the house to the plane.

When we reached the plane, we silently shook hands with Tex, Luis, José and Raul. Maria and Lupe made the sign of the cross on both Jim and me. They didn't have to ask us to kiss the cross when they put their thumbs to our lips.

No man could live through what Jim and I had experienced on our previous flight without knowing God's love, and how He had put His protecting arms around us in our greatest danger.

I gave Maria a little squeeze and kiss, then got into the plane. Jim followed. I started both engines, taxied to the far end of the runway, then pushed all the throttles wide open. I held the brakes until the plane was vibrating so that it was fixing to start tearing the motors from their mounts. I then released the brakes and we were headed down the runway and on our way.

I didn't glance at the speed indicator until we were about three hundred feet from the end of the runway—seventy miles an hour. I eased the nose wheel off the ground and when the nose blanked out the lights at the end of the runway, I pulled back on the stick and we were flying. This time the warning buzzer didn't come on.

I eased the nose down and picked up flying speed. Then I released ten degrees of flaps and started to climb up. After releasing all flaps, I circled out over the ocean and back over the ranch. The flashlights looked like a small string of light-ning bugs on the ground far below. Four more circles and I was up to twelve thousand and five hundred feet.

After trimming out and setting the automatic pilot, I slapped Jim on the shoulder, told him the course we were to fly and to please take over. I was going to catch forty winks if I could trust him not to fly into another storm.

He put both hands on the controls, didn't answer me, but started growling to himself that if the younger generation had enough sense to get more sleep and less loving, they would be able to stay awake and not impose on their elders.

I laid my head against the window of the plane, and, just as I was going to sleep, Jim gently pulled my head over and put his Stetson between my head and the window. In a very low breath, said, "I don't blame you, son. It's all right. Get all the loving you can while you are young. Hell, you can fly when you get old."

Voices awoke me. It was Jim calling the control tower in Tegucigalpa. We were only about twenty miles from our destination. I had slept all the way.

It was daylight and the sun was shining. It was a beautiful day.

"Where are we?" I asked. "I'll bet you are lost and have flown a circle, and we are over Canada or Alaska."

Jim gave me a go to hell look, acknowledged the tower's reply in Tegucigalpa, then told me to keep my damned hands off the controls.

In five minutes, we sighted Tegucigalpa. Jim made a perfect landing and taxied toward where *Señor* Perez, *Señor* Padilla, and Ramon were waving to us.

I turned around and reached for the saddlebags of jewels and put it inside my suitcase.

In just a few minutes all the gold had been transferred from the plane to the armored car. Perez didn't show any interest whatsoever in the gold. All his interest was in the jewels.

He was so interested that I became suspicious. I winked at Jim and shook my head, then I told Perez that the buyer and appraiser in Acapulco would be waiting tonight to make us an offer on the jewels.

If we could get the gold assayed in time to fly back to

Mexico late this afternoon, then we would be back early tomorrow with the jewels. *Señor* Perez was very disappointed; then he assured me he would have the assayer rush the reports so we could depart for Mexico no later than 5:00 P.M.

Jim, Ramon and I stopped at the hotel for breakfast. Once we were alone, Jim started giving me hell. "Why did you tell Perez we didn't bring the jewels?"

"Look, Jim, he was too anxious. Also, the gold and the jewels are worth a small fortune. I was afraid we wouldn't be allowed to get out of the city with so much money.

"Let's play it safe. This afternoon, we will get our money from the gold, fly up to Juticalpa, which is about ninety miles, spend the night there, and hide the money from the sale of the gold in the tail of the plane, then in the morning, we will come back here. We tell Perez we have only brought about one-third of the jewels and if we can make a deal on these, we will bring the other two-thirds within three days.

"This way, we will complete the deal, have all of our money, and be back safe in Mexico before Perez realizes we aren't coming back, and have no more jewels. For some reason, I'm suspicious and don't trust Perez."

Jim took about five minutes over coffee to think over what I had said. He finally agreed to go along with my idea.

I had to kid Jim and asked him what he would do without me. He turned red in the face and said, "That's not the question. The question is, what in the hell am I going to do with you?"

I got up, patted him on the back, and told him while he was figuring that one out to pay the bill. I was going to my room and get some sleep. I heard him swearing to himself as I left the room.

At 2:00 P.M., the phone awoke me. Señor Perez was calling from the bank to inform me the assays were ready on the gold and to please come to the bank.

On the way to the bank, Jim asked if the assay reports hadn't been made too quick.

"Sure thing," I replied. "The banker is very anxious to get those jewels." Jim wanted to know what I expected once we reached the bank.

"This is my idea, Jim. Perez is smart. The reports will be practically the same as the first ones were. I believe he wants the jewels more than he wants the gold."

Perez met us at the door of the bank and showed us to his private office. Jim's banker, *Señor* Padilla was very busy counting money. There were several large stacks of money on the desk.

Perez got right down to business. The gold averaged the same as the first did. There were sixteen thousand, three hundred and ninety two ounces at four hundred forty-five dollars and twenty cents per ounce for a total of seven million, three hundred four thousand, four hundred and forty dollars.

Once again, Señor Perez offered us the protection of the armored car to the airport, which we gratefully accepted and assured him we would be back no later than 8:00 tomorrow morning.

Chapter 37

IT TOOK Jim and me about thirty minutes to remove the lining from behind the back seat in the plane. We had to tie the suitcases of money so they would not get tangled up in the control cables. We then replaced the lining.

We had a nice thirty minute flight from Tegucigalpa to Juticalpa. The little grass runway at Juticalpa is about a mile from the town and right beside the army barracks. We didn't have to worry about anyone trying to steal or break into the plane. All passengers walked to town. There were no taxies, although an ox drawn cart did carry the passengers' luggage from the airport to the little town of 15,000 population.

We checked into the best of the three hotels. This hotel was at least a hundred years old, very beautiful and surprisingly clean. We decided to look the town over. Very few Americans had ever been in this village. We really created a great deal of excitement. I don't know who enjoyed themselves more, Jim and I or the natives. The people were very friendly. We had no problem in communicating since Jim and I both spoke Spanish.

It was dark before we returned to the hotel. While having dinner, I asked the waiter if there was a nice nightclub in town. He told us there was, and offered to go personally and show us where it was.

We finished dinner, went to our room, showered, shaved and dressed. At 9:00, we were ready for what night life Juticalpa had to offer. The waiter, true to his promise, went with us to the nightclub, which was only two blocks from the hotel.

Once inside the club, it was plain to see it served a triple purpose. One, as a dancehall, two as a bar and club, and three, as the local cat house.

There were at least twenty-five young girls sitting along the walls. Some of them were very well dressed and showing their Spanish and Portuguese ancestry. They were very beautiful.

After I had a couple of beers, I asked the waiter where the men's room was. He showed me outside. I had to leave the room and go across the patio. When I came out of the toilet, a very pretty young girl was standing outside the door to the nightclub.

She was very light complected and built like a government post office, everything in the right place.

She spoke to me in Spanish. "Forgive me, Senor, for following you. But never do we have the honor here of having men such as you and your friend.

"We girls make very little money here. Only a few men here can afford to spend money on us, and the two girls that you and your friend chose for tonight, will be envied by all the other girls in this town. The lucky girls will be the talk of the town for many years. Please, *Señor* will you choose me?

"We are very poor, but for this honor, if I am pretty enough, I am yours for whatever you want to give me. I assure you, I am very clean and know how to please a man."

I laid both hands on her shoulders and asked her how much she usually made in one night.

"We get one half of the price of the drinks if a man can afford to buy us a drink, and for loving a man, as I have said, this is a poor village. Sometimes on a good night, all together we make ten dollars. But other nights, we have to take whatever we can get or we don't eat the next day."

I knew, even though she was a prostitute, that she was being truthful with me. I felt sorry for her. "Look" I told her, "and clearly understand everything I say.

"You are a very beautiful and desirable woman, but you see, I have just married a beautiful Mexican girl, that I love and respect with all my heart. I will always went to be worthy of her love and respect, so it isn't possible for me to have you tonight. I love my wife too much to cheat on her."

She raised her face up and looked into my eyes and decided I was telling the truth. She said, "*Señor,* thank you for telling me. I only wish I could meet your wife and tell her what a wonderful husband she has.

"If the no-good *cabron* I loved and gave my virginity to had been only a small part of a man, I would not be here as a whore tonight. I hate this life." She started crying and turned to enter the nightclub.

I took her by the arm and gently turned her around facing me. She wasn't acting. She was crying her heart out. "Look, you say you hate this life, then why are you here?"

"Senor, you don't understand. Once a girl gives her virginity to a man, and her father finds out, he makes her leave his house. She is no longer his daughter or a member of his family. This is the only thing a girl can do to live. I have saved one hundred and fifty *liemprias.* I am a very good seamstress. This gown I am wearing, I make it. My girlfriend, who hates this life as much as I do, is also a good seamstress. She has saved one hundred fifty *liemprias.* When we have saved one thousand *liemprias,* we go to Tegucigalpa and put in a beautiful dress shop and make a good, decent living. Maybe we can even find good men and marry and have a home. Here, we have nothing to live for."

I put my hand under her chin and raised her face up to where I could look down into her eyes. Tears were streaming down her face. "Look, little lady, this is your lucky night."

I took ten one hundred liempria bills from my pocket. "Here's a thousand liempria. You said you had saved one hundred fifty liemprias and your girl friend has saved the same amount, so now you have three hundred liempria more than you need to go into business. If you aren't lying to me, you have just retired from your profession."

To my surprise, she refused to take the money.

"Look," I told her, "this can be a loan. I believe you and I want to see you have a chance. So, take it as a loan."

She agreed and put the money in two banks, both sides of her bra. "Will you do me a favor?" I asked.

"Oh, si, Senor, anything. What do you wish?"

"Go back inside and get your girlfriend. The two of you

come over to the table and join me and my friend. My friend is a little old and bashful. You sit with me and I want your friend to really warm up and love my friend. Understand?'' She nodded her head.

"When my friend and I get ready to leave, we will tell you the name and number of our hotel rooms so everyone will hear and give you each twenty liemprias and tell you to come to our room when you are through working for the night, but don't you come. This way all your friends will think that you are spending the night with us, and you can go to wherever you live, pack your clothes and leave this town tomorrow.

"If anyone should ask you where you are going, tell everyone you are going to Tegucigalpa to buy a new dress and that you made a lot of money from the two Americans, savvy?''

"*Si, Señor,*'' she replied. "It is a very good idea, and we will do it.''

She took a handkerchief from her purse and removed her lipstick. Then, like a little girl, she looked up and said, "*Señor,* tonight, for the first time in my life, I have met a man. You will never know what a privilege and how much I would like to give myself to you, but I understand and respect you.

"As a favor, *Señor*, do you think your wife would mind if I kissed you? I want to so very much.''

"Of course not,'' I replied.

I put both arms around her. She stood up on her tiptoes and pressed her lips against mine. She stepped back, looked at me and burst out crying. She held out her arms to me.

I am only human and have never been able to resist temptation. So, I gently turned her around, slapped her on her shapely bottom and pushed her toward the door. I told her to hurry and get her friend and join Jim and me.

I had a smoke and waited a minute, then went inside. Jim asked where I had been and said, "You were gone so long I thought you had gone to take a crap and the hogs ate you.''

I asked Jim why he didn't invite two of the girls over for company. Before he could answer, I motioned to Marta, the girl I had met outside.

Marta and her girlfriend hurried over. When they introduced themselves, they both squeezed my hand and said thanks. I knew Marta had already given her friend the wonderful news.

Marta's friend, Yolanda, really warmed up to Jim. After the second round of drinks, we decided to dance. When we came back to our table, Yolanda sat down in Jim's lap. It was very hard for me to keep from laughing at Jim.

He was sitting as straight and stiff as a statue. Both his arms were hanging down limp and almost reaching the floor. The old boy was gazing straight ahead and acting as unconcerned as if he were sitting all alone and watching a T.V. program.

Yolanda put both arms around his neck and started biting the lobe of his ear. I winked at her. All I could see was one big black eye peeking around Jim's head. Her eye lit up like a star and she started kissing Jim's ear.

I could see her pink tongue darting in and out of Jim's ear, as fast as a hummingbird extracting nectar from a blossom.

In just a second, Jim raised one arm and almost encircled her waist. Then let his arm fall down to his side. Yolanda opened her mouth and almost all of Jim's ear disappeared inside.

Jim quivered like a palm tree in a tropical gale. One of his arms went around her shoulders, the other under her knees.

He stood up and said, "That done it, by God, that done it." With Yolanda held closely in his arms, he headed for the door.

I shouted and asked him where he was going. He looked back over his shoulder as he went out the door.

"None of your damn business, and if I didn't like you, I wouldn't even tell you that much."

I was sure Yolanda overplayed her hand, but the way she was clinging around Jim's neck and trying to eat his ear off, it was plain to see this was one bluff she wasn't sorry she had made.

Everyone started laughing. I called the waiter and paid the check. Marta popped her little round butt in my lap. I had noticed earlier it stuck out like a spare tire on a Volkswagon. She put both arms around my neck and whispered in my ear for me to carry her out as Jim had Yolanda.

I gathered her up in my arms and headed for the door. All the other girls started shouting their approval and encouragement.

As I went out he door, I heard one girl complimenting the Americanos for being so *macho*. Once outside, I set Marta down, took her by the arm, and started toward the hotel.

I walked so fast, Marta almost had to run to keep up. I was in a hurry to get rid of her, before I changed my mind and did something I would regret.

As I've said before, there's two things I can't stand and temptation is both. When we reached the hotel, I stopped and told Marta that this was goodbye.

She raised her face to mine and said, "*Señor,* are you sure you don't want me tonight?"

I was very tempted, but I couldn't keep from seeing and remembering Maria's beautiful and innocent face and the love and confidence in her eyes.

"I am very sorry, Marta. You are a very beautiful and desirable girl. I have already told you how much I love and respect my wife. Don't you see, as much as I want you, that I would be thinking of my wife when I made love to you, and never could I get over the guilty feeling. This you could also sense, so we would be a disappointment to each other."

"*Si, Señor,* I understand. Always, I will remember and respect you for being such an honest man, and always, I can dream of how beautiful and great it would have been for us to have had each other. And each night for all the rest of the nights of my life, I will pray to my God to protect you and grant you the peace and happiness that you so deserve."

"Thank you, Marta. If I hear of you ever entering, regardless of the reason, another place such as you are leaving tonight, I make you this promise. I'll come back and beat your little butt off! Do you understand?"

"*Si, Señor,* I do. And now, on the cross and before the blessed Virgin, I make you a promise. Never will I enter such a place again, or even knowingly walk on the same side of the street where such a place is."

I kissed her on the forehead as you would a little girl.

"Goodbye, Marta, and good luck." I turned and started back to the hotel. To me, the most beautiful sentence or benediction I've ever heard is "Vaya Con Dios." I turned, and as I walked away, I heard Marta say, *"Buena suerte, Señor, y vaya con Dios!"*

My intentions were good in trying to help Marta straighten out. If I've been a sucker, this one blessing was worth the five hundred dollars I had given her.

As I lay down in bed, out loud I said to myself, "Maria, my darling, this night I can never tell you about. But, if you could know the truth as it actually happened, I am sure you would be as proud of me for resisting temptation as I am of myself."

Chapter 38

AT 6:00 the next morning, the alarm went off. True to form, Jim was banging and kicking on the door and making more noise than a jackass in a tin barn.

"Okay, okay," I told him, "go order coffee and I'll meet you in the dining room."

When I entered the dining room, Jim was already having his breakfast. As I sat down, he asked me if my date had already left the hotel. I didn't tell Jim that Marta didn't spend the night with me.

I replied that I wasn't so damned old that I couldn't love and satisfy a woman without taking all night to do the job.

"Hmmmmmm . . ." was Jim's only reply.

I could see he was getting red in the face. I started to kid him a little more, then changed my mind. I didn't want to get him all shook up and have to listen to him cuss, complain and bitch on the flight back to Tegucigalpa, so I quickly changed the subject and gave the old boy a snow job.

An hour later, as we finished breakfast, he was in a very good humor and we were laughing and reliving last night's experience. We checked out of the hotel and were off to the airport.

At 7:45 we took off for Tegucigalpa. Thirty minutes later, we were on the ground taxiing toward where *Señor* Perez, *Señor* Padilla and Ramon were waving to us as they had on our previous arrivals. The only difference this time was that they didn't bring the armored truck.

I insisted on gassing up the plane before we went downtown to have the jewels appraised. I sure as hell didn't want to have to take off in a hurry with almost empty gas tanks.

While we were gassing up the plane, I slipped Ramon some money and told him to take a taxi to the hotel, pay his bill, then hurry back to the airport to guard the plane until Jim and I arrived.

We had no more than gotten into the car for the drive downtown to the bank when Perez started asking us how much the jewels had been appraised for and what offer the jeweler in Acapulco had made.

I told Perez that we had brought approximately one third of the jewels and that it would take the jeweler in Acapulco another two days to complete his appraisal on the rest of the jewelry.

If we could do business with him, fine. We would take our money and go back to Mexico and be back in three days with the rest of the jewels. If he couldn't meet the price offered by the jeweler in Acapulco, then we would take our jewels and vamoose for Mexico.

Perez started getting nasty. He informed me he had hired a jewelry man to make the appraisal, and we had misrepresented the deal, since we hadn't brought all the jewels as we had promised to do.

Jim told him, "Look, Mister, if you think we are going to bring all the jewels to you before we have our appraiser determine their value, you are very sadly mistaken, for neither my friends nor I are qualified to determine their value.

"If you ain't satisfied with this arrangement, have the car turn around and take us back to the airport. we don't have to do business with you. Is that clear?" This really made Perez mad.

He started telling us how he had helped and accommodated us by buying the gold. I told him I was under the impression that he was also making a profit. I had never known of a banker losing money on a deal where he made ten dollars an ounce commission.

Señor Perez was sitting in the back seat between Jim and me.

He turned to me and said, "Unless I am willing, you

cannot leave this country with the jewels. I could take them and have you thrown out of our country."

On a mission such as this one, I always carry a little snub-nose thirty eight in the top of my boot. I had crossed my legs while the good banker was talking, and my hand was inside my boot top and around the little pistol. I jerked the pistol out and socked it into Perez's belly, all the way to the cylinder. He sounded like a punctured balloon. "Whoosh," as all the air went out of him.

He looked down at the pistol and turned as pale as a corpse. He tried to grin and said, "*Señor* Mark, I was only kidding."

"Maybe you are," I told him, "but, I sure as hell ain't. The only benefit those jewels will be to any man who tries to take them from us will be as a crown or halo, because he will be a dead son-of-a-bitch!"

The chauffeur threw on the brakes and stopped the car. He turned around to where he could see the back seat, and Jim stuck his pistol between his eyes and told him, "Quick, let's see both your hands, or you'll be the only son-of-a-bitch in Tegucigalpa with three eyes."

The chauffeur almost knocked the car top off, he threw his hands up so fast. Padilla, Jim's friend and banker from Chihuahua started talking, trying to assure us that Perez was honest and we had all made a mistake. Perez assured us he was only kidding and asked us to put away our guns and continue on to the bank and complete our business.

I pulled my pistol out of his belly and put it back into my boot. Jim did the same, only he kept his hand under his coat and told the chauffeur to take off for the bank and that any damn fool should know business was what we were down here for.

Before reaching the bank, I asked *Señor* Padilla if he wanted to stop at his hotel, check out and meet us at the bank. He could go back with us today or wait for us to return in three days.

He talked it over with Perez, and they both agreed that, since he was neglecting his bank in Chihuahua, it wouldn't be necessary for him to wait and be present at the final transaction.

This was good news to my ears, for *Señor* Padilla was the best insurance we could possibly have for being safely returned to the airport and on our way.

Padilla got out of the hotel and promised to come to the bank as soon as he packed and checked out. Perez told us if we wanted to have breakfast and rest, that, as soon as the jewels had been appraised, he would call us at the hotel.

I winked at Jim and started getting out of the car. Jim followed me. I thanked Perez for his thoughtfulness. Once inside the hotel, Jim asked me if I thought we would ever see the jewels again.

"Yes, I do, and this is the reason. *Señor* Perez will be very reluctant to pull a crooked deal in *Señor* Padilla's presence." I winked at Jim, "But, when we return with the rest of the jewels, I don't know what will happen."

Jim grinned and said, "We will worry about that when the time comes."

In about three hours, Perez called us from the bank. When Jim, Padilla and I arrived at the bank, we were greeted personally by *Señor* Perez. He was all smiles just as if nothing had happened.

Once again, we followed him back to his private office. He had all the jewels very neatly displayed on the top of his desk. He asked how much the jewelry man in Acapulco had appraised and offered for all the jewels.

"Look, *Señor* Perez," I replied, "I would not quote your offer to anyone else, and I feel I should respect and keep in confidence the other man's offer. So if you care to bid on the jewels and your offer is higher than his, you have bought them. If your offer is below his, we take the jewels back to him."

Senor Perez asked permission to speak privately with his appraiser. We all left the room.

In about five minutes, he asked us back into the office and offered one million dollars for the jewels. I thanked him for his offer, but told him his offer was far below the one we had received in Acapulco.

I reached for the saddlebag and started to reach for the

jewels. He raised his offer two hundred and fifty thousand dollars. I shook my head and started putting the jewels in the bag. Before I had all the jewels packed, he raised his offer another two hundred and fifty thousand dollars. I shook my head again and started again putting the jewels in the bag.

As I finished packing the last of the jewels, he again raised his offer to one million six hundred and fifty thousand dollars. Again, I shook my head, extended my hand and told him we really appreciated his offer, but I was taking them back to Mexico if this was his final offer. He assured me it was.

We shook hands all around and said goodbye. We were going through the door when *Señor* Perez called us back. He wanted to know the very least we would take.

"One million seven hundred and fifty thousand dollars," I replied. He started trying to negotiate. Once again, I thanked him, and then asked Jim and Padilla if they were ready to go.

As I opened the door, *Señor* Perez said, "Very well, Senor Mark, if you promise to bring the other jewels and give me a chance to bid on them, it's a deal. But, I have gone three hundred thousand dollars above the price my appraiser advised me to give."

I set the bag of jewels back on his desk. He called a teller and had the money brought to his office. We had to take most of our pay in Mexican pesos for he didn't have any more American money.

Once again, we shook hands and assured the banker we would be back in three days. Perez then volunteered to go with us to the airport. I sure breathed a sigh of relief.

We all laughed and joked on the ride to the airport. I asked Jim to check and pre-flight the plane while I filed a flight plan to Mexico. Fifteen minutes later we were ready for take-off.

Señor Perez gave us a big brazo and assured us he would personally be waiting for us on the third morning at 8:00 A.M. Jim winked at me, then told him to be sure and be at the airport at 7:00 A.M. and wait until we arrived. He smilingly agreed.

I could read Jim's mind. Since we had no more jewels and

wouldn't be coming back, Jim wanted Perez to have to wait as long as possible for having been so snooty to us.

I still wasn't convinced that we would be allowed to take off. I am sure Jim felt the same way. I started both engines and called the control tower. The tower answered back. "Five-two-Sugar, you will hold your position until further advised."

Jim and I looked at each other. Jim told Ramon to unsnap the curtain behind the back seat and locate the two pump shot-guns and if he asked for them to hand them to us fast.

I glanced at the end of the runway. A commercial airliner was on about a two mile final. The commercial liner landed and taxied off the runway just as I reached for the mike. The control tower came in and I heard the sweetest words ever spoken, "Thank you for waiting and good day five-two-Sugar. You are clear for take-off."

They didn't have to tell me twice. I was rolling before I acknowledged.

I held the nose of the plane on the runway for at least three thousand feet. Jim asked if I was going to fly home or taxi home.

I glanced at the speed indicator—one hundred twenty miles an hour. I eased the plane off the ground, jerked the gear up, and headed straight up like a homesick angel.

That altitude between me and the ground sure did feel and look good. We were all very happy and really had a ball on the flight.

Señor Padilla congratulated us on having made a fortune and started to caution us on our return. Jim laughed and told Padilla this was the last trip—that we were afraid to let Perez know we didn't have any more jewels.

Señor Padilla agreed we had been very wise, especially since he wouldn't be there to help protect our interest.

We had almost done the impossible, but actually, we had paid a bitter price. There was Carlos, Luis' brother, who was killed in the car accident when Tex and I were injured; poor Pepe, who had died from the sting of a scorpion; then Snider and Block, who had stolen the first half of the treasure.

Even thieves, men as sorry as they were, somewhere have

someone who loves them, and for all eternity, will lie in unmarked graves, with no one except Jim and God knowing their final resting place.

And, last, but not forgotten, Juan, José's brother, who was so brutally beaten to death and murdered by Flores. That makes five dead men, which is a bed full for any man to have to sleep with every night. And, there was one more to go, Tino Flores.

Now that we had successfully sold all the treasure, I knew I couldn't rest until we met. This world is a big place, but it's too small for the two of us. I also knew there was a chance he might kill me, but I sure as hell wouldn't go alone, for I would take him with me.

If we had been five minutes later, we would have had to fly on to Acapulco to land. It was getting dark, I could just recognize the ranch house when we reached Agua Blanca.

I had to leave the landing lights on to see how to taxi back to the house. Once again, we were all together.

If we had all been blood relations, we could not have loved each other more or had a happier reunion or more enjoyable evening. Everyone had been expecting us. The tables were loaded down with food and I've never seen so much champagne for so few people. I had to agree that a celebration was in order.

After dinner, I had a couple of drinks, but I felt tired. Maria asked me what was wrong and why I wasn't enjoying myself.

"Nothing is wrong," I assured her. "On the contrary, everything is wonderful and right. We have all had quite an experience and now that the battle has been won and the victory ours I am a little tired."

Maria pulled my head down and kissed me. "Of course, my Marek. I am fool woman that I didn't realize how much worry and strain you have gone through. Come, my darling, we go to our room, so you can rest."

I looked around. As drunk as everyone was, we wouldn't be missed.

As usual, José had to upset the applecart. He was sittng flat on his butt on the floor in a corner, by the door. His head was bent over to one side and resting against the wall, trying to hold in both hands a half-full bottle of champagne.

He turned the bottle up to take another drink, forgot to turn his head, and missed his mouth, pouring most of the champagne in his ear and down his shirt collar.

This small incident didn't dampen his spirits in the least. As far as José was concerned, there were only two things in life —women, and booze. These two subjects were all he ever thought about.

I really wasn't surprised when he said, "Look everyone, my brother is the only one here man enough to take his woman." Then added, "Just a minute, my brother, I want to shake the hand of yours and say to you thanks and goodnight."

José managed to brace himself against the wall and get to his feet. He turned the bottle up and this time hit his mouth, drank it all, then staggered two steps toward me extending his hand.

I reached out to shake his hand just as his eyes turned glossy and crossed. Before I could catch him, he hiccupped and fell full length, face-down at our feet and passed out cold. We all knew that the party had been a success as far as José was concerned.

We went to our room and after a shower, I slipped into bed. Maria was waiting there. As she came into my arms, I could feel her warm body and then her full, ripe breasts against my chest. I told her she should be ashamed, going to bed with only her panties on.

"It is true, Marek, but what about you? You don't even have on the panties!"

Which was very true. I was as naked as a master of ceremonies at a nudist convention.

Maria lay in my arms for just a minute, then wiggled herself up to where she could look into my eyes, and asked, "Marek, why we don't kiss each other?"

The moon was shining through the window and as I looked on her beautiful face, I remembered last night in Juticalpa and Marta, the prostitute. I was very thankful as I kissed Maria's sweet innocent lips, that I hadn't betrayed her confidence and was worthy of her kisses.

Later, with my eyes heavy with sleep and Maria lying in my arms, I laid the blanket back to our waists and with the beautiful moonlight shining through the window and with an angel in my arms, I drifted off to the heavenly world of sleep.

Chapter 39

EARLY THE next morning all of us men gathered around the table for our last conference. They all elected me spokesman and asked me to preside over the meeting.

I thanked them and said, "Before I open the meeting, I would consider it a pleasure to have the honor of shaking hands with each of you, for never again will we be as close a team as we have been in the past months.

"I want to thank each of you for your loyalty, and for being so honest, for it's unbelievable that a group of men could have worked together and handled so much gold and jewels as we have, without anyone of us getting greedy. This is why we succeeded. Now, it's time we go our separate ways.

"Gentlemen, we received fourteen million, one hundred sixty-eight thousand and forty-four dollars and eighty cents from the first sale of gold we flew to Honduras. We received seven million three hundred four thousand and four hundred dollars for the second sale. We received one million, seven hundred fifty thousand dollars from the sale of the jewels. This makes a total of twenty-three million, two hundred twenty-two thousand four hundred forty-four dollars and eighty cents, which is quite a bundle.

"Now comes the time to divide up the money. Each of us has suffered enough tears and heartaches, not to mention the hardships, that we have earned every penny we will receive. We also have a balance of thirty thousand dollars left in the expense kitty."

I continued, "Well, men my first suggestion is that we pay *Señor* Padilla twenty four thousand dollars for his service in

354

helping us sell the gold. Secondly, but not least, we take six thousand, which is the amount the Mortuary in Acapulco has agreed upon, to move Pepe to wherever Ramon wants him moved to his final resting place." (Pepe's burial was completed in a month).

We all agreed that Carlos, Luis' brother, and Juan, José's brother should receive an equal share, with the money going to their wives and children.

Now came the big question. How was the big money to be divided? I asked *Señor* Padilla, to please figure out a plan of division that would be fair and just to all parties concerned.

I excused myself and left the room, for I didn't intend to help figure up each person's share. I had carried almost the entire responsibility in the complete operation. No more for me.

About an hour later, Tex came to where Maria and I were sitting in the patio and asked me to come inside the room. They had all come to an agreement, if it was acceptable to me.

When I re-entered the room, *Señor* Padilla had a large sheet of figures before him and told me, "*Señor* Mark, this is what we have agreed upon, subject to your approval."

"For José, Ramon, Raul, Juan's family and Carlos' family, eleven percent each, or each person receiving two million dollars each. I assure you, *Señor* Mark, in Mexico, two million dollars is a fortune.

"The same for *Señors* Jim, Tex, and Luis, eleven percent each, or two million. And for you, Senor, everyone would have it no other way. You are to receive twelve percent, or a total of more than two and one half million dollars."

I was overcome by their generosity and thoughtfulness. I started to object, when Jim asked me if I was satisfied with the percentages and if my share was enough.

"More than enough," I replied, "But I won't accept a larger share than . . ."

Jim interrupted me before I could finish and said, "If you are satisfied, shut your damn mouth and go ahead with the meeting. We ain't got all day."

Everyone started clapping and shouting their approval. It

took me a minute to get the lump out of my throat. I cautioned everyone to invest their money wisely and reminded them that once upon a time, José had owned a ranch, but had let the whores and tequila break him.

José spoke up and said, "Maybe I take mine and Juan's wife's money and buy another rancho, bigger and better than the one we had before."

"Oh, no you don't, José, not this time," I told him. "This time, my brother, I personally am making sure of your family and Juan's family's future security."

I then asked Raul if he would trust me and the banker to figure out a time-deposit and interest rate on their money so they would have a nice income each month to live on for all their lives.

Raul didn't understand. "What this is?" he wanted to know.

José patted my shoulder and told Raul his brother's idea was a very good one and not to be the fool, that I would take care of everything.

Senor Padilla asked José and Raul how they would like to live in Mazatlan for the rest of their lives.

They had one question: Could they get a job and make a little money?

When Padilla explained no job would be needed, they both really went for the idea.

"All right. Here's what we have figured for you two and Juan's family. You can each buy a big, beautiful home and pay for it, have maids, and your wives will also have money to buy all the beautiful furniture it takes to furnish the home.

"You will have plenty of money to live for one month, and each month you come to my bank, and by only signing a piece of paper, you and Raul will receive ten thousand pesos each. That is yours for beer, cigarettes and the muchachas and your wives will sign a paper and receive more than two hundred fifty thousand pesos each month.

"With this money, they will pay the taxes on the house, pay all the bills, servants, food and clothing, and have enough left over to send your kids to the best college in Mexico."

"How many times we do this?" Raul wanted to know.

They couldn't believe it when I told them each month for as long as they lived, regardless of how old they were or how many years they lived.

I didn't want them to know they had more than one and a half million dollars each on a life time deposit. This I could explain to their wives, and of course, their children would get a good education and know how to handle the estate upon their deaths.

Jim, *Señor* Padilla, Tex and I would make sure of their interest until the children were capable of managing their own affairs.

When José and Raul came back into the room, they sat down on each side of me. José spoke up and said, "Say to me again, my brother, how much money we get each month by only signing the paper at the bank. Me and Raul don't drink nothing, but still we think we are drunk and do not hear so good."

"All right, José. You and Raul listen carefully. I'll explain again. Each month, for as long as you live, you will receive ten thousand pesos a month. All you and Raul have to do is buy your cigarettes. The rest you can spend on beer and the girls."

"Is good!" they both agreed. They only had one small problem. If they spent all the money on beer and girls, who would feed and clothe their families and pay the expenses on the casas?

"Look," I told them, "as *Señor* Padilla explained before, each month, your wives sign a paper. They receive more than two hundred fifty thousand pesos each. Also, Juan's wife will receive the same amount, and with this money they will pay the maids, food, clothing and all the expenses." When they finally understood, they were two happy men.

José had to brag a little. He stuck his chest out, turned toward Raul and told him, "See what I say to you. My brother is the smartest man in the world. Already he has made the interest that don't deposit, and this fast. We are rich with fine homes."

Raul agreed it was too good to be true, and he was very

happy. Also, very honest.

"But, José, tell me," he asked, "how we only sign this paper each month? And how the deposit makes the money to pay us when we have no interest?"

Of course, José was dense as dog shit. He didn't understand it either, but he wasn't going to admit to his stupidity.

José tried to look very dignified, then answered, "*Por favor,* Raul, someday when I am not too busy, all this I explain to you so you are not fool all your life."

That's one conversation I would like to eavesdrop on.

José came up with a question I was afraid he would ask. "Why, my brother, we only get ten thousand pesos each month and our wives get over two hundred and fifty thousand pesos?" I had my answer ready.

I tried to look shocked and surprised. I threw an arm around each of them and clamped my hands over their mouths and stood up. Of course, they were forced to get to their feet. I half ran and had dragged them to the far corner of the room.

I continued to hold my hands over their mouths, pulled their heads close together, and loud enough for everyone to hear, told José and Raul never to even think of this matter again.

I asked them both to promise me they would never tell anyone about them or their wives signing the paper at the bank each month, that they knew how hard the Mexican Government was trying to educate all the children, and if they told anyone or didn't make all their children go to school and get a good education, the government would make *Señor* Padilla stop letting them sign the paper for the money.

And, furthermore, if they ever asked their wives for any of the money to buy beer and spend on the girls, that they both knew how sneaky the government was, and the government would be sure to find out, and then, no more money.

"Now, José, you and Raul, both promise me to never think of this again, much less tell anyone. Do you promise?"

They both agreed by nodding their heads.

I knew the subject would never be discussed again, because

as loyal as José and Raul were, drunk or sober, you couldn't get anything out of them with a corkscrew.

I released them and told them to hurry outside and make sure no one had heard our conversation. Without a word, they both took off. Once they were out of the room, Tex and Luis started to laugh.

Jim slammed his fist down on the table and wanted to know what was so damn funny. Luis, still laughing, wanted to know if Jim didn't understand what I had told José and Raul, and "Did you see the way they took off?"

"Hell, yes," Jim replied, "I saw and understood. You and Tex heard but didn't understand. You thought it was funny. I didn't find it funny and you don't see Mark or *Señor* Padilla laughing, do you?" Jim was really getting worked up.

"Hell, no, you don't!" Tex's mouth was open in astonishment.

Luis said, "I don't understand."

Jim said, "Well, since you and Tex are both damn idiots and dumber than a milk cow, I'll explain. We all have trust and confidence in Mark but those two worship him. Look at José. Even now, his face is still scarred and black from the beating he took, which a lot of men wouldn't have taken before squealing on a friend.

"Now, ask yourself this question. How many men could stand and see their brother beat to death before their eyes as José did when that goddamn sorry son-of-a-bitch Tino Flores murdered Juan.

"José never betrayed Mark, all the time knowing one word would have saved Juan's live. Do you think any man could ever get José and Raul to reveal the source of their money?"

"What Mark did was to make sure their wives and children were well cared for, leaving José and Raul party money. And, they will always be too afraid to take money from their families to party on, or discuss this with anyone. Who would be smart enough to wise them up?"

Before Jim could continue, José and Raul came in.

José marched up and very proudly informed me that no one was outside. "But, my brother, I am very much afraid and worried."

"Why, José?" I asked.

"You do not know this, but my three oldest childrens, I make them stop going to school."

"Why?" I wanted to know.

"For this reason," José replied. "They were learning too much, and if I don't quit them from school, pretty soon they be smarter than their papa."

I was shocked, but knowing José, I knew that was exactly the way he thought. I hung my head down, and started shaking it from side to side as I walked across the room as if in deep thought.

Finally, José couldn't stand the suspense any longer. He caught me by the arm.

"What we can say? What we can do?" He wanted to know.

I ignored José and asked Señor Padilla: since no one in Mazatlan would know José's children, couldn't we start them to school and no one would ever know.

He took about a minute to think it over, then answered that he was sure he could, if José and Raul promised to keep all their kids as well as Juan's kids in school. José's face lit up like a Christmas tree. He and Raul assured us only sickness would spoil a perfect attendance.

Chapter 40

NOW THAT everything was settled and agreed upon, we called all the women together and told them to be packed and ready to leave for Mazatlan early tomorrow morning.

Jim, Tex and I drove about ten miles to say thanks and pay Sanford Parks the rent on the house which we had been using the past month.

He was a typical big-hearted rancher. He invited us in for coffee and threw a fit when we tried to pay him rent on the house.

He and Jim had a cussing contest for about ten minutes and since neither could outswear the other, it ended in a "Mexican stand-off," with Sanford promising to bring his family and visit with Jim for at least a month in the very near future.

On the way back to the ranch, we decided to start José, Raul and Ramon in the car for Mazatlan. By driving all night, they could be there tomorrow morning before we arrived in the two planes.

As soon as we were back at the house, Jim corralled everyone and told them of our plans. In thirty minutes, we had the car loaded and the three on their way. We spent a very quiet and relaxing evening. Everyone was very sad to leave.

Each of us, in our own way, would always remember our stay at this house and the moments of fear, waiting, love and friendship would stay with us for the rest of our lives.

We took off early the next morning and had a good, smooth flight to Mazatlan. When we landed there at 9:50, José, Ramon and Raul were waiting for us. I went to the control tower, closed my flight plan and had just joined the group when Jim and party arrived.

I asked Ramon to drive the women around until they found a motel they wanted to stay at, deliver our luggage to the motel, and come to the bank and wait for us.

Tex, *Señor* Padilla, and I carried two suitcases of money, each. We caught two cabs and went directly to the bank. When we arrived, it took *Señor* Padilla until noon to complete the merger, or sale of the bank, or whatever he did to assume management of the bank.

Finally, at 2:00 P.M., all the papers were in order and we were all called into the President's office.

It took another two hours to get all the money deposited to our accounts and the time-deposits set up correctly for all of us. We were all tired and hungry. We had been in the bank for six hours.

Jim was complaining to himself that he never realized it was easier to make money than to get it deposited in a bank after you had it. We couldn't all ride in the car, so Tex, Luis and Raul followed us in a taxi.

When we arrived at the motel, which was a very nice place and right on the beach, I had to compliment the girls on their choice. They had been able to rent three-room apartments, complete with kitchenettes.

Maria met me at the door and put those warm loving arms around my neck, kissed me and told me to hurry and wash up for dinner.

She took my face in her hands and said, ''My poor husband, you are so exhausted. Please, Marek, tonight no business talks, only rest.''

I went into the bathroom and when I looked in the mirror, I could see what Maria meant. Holy Hell! My face was as wrinkled as a prune. I had aged five years in the past three months, which wasn't surprising considering the physical and mental strain I had gone through, not to mention the responsibility I had carried for all of us.

Maria was very happy. This was the first meal that she had ever cooked herself. It was a delicious dinner, I really put the food away and praised her cooking.

"Look, honey," I told her, "you are the best cook in all Mexico and the best wife, if only you were not so ugly, you would be perfect."

Maria came and put her arms around me and started kissing and biting my ear. Between kisses, she was whispering in my ear, "What you . . . say is . . . true . . . my husband. I am ashamed to be . . . so ugly."

I pulled her down on my lap and started to kiss her throat and unbutton her blouse. "Don't do that, Marek," she said, "for in the refrigerator I have for you the dessert."

I ignored her and unbuttoned her blouse. She started fighting like a cat. I only held her more firmly against me and very gently raised up her bra. She was wiggling and fighting. I started kissing her lovely full breasts.

Both her arms went around my neck. In another minute it seemed we were melted together. Maria whispered in my ear, "Marek, why we don't have dessert in bed?" With the sweet delicious, pink strawberry that I had in my mouth, I was all for dessert in bed.

We had just gotten up and dressed when Jim and Lupe came over. Maria served pie and coffee. After I tasted the pie, which was delicious, I winked at Maria and told her this dessert wasn't as good as the last dessert I had.

Jim rose to Maria's defense. "What the hell is the matter with you, Mark? This pie is perfect. Dammit, you don't appreciate good food!"

I ignored Jim and told Maria, "Look, woman, you will serve your husband the dessert of his choice. Understand?"

Maria was trying very hard to keep a straight face and not laugh. "Yes, my husband," she replied, "and each night when you return home for your dinner, your dessert will be sitting on your plate ready for you."

I almost laughed out loud. I could just see Maria sitting on my plate on the table with only her panties on and her lovely breasts standing straight out at attention.

I was grateful when Jim told Maria to ignore me and make me eat out every night. This gave me the needed excuse to laugh, without Jim becoming wise to what Maria and I were really thinking.

We finished our coffee, then Jim told me that Senor Padilla, Ramon, Lupe and he were leaving for Chihuahua early the next morning. He was very anxious to get back to his ranch, and lamented no one would ever know how happy he was to get the mortgage paid off.

"Why don't you and Maria come and visit for a few days?" I thanked Jim for his invitation, but reminded him that I had to help José and Raul buy their houses and figure some way to get their families and Juan's family out of Loreto. When I said Loreto, Jim jumped up and stuck his finger under my nose.

"How in the hell are you going to do it?" he wanted to know. Before I could answer, he started cussing me for being the dumbest, stupidest, s.o.b. it had ever been his misfortune to meet.

I pushed his hand out of my face and informed him that if he placed any value on his finger, to keep it out of my mouth, or he would draw back a stub. And furthermore, I wanted to know what brought on this cussing seizure he had just had.

"You're going to Loreto," he replied.

"Look, Jim, I just said we were going to figure some way to get José, Raul and Juan's family out of Loreto. I am not going there."

"How are you going to do it?" he wanted to know. "I don't know at this time, Jim, but give us a little time, and I am sure we will find a way."

Jim interrupted me, "Look, Mark, I've never asked you to make me a promise, but will you promise me to be careful and under no circumstances, go anywhere near Loreto? I know, and you know, that it's only a question of time until Flores finds out where you and Maria are.

"I also know you are as good a shot with a pistol or rifle as I ever saw. Don't fool yourself for one single second that Flores don't know this too. Never get careless or let your guard down or both of you will die when you meet.

"And, when you do meet, don't hesitate. Shoot him. It don't make a damn if it's in the back, belly or side. Just get the bullet in him. Then really get ready for action, for Flores won't be by himself. He will have one, and probably two killers with him. They will shoot you down like a trapped coyote.''

I thanked Jim for the warning and advice. Then I told him, ''When the time comes, I'll try to make it my choice and not his. As soon as I can get José, Raul and Juan's families out of Loreto, I am going for Flores.

''I intend to be the hunter, not the hunted. I know if he finds me first, I haven't got as much chance as a snowball in hell.''

Jim agreed this would be the best way and that it would increase my chances of being the one to walk away alive. Tex, Jackie, Luis and Carmen came in and stopped any further discussion.

We all drank coffee and talked until after 10:00. When Jim realized how late it was, he asked if I would drive them to the airport in the morning.

''What time?'' I asked.

''Before 6:00,'' her replied.

''Look, Jim, if you are broke, I'll lend you taxi fare to the airport, but I'll be damned if I'll get up in the middle of the night and drive you myself.''

He turned red in the face, but before he could throw a fit, Tex saved the day by telling Jim he would be up early and would drive them to the airport.

As Jim and I shook hands, he told me that he and Lupe would be back the following week for a visit, and would I please wait to start my hunt for Flores until he arrived. ''It's a deal, Jim, and thanks, I really appreciate it.''

Jim Dunlap might be fifty-five years old, but he is as active as most men of thirty-five, and I have seen him in a lot of tough tight spots, and if he ever knew the meaning of fear, he never showed it.

I would need someone to watch my back when the showdown came, and I would rather have Jim than anyone I know.

Chapter 41

I AWOKE the next morning with Maria's hand over my mouth. She was almost hysterical, she was laughing so hard. She finally regained her speech. "Please, Marek, you get up and go to the door. We have two very important guests. This you will see, but no believe."

When I looked out the door, I couldn't believe my eyes. There stood José and Raul dressed in their best and only suits. I have never in my life seen suits so wrinkled. Their shirts looked like they had slept in them.

Both wore black suits. Raul's shirt was blue and his wide tie was as yellow as a canary. José was very proud and had every reason to be. He had on a bright purple western shirt and a wide tie, redder than a rooster's butt!

It took me a couple of minutes to get control of myself. I opened the door and invited them in. Maria came in and José stood up and spoke like a little gentleman, then grabbed Raul by the arm and gave him a cussing. Raul wanted to know what he did wrong.

José explained that a gentleman always rose to his feet to greet a lady.

"Por qué?" Raul asked. They both sat down, arose, and very dignified said, "Buenas Días, Señora." Maria invited them for breakfast.

As she entered the kitchen, she turned and complimented them on looking so nice and dressed up, and asked if today was a special occasion. They both grinned like jackasses eating dill pickles.

I don't think Maria was prepared for José's answer. At least

I wasn't. "*Gracias,* for the compliment, *Señora.* Me and Raul come to see if this day my brother will go and help us look for the homes we are going to buy.

"So, *Señora,* I say to Raul, that now we are important wealthy men and that always we must be very careful and dress very good when on business and we go out to meet the public."

I glanced at their attire and goddamn near ruptured myself laughing. Maria brought us coffee. While drinking our coffee and waiting for breakfast, I picked up a magazine that had a picture of Napoleon.

I showed José the picture and told him that Napoleon was a great general. Raul didn't understand English, so he asked José in Spanish who this man was.

José stuck out his chest and told Raul he was the biggest fool in all Mexico. That everyone knew he was the Great American General who fought the Indians at the Battle of Bull Run.

José had all the names of places and people in western movies he had seen in the States all mixed up.

Raul didn't understand, "But, why José, the general fight the Indians if already the bull she don't fight and has run. The bull is not brave, no?"

José replied, "Raul, you fool, of course the bull was brave, but if the frigging Indians had scared the shit out of you with that ferocious Masondickson lion, like they scared the poor bull, then by the God, you run too, no?"

Raul was so hypnotized by José's speech, his eyes were big as baseballs and his mouth wide open.

José continued. "Then," he informed Raul, "was when the brave general fights all the Indians."

Raul jumped up clapping his hands and shouting, "*Bravo, Bravo, Olé!*" at the top of his voice. "Why, José, you and me with some of our money do not build a statue of such a brave man here in Mexico beside our own Pancho Villa?"

I was laughing so hard I fell out of my chair. Maria's call to breakfast saved the day. I had laughed so much my stomach and sides were hurting. I finally managed to stand, and followed everyone in to breakfast.

After breakfast, I sent Raul to see if Tex and Luis wanted to go house-hunting with us. In just a few minutes, they drove up. I invited them in for coffee. We all agreed to go to the bank where we had our money deposited and see if the manger would give us a lead on any houses for sale.

When we arrived at the bank, we were received like royalty. After talking for a few minutes, I told the manager we were interested in buying three or four nice houses. His face lit up like a Halloween pumpkin.

"*Bueno, Señors,* you are very lucky. It so happens this bank has helped finance four houses. Three of them are already completed and within five days, the fourth will also be completed."

I asked for directions. Then the manager offered to go and show the houses to us personally. I was surprised at the location. It was only three blocks from the beach and two blocks from a good school.

The houses were very nice. Four bedrooms, two baths, kitchen, dining room, den, living room, and a nice patio and servant quarters in the rear. The lots were very large. Actually, the four houses covered the entire front of the block.

I almost swallowed my cigar when he said two million three hundred thousand pesos each. That was only fourty-four thousand dollars, which is a lot of money, but in the States, the houses alone would have cost at least ninety thousand dollars.

Tex, Luis and I went into a huddle. Luis told us he had talked by phone to the wife of his dead brother, Carlos. She was very happy over her good fortune and was very anxious to return to Mexico to live and he would like to have one of the four houses for her.

We called the bank manager over and told him if they wanted to sell all four houses together, we would give forty thousand dollars, or two million pesos for each house, and for him to get the contractor and give us an answer in thirty minutes. We were going to inspect the three houses that were completed.

We had inspected two of the houses and were going into

the third when the bank manager and the contractor came and told me that it was impossible to consider my offer. Forty-one thousand dollars was their bottom price.

The bank manager, contractor and I argued for almost two hours. Finally, the bank manager told me, "*Señor* Mark, I can go no lower. How you say in English—I have had the intercourse? If I lose your big account, I am fired. If I lost money for the bank, I am fired. Please believe me, *Señor*, forty one thousand dollars is the best I can do, even if I lose the sale."

I assured him we didn't want to be the cause of his losing his job, and asked him to make out the bill of sale to José and his heirs, Raul and his heirs, Juan's wife and her heirs, and to Carlos' wife and heirs, and have everything ready to sign at 4:00 P.M. We would be at the bank at that time to complete the transaction. He was the happiest man I ever saw!

As we drove off, Luis asked what the maximum price I would have given for each house. "The original asking price," I replied.

José didn't understand. "My brother, the *Señor* Banker, I think he say only forty-one thousand each. So why we argue?"

"Look, José, I saved us twelve thousand dollars by arguing two hours, and that's a lot of money."

Then it dawned on José. He spent the next ten minutes in Spanish explaining to Raul how smart his brother was and how I had screwed the banker out of twelve thousand dollars.

Then José had his bright idea. "My brother, you say you save all this money, then why we don't make the big party?"

"All right, José, it's a deal. We'll have the biggest and best party anyone ever had in Mazatlan."

This made José very happy. He started telling Raul. Raul subscribed to the idea with the same enthusiasm.

José asked permissing to borrow the car as soon as we were back at the motel so he and Raul could have the music, and girls ready before it got dark.

"Just a minute, José, just a minute. We are going to have the big party, but only when the time comes."

"When is the time come, my brother?" José wanted to

know.

"When we have your family, Raul's family and Juan's family safe in Mazatlan, and I have met Flores and put the son-of-a-bitch in Hell where he belongs."

Poor little José; he reached over the seat, took one of my hands and kissed it, and with tears running down his cheeks, he said, "*Gracias a Dios,* you have not forgot and always you keep your promise, and as always, my brother, you are right. That will be the time for the most wonderful party we will ever have."

I didn't answer, but I hoped and prayed I would be present at the shindig.

When we arrived at the motel, José wanted to know when we were going to look for houses for him and Raul.

"We have just bought them, one for you, one for Raul, one for Juan's wife and kids and one for Carlos' wife and children."

As usual, José and Raul were confused. They thought the houses were for Tex, Luis and me. They couldn't imagine owning such beautiful homes. It took a little while to convince Raul.

José came to my rescue and told Raul that if his brother said they were theirs, then they were very respected men and would have the nicest homes in Mazatlan. Once again, I assured them that they were their houses.

José was so happy. He ran to tell Maria the wonderful news. They both came running back to the car.

José insisted we go at once and show the new homes to Maria. By this time, Carmen had joined the excitement. Tex said he would stay with Jackie and we could all go back and see the houses. José started pointing them out while we were still five blocks away.

Señor Nava, the contractor, asked me if I would be interested in buying the most beautiful house in Mazatlan. He went on to describe the place. There were supposed to be three hectares, or six and three-quarters acres of land with nine hundred feet of private beach.

Señor Nava asked why we didn't go look at the property while the women and José were looking at the houses. It was only about two miles to the property.

When we got there, I got the surprise of my life. It was the most beautiful place I have ever seen. This mountain, or hill, was about two hundred feet high, above the beach and on top of the hill, about two and one-half acres was very flat and ideal for building. There were palm and coconut trees everywhere. The view was out of this world.

The way the little cove came around the property, you had a perfect view of the city and the ocean. The house was beautiful and very elegant, adorned with quantities of marble. The master bedroom and guest room were so large you could get lost in them. These rooms and the living room and den were completed.

The kitchen and dining room had not been finished. The patio was very large and one of the most luxurious I had ever seen.

Before I could ask the price, *Señor* Nava told me his company had built the house, but they had to stop work about three months before when the owner ran out of money.

"*Señor* Mark, only last week, the man who owns the property came and tried to sell it to me. It is very valuable and I personally know this man has, besides the land, over ninety thousand dollars in the house, boat dock and picnic house. All this and the land included, he offers me for eighty thousand dollars, cash. But, I am a poor man and do not have that much money."

"What about this boat dock and picnic house?" I asked. *Señor* Nava smiled and asked me to follow him to the beach. I had an idea. I asked Luis to take the car and go get Tex and Jackie, and hurry back.

I followed Señor Nava down the path to the beach. This path was at least six feet wide and part of it had been hued out of solid granite. The rest was flat rock, very neatly cemented together.

When we reached the beach, I couldn't believe my eyes. There was a nice sandy stretch about nine hundred feet long, and over fifty large palm and coconut trees growing on the beach and on the hillside.

Where the granite cliff rose out of the sea, they had built a boat dock. I had never heard of a picnic house, but we live and learn.

About fifteen feet above the beautiful clear blue water and blasted out of the solid granite cliff was a room at least fifty feet long and forty feet wide, and about ten feet high. The floor and ceiling had been buffed and honed until they shone like polished marble.

The back wall, both the sides and overhead had been reinforced with one inch steel, and cemented. This cement had been colored as blue as the water below.

There were four picnic tables and two barbeque pits. There was also a large fresh water shower and bath.

The way everything was made, even in case of a storm, or flooding, nothing would be damaged or destroyed. There was no doubt about it, they had spent a lot of money.

I sat down at one of the tables and lit a cigar. The soft cool breeze was blowing in my face. This was the most comfortable, quiet, peaceful and relaxing spot I had ever been in my life. I could just imagine having good food and some bedding down here, and how happy I would be. I had found my haven.

I told *Señor* Nava I wanted the property and to take the owner to my bank. The banker was to pay him from my account one thousand dollars to bind the sale and set the rest in escrow to be released when the man furnished definite proof of ownership and proved there were no liens or mortgages on the property or buildings.

Señor Nava assured me that the only mortgage was held by our bank. I wanted to know if he could do all this that afternoon.

When I told him there was two thousand dollars commission for him if he did, that did the trick. He assured me he would have everything ready for me when I went back to the bank at 4:00 P.M. to close the deal on the other four houses.

"One more thing."

"What is that, *Señor* Mark?" he wanted to know.

"Will you personally oversee and help complete the kitchen and dining room? I will want the best material available."

"*Si, Señor* Mark, I go to work tonight if you want me to."

I told him to give me a week or two to buy the materials I wanted. We walked back up to the house. Tex, Jackie and Luis were just arriving. Jackie really loved the house and the view. I asked Tex and Luis how they would like to have homes built here also, and when I quoted the price, they couldn't believe it. Jackie settled the question.

She told Tex, "Look, my worthless husband, we have been married almost six years. We could never afford a home or children. Now we can. Here's where I want to have them."

Jackie was thinking of a smaller house. Luis wanted the same size house. While *Señor* Nava was making a rough estimate, I told Tex and Luis we would divide the land three ways, and since I had the choice lot, if they were willing to pay five thousand dollars each for their property, it was a deal.

Before they could answer, *Señor* Nava assured Jackie the house wouldn't cost more than sixty thousand dollars. "We'll take it," she announced for both Tex and Luis.

I asked Jackie, Tex and Luis why they didn't take a walk down to the beach while I took *Señor* Nava back to the bank so he could cinch the deal. I would pick up Maria and Carmen and bring them back here and, after seeing the beach (I didn't mention the boat dock or picnic house), if the guys wanted to back out of the deal, they could.

When *Señor* Nava and I got back to town, Maria and Carmen came running to the car. They were very proud of José and Raul.

They each admired the houses. Then Carmen asked where Luis was. I wanted to surprise them, so I told her we would pick Luis up on the way home. Maria and Carmen kept up constant chatter talking about the beautiful houses and how lucky José, Raul and Juan's wives were that I was their friend.

Finally, Maria asked me, "Marek, do you think that some day when you can afford it, maybe we can buy a little house not so expensive or beautiful as José's, but our own little home?"

I thought to myself, if only you knew, my darling, and in a few minutes more you will. Instead, I told Maria always to remember this day, month and year, and never to ask me for anything else as long as she lived. For as of this day, I could afford but very little for the rest of our lives.

She looked up at me with those beautiful big eyes and a big tear slid down her cheek. She was so surprised and hurt, her chin quivered like a little girl's. She said, "Marek, forgive me, I am ashamed. I do not again ask for anything."

"Make sure you don't," I told her.

By this time, we had reached our home. Carmen had overheard our conversation. She and Maria were so surprised, they didn't notice where we were until I stopped. When they saw the house, Carmen said, "Look at that big mansion."

Maria said, "It's the most beautiful house in all the world! Look at the view."

I very gruffly told Maria to get out of the car and come with me. She did, without a word. I offered her my arm. She slipped her little hand in my arm and looked at me with those big beautiful eyes, just like a little puppy dog that had been kicked for something it didn't do, as if to say, "Why are you being so mean to me?"

Without a word, I led Maria around the house. As we passed through the patio, she swooned. I had to drag her through the patio. When we completed the circle back to the front door, I pointed out the ocean and the city. Not a word had we spoken.

I let her enjoy the view for a minute, then looked down, smiled and asked her how she liked the place.

"Oh, Marek, it's the most beautiful home in all the world." I picked Maria up in my arms and held her very close to me. She started wiggling. "Let me down, Marek, what these people will think?"

I crushed her to me and told her, "Look, woman, stop that damn wiggling before I bust your butt." She lay perfectly still. "And furthermore, I don't give a damn what people think, 'cause when I pay eighty thousand dollars for a new home for my wife, I'm sure as hell going to carry her over the threshold."

I carried her inside. She was speechless. I set her down and asked what kind of hostess she was, not inviting the people to see her new home. She looked at me. I have never seen anyone as surprised as Maria.

She whispered, "Say it again, Marek."

"Yes, my darling, this is your new home." She flew into my arms and almost squeezed my ribs in. She was crying like her heart was broken. I finally got loose. She turned around and there stood Carmen. They embraced and both were bawling like two little kids. They finally quited down, as I asked what was wrong.

Maria put her arms around me and said, "Oh, Marek, you are so fool about women. Only when they are so happy can they cry and enjoy it so much."

I then showed her the unfinished kitchen and dining room. I told her I was proud it wasn't finished, for she could have it done exactly the way she wanted it, and also that she had a blank check to furnish her house.

Maria came back into my arms and said, "Marek, I do not deserve you and this beautiful house, but I love you and my home so much, and you will see always I be the good faithful wife."

Tex, Luis and Jackie came in. I asked how they liked the beach and if they wanted to back out of the deal. They all answered "no" at the same time. Luis started telling Carmen they were going to build a home here, too. She was almost as happy as Maria.

Tex, Jackie, Luis and Carmen hurried outside to select a location for their new homes. I took Maria by the hand and asked her if she would like to see our beach. She was so happy, she danced and sang as we went down the path. When she saw the beach and beach house, she could hardly restrain herself.

We were so happy that we lost all track of time. José came running down and informed me it was almost 4:00 and time to go to the bank. The girls were so happy on the trip, they chattered like a flock of sparrows. I finally got everyone's attention. "Say, how about everyone being our guests for dinner at our new home?"

"But, Marek," Maria interrupted me, "our kitchen is not finished and we have no furniture."

"That's no problem," I told her. "Look, you and the girls go to the market and we'll have a cook-out."

Everyone started shouting their approval. I stopped and let the girls off at the market. There was a big hardware store just across the street from the bank. The bank manager and *Señor* Nava met me at the door. Every document was in order and ready to be signed.

The man who owned the property we were buying accepted his one thousand dollars and assured me the Bill of Sale for the building, material, labor and land deed, including his Bill of Sale to me, was in the bank and in order, and that he had signed the property to me.

I told the cashier to have an abstract made and then call me, and have the deed made to Maria Vargas de Mark. A foreigner couldn't legally own property within fifty miles of the coastline, but Maria was a citizen. I gave *Señor* Nava one thousand dollars towards his commission and told him he would get the other thousand when the deal was completed.

José received the deed to his house, Juan's wife's house, and also Raul's. Luis accepted the deed for Carlos' wife. We were through in thirty minutes. I walked across the street to tell Maria we were ready to go.

Next door to the hardware store was a furniture store. There was a nice big comfortable lawn chair in the window. I went inside. The chairs were so cheap, I bought all seven they had in stock.

The salesman was really on his toes. I stopped to admire a nice three-quarter rollaway bed and mattress. I bought the bed after he promised to deliver the chairs and bed to our newly purchased home within the hour.

When we got to the market, the girls were actually waiting for us. We went to the motel and Tex suggested, since it was so early, that we all take our bathing suits and try out our beach. We were only a few minutes at the motel.

Maria and I were in the car waiting for the others. She started laughing. "Now what?" I asked her.

She pulled my head down, kissed me and said, "Oh, Marek, today I didn't understand, and it hurt so much when you were, how you say it, like the sore tail of a bear.

"And you are so right. Always I remember this day, month and year and never again ask you for nothing.

"If I am good and don't do something to make you angry," she cuddled up to me and said, "Marek, can I ask you for something?"

"Look, woman, I just told you to never again ask me for anything. I am a poor man."

"But, this, my husband, don't cost nothing. Can I kiss you?" She did, and was doing a real good job until the other guys came and very rudely interrupted us. As we drove off, Maria put her arm around me and said, "I am so happy, my husband. Just think, for the first time, we are going to our new home."

Chapter 42

WE FOLLOWED the delivery truck to our house. Maria was thrilled over the chairs and bed. After we carried everything down to the beach house, I suggested the girls put on their bathing suits while we men filled the oil lanterns and got everything ready to start dinner after our swim.

It was a wonderful feeling to wiggle your toes in the sand and know it was your own beach. We swam and played until almost dark and everyone really had a ball. I went and took a shower and was lighting the lanterns when Maria came.

She told me she was embarrassed. "Why," I asked her.

"You see, Marek, I have never been to a picnic like this, and I do not know how to make the fire or cook the steaks."

"Don't worry," I told her. "Hurry and change out of your bathing suit and tonight you watch me, and the next time you will know."

I had a smoke while she changed. Then, I showed her how to light the charcoal.

Jackie and Carmen made a delicious salad. Finally the coals were ready. The steaks were huge, and for once, I got them just right. We really enjoyed our dinner.

We all ate so much, we were drowsy and at 10:00, we decided to go back to the motel and return tomorrow for the dishes and utensils.

Tex kidded Maria and tried to get her to let him hire me as a chef. After telling everyone goodnight, and before we reached our room, I heard my phone ringing. It was my lawyer from the States.

After completing the call, I took Maria in my arms and she

started crying. "What's wrong, angel?"

"Oh, Marek, I am so sad, for my beautiful home is so empty. We have a new bed and mattress in the little picnic house. Why we don't go to sleep in our new home?"

I didn't answer, but went in the bedroom and got two sheets and a blanket and the pump shotgun.

I tossed the blanket and sheets to Maria, laid the shotgun across the bundle, then picked Maria and the luggage up. She giggled like a schoolgirl on her first date. We sang and kissed on the drive to our new home.

I parked the car, reached under the seat and put the old 357 Magnum pistol under my belt. I went around, opened the door, picked up Maria and the stuff and headed down the path to the beach house.

I lit one of the lanterns, then unfolded the bed and helped Maria put on the sheets. I pulled off my shirt, shoes, and trousers, and lay back on the bed. Maria removed all her clothes except her bra and panties. I motioned for her to sit beside me.

"I have something very important to tell you. Do you know who was calling me from the States tonight?" She shook her head.

"It was my lawyer. I have been moving around so much, he couldn't find me. He called to tell me my wife had sued me for and received a divorce. The divorce will be final in two weeks. Tomorrow, Maria, I am mailing her a check. This money will be put in trust so my sons are well cared for and educated."

I was very proud of Maria when she assured me this was the right thing to do and went on to say that if I needed the money, I shouldn't buy the house, for we could live anywhere. I told her we could afford to buy and furnish the house and still have enough to live on all our lives.

"Just one request, Maria. When my sons come to visit us, and if they should decide to live with us, they will have to respect you and I will expect you to respect them and make them as welcome in our home as if they were your own sons."

"Oh, Marek, you don't need to say this. You know I will love and respect them, even more than my own, and if I can't make them love me, then it is my fault, and gladly I will go away, for never would I come between you and your sons, for I know how much you love them.''

I gently took Maria in my arms, kissed her sweet lips and tried to tell her how I loved and worshipped her, then I asked her if she realized that in only two weeks we could be legally married. I thought she was kidding when she murmured in my ear, ''Oh, Marek, I can never marry you.''

I raised up and looked down at her. Never have I seen in anyone's face so much pain and regret. Maria's answer almost knocked me out of bed. She sat up in bed and looked me right in the eye.

''I am so sorry, Marek, but I am not a virgin.'' I pulled her to me and kissed her and assured her that it didn't matter.

I kissed her neck and started to kiss her breast. She really came unwound! ''Don't you do dat Marek. Don't kiss my titty when we have the important things to talk of.''

''All right, Maria, what do you want to talk about?''

''Oh, Marek, I say again, I am not a virgin, so you see, I can never marry you, for every man on his wedding night deserves a virgin.''

''Are you finished?''

''Yes,'' she replied.

''All right then, my beautiful, stupid darling. Listen carefully to what I have to say. The first time I put you in bed, you were a virgin. Correct?''

''Of course I was, Marek. You know this is true. And I never tell you this before, but with the Blessed Virgin as my witness and on my hope of heaven.'' She made the sign of the cross. ''I swear never had any man so much as had his hands on my body all my life.''

''All right, darling, I believe you, and since you have known me, you haven't loved another man?''

''Of course not,'' she replied. ''And you know I love you so much I will never know no man but you. You must always know this is true.''

''Yes, darling, I believe you. Now, look, as far as I am concerned, you have been my wife since the first time I put you in bed. Haven't I respected and treated you as a man would his wife?''

"Oh, Marek, yes, and this is why I love you more each day."

"All right, Maria, I love you, and to my way of thinking, we have been married all this time. In two weeks, we can get married so it will be legally recognized by the law of the land, and no one can ever hurt or embarrass you. Understand?" She laid her face against mine. I could feel her tears on my cheek.

Finally, she asked me, "Marek, promise me that never you will feel as if you were cheated on your wedding night."

"I promise, darling, so don't be a fool all night. Say 'yes' or 'no'."

"Oh, Marek, I say yes, yes, yes, my love, and I am the happiest and luckiest woman in all the world. Now, my husband, why we don't kiss each other?" I couldn't see anything wrong with that, so I went for it. In about five minutes, I was panting like a hound dog, chasing a rabbit on a hot day.

Maria raised up and removed her bra and placed a lovely breast against my mouth. "Why don't you kiss my titty?" she asked.

"I don't understand you women. First you tell me not to kiss your titty, then you tell me to kiss it."

She pressed her breast against my mouth. "Shut up, you, and do it."

I opened my mouth, but instead of words coming out, a ripe pink nipple went in. I gently kissed that sweet lovely firm breast, then ran my tongue around and over the nipple. I could feel it getting hard in my mouth. In a minute, Maria could no longer control her desire.

"Please, Marek, turn me on my back and take off my panties."

"Now, darling?" I asked.

"Oh, yes, Marek, I am yours. Do what you want, my darling, and always you will know no other man can ever have me. Now, please, Marek, I cannot wait no more."

She wasn't the only one. Afterwards we lay in each other's arms too exhausted to move. I finally got up and put on my shorts and got us a drink of water. It was hot, but we were hotter.

We lay on our tummies, smoking, and looked out over the

ocean. The breeze was very cool and refreshing. The white sand on the beach was breathtaking with the full moon shining down on it, and the small waves gently rolling on and off the beach.

I asked Maria how she would like to go swimming. "Oh, I would Marek, but we forgot to bring our bathing suits."

"Look, sweetheart, we are all alone. This beach is our very own. I will have to admit, I've never gone swimming naked with a woman before, but there is a first time for everything."

Maria laughed and said she had never gone skinny dipping with a man either. She jumped out of bed, pulled off her panties and said, "My husband, five minutes from now, I can't say dat." Stark bare-butt naked, we ran hand-in-hand to our beach and dove into the water together.

We spent a wonderful, unforgettable hour skinny-dipping and playing in the sand, then fell asleep. We awoke at 8:00 A.M. with the sun shining in our faces.

When we got back to the motel, the other guys were waiting for us. We had given them quite a scare, since they didn't know where we were.

While having coffee, we discovered several ways to try and get José, Raul and Juan's families out of Loreto.

We finally decided that our best plan was to fly to San Luis Potosi, where José's mother was living and get José's brother-in-law to drive to Loreto and tell everyone José's mother had died.

Everyone agreed on the plan. I asked why we didn't fly over to San Luis today and get the show on the road, for if this idea didn't work, we would have to try something else.

I called Maria and told her I had to go to San Luis Potosi and asked her if she would go with me. This made her very happy. Luis asked if he and Carmen could go along. "Sure thing," I answered. "We will only take José, and the plane carries five passengers." Maria and Carmen were all excited and started to pack.

I told them we wouldn't be gone for more than two nights. Thirty minutes later, they were ready and had only packed two suitcases each. I wondered how much luggage they would have taken if we had planned on being gone a week.

At 11:00, Tex drove us to the airport. I took off and circled over our house. I laid the plane over on the right side where Maria could get a good look, and told her to look at her home from the air.

This was a mistake. She looked and then started crying and said, "Oh, Marek, I am so sad to leave my home alone. It will be so *thriste* (lonesome)." It took fifteen minutes to kid her out of her despondent mood and back to her usual smiling and happy self. Two hours and forty minutes later, we were in San Luis Potosi. We took a cab to José's mother's home.

Chapter 43

JOSÉ OPENED the door and we all went inside. The first thing I noticed was a picture of Juan and a candle burning beneath the picture. Not even time could ease the pain in the old lady's heart, or dim the memories of her love for the son that Tino Flores had murdered.

When José's Mama came into the room, it almost broke my heart to see how old, frail and stooped she was. The years of toil and hard work had certainly taken its toll.

I took her in my arms. She was crying so, she couldn't talk. She reached for José, and with her arms around both of us, she raised her eyes toward heaven and prayed, "I thank you, God, for answering my prayers and bringing my sons back safely to me so we could be together once more in our home before I die."

We introduced Luis, Carmen and Maria. When Mama finally understood Maria was my wife, she had her come and sit beside her. She put her poor, old calloused, and wrinkled hands on Maria's face and told her, "My son, you are a lucky man. This is the most beautiful girl I have seen in all the years I have lived."

"You are right, Mama." I agreed. "She is beautiful, but not one-half as pretty as you were when you were a girl, and you are still the most beautiful Mama in the world."

Mama very gently spanked my leg and told me I should be ashamed to lie to my Mama. She smiled, patted my hand and said, "Even if it's not true, it makes a Mama feel good for her son to say such a nice thing."

José interrupted and began telling Mama about his, Raul

and Juan's wives' new homes and how always Juan's wife and children were sure of a good living and education. And, how each family had more money now than they needed to live on for as long as they lived, and as long as their children lived.

Mama wanted to know how such a miracle was possible. José smiled and pointed at me. "Ah, Mama, my brother, he fix everything. He is a smart man."

"Si," Mama agreed, "beyond a doubt, he has always been my wisest and smartest son."

We went next door for José's brother-in-law. After visiting with him for a while, I told him of the new homes José, Raul and Juan's wife had in Mazatlan, and asked if he would help us to get them out of Loreto.

He was very happy to help and assured me he would do anything I wanted him to do. "All right, here's what I want you to do. You and José leave at once for Loreto." José jumped straight up. I told him to sit down and listen, that he wasn't going to Loreto.

"If you all leave at once and drive all night, you can be in Loreto before the bus leaves in the morning for Durango.

"When you all get to where the road goes to Loreto, drive a mile or two on the highway toward Durango, find a landmark that you will be sure to remember. Then, José, you get out of the car and hide far enough from the highway so you can't be seen. Your brother-in-law will go alone to Loreto.

"When he gets to Loreto, he will tell everyone that your Mama has died and they are to all come to San Luis Potosi for the funeral. Don't even tell José and Juan's wives the truth, for they might get scared if Flores should become suspicious and question them.

"I know how much they love Mama, and I hate to hurt and deceive them, but the more grief and emotion they show, the better our chances are of getting them out.

"Go get José's cousin to look after the goats and you go personally to the bus station and buy all the tickets to San Luis Potosi. You bring José and Juan's wives and their two youngest children in the car with you. Have Raul's wife ride the bus with the rest of José's and Juan's children, as well as her own."

I knew the three families together had about twenty children. "You wait until Raul's wife and all the kids are on the bus, then follow the bus out of Loreto and watch very closely to see if Flores or one of the policemen get on the bus.

"If they do, it's all right. Just don't get excited. Follow the bus for three or four miles, then pass it, and don't drive fast enough to blow a tire or have an accident, for as slow as the bus travels, you will be at the highway at least fifteen minutes before the bus reaches the highway.

"Go get José and you can then tell the women the truth. Now, clearly understand me. This is very important. If there is no suspicion, or policemen on the bus, then you all drive on to Durango.

"If there are policemen on the bus, you turn around and go back toward Fresnillo and come straight back to San Luis Potosi.

"Raul's wife and all the children are safe, no one will bother them and they will reach San Luis Potosi. What time does the bus leave Loreto?"

"8:00 A.M." José replied. "All right, it will take the bus from two hours and forty-five minutes to three hours to reach the highway."

"We will leave San Luis Potosi and fly to where we can see where the road from Loreto intersects the highway. I'll circle until I see you drive on the highway, then I'll come down real low to be sure it's you, and I'll see José get in the car. Now, remember, if it's safe, you go on to Durango, and I'll head for Mazatlan. If it isn't safe, turn around and go back to Fresnillo.

"If you turn around, I will come back to San Luis Potosi, and if Flores or any police follow Raul's wife and the children, on to San Luis Potosi, I'll be ready for them when they arrive."

I had them both repeat their instructions three times. They had it down pat.

"All right, now, for the last instruction. If it's safe, and you go on to Durango, as quick as you get there, check all four bus companies and count up how many tickets it will take for all of you, and be sure to take the first bus to Mazatlan.

"Don't go anywhere, or be seen on the streets. We will have rooms ready when you get to Mazatlan, so come straight to our motel."

I borrowed one of Jim's expressions and told José if he even thought about having a beer, I'd wring his neck. José said if I would give them money for expenses, they were ready to go. José asked how Mama was going to go to Mazatlan.

I asked her if she would be afraid to fly over with us. "No, my son," she replied, "And what kind of Mama do you think I am to be afraid to go with my son anywhere he wants to take me? If it wasn't safe, you wouldn't let me go."

I had to admit the old girl had something there. After José and his brother-in-law took off, we finally managed to stop a taxi, told Mama goodbye, and to be sure and be ready in the morning, no later than 8:30, and we would come for her.

I'd always loved San Luis Potosi. It is a beautiful historic old city. We spent the evening sightseeing, had a delicious dinner and went to a nice night club to dance. At 11:00, I suggested we call it a night and go to our hotel, for we had a long day ahead of us tomorrow.

We were very tired and went right to sleep. We almost overslept, and by the time we hurried through breakfast, it was 8:20.

I asked Maria and Carmen to take a cab and go bring Mama to the airport. While Luis had the plane refueled and stowed aboard our luggage, I filed my flight plan. We had at least one and one half hours flight to where we rendezvoused with José. This was one time we couldn't afford to be late.

For once, we were lucky and had no trouble in getting two cabs. I had filed my flight plan and walked back to the plane and just finished my pre-flight when Maria, Carmen and Mama arrived.

Luis rode in the back seat by himself, so Mama could ride beside Carmen. My idea was if the old girl got sick or scared, Carmen and Maria could help her, but my precautions proved unnecessary.

There was no wind, so we had a perfect take-off. After raising the gear, I looked back to see how Mama was taking her very first plane ride. By this time, I was about five hundred feet off the ground.

Mama looked out and for the first time, she realized we were off the ground. She started laughing and said, "Look close my son, and see if I have on the feathers, for I am flying like the bird."

I circled over the town and she recognized many places on the ground. She would laugh every time she could see a car or truck on the highway below and damn near drove me nuts. Every house or ranch she could spot, she wanted to know what the people's name was and who lived there, plus the name of every little village we flew over.

Mama finally asked me if we were lost. "No, Mama," I replied. "Why?"

"Well, my son, you don't know anyone's name or the names of the little village, and you have no road to follow. How you know where we go?"

"Do you see this, Mama?" I pointed to the instrument panel. She tried to raise up, but her seat belt was too tight.

Carmen removed her seat belt, then the old girl stuck her head up front between Maria and me. She looked at the panel where I was pointing. She didn't say a word for at least five minutes, she was so intent on the instruments.

She finally said, "My son, why do you waste your money on so many clocks, and they are no good? I just look, and no two has the same time." Since I had nothing else to do for an hour, I decided to give Mama her first lesson in navigation.

I explained the use of each instrument. I showed Maria that if you push the stick forward, the plane went down; pull it back and it would go up, etc.

At 10:30, we were at our rendezvous point. I descended to where the mountain blocked our view of Loreto and started to circle. In about five minute, I spotted José's brother-in-law's car. He was only about ten minutes from the highway.

I pointed and showed Maria the car. By the time I had completed my second circle, the car had reached the highway and turned toward Durango and stopped. I told Mama to look close and see if she could see José.

I came down to no more than five hundred feet above the highway. José waved and started running and pointing toward Durango. I sure breathed a sigh of relief. Everything was going as planned.

I circled back toward Mazatlan. The bus coming from Loreto had almost reached the highway and was heading for Durango. This made me very confident, 'cause I knew there was no way Flores could possibly leave Loreto and get to Durango before José and his clan were half way to Mazatlan.

We had a very nice flight. Mama sure loved the view when we flew over the Sierra Madre Mountains. We landed in Mazatlan and went straight to the motel.

Mama had never seen the ocean before, and it really fascinated her. She walked down to the beach and stood gazing out over the water the entire time Maria was fixing our lunch. I went to tell her that lunch was ready. When I walked up beside her, Mama said, "All my life I hear of the ocean. Just look at it. It is so big, you can't see across it."

I asked Mama what she thought of the ocean. Her explanation was as good as I ever heard, even though I had to laugh when she replied, "So far as I can tell, my son, it is mostly water."

After lunch, Mama went back to further observe the mystery and beauty of the ocean. Tex and I rented another six motel rooms and sat back anxiously to await José's arrival. They arrived at 2:00 A.M., tired but happy.

I finally persuaded them to go to bed and rest a while. They were very anxious to see their new homes. At 7:00, José was banging on my door, ready to show the women their new homes.

Maria wanted to go with us. All seven of us sure made a car load! Maria and I, José and his wife, Raul and his wife, and Juan's wife.

The women couldn't believe their eyes. They were very happy with their new homes. I explained to the women, after swearing them to secrecy, how on the first day of each month, they would go to the bank and sign a paper, and the amount of money they would receive, and the amount José and Raul would receive. I cautioned them to never lend or give José and Raul one cent, or they would lose everything.

I also told Juan's wife she could never tell anyone or remarry, or she would lose everything.

"Don't worry," she told me, "eight kids are all any woman needs and now that I never have to worry about food and clothing and can educate them, I don't even want or need a man, for always in my heart, there will only be my Juan."

Maria insisted I drive by and show them her new home. They were impressed and started calling Maria "Señora Marks." Maria smiled and said, "See, I know how to handle my people."

I stopped at a small cafe and invited everyone for breakfast. While having breakfast, the women asked Maria if she and the other two Señoras, Jackie and Carmen, would please help them shop for furniture and everything they needed to furnish their houses, and admitted they didn't know what to buy or how to go about buying it. Maria was very pleased. I reckon all women love to shop.

When we got back to the motel, all twenty-two kids were having a ball playing on the beach and wading in the surf. Since today was Sunday and they couldn't go shopping, I suggested to Tex and Luis we take our wives and beat a hasty retreat to our beach house.

I love kids, but twenty-two that have never been around the beach before was too many. We grabbed our bathing suits. I gave José and Raul money for food, and we made a quick exit.

We stopped by the market and bought some steaks and took off for our new home and beach house. We had a great picnic in addition to the fun we had playing on the beach and swimming.

By 10:00, we were all tired and agreed the kids should be in bed. We went back to the motel, and as silently as thieves, we sneaked into our rooms.

Chapter 44

THE NEXT morning, I was still having breakfast when all the women arrived, ready to start their shopping. José's wife, Melinda and Raul's wife, Requel, insisted their husbands come along. I certainly wasn't envious of them.

I suggested to Tex and Luis that we go fishing. We took our fly rods, rented a boat and found a nice little cove. This was our day.

We hit school after school of Spanish Mackerel, from one and a half to four pounds. Tex wanted to know what we were going to do with all the fish. That was no problem, with all the kids. I could account for thirty of the fifty-four we had caught. We gave the rest to the boys at the boat dock, and we were back home at 2:00.

In another hour, the girls and José and Raul arrived, tired but happy and informed us that in one hour the furniture would start arriving at their homes. We went to help them unload and arrange it. I have never moved so much furniture in my life. I am sure Mayflower would offer me a seat on their Board of Directors. It's quite a job furnishing four houses and moving the same couch or bed forty-three times before you please six women. Man, I was beat!

Finally, after three days they announced everything was secure and ready to move in. I winked at Tex and Luis. We took off, and as we went through town, we got four taxis and went to the motel for Mama and the kids. I sure as hell wasn't taking any chances on anyone changing their mind.

When we got back to the houses with Mama and the kids, everyone except Tex, Luis and I cried a little—they were so pleased and happy. We three felt like shouting with joy.

While José and Raul acted as baby sitters, we carried their wives back to pack so the move would be absolutely completed. Finally, at 7:00, they were ready for two more taxis. Thank God, the ordeal was over! I asked Tex, Jackie, Maria, Luis and Carmen if they could get ready in one hour for dinner, and if so, I invited them to be my guests at the Copa de Leche Cafe and Night Club.

In my opinion, this is the best seafood restaurant in the world. They were all ready, with fifteen minutes to spare. We had two drinks, then the best large fried shrimp dinner I ever ate. We danced and talked until they closed at 1:00 A.M.

We didn't get up until noon the next day. After breakfast, Maria asked me to go shopping with her. "Haven't you had enough shopping?" I asked.

"Oh, Marek, you know I have to look at material to finish my kitchen." Maria sat down in my lap, put both arms around my neck and gave me a big kiss, then smiled and asked, "You like?" I did.

Maria told me if I were a good boy and would go shopping with her, she would give me all the kisses I wanted. "When?" I wanted to know. She jumped out of my lap and said, "When we come back, for if I give you more kisses now, we go to bed and don't go shopping."

We drove to the largest builder in town. They had all kinds of material, blueprints and pictures. Maria was very impressed by all the material and she very carefully and very slowly went through each design step-by-step.

At 3:00, I excused myself on the pretense of going to buy a cigar. I had some shopping of my own to do. I took a cab and told the driver to take me to the nicest dress shop in town.

Once there, I told the sales lady I wanted to see the most beautiful wedding gown she had. She took me at my word. I have never seen such a lovely gown.

When she told me the price I damn near had a fainting spell. The saleslady wanted to know if I could bring my sweetheart in for a measurement.

I hurried back to get Maria. She had narrowed her selection down to three different designs. I asked her to go home to discuss her selection. The saleman was happy to lend us several samples and different colors of material. I have a hunch he was so tired he would have given us the selection of our choice just to get rid of us.

When I stopped at the dress shop, Maria wanted to know why we were stopping. "To buy you a dress."

"But Marek, I have so many new clothes, I do not need any more." I didn't answer. I parked and opened the door, then helped Maria out of the car and led her inside.

The saleslady met us. "Ah, Señor, now I see why you want such a lovely wedding gown. I am sorry we have no gown that could do your future bride justice." That was as nicely turned a business compliment as I ever heard.

When Maria saw the gown, she was so happy she almost cried. The lady took her into the back to try it on. In twenty minutes they were back. The saleslady told me the gown was made for Maria, that it was almost a perfect fit, and with only a few small alterations, the gown would be ready at 4:00 tomorrow evening.

Maria said, "Oh, Marek, you are so fool! Five hundred and eighty dollars is a fortune for this dress."

"Don't you like it?" I asked.

"Of course," she replied. "It is the most beautiful gown in the world."

"All right, my darling. Look, I have the most beautiful wife in the world. My wife says she has the most beautiful home in the world, so I can do no less than buy her the most beautiful gown in the world. Right?"

Once again, tears of love and happiness were in her eyes. "I do not deserve you, Marek. And, I accept the gown only if you promise our daughter can wear it when she gets married."

"Where do you get this daughter business?" I wanted to know.

"Oh, Marek, we have two sons, and in two weeks, we are legally married. I am sorry to be disobedient, my husband. I want to do what you tell me to do, but never again will I do it."

"Look, Maria, I don't know what you are talking about.

393

What is it you will never do again?"

"This my husband. After we make love, go to the bathroom and wash out the baby. I won't do it, you hear?"

Then she put her arms around me and said, Marek, please. I want our baby so much. You are very white, and so am I, but if our baby should be a little dark and you are embarrassed, we go away and never cause you to be ashamed."

"Look, Maria, if our baby has a yellow face, and a plaid butt, we will love it, for it will be ours."

She burst out crying, "Oh, Marek, you say the nicest, sweetest things at the right time. Now, my husband, why we don't kiss each other?"

It seemed Maria's lips were sweeter and I felt more love every time I kissed them. I looked down into her innocent eyes and told her, "Well, don't stand here woman, let's go. How do you expect to get pregnant here?"

She almost smothered me with kisses. I could feel those firm breasts on my chest and her smooth flat tummy against mine. She finally stopped kissing me, grabbed me by the hand, and said, "Quickly, Marek, let us hurry to our home and make the baby." Five minutes later we were on our way. Fifteen minutes later we were in bed.

I don't know if we made a baby, nor will I ever know, but we both put all we had into the project. After we finished, I noticed Maria was on her knees in bed, but I didn't think anything of it. "Do you want a cigarette?" I asked her. Her reply almost knocked me out of bed.

"Please you shut up, Marek. I am praying to God that we did make the baby and now I have to promise him to be the good mother and always keep the baby clean and smelling good."

I wanted to laugh, but didn't dare.

The next morning, at 7:00, the phone started ringing. I pulled the blanket up over my head. Finally, Maria got up and answered it. It was Jim.

I asked him why he had so little consideration for a friend as to call him in the middle of the night. For once, he ignored my sarcastic remark and inquired about José, Raul and Juan's families.

I heard him breathe a sigh of relief when I told him they were here in Mazatlan and in their new homes.

Then Jim asked if I was ready to start my hunting trip "for Flores." I told him, "Yes, I am, and the sooner the better, for I have a feeling I don't have much time if I intend to be the hunter."

"I have the same feeling," Jim replied. "Me and Lupe will leave here early in the morning and fly down, so get your damn lazy carcass out of the bed and meet us no later than 9:00 at the airport." Before I could answer, he hung up.

Maria was very happy that Lupe was coming to visit her so she could show her and Jim our new house.

We spent the day at home, trying to decide what material was best to finish the kitchen and dining room areas. at 3:00 Maria reminded me we had to be at the dress shop before 4:00 to get her wedding gown.

When I stopped the car at the motel. Maria started calling Jackie and Carmen to show them her new gown. I went over and had coffee with Tex and Luis, while the girls had their little party.

I suggested we all go to the beach house for another cookout. Jackie and Carmen declined. I am sure they realized this was a very special occasion and Maria and I would rather be alone. I winked at Maria and told her to be sure and not forget out bathing suits.

"All right," she answered, "but maybe we don't use them." I knew what she meant, and once it was dark, I was sure she was right.

We arrived at the beach house as hungry as two bears. After supper, we lay back on the bed and, with the cool breeze blowing on us, we were asleep before you could say "Jack Robinson."

Chapter 45

ABOUT THREE hours later, I awoke with two soft arms around my neck and sweet, demanding lips pressed against mine. If I live to be older than Methuselah, I'll never know another night like that night.

I never thought it was possible for a woman and man to feel so much love and desire for each other. We forgot to put on our bathing suits and went swimming. We were only at the beach for a very short time. Our need for each other was too great.

The rest of the night, we lay in each other's arms, talked, or made love. We were so happy and so much in love. Neither of us even thought abut going to sleep.

We watched the sun come up. It was a beautiful sight and we promised each other, that we would stay awake all night more often. Maria looked into my eyes, and asked, ''Marek, why Jim and Lupe is coming and is true, that you and Jim are going to find a way to kill Flores?''

I knew Maria would have to know the truth sometime, and now was as good a time as any. I looked up and met her beautiful eyes and nodded my head.

Before I could speak, Maria told me that ever since she had run away from Loreto and come to me, that she lived in constant fear of being found by Flores.

''Marek, you do not realize what a cruel, evil man he really is. It is best you go now, as you have planned, for it will be too late if he ever finds out where we are, and Marek, please be careful.

''This I promise you, my husband, if anything should happen to you, then I will return to Loreto and be very nice to

Flores until he relaxes his guard, and then I will kill him.

"I am so thankful that my dear friend Lupe will be with me so we can go every morning and evening to our Church to pray for you and Jim's safe return."

Big tears were in Maria's beautiful eyes. I kissed them and told her not to worry, that Jim and I would be careful and we knew how to take care of ourselves.

"I know you do, Marek. This way, you have a chance and I know you are better man than Tino Flores.

"Please remember this, my husband. He would rather shoot you in the back when you are asleep, so be very careful, and when you see him, give to him no more chance than you would give a mad dog, for this man is more dangerous."

I kissed away Maria's tears and assured her I would be fine. We had been so busy talking, I didn't realize it was 8:00. I only had an hour to shave, dress and meet Jim and Lupe at the airport.

We hurried back to the motel. Maria didn't have time to dress, so she insisted I go without her and she would dress and have breakfast ready when we got back. I was already outside when Maria called after me and reminded me that we had forgotten to kiss each other.

I went back inside. Maria held me very close for a long time. I asked her why she didn't change her mind and go with me. She laughed, pushed me toward the door and told me she had to dress and look nice.

Before I reached the car, I met Tex and Luis. I asked them to come with me to the airport. On the way, we discussed the best way to get Flores out of Loreto. We hadn't reached any definite plan before arriving at the airport. Jim hadn't arrived. We all sat in the car talking.

In about ten minutes, Luis spotted Jim's plane. He was on short final and no more than half a mile from touchdown. We walked to the parking area to help tie down the plane.

Jim had just goteen out of the plane. We shook hands and I had started around to help Lupe out when I heard someone shout. I looked up, and here came José running and screaming at the top of his lungs.

José grabbed me around the shoulders and was so out of

breath he couldn't say a word, and so scared he was trembling. I shook him.

"What's wrong, José?"

He looked like he had seen a ghost. I shook him until his teeth rattled.

He finally regained his speech. "This morning I know *Señor* Jim he is coming so I go to your house to see my friend, but when I get to this little cafe about one block from your motel, I can see the car, she ees not at your house.

"Since the car ees not there, I know you are here to the airport to meet *Señor* Jim, so I go in this little cafe to have a coffee and wait until I see you return. I have been here only a little time." Once again, José started shaking from fright.

"Then, my brother, I cannot believe my eyes. I go look out the window to be sure, and across the street, sneaking toward your home goes that sorry son-of-a-bitch, Tino Flores, and the fat cop Alfonso."

"Are you sure, José?" I asked him. "How long ago was this?"

"*Si,* my brother, only a few minutes ago. I am lucky and get the taxi and hurry here to warn you." I started running to the car and shouted to José to help Lupe with the luggage and go to Carmen's house, not mine.

Jim, Tex and Luis were right behind me. I jerked the front door open, and Tex said, "No, Mark, let me drive, you will have more room in the back." I reached under the seat, grabbed my pistol and jumped in the back seat. Jim followed me. As Tex took off, for the only time in all the years I had known him, I heard Jim say "Thank God."

I looked and he was lovingly rubbing his hands over the pump shotgun that I had forgotten to take out of the car this morning when Maria and I returned from the beach house.

Jim reached down and got he box of buckshot, checked to see if the shotgun was fully loaded. Then he filled both his front pockets with extra shells.

I asked Luis to hand me my pistol shells out of the glove box. Tex was literally flying, he was driving so fast. I told him to slow down and when we were about two blocks from the motel, to turn off the motor and very quietly coast to the back entrance trying not to make any noise.

Jim told Tex and Luis to go to their houses, get their guns and keep a sharp lookout in case there were others besides Flores and Alfonso.

"How do you want to handle it, Mark?" Jim asked.

"Let's try to enter the house by the back door which leads to the kitchenette. Maybe they haven't gotten inside the house, but if they have, Jim, I'll enter first, you right behind me. Regardless of how many there are, I'll go for Flores."

Jim slapped me on the shoulder, then patted the shotgun and said, "That's the thing to do. Just be damn sure and get that S.O.B. Me and Old Betsy here (he patted the shotgun again) will take care of the rest."

Tex turned off the ignition and very quietly and slowly coasted to the back door of our motel room. When I reached the back door, I looked back, Jim was right behind me. I saw Tex and Luis running toward their houses. Very slowly, I took hold of the doorknob.

Thank God it turned and I nodded to Jim that the door was unlocked. Then I very slowly pulled the hammer back on my pistol to full cock.

I slowly opened the door. There was no one in the kitchenette and the door from the kitchenette that opened into the living room was closed. Before I reached the door, I heard Maria moan, and a man's voice in Spanish. I couldn't understand what he said.

I glanced at Jim. He had raised his shotgun waist high. Very faintly I heard him push off the safety and from the angle of his clamped jaw and the look in his eyes, I knew he had heard. I very slowly and quietly pushed the door. It opened, just a crack, no more than an inch.

A man's side and leg were blocking my view of the room. Someone was standing with his back very close to the door. The person moved slightly and no one, in his wildest dreams could imagine the horrifying sight that met my eyes.

Maria's clothes were torn in shreds and scattered all over the floor. Part of her slip was bound around her mouth to keep her from screaming. As long as I live, it will make me physically sick to remember that moment.

Poor Maria was on the floor on her hands and knees. Flores was down on his knees and had both arms locked around her waist, and was trying, like an animal, to rape her. Maria was bucking, kicking, elbowing and fighting him off with all her strength.

I hit the door with my left shoulder and landed within four feet of Flores. He jumped to his feet. His eyes were glued on the pistol leveled at his belly. He threw both arms up and said, "Por favor, no!"

I had very gently started to squeeze the trigger when Maria groaned. I glanced down and she was trying to sit up. I couldn't believe the way she had been beaten.

I slowly eased the hammer down on my pistol and took it in my left hand. Goddamn Flores' soul to Hell, he wasn't fixing to die that fast and easy. I was going to have the pleasure of beating him to death with my own hands.

I glanced down and his penis was sticking out of his pants about two inches. He glanced down and lowered his hands to cover himself.

I slowly feinted with my right hand like I was going to punch him in the face. He fell for the fake and jerked his hands up to protect his face.

I stepped forward as fast as a striking snake and struck down with the pistol. When the barrel connected with his penis, he screamed as he doubled over with pain. I started from my boot tops and caught him full in the face with a right upper cut.

When the punch landed, the nicest sensation I ever felt was the pain running all the way up my arm and into my shoulder.

I raised him at least six inches off the floor. He hit the wall and slid down in a sitting position. I'll never understand why it didn't knock him out.

He was sitting flat on the floor, his nose busted and spread all over his face. Blood was running out of his nose and ears, and the blow to his penis had made him so sick, he was vomitting down his shirt.

I heard something that sounded like a blimp being punctured. I looked, just in time to see Jim pull the shotgun tock out of Alfonso's fat belly. He doubled up on the floor beside Flores.

I picked my darling Maria up in my arms and told Jim to watch our guests.

"Will do," Jim told me, "you just take care of Maria. The only place these two sorry bastards are going is to hell."

I gently laid Maria on the bed and removed the gag. Her lovely lips were bruised. One side of her face was bleeding and both of her eyes were black and almost swollen shut.

Choke marks were on her lovely soft neck and each beautiful breast had black and blue pinch marks all over them. Flores had pinched one lovely pink nipple until it was bleeding.

Her stomach, back and legs had welts all over them. I rushed into the bathroom for a wet towel. Very gently, I started to wash her face.

She opened her eyes. "Oh, my Marek, I am so sorry and I fight so hard."

I bent over, kissed her cheek and very softly told her not to talk, that now everything was going to be all right.

"Oh, my Marek, I fight him so hard. I can never be sure, but I think once, for just a second, he was able to put a little inside me, then I jump and he can do no more."

I gently laid her back on the bed and covered her poor bruised and tortured body with a sheet. Then, I very gently put my hands on her face and told her she was very wrong. Nothing had happened. Being a man, I knew it was impossible. "Maybe he touched you, but nothing more, and I am so proud of you and the way you fought him."

Maria put her arms around my neck and said, "Now, my Marek, you must go and destroy this animal so he can never harm us again, but please, Marek, don't kill Alfonso."

"Why not?" I asked.

"He only hold me while Flores put the gag in my mouth, and he begs Flores to let me alone, and Flores curses him and tells him I am like a female dog in heat and he will love me like a bitch dog. But Alfonso refused to hold me. Flores knocks him down, but still he will not hold me."

I very gently kissed Maria's poor bruised and swollen lips

and told her to stay in bed and not get up until I came back to take her to the doctor.

I closed the bedroom door behind me. I didn't want her to see what was about to happen to Flores. I heard someone in the kitchen. I turned to see Tex, Luis, and José. "How's Maria?" Jim asked.

"She's almost beaten to death, but I think she will be all right."

José stopped beside Flores and said, "Remember me, you son-of-a-bitch of a dog? I am José, the man you almost beat to death, and my brother, Juan, you beat to death before my eyes."

I asked José if he wanted to kill Flores. He didn't answer me, but took a swing at Flores and hit him on the jaw. The punch wouldn't have hurt a ten year old schoolboy. José wasn't a fighter.

Flores started begging and praying for us to spare his life. José laughed and said, "Look, my brother, this big coward and son-of-a-bitch is more scared than me and Juan. We did not say one word while he beat us."

In Spanish, so Flores and Alfonso would understand, I told everyone how Flores had tried to rape Maria and what he had said about her being a bitch in heat.

I grabbed Jim with both arms and bear-hugged him. He had drawn back the shotgun like a baseball bat and was fixing to bust Flores skull with it. We got Jim quieted down and I told him that Flores was my meat and to leave him alone.

Jim gave me a go to hell look and asked if I was going to kill Flores or let him die of old age. I ignored Jim and told them that Maria had asked for Alfonso's life to be spared, and how he had refused to help Flores.

All this time, Flores had been crying and praying to God to spare his life. I reached down, grabbed Flores by the hair and jerked him up on his feet.

He was whining like a hurt puppy. I told him to shut up and listen, that I wasn't going to kill, not yet—not today.

When I saw the fear in his face, an inhuman idea came to me. How to hurt and humiliate him more than killing him at this time, and to let him live in fear and embarrassment, until I was ready to kill him.

I knew he would never have the nerve to try to kill me again, for if ever a man had been conquered it was Tino Flores.

I then told Alfonso that since he hadn't helped Flores, I would remember that in his favor; but since he wouldn't help Maria fight for her life, I considered him to be only half a man, and that was exactly what I was going to make him.

For the first time, Alfonso spoke, "*Señor* Mark, I think I know what you mean, and it is more than I deserve. For years, all of Loreto has been afraid of this man." He pointed to Flores. "All this time, he is only a yellow coward. And all my life, *Señor,* I will live in shame, for I was not a man but stood by and let this poor girl be tortured by such an animal.

"I assure you, *Señor* Mark, had you done to my wife what we have done to yours, and I got the upper hand as you have, I would kill you like a dog. This we deserve. I have lived like a fool and a coward, but *Señor*, I will try to die like a man."

Flores begged me not to listen to Alfonso and said he would do anything to amend the wrong he had done. "Shut up, Flores, and listen well. You now stand before me, the biggest coward and sorriest man I have seen in my life. The only reason I don't kill you this instant is because I want you to live in fear. You have one week to one year to live.

"Now you will have to guess when I will come and kill you. I don't care where you go, for the farther and faster you run, the more afraid you will be. I will hunt you down, and when I am ready, I will kill you like the animal you are.

"Every night, I want you to remember the promise I am making to you. After I kill and bury you, I am going to piss on your grave, just like a good sheep dog does after he kills a wild coyote."

A little color had returned to Flores' face. He was nodding and agreeing. I could read his mind. "Just turn me loose now, and then try to find me."

"And now, Flores, my revenge! For years you have bullied and scared everyone in Loreto because you were so much a man and so tough and brave. I am sure you told everyone in Loreto how you were going to bring back the *gringo,* so, my friend, I won't disappoint you.

"I am going to take you back to Loreto. I can land and take

403

off on the dirt road by the river. It's only a short distance to the village."

I tightened my hold on his hair, and pulled his head back to where he had to look in my eyes. "And now, you goddamn son-of-a-bitch, I am going to castrate you, and when I land at the river at Loreto, I am going to kick your ass out of the plane.

"You will be weak and sick as a drowned cat, and you will have to walk to the village or bleed to death. Be sure to tell everyone how much of a man you are to beat and rape a helpless woman."

Jim laughed and said, "By God, Mark, that's the thing to do. Now I understand what you meant when you told Alfonso you would leave him half a man. Are you really going to cut out one of his nuts?"

Before I could answer, Flores started screaming. I slapped him backward, jerked out my handkerchief and crammed it in his mouth. Jim handed me a piece of Maria's torn dress. I tied this around his face to keep the gag in place. I gave Luis the shotgun to keep close watch on Alfonso.

I went to the dresser, took out a big spool of nylon fishing cord and my large bowie knife. I told Jim to lock the back door and bring me one of the straight wooden chairs out of the kitchen.

When Jim brought the chair, we set Flores down. I took a large pillow from the couch and put it behind Flores' back, forcing him to sit on the front edge of the chair.

We tied each hand separately to the back of the chair, then pulled his legs up and tied them to the back legs of the chair.

I got the bowie knife off the dresser and told Tex to get behind the chair and lean it back, that Old Doctor Mark was ready to operate.

Someone knocked on the door. Luis asked who it was.

"Police, open the door," was the reply.

I went to the window and carefully peeked out. Sure enough, there stood two policemen.

I told Luis to tell them he hadn't called the police and everything was fine, and to stall them for as long as he could.

I glanced around the room. It was in too big a mess to ever

404

clean up. If the cops got inside, they would know something had happened here and would search the house. Luis was giving them the best sales pitch, but they weren't buying.

We realized that in another minute, they would demand to enter and use force if necessary. I told Tex to stand to one side of the door, and I would stand on the other side, and when Luis opened the door, I was sure both cops would rush inside and they would be so shocked at what they would see that we should have a split-second advantage.

"Jim, you go stand behind Flores. Here, take my pistol and cut Flores' right hand free and hold it.

"Look, you guys, we have to get the drop on these two cops, regardless of the risk. For what has happened here, there is no way we can justify our actions in court. Flores has to be killed so he can't testify against us. If he lives, we will all go to prison.

"Now, Jim, do as I say. Once Tex and I have disarmed the cops, I will swing the shotgun barrel and break this window. When the glass breaks, everyone will look. You have a good grip on Flores' arm. When I break the window, put my pistol in his hand. Then shout, "look out," and jump to one side. I will blow the bastard in half with the shotgun."

Jim nodded his head. I told Luis to be very careful and slowly open the door just enough to look out and refuse to let the cops enter. Tex and I took our stand on each side of the door.

When Luis refused to let them enter, they both hit the door and practically fell inside. Neither had drawn their guns. Before they knew what had happened, Tex and I had them covered.

Luis slammed the door shut, grabbed both their pistols and it was then that they noticed Flores. Before they could ask what was going on, I pointed to Flores and told them he had broken into my home and beat my wife almost to death. We had found him this way and were just fixing to call the police.

I winked at Jim and started a slow arch with the shotgun. All eyes except Jim's were following the barrel of the shotgun. As the window broke, and above the sound of the breaking glass, I heard Jim shout, "No, Mark, No! For God's sake, don't shoot!"

I was already turning very fast with my finger starting to squeeze the trigger. In one-hundredth of a second more, it would have been too late and the gun would have fired.

Jim's warning registered on me just in time, for there, between me and Flores, stood Maria. I had almost shot her!

I was paralyzed with fright. When I could speak, I told Maria to please go to her room and stay there until I came for her.

"No Marek, now I talk." She turned to the two policemen and told them how she had been beaten and raped by Flores. She said, "Then my husband and these men come and tie him up. They were fixing to call the police when you come."

Alfonso spoke up and said, "*Señor* Policemen, this man and I are also policemen from the little village of Loreto. This young lady is from our village. When she leaves to marry the *Señor* Mark, this man Flores goes *loco*. We come here together, but I do not know this man would do such a thing as this. What the lady says is true, for I am with these men and together we find Flores as he is now, and the beautiful young wife of *Señor* Mark so beaten and abused."

The policemen were really confused. The cop who was standing beside Flores told his partner someone was lying and to go call their Chief and tell him to come at once.

Maria said, "Just a minute. I prove to you who is the liar. When you see how that animal bruised my body, then you will know."

The policemen told Maria to please open her housecoat so they could see for themselves. Maria really gave them a piece of her mind.

"Look, you two stupid and ignorant men, are you so poorly raised that you don't know how to treat a lady when you see one, and expect a lady to undress before you?

"All you men, walk over and face the wall and when I have my clothes arranged then I will tell you to turn around and you can see that I am telling the truth. Now, all of you face the wall."

Very obediently, we all walked over and faced the wall. We had no sooner faced the wall than the loudest and most blood-curdling scream split the silence of the room. I wouldn't have believed such a scream of pain and fear could come from the throat of a human being.

Once we all turned and looked the other way, Maria had grabbed the large bowie knife off the dresser and drove it into Flores' chest all the way up to the handle. All the hate and revenge of her Indian heritage was gleaming in her eyes. She still had both hands on the knife handle and was slowly turning the long knife blade in Flores' heart.

Maria looked up and when she saw we were looking, she turned as quickly as a cat, took my pistol off the dresser and put the muzzle against her breast. I shouted "No!" and jumped toward her, but before I could reach her, she pulled the trigger. The gun jumped out of her small hand as the heavy magnum slug knocked her over backward.

Very quickly, I lifted her up. Both her loving arms, for the last time on this earth, went around my neck.

Maria said, "Was the only way, my Marek. Now, you are safe. No one can ever hurt you now." Her lovely arms tightened around my neck. I looked down into her beautiful eyes. Maria was strangling as she said, "Oh, my husband, oh, my Marek."

Then she actually smiled and, in a voice which was just above a whisper, she said, "My Marek, why we don't kiss each other?"

As I softly and gently pressed my lips to hers, I felt a slight quiver run through her body. I had heard many times before and recognized the little rattle I heard in her throat.

I raised up my head and looked down at her beautiful and peaceful face. As I kissed the trickles of blood flowing from her lovely mouth, my eyes were so full of tears, I could no longer see for I knew my darling had just died in my arms.

I carried her back into our bedroom and very gently laid her on the bed. Then I ran back into the other room. I kicked Flores in the side so hard, the chair fell over and the bowie knife came out and dropped on the floor. There was a whooshing sound as a stream of blood gushed from his wound. I reached down, picked up the knife, and almost dropped it—it was so slick and covered with blood.

I grabbed Flores by the hair and placed the knife across his throat, then went crazy from pain and grief. I can just barely remember beating his head against the floor and telling him to open his eyes and breathe once more. He had to breathe once more to know I was the one to finish him off. I was going to cut his damn head off.

Tex grabbed my arm and Jim got me around the neck with a hammerlock and started shouting for everyone else to help.

I guess I fought like a crazy man for I was almost choked to death before I heard Jim telling me over and over again to stop it and turn Flores loose—that he was dead and could not feel or hear me.

Tex still had a hold on my arm, but I still had Flores by the hair with my other hand and was kicking him every time I could get a leg free. Everyone except Alfonso was trying to help hold me.

Jim relaxed his choke hold. "Are you all right now, Mark?" he asked me.

I couldn't speak, but nodded my head. They turned me loose and I fell to the floor. While I was getting my wind back, they cut Flores loose from the chair.

Alfonso started telling the two cops that everything was closed since both Maria and Flores were dead and he could swear no one else was involved, that everything was over. The two policemen agreed, but they would still have to bring their Chief of Police to officially close the case.

Both policemen removed their caps, offered their sympathy and apologized for having to bother me in my time of grief and sorrow. They would return in a short time with their Chief and officially close the case.

I asked Tex to please go and bring Jackie, Carmen, and Lupe to stay with Maria and me for a while.

The policemen removed the carcass of that miserable bastard and no one was sorry to see the last of him.

Lupe, Jackie and Carmen arrived a little later and were heart-broken over the terrible thing that had happened. Of course, Lupe and Maria had grown to love each other like sisters. When Lupe came in, we put our arms around each other and cried like two grief-stricken children.

Jackie showed Maria's wedding gown to Lupe. She pressed the gown to her face and said they would bathe Maria and dress her in the wedding gown, that she was sure Maria would want to be buried in her beautiful gown. I agreed, and left the room.

Chapter 46

THE NEWS has sure traveled fast. My banker, *Señor* Nava, the contractor and the Chief of Police were outside to offer their assistance and condolences. The police were very helpful. They didn't ask me even one question.

The police had a short conversation with Jim, Tex, Luis and Alfonso. The chief came and told me the investigation was closed and he was sorry that they had been unable to prevent such a horrible thing from happening.

My banker insisted that I give him instructions, then leave all arrangements to him. An ambulance arrived for Flores. The ambulance driver agreed to take the remains to Loreto.

I told Alfonso to go with the ambulance to Loreto. Go and see Maria's family and tell them that Maria and I will arrive late Monday evening."

I wanted Maria to spend her last night in her home with her family. "And, Alfonso, you be damn sure you tell the truth. You have been lucky to come out of this as easy as you have. If you lie, I promise you . . ."

Alfonso interrupted me and said, "*Señor* Mark, I know how lucky I am and I do not lie to the policemen to try and save myself, but to help you and your friends.

"I know how much love you had for Maria. All my life, I have to live knowing I could have helped Maria, so I will be man enough to admit all, even my own cowardice. I will hold back nothing and tell everything.

"I also know, *Señor*, my life hangs on a very small thread. Remember, I have seen you in action twice in my life, and I realize you could and would kill me in a minute.

"My prayer, *Señor* Mark, is that someday in your heart you can forgive me and do me the honor of shaking my hand and calling me friend."

"One other thing, Alfonso, tell Maria's family, if it's agreeable with them, to please have the Rosary Tuesday morning. Also, Monday morning, Maria's monument will arrive and please see that it is properly installed at the gravesite before the funeral. I intend for everyone to think we were married. Now get in the ambulance and go."

Alfonso assured me everything would be taken care of exactly as I wished. I asked Nava if he knew where we could buy a beautiful monument for Maria.

"*Si, señor,*" he replied. "Please get in the car and I will drive you there."

I don't suppose anyone could ever call a tombstone beautiful, but they had one that was life sized, an angel in polished marble. This was my selection. Nava pulled the right strings and they promised to have the monument in Loreto early Monday morning.

I had the monument inscribed "MARIA VARGAS DE MARK—Beloved Wife of . . ." and then my name and the date of Maria's birth and death. They promised to consult with Maria's Mama and add any verse from the Bible she wanted them to.

We then went back to the motel. Lupe came and took me by the hand and led me into the room and said, "Look, Mark, doesn't Maria in her white gown look just like a beautiful sleeping angel?" She certainly did. I only saw my darling a second before my eyes filled with tears.

When the hearse came and took Maria to the funeral home, I have never felt so heart-broken, helpless and all alone. I staggered into the kitchen, laid my head on the table and cried until I had no more tears to shed.

Jim and Tex came and brought me to Tex's house. They tried to get me to eat, but I couldn't swallow the food, although I did drink some coffee.

I walked down to the beach. I was like a zombie and had no conception of time.

The next thing I realized, it was daylight and Jim was walking

411

toward me. He put his arm around my shoulders and as w
walked toward the house, he told me he had to leave at once fe
his ranch, but Lupe would stay and go with Maria and me, an
he would be waiting for us tomorrow in Durango from 11:0
A.M. and go on with us to Loreto.

Jackie gave me hot coffee. After drinking the coffee, I wen
back to walk and sit on the beach. Late in the afternoon, Jack
and Lupe came and asked me to come with them. I followe
them to their house. They gave me a big bowl of hot soup.
didn't realize how hungry I was.

After I ate, I sat down on the couch. I was so tired I didn
even realize when I keeled over and went to sleep.

At 5:00 the next morning, Tex awoke me and told me it wa
time to shower, shave, dress and get ready to go. I was ve
thankful he went with me to my house. I don't believe I coul
have entered it alone—that house which had once known
much love and now was so sad and lonesome.

While I was shaving, Lupe came and packed my suitcase.
At last we were ready to leave. Lupe and I rode in the hearse
with Maria. Tex, Jackie, Luis, Carmen, José and Melinda
followed in their car. It was a long ride. When we arrived in
Durango, true to his promise, Jim was waiting.

Outside Durango on the way to Loreto, I noticed that two
cars were ahead of the hearse and three, counting Tex's car
were following us. Jim rode in the hearse with Lupe and me.

At 4:00 P.M. we came around the end of the little
mountain and there across the river was the little village of
Loreto. My darling, Maria, had for the last time and for all
eternity, returned home.

I had no way of knowing how Maria's family would receive
me. When we stopped at her house, her Father and brother
slowly walked to meet the hearse. Señor Vargas opened his
arms and embraced me and said, "I thank you, my son, for
bringing our daughter back to us."

Pablo, Maria's brother, also embraced me, but words failed
him.

Then Señora Vargas, Maria's mother came to me. As she
embraced me, neither of us could hold back our tears. She

pulled my head down and kissed my cheek and said, "Oh, my son, I know how great our love and grief is for our daughter, but I know you loved her as much as we did."

As Jim, Tex, Luis and José carried the casket into the house, the street and patio were lined with people and not a dry eye was in the crowd. We passed by Alfonso, bareheaded and holding his hat over his heart. Tears were running down both cheeks.

I had noticed ever since we arrived that there were two bands of musicians carrying instruments in their cases and four of them had kept me completely boxed in. Two were always in front of me and two behind me. I couldn't turn around and walk without almost bumping into one of them.

I grabbed one by the shirt collar and told him this was no time for music or a fiesta. When he answered, I was surprised to see tears in his eyes.

"Don't you recognize me, *Señor* Mark? I am from the ranch of *Señor* Jim. We are all so sorry over the loss of your wife."

Then I recognized him and as I looked at the others, I remembered them from the roundup on Jim's ranch, when we had vaccinated all the cattle.

As I looked at each, I noticed they were holding the cases that contained their guitars, violins, etc., under one arm, and every one had his other hand inside the case.

The cowboy said, "Look quickly, *Señor* Mark, if need be, we are here to play a different kind of music than anyone thinks."

As the cowboy carefully raised the lid of his violin case, I saw the hand wrapped around the handle of a forty-five automatic pistol. Then it dawned on me, in all ten of the instrument cases were pistols, rifles and sawed off shotguns.

Then I understood why two cars went ahead of us all the way from Durango and why the other two cars followed behind with Tex. I also realized why Jim had to make his unexplained business trip to the ranch.

He had recruited ten of the bravest, toughest and most loyal cowboys that he knew in Chihuahua, dressed them as musicians, complete with musical instrument cases, and rented enough cars to transport them to Loreto for my protection.

After all the village had come and paid their respects, *Señor* and *Señora* Vargas asked me to come with them to the dining room. Maria's mother handed me a letter. I opened it and there were polaroid pictures of our new home in Mazatlan, including the picnic house, boat dock and beach. There were also three pictures of me. One asleep on the bed, and two where I was cooking steaks. I hadn't even caught Maria making the pictures. Once again, tears ran down my face.

As I read the letter Maria had written her family, I didn't know a woman could find the words to describe her happiness and love for a man as many ways as Maria had.

Maria had been so much in love and so happy with me, but at the same time, loved her family and home so dearly, she had to write and let them know she was well and happy. I looked at the postmark. It had only been ten days since she had written the letter. If only she had told me she had written the letter, I would have been on guard. I will always believe this is how Flores found out where we were.

When Maria closed her letter, she had signed in large letters, "Love, your daughter, *Señora* Maria Mark." I was so glad I had had that inscription put on her stone. Now, no one would ever know that we were not married.

Maria's parents and I talked of Maria for hours. None of us wanted to be alone. Finally, *Señor* Vargas suggested we all rest a while. As he showed me to my room, he informed me that Flores had been buried this morning before we arrived.

When I entered the room, there sat the cowboy from Jim's ranch that I had talked to earlier. The violin case was open and the forty-five automatic was in it. Laying on the table within easy reach was a sawed off pump shotgun. He got up and shook hands and wanted to know if it would be all right if he smoked during the night.

From this request, I knew Jim had posted an all-night guard in my room. I started to protest and then decided it would be better to tolerate the guy than to try to get rid of him. I was sure he had been ordered by Jim not to leave me alone for even one second.

The next morning, the maid awoke me as she put a pot of coffee on the table. She told me that we were to be at the church in one hour.

The people of Loreto were very poor and couldn't afford to buy flowers even if they had had a florist shop in the village. All the same, when we entered the church, it was filled with flowers. The people had gathered wild flowers from the surrounding country and mountain sides ever since Maria's death.

I couldn't really believe she was gone. It was just like a bad dream, and I would finally awaken.

When I walked up to look at Maria for the last time, I had to face reality. As I gazed down at her beautiful face, she really looked like a sleeping angel.

Only a strong man who realizes that God has seen fit to take from him, can stand unashamed and let the tears flow freely down his cheeks. As I stood at the casket, I was not ashamed, nor did I try to hide tears.

When we reached the cemetery, the first thing I noticed was that Maria's monument had been properly placed at the head of the grave. After we laid Maria to rest, I returned home with her family.

Two hours later, Jim came and asked if I was ready to go. Each member of Maria's family embraced and kissed me and made me promise that I would return as often as I could to visit them, assuring me their home was my home.

I told Jim I wanted to stop by the cemetery and say goodbye to Maria. When Tex stopped the car, I noticed Jim and his three car loads of musicians were right behind me.

As I knelt and prayed, my tears fell on the newly made grave. I knew my soul, heart, love and happiness would always remain in this grave with my darling, Maria. I started walking across the cemetery until I located another newly made grave.

I checked the small marker to make sure it was Tino Flores. I hadn't forgotten the promise I had made him. Now, I intended to keep that promise; which I did.

As I started to walk away from his grave, I saw Alfonso running toward me.

"Take this, quick, *Señor* Mark. Those five men coming toward you are Flores' father and four brothers."

As I turned around, I opened the cylinder of the pistol to make sure it was loaded. It was.

When the five men were about fifty feet from where I stood, a loud voice in Spanish said, "If you want to all go to hell together, make one more step toward Mark."

I recognized the voice. I turned around. About a hundred feet behind me, and on each side of me, stood Jim and his ten musicians, but this time, they didn't have their instrument cases, although every one had his favorite instrument in hand and aimed at the five approaching men.

I had to grin. As I looked at them, they were strictly a three piece band—pistols, rifles, and sawed off shotguns.

The old man, Flores' father, spread his hands, then said, "Please, notice none of us are armed. We only come here to apologize and tell *Señor* Mark we are sorry. We loved our son, but we are ashamed of what he did."

The old man walked up and extended his hand. "*Señor* Mark, we are sorry and never will me or my family cause you trouble. Come back as often as you like."

As I turned away, I heard Jim tell the old man he had made a wise decision, for this graveyard wasn't half full.

I walked very slowly toward the car. When I reached the car, Alfonso had hurried on ahead of me. He was holding the car door open for me. His hat off, I could see tears in his eyes.

I realized he had made a courageous gesture in warning me and bringing me the pistol; if Flores' father and brothers had been angry, he would have been killed or left alone to face the remaining clan after we were gone.

I remembered the last words he had said to me when he left Mazatlan to return to Loreto with Flores' body. As far as I was concerned, Alfonso had done all a man could do toward righting the wrong he had helped do.

I returned his pistol, extended my hand and said, "*Gracias, amigo.*"

Alfonso grabbed my hand and actually kissed it. "*Gracias, Señor* Mark. "Now, that I have your fogiveness, my shame will be easier for me to bear."

Chapter 47

WHEN WE reached Durango, Lupe and Jim invited me back to their ranch to stay a while. I very gratefully accepted. There were too many heartaches and memories for me to return to Mazatlan.

I told Tex and Luis if they wanted the house which I was buying for Maria, to buy it and forget the deposit I had placed on it. They thanked me and said they definitely wanted the property.

I asked Tex to call Russ in El Paso and have him fly down to get the plane we had used to transport the gold to Honduras, and settle my accounts there.

We drove all night and arrived at Jim's ranch late in the evening.

I was very edgy at the ranch. Every night I would go down to the bunkhouse and listen to the cowboys tell their hair-raising tales.

Still cooking for the crew was that colorful, tough old character known as "Old Filthy." In one of many youthful escapades, Old Filthy claimed he had three of the most beautiful *señoritas* in his village pregnant at the same time, and admitted this created quite a problem since he couldn't marry all three of them.

One of the *señoritas'* papas found out who was responsible for his daughter's condition and came hunting for Old Filthy with a machete. The fight was on, and the old man was killed.

Old Filthy escaped and fled to the wilds of the Sierra Madre and, for more than ten years, lived like an animal in the unpopulated wilderness.

He painted a beautiful picture of the Sierra Madre, with its mineral resources, fishing and all types of wild game that had never heard the sound of a hunter's gun.

The Sierra Madre sounded like what I was looking for. A place to get away, with plenty of time to think and accept life again.

I asked Old Filthy how he would like to take a pack trip through the Sierra Madre, and he was all for it. If Jim would let him take a leave of absence from his job, he would go.

Old Filthy and I talked over our adventure with Jim. He thought it was a good idea. He told me he had all the pack mules, horses and camping equipment I needed and to help myself to supplies from the store room.

Old Filthy and I were up early, and by 9:00 we had all our camping gear and supplies packed on four large mules, and our horses saddled. We were ready to go. I was wearing my pistol, a 357 Magnum, and carrying a 243 rifle, with a four power scope. Old Filthy was carrying a pump shotgun and his old single action forty-four pistol.

Two days later, we were in the foot hills of the Sierra Madre. The Sierra Madre is a large range of mountains, covering four states in Mexico; Chihuahua, Senora, Sinola and Durango. Approximately four hundred miles wide and one thousand miles long, these mountains are just as wild, rough and beautiful as the Rockies.

Old Filthy and I hunted, fished, and prospected. I found enough gold and silver prospects to refill Ft. Knox.

We lost all track of time and we never got in a hurry. We had no idea where we were and we didn't care. We knew the Pacific Ocean was to the West, so we just followed the sun.

Late one afternoon, we rode through a divide in the mountains and about sixty or seventy miles to the West, we could see the sun setting on the ocean. Three days later we were in Culiacan Sinaloa. We had made about a four hundred fifty-mile pack trip.

On the outskirts of Culiacan, we found a small goat herder's place and rented a corral. After corraling our horses and pack mules, we went downtown and checked into a hotel.

When we had settled into our room, I called Jim. He really gave me a cussing and asked if I knew what the date was, and how long we had been gone. I didn't.

Jim really came unwound and informed me it was the first of July and that we had been gone for three months. Furthermore, my parents, ex-wife, and my two sons were very worried about us. They had called him at least four or five times every week for the past two months.

I asked Jim's permission to sell the horses, pack mules and the camping equipment. Old Filthy and I would take the early flight to Chihuahua.

"Don't give a damn if you give them away, just be on that flight. I'll be in Chihuahua when you land." Jim cussed me another five minutes before hanging up.

I told Old Filthy to go and sell the horses, pack mules and the camping equipment for whatever price he could get and I would make our reservations for the flight to Chihuahua. I also wanted to call my family.

My sons were overjoyed to hear from me and asked me more questions in thirty seconds than I could have answered in a week. They damn near made a pauper out of me because I couldn't get them to hang up the phone.

They both asked me at least twenty times when I was coming home. I told them if they could get their Mother to drive them to Hot Springs tomorrow, I would be on the 5:00 P.M. flight and we would take that vacation and fishing trip to Yellowstone Park and Montana I had promised them.

I reminded the boys they both only had drivers' permits and were not old enough to get their license.

I asked them if it would be too much trouble for them to go to the Auto Dealer and select that sports car they had been telling me they wanted, and have old Cuzzin Cliff have the car licensed, insured, serviced and ready to go when I arrived tomorrow evening.

They both shouted, "No, Daddy. 'Bye, Daddy. We will go right now . . ."

Both receivers clicked. That's one way to stop a long distance call.

The next morning at 9:30, we landed in Chihuahua. Jim was all smiles as we shook hands. We had only fifteen minutes to have a quick coffee and talk before my flight continued to El Paso.

During this time, Jim was a perfect gentleman. He didn't have a single temper tantrum, and only cussed fifteen or twenty times. I couldn't take that kind of memory of Jim with me.

They were calling my flight as Jim and Old Filthy walked with me to the boarding gate. I was the last one to board.

I stopped in the door of the plane and pointed to Old Filthy. I told Jim to let him drive back to the ranch.

"Why?" Jim asked.

"Well, Jim, you might exert yourself and have a stroke. You have been a fugitive from the undertaker for years."

That did it. Jim threw his hat on the ground. The plane started the engines, making it impossible for me to hear what Jim was saying. But from the way he was stomping his hat, I knew the fast flowing words would never be heard by any youngster in Sunday School. Jim had been proud to see me.

When I landed in Hot Springs, my sons were waiting, all smiles. They informed me they had everything ready for us to leave on our vacation early the next morning.

I had dinner with Nita, Randy and Rickey. After dinner, Nita said she would drive me to my mother's to spend the night.

On the way, Nita stopped at a drive-in for coffee. I couldn't have been more surprised when she started talking about our past.

"I know I shouldn't have divorced you the way I did," she said. "I will also admit that the last three months you were with us, before going to Mexico, that I wasn't much of a wife to you. Can't you see I was only trying to make you realize how much you needed me? But, I know now, I only drove you further away.

"I am going to wait a year for you to get over your loss and memories of Maria, and when you do, remember, I love you and we have two fine sons who love you, too, and we can be a happy family again.

"One more thing, and this is a promise. If we have a second chance, I'll never mention Maria's name. I know you loved her, and in my heart, I can't blame her for taking you, after I refused you the love a woman should gladly give to her husband. I know you were worthy of the love I didn't give you."

In silence, we finished drinking our coffee and without another word, she started the car and drove me to my mother's home. I thanked her for the delicious dinner, then went into the house.

The next morning, I was still asleep when my two sons came tearing into my bedroom and informed me they were all packed and ready to go. They were so anxious to get started they couldn't wait for breakfast.

We had only driven about twenty miles when they both started complaining they were hungry, so we stopped and ate, "for the first time." I would give four-to-one odds we didn't pass by a single drive-in from Langley all the way to the Yellowstone National Park.

I still can't believe it is possible for two teen-aged boys to eat as many hamburgers, drink as much root beer, and pee as often as those two kids.

I shouldn't complain, for if there was enough vegetation along the side of the highway to conceal them, I only had to stop at every third service station for them to use the restroom.

At 5:00 P.M. on the third day, we finally arrived at our motel at West Yellowstone. I told the boys to unpack the car while I went to buy flies and tackle. I wanted to get an early start fishing in the morning.

In a sporting goods store, I am just like a fat lady in a girdle shop—never know when to leave, and keep hoping to find something to better the cause.

It was getting dark, as I started back to the hotel. The boys were running out to meet me. "Hurry, Daddy. Hurry, Daddy," they both shouted. "We knew you were tired, so we went and bought our dinner and have everything on the table ready to eat." I was very pleased and flattered over their thoughtfulness.

When I entered the kitchenette, I damn near had heart failure. There, in the center of the table was a gallon jug of root beer, and a pile of at least a dozen hamburgers! I wanted to sit down and cry.

I had had hamburgers and root beer for breakfast, dinner, lunch and at least three times in between meals for the past three days.

I very bravely sat down and joined my sons for the Passover. I promised myself that starting tomorrow, we were going to eat a little higher on the bull!

We spent a wonderful ten days fishing the Firehole and Madison River, as well as Quake Lake. The fishing was great. On the eleventh night, Nita called me and told me it was very important that I leave at once for El Paso. Jim had some kind of emergency and would be waiting there for me. She also said she was flying out to be there when we arrived. She wouldn't tell me what was wrong, just kept insisting it was an emergency and she couldn't discuss it over the phone.

"All right," I told her. "We will leave at once, but it will take me two days to drive from here to El Paso." I started worrying. I couldn't imagine what had happened unless something had come up pertaining to the treasure. But I knew it was serious or Jim wouldn't have had Nita call me and interrupt our vacation.

Chapter 48

I HAD two days to worry before we reached El Paso. On the third morning, my sons and I arrived in El Paso. I had just parked at the motel where we were to meet, when Nita and Lupe drove up and parked alongside.

The boys were very happy to see their mother. After talking to her for a few minutes, they put on their bathing suits. As they started for the pool, in came Jim. We only had a chance to say hello before the boys took over and invited Uncle Jim to go out to the pool and watch a new dive they had learned.

Without a word, he followed them out of the room. I was surprised and couldn't figure out what was wrong. I asked Nita what was going on and why the hell they had interrupted our vacation if it wasn't important enough to discuss, after me practically driving two days and nights in order to get here at the earliest possible time.

She smiled, and looked at Lupe, and without answering, she took my arm and led me over to a chair.

"Sit down, Mark," Nita said. "What I have to tell you will knock you off your feet. We led Jim to believe that you were in some kind of trouble to get him to meet everyone here. Lupe and I are solely responsible.

"Lupe called me five days ago and we hatched up our little conspiracy. Do you know where we had just come from when you arrived?"

I couldn't imagine, so I just shook my head.

"From shopping, and from the doctor's office." Nita looked at Lupe and they both giggled. I told them the shopping didn't surprise me, but what was the deal about going to the doctor?

Nita got all carried away with herself, threw her arms around my neck and said, "Oh, Mark, I have the most precious news for you. Lupe and Jim are going to have a baby!"

Nita was right. I have never been more surprised. Nita smiled very sweetly, told me to close my mouth, that I looked very foolish. Then she told me that five days ago Lupe had called her and told her she knew she was pregnant and afraid to tell Jim.

Jim would never let her have a baby and she hadn't told anyone, but when she started to get a little big, she was afraid Jim would notice her condition. "Lupe wanted you and me to be here when she told Jim. She was afraid Jim would run her off."

Lupe was very nervous. She started unwrapping a package and was showing me a little pair of baby shoes and a dress when Jim came in.

He took one look and in Spanish said, "Lupe, if I've told you once, I've told you a thousand times that those damn gossipy old women are going to extremes having so many baby showers." Jim took me by the arm and said, "Let's go have a beer and a talk. What is the problem?"

Before I could answer, Lupe stood up and dangled the baby shoes in Jim's face.

"Aren't they pretty?" she asked him.

Without even looking at the little shoes, or Lupe, Jim replied, "Si, Lupe. Who are they for?"

"For our little baby, Yemmy," she almost whispered.

Jim was getting all worked up and started pulling me towards the door. "I don't give a damn whose baby they are for, I still say there's no sense in having so many showers!"

Then it finally dawned on him what Lupe had said. He stopped like he had hit a brick wall, turned my arm loose and very slowly turned around to face Lupe. He was white as a sheet. With his mouth wide open, he mumbled, "What did you say, Lupe?"

Poor Lupe was so nervous and scared she started crying. "It is true. Yemmy, I know always you say, I can never have a baby, but this very morning, Nita and I go to the doctor, and we are going to have a baby."

Jim stood as still as if he were hypnotized. His color started coming back and he regained his speech. He gave me a big push toward the door.

"Dammit, Mark, didn't you hear what Lupe just said? Don't stand there like the damn idiot you are. Go get a doctor."

He changed his mind, then ran and grabbed me. "No, don't go, it will take too long!" The old boy was really excited and mixed up. "Get on that damn telephone and call the hospital and tell them to send an ambulance!"

Nita and I started laughing. Jim realized what he had said and with a "go to hell" stare, he told us to shut up and he would make the calls himself.

Lupe came to our rescue. She put her arms around Jim and told him she was fine and didn't need a doctor or the hospital for at least another four to five months.

Jim very gently took Lupe by the arm and led her over to the couch and told her to sit down and take care of herself. He sat down beside her.

Nita went over, kissed and congratulated both of them. I kissed Lupe, and when I started to shake Jim's hand, he was as embarrassed as a school boy on his first date.

"What the hell are we all out here for?" he asked me.

"For the wedding," I replied.

Jim grinned and got up. "Well, now, let me congatulate you and Nita, and it's about time you two idiots came to your senses, if you got any senses, which I doubt. But it don't matter anyway. The boys are big enough now to raise both of you damn fools."

I interrupted him. "Just a minute, Jim, just a minute. I am not getting married, but you are, my friend."

"What the hell's the matter with you, Mark? Have you gone crazy or something? What the hell would I want to get married for?"

"Look, Jim, there's been a lot of excitement and surprises around here for the past hour. Haven't you ever realized that Lupe is a good woman, and have you forgotten that she is carrying your child? Do you want your baby to go through life stamped 'illegitimate?'

"Ate you going to be a man and assume your responsibilities as a father and a husband, so your wife and child will be proud of you? Well, are you or aren't you a man?" Jim was getting red in the face.

"You're damn right, I'm a man!" he replied, "and any s.o.b. that says I ain't, I'll beat the living hell out of him to prove it!"

"Easy, Jim, easy."

I grabbed Nita by the arm and as I started out the door, I told Jim now was his chance to prove that what he had just said was true. "So get down on your knees like a man, and ask Lupe to marry you."

I stopped just outside the door and didn't close the door. You can call us nosey, an eavesdropper, or whatever you like. Nita bent over and put her head under my arm so she could also see into the room. We intended to hear Jim when he proposed to Lupe.

Jim got down on his knees, cleared his throat and finally said, "Lupe, I want you to know that I am a mean, tough man and I drink, cuss, gamble, throw fits and fight, but hell, every man has a few faults.

"I know I should have married you fifteen years ago, and all this time we have lived together, well . . . hell, I didn't have to tell you. You knowed how much you meant to me, so what do you say? I'll even try to stop cussing, drinking, fighting, and chewing tobacco in the house, so the little baby will be proud of his Poppa."

Lupe didn't make any reply. Finally, Jim said, "Dammit, Lupe, I feel silly as hell down here on my knees, so are you or ain't you going to marry me?"

Lupe started crying.

"Now what did I say or do wrong?" Jim wanted to know.

"Nothing, Yemmy," Lupe replied, "but you are such a fool and I am so happy and love you so much, and we will be so happy with our baby and he will love you so much."

Jim shouted for me at the top of his voice. Nita and I went back into the room. Jim jumped up off the floor, all excited, gave me a big hug and told us he and Lupe were going to have a baby and get married.

"That's fine, Jim, and congratulations. I was afraid Lupe would refuse your proposal."

He was too happy to blow a fuse. "Just think, Mark, I am going to finally have a son after all these years. Hell, I'm only fifty-five and good for at least another thirty years!"

Lupe could understand but very little English, so he switched back to Spanish. "Just think how much fun I'll have teaching the little fellow to hunt, fish, and ride." He went over and sat down by Lupe and put his arm around her.

Lupe was very happy and gave Jim a big kiss. "Why, Yemmy, we do not name him after your dearest and best friend, and the man you have loved and treated like the son you never expected to have? Just think how nice it will sound to call our son Marketo, Little Mark."

Jim stared at me, and then told Lupe he liked the name and she could name the baby whatever she liked, but he damned sure wanted it understood that he wasn't naming his son after a certain little upstart he knew by the name of Mark.

I winked at Lupe and told her I appreciated her thoughtfulness, wholeheartedly approved of the baby's name, and I would keep in close touch with her, and as soon as the baby came, I would come and get it.

"What fur?" Jim asked.

"Why to raise the little boy and bring it up right, Jim. You don't expect me to let my namesake be raised up by a cussing, fighting, fit-throwing, tobacco-chewing, mean old man like you, do you?"

Jim was wearing an expensive Stetson hat. He jumped up, threw his hat on the floor, and said, "Listen you cocky little bastard, I'll have you know, by God, that no s.o.b. will ever take my baby. I'll . . ."

That's as far as he got.

I had always wanted to stomp his hat when he threw one of his cussing fits. I could tell this was going to be as big a fit as he ever threw. I pushed him over backward onto the couch and tried to stomp his nice, new Stetson through the floor.

Jim was so surprised at me, he sat open-mouthed and speechless. When I stopped stomping his hat, he looked at me and very innocently asked, "Why the hell did you stomp my new hat?"

"Well, Jim," I replied, "I've seen you stomp your hat a hundred times. I figured you were getting tired and I would save you the trouble."

"Hummmm . . . ." Was his only comment.

Nita and Lupe were laughing so hard I was afraid they would split their girdles. Lupe winked at me and said, "What you say, Mark is true. You can have the baby."

Jim started to get up and was cussing something terrible. In Spanish, Lupe said, "See, Yemmy, how you cuss and throw the fits? Just think how embarrassed I will be when we have company and we are waiting dinner for you, then little Marketo gets hungry and throws his little *sombreto* on the floor."

I had never heard Lupe try to speak a sentence in English before, but in the fifteen years she had lived with Jim, she had heard these words so often and I shouldn't have been surprised. "And, when Marketo, he starts cussing and stomping his *sombreto*, and I can just hear what he will say."

Then in English, she said, "He say, 'Goddamn to 'ell, Mommie dear, I hungrier dan de lettel coky bastard, were de 'ell my sun of a bichen poppa ees?' "

Nita and I laughed so hard, we damn near ruptured ourselves. Even Jim laughed until the tears ran down his cheeks. I finally suggested that we go downtown; I wanted to have the privilege of buying their wedding rings.

We started to leave the room; then Lupe reminded Jim he had forgotten something. Jim turned around, and looked at his hat, which was stomped as flat as the proverbial pancake, and still lying on the floor.

"No, I ain't," he told Lupe, "and furthermore, I am not fixing to wear that damned hat. It's stomped flatter than a cow turd. But I'll tell you something else," he pointed to me, "that cocky little bastard is damn sure fixing to buy me a new one, or I am going to stomp his rear end as flat as my hat!"

"No, Yemmy, it is not the *sombrero*, but you forgot to kiss me goodbye."

"Well, I'll be damned," Jim said, "we are not even married yet and already I am being tied and branded. After little Marketo gets here, I'll know how a branded calf feels." He bent over and kissed Lupe on the cheek and strutted out of the room.

After buying the set of rings, Jim bought us both a new Stetson. As we were walking back to the parking lot, we passed a garbage can. I stopped, lifted the lid off, and told Jim to stick his head down inside the garbage can.

"What the hell fur?" He wanted to know.

I told him to go stick his head in and shout 'DADDY', just to see how it was going to sound to him.

Jim grinned and placed his arm around my shoulder. "You know, Mark, it's going to sound wonderful." We stood silent for a long time. Finally, Jim broke the silence.

"Mark, I was just thinking of all we've lived through together and how lucky we are to be alive. We have truly been the last of the Soldiers of Fortune. I doubt if two men ever lived who have shared so many dangers and risks together, and now, we wind up with a baby, and everything is perfect. What does it all mean, Mark?"

I could only answer, "Well, Jim, I guess my brother José would have as good an answer as anyone. *Quien sabe?*"

As I lifted my eyes toward heaven and silently started to thank God for his protection and blessing, I glanced at Jim. He, too was gazing toward heaven, and, as I watched his lips move, I realized Jim also knew to whom we owed our lives, our success, our families and our future. To a grand old man upstairs, who wears a beard and a long white robe.

I was trying to think of some way, unworthy as I was to express my gratitude and appreciation, when Jim once again looked up and very softly said, *"Por Todo. Gracias a Dios."*

I have never been more sincere then when I answered "Amen." For I couldn't add any more than what Jim had just said: "For everything. Thank you God."